Bogmeadow's Wish

Also by Terry Kay

Terry Kay

Bogmeadow's Wish

A novel

Mercer University Press
Macon, Georgia

MUP/H821

First Edition.

Books published by Mercer University Press are printed on acid free
paper that meets the requirements of American National Standard for
Information Sciences—Permanence of Paper for Printed Library
Materials.

Mercer University Press is a member of Green Press initiative
(greenpressinitiative.org), a nonprofit organization working to help
publishers and printers increase their use of recycled paper and
decrease their use of fiber derived from endangered forests. This
book is printed on recycled paper.

Cataloging-in-Publication Data
Kay, Terry.
Bogmeadow's wish / Terry Kay. -- 1st ed.
p. cm.
ISBN-13: 978-0-88146-230-2 (acid free paper)
ISBN-10: 0-88146-230-6 (acid free paper)
1. Americans—Ireland—Fiction. 2. Grandfathers—Death—Fiction.
3. Family secrets—Fiction. I. Title.
PS3561.A885B64 2010
813'.54--dc22
2010045511

This story is dedicated to Norman Arey, Robert Coram, Grady Thrasher, and Lee Walburn, the original Boy Dogs, so named on a trip to Ireland in 1995. Yet, to quell potential guessing games from those who know them well, I offer this disclaimer: none of them carry a scintilla of similarity to the Boy Dogs of *Bogmeadow's Wish*. However, if friendships enrich lives as we are advised, then they have made me a wealthy man.

I also wish to acknowledge the helpful and insightful comments of Ann Davis, a grand lady born of Ireland, but now living in Georgia. And to my friends and gifted readers, Deidre deLaughter and Denise Jordan Lane, a sincere and grateful Thank You for catching annoying errors of spelling and punctuation and other rules of grammar that baffle me but seem to thrill teachers of English. The errors that remain are the failure of the editor known as Somebody.

Author's Note

I love Ireland.

Thinking back—putting the bits and pieces of it together—I am sure I love Ireland in great part because my mother loved it.

Or she loved what she knew of it, mainly its music, and that music was mainly from the mesmerizing tenor voice of Dennis Day, the popular sidekick to Jack Benny in the golden era of radio.

My mother believed he was from Ireland. He wasn't. He was born in New York City to Irish immigrants. His real name was Owen Patrick Eugene McNulty, a fine enough name for an Irishman, but lacking the show-business luster of a Dennis Day.

Yet, when you pit fact against Irish magic, there's no match to be had. For my mother there was something about that music that could cause a smile to grow across her face while a mist made a shining in her eyes. Irish music can do that.

Early on, when people asked me of my ancestral home and cultural persuasion, I would tell them I was Irish. I still cling to that boast, but truth is, it's more probable that I am predominately from British stock, with a couple of trips into Scotland to flavor the genetic brew.

Still, it was Ireland that my mother loved, and that is good enough for me.

I first went there in May of 1995, with four male friends—Lee Walburn, Robert Coram, Grady Thrasher, and Norman Arey. We had something of a high-brow excuse for the trip: to discover our literary heritage—such fellows as Shaw and Beckett and Yeats and Joyce. Of course, it was a sham. We were there not for literature—not even for celebration of Molly Bloom's titillating monologue in *Ulysses*. We were there in search of merriment and good ale.

We found both.

Because I had designated some of the expense of the trip for research, it occurred to me that I needed to write something to ward off possible IRS inquiry. I decided to outline a screenplay, a quick and easy project. To my surprise, I liked the story that came out of hiding, and I turned it from screenplay to short story, and, finding it even more pleasing, I began to stretch the short story until it took on the size of a fat novella.

For two or three years, it was my play-with writing – the kind of pleasant word-chase that writers use in escape, a little like artists doing idle sketches, letting their pencils have some freedom while their minds are noodling over another landscape in another country.

It was fun. I enjoyed the characters that materialized. I cherished hearing again the music my mother loved so well. I liked the veneer of Irish folklore—the outrageous tales, the mix of jubilation and pathos—that seemed to find its way into every circumstance of the story.

But it was only play-with writing.

And then my wife and I returned to Ireland with Norman and Peg Arey in 2004.

To my surprise, *Bogmeadow's Wish* was waiting there for me. The whole of it, I mean. It was there in Dublin and in Waterford and in Dingle and in Limerick, there in the Mountains of Mourne, in every tucked-away village, in every field of grazing sheep, in every pub and in every fiddle and flute and guitar, and in every cheery greeting, offered at near-shout through faces lined with laughter.

Call it what you wish. Call it realization. Realization is a good word.

Call it romantic meandering. I like that. Romantic meandering is a fine thing for a writer.

Or call it what I want it to be: Irish magic.

I finished the book quickly after returning home, but did nothing with it because I realized it was radically different from anything I had published. It was a light romance with the kind of exaggerated spirit one expects of the Irish. It had a leprechaun named Bogmeadow and a flying unicorn from the Land of the Ever Young. It had sweetness and sadness. It had despair and confusion and hope and—yes, it had a wish. One magical wish. I had never dealt with any of that in my writing.

Yet, it is a story I enjoyed discovering, one that left me happy with the experience.

I think it is because I still want to believe I'm Irish—full-blood, to-the-core Irish.

And I think my mother would have liked what I have written.
I even have a few words from *Toora Loora Looral* in it.
She used to sing it to me.

Terry Kay
June 7, 2010

Bogmeadow's Wish

1

At the moment of his death, Michael Finn Coghlan's life slipped quietly out of his body, like the gentle release of a small, cool fish into dark waters.

Cooper Finn Coghlan could feel the leaving.

Cooper was holding his grandfather's hand.

His grandfather had opened his eyes from a still, narcotic sleep, had smiled a faint, warm smile and blinked once, a sheen washing over his eyes. He had whispered a single word that Cooper did not understand.

There was the sound of a gurgle, then nothing.

The faint, warm smile stayed locked on his face.

Cooper did not move from the side of the hospital bed where he had been sitting, did not pull his hand away from his grandfather's hand. He closed his eyes and waited for what he believed would be the terror of loss, a tremor, a rush of pain. Yet he did not feel terror. He felt calm, tranquil.

What his grandfather had said was true, he thought.

About the Irish. About dying.

Once, in Dugan's Tavern, with a congregation of merry-makers reverently listening, his grandfather had declared, "When the Irish die, the world loses a song, and all that's left is the silence only a deaf man has ever heard."

His grandfather had smiled proudly over his pronouncement and he had added as assurance, "But it's not long-kept. Just a small waiting for it all to sink in, and then there's a sigh from one of the watchers—like the wind of a morning, it is—and soon enough there's somebody offering up a tale about the dear departed, and them that's listening feel the words of the telling resting warm across their shoulders, and if it's the right place and the right time there'll be a fiddler tucking his fiddle up to his chin and drawing his bow across the strings, and you'd swear you can hear the dead talking again."

He had paused, letting the words drift among his listeners, and then he had sighed, "Sweet mother of Jesus, I can't imagine what dying's like if you're not Irish."

Cooper released his grandfather's hand, slipped from the bed and moved to his grandmother, who was seated in a hospital-issue armchair of imitation leather. She was holding a rolled magazine, her fingers absently playing against it. Cooper knelt in front of her, put his hands over her hands. He said quietly, "He's gone."

His grandmother inhaled suddenly, the sound of a gasp.

Cooper reached to touch her face. "I should tell the nurses," he said.

His grandmother nodded stiffly.

He stood. "I'll be right back," he added.

His grandmother turned her face to the bed. "I hope he's there," she whispered.

"Where?" asked Cooper.

"Ireland," his grandmother answered. She sounded weary. Or bitter. Or both.

"Ireland?"

"He used to say he wouldn't go to heaven without making a detour to Ireland."

"I always thought he believed one was pretty much the same as the other," Cooper said softly.

For a moment, his grandmother did not answer. Then she said, "To hear him tell it, heaven was a distant second." She looked up at Cooper. "Find your mother and father. They're probably in the cafeteria."

"Are you all right?" asked Cooper.

His grandmother did not speak or move. Her eyes stayed on Cooper.

"Nana?" Cooper said.

"It's over," his grandmother whispered. "All these years. It's over."

Cooper again touched his grandmother's face. He leaned to her, kissed her on the temple, and then he left the room.

Dottie Cooper Coghlan sat motionless, holding her magazine—an old *New Yorker* someone had abandoned—and gazed at the lifeless form of her husband, his head resting peacefully against the bed's pillow. She

2

could see his smile. And then she pulled her body erect in a proud posture, raised her chin, swallowed against a quiver in her throat. She stood and crossed to the bed and looked down at the body.

"Finn," she said quietly. "Why did you ever come into my life?"

It was a question she had wanted to ask for many years.

Dorothy Jean Cooper of the Druid Hills suburb of Atlanta, Georgia, had married Michael Finn Coghlan of Ireland on September 18, 1941, in a solemn, tense ceremony at the Glendale Presbyterian Church. It was not a marriage joyously endorsed by Dorothy's parents, whose ancestry from both families was believed to be upper-deck British. To Hart and Joyce Cooper, the only asset that Finn Coghlan, the stonemason, brought to the marriage was the fact that he was not Catholic, but Presbyterian.

They were, however, in concert about the rest of Finn Coghlan's existence. He was not simply an emigrant from Ireland claiming to seek a better life; he was *Irish* Irish, his time spent jabbering in his dreamy, blarney way about things that did not matter. *Irish* Irish. It was in his manner and in his look—gangly muscled, fair-skinned, his hair a deep crimson and always in need of combing, a smile working across his face like a hinge. As Irish as a shamrock. Nothing at all extraordinary about him. Nothing but his eyes. His eyes were the blue of sky when the sky is sun-bleached. Yet, blue eyes did not fool Hart and Joyce Cooper. Finn Coghlan was *Irish* Irish, and he had invaded their lives with the boisterous, tongue-dancing language of his native country, had changed their daughter's name from Dorothy to Dottie, knowing their objections, calling her Dottie openly, cooing it like a mourning dove—"Dottie, me love…"

"He's cast a spell on you," her mother had warned. "That's what it is, a spell."

And that was what it had been: a spell. In the beginning, it had been as mesmerizing as music. Finn Coghlan had come into her life not with bouquets of flowers and gifts of jewelry in velvet-lined boxes, but with sweet, erotic whispers that had numbed her, and rushed her—to her great surprise—to the narrow bed in his cheap apartment near Ansley Park. They had married with the squeaking of Finn Coghlan's bedsprings playing a stronger refrain than Nellie Harrison's rendition of the

3

Wedding March on the Glendale Presbyterian Church organ.

Even after she realized the power of Finn Coghlan's spell and had become numb to it, she was still Mrs. Michael Finn Coghlan—Dottie Coghlan—and, for better or worse, as she had promised, she would remain Dottie Coghlan until death parted them. Her greatest comfort was in the knowledge that she had reared their only child, David Damian Coghlan, to be as Americanized as a Ford automobile, a man holding a responsible position with a major bank, properly married to an Agnes Scott College professor of American literature named Christine. Yet, her greatest regret was that she had failed to do the same with her grandson, Cooper. It was not her fault. She had had no chance. Cooper was Finn Coghlan reborn, the product of a leapfrogging gene that had streaked the chromosome sky like a comet, landing in the warm puddle of Christine Coghlan's egg, where it had formed itself into Cooper, and Cooper had emerged from Christine's womb with a wisp of crimson hair covering his head and Finn Coghlan's smile dangling from his lips.

She had even agreed to the name selected by his mother: Cooper Finn Coghlan. Finn. *Finn.*

"You look like you're laughing at me," Dottie Coghlan said softly. "Are you, Finn? Are you laughing at me?"

She had tried to be what he had needed, tried as best she could; yet she had always known something was missing between them. Had even talked to him about it in timid, jittery moments. He had smiled away the questions, teasing her about imagining things. Had declared that his life was too full to cram another thing into it. Had used the wizardry of his words, like incantations from a hypnotist, to make the questions disappear. Still, something was missing. She knew it.

She tugged the bedcovering neatly over his chest in the way of a mother calming a child who has had a disturbing dream. She would do what he had asked her to do. She did not like it, but she would do it. She put the palm of her hand over his chest and believed she could feel the muscles contracting, quitting their work. "I hope you've got your peace, Finn," she whispered. "I pray to God you do. You never had it here, no matter how you acted. But I did love you. In spite of everything, I did love you."

4

2

There was a howl in the February weather. A cold, gray day. Cloud sacks holding water, or sleet. The after-lunch traffic wiggling along the streets of Decatur was slow-rolling, clogged. No one said it, because saying it would have seemed indecent, but the gathering of mourners who had steered out of the traffic and parked and then drifted into the sanctuary of the Glendale Presbyterian Church for Finn Coghlan's memorial service was grateful there would not be a gravesite ritual.

Finn Coghlan had been cremated. His wife had called it a deathbed wish, requested in a moment of privacy between the two of them on the day before he died.

The wish had shocked Cooper. His grandfather had often talked of how he wanted to be escorted to the gate-station of heaven, and the description had been of a lavish, almost comic affair. Dressed in his finest, with a shamrock in the lapel buttonhole of his suit coat. A colored-on rosy face from an embalmer's makeup kit. A smile fixed between a grin and a laugh. Hair brushed up, as though caught in a happy wind. Foot-tapping Irish music, the kind found in a tavern, not a church.

"He had his reasons," his grandmother had said firmly. "I'm only doing what he wanted." The tone of her voice had dared anyone to doubt her.

The ashes were contained in an ornate urn displayed on a small mahogany table that had been placed in front of the altar. A Bible, opened to the twenty-third psalm, was beside the urn.

Cooper sat beside his grandmother on the first row of pews, right side of the center aisle. On the opposite side of his grandmother was his father and, beside his father, his mother. They were all dressed in the dark clothing of a funeral service. His grandmother and his mother held tissues, as though the tissues were part of their ensembles, like small, tattered bouquets.

Behind the family, fanned out on both sides of the aisle, a small gathering of mourners sat patiently, politely. An odd group, Cooper thought. His grandmother's friends, very proper, very sophisticated. His grandfather's friends, a look of discomfort on their faces, bunched together, whispering among themselves. Finn Coghlan's friends were old brick layers and stone masons, their suits as wrinkled as their skin, and a few of the regulars at Dugan's Tavern, where his grandfather had had his daily ale and was a legend. The regulars from Dugan's wore the saddest expressions, Cooper thought. Rightly so. The stories of Finn Coghlan were over for them.

Cooper was certain the soft sobbing he heard behind him was from Kevin Dugan.

Behind the altar and the pulpit, in a high, imposing chair, sat the Reverend Robert Joyner, senior minister of the church.

Cooper did not like the Reverend Joyner. The Reverend Joyner had an air of superiority that was less than godly. It was in his look, a slow-blink gaze that seemed to contain a sneer. It was also in his posturing, in his habit of always pausing before he began to speak, as though commanding everyone to become subservient in his presence. It made the Reverend Joyner appear haughty and bored, like a slick-haired television evangelist ticking his face to the nearest light-on camera.

Erin O'Connell and Davy Kildare were playing a melancholy fiddle-and-flute rendition of *Amazing Grace*—music that was eerily beautiful, sliding across the curved dome of the church.

The Reverend Joyner had his eyes closed, his head slightly bowed. The jowls of his cheeks folded over the stiff collar of his shirt. To Cooper, he had the impatient look of a man who wanted to be elsewhere.

Cooper was right.

The memorial service for Finn Coghlan—Friday, February 18, 4:30 p.m., six days following his death—was not pleasing to the Reverend Joyner. Privately, he did not approve of cremation. God's likeness was not in a pile of ashes, and to have an urn full of them as the centerpiece for a holy service seemed no different than performing an exorcism over an anthill. How could one shepherd the spirit of the dead heavenward when all that existed was ash? Maybe with a leaf blower, the Reverend Joyner thought cynically.

A pain, like a small stroke, jabbed at his chest and he accepted it as the pain of shame. Shame for allowing his mind to conjure an absurd image during the solemn duty of presiding over the death service of a church member, even one as annoying as Finn Coghlan. He had to remember that Dottie Coghlan was Finn's widow, and Dottie Coghlan was in every way a special woman, the kind of person God would warmly embrace and forgive of all sins. She deserved honor—and pity. She had been married to Finn.

The Reverend Joyner bobbed his head, quickly begged God's forgive-ness for the trickery of his wandering imagination. And then the thought of the leaf blower blossomed again and he bit at the grin that slipped humorously across his face. He could see himself holding his leaf blower over the urn, aiming the nozzle of it into the narrow, lidless top. One blast would send Finn Coghlan's remains to the church ceiling, and that would be far closer to God than Finn had ever appeared to be in life.

He shifted in his chair, sighed softly, grateful that he was adept at turning a silly smile into a pontifical frown.

When the music ended, the Reverend Joyner moved to the pulpit holding a single index card in the palm of his hand. He said, in his flat, nasal voice, "Dear friends, we are here this afternoon to celebrate the life of Michael Finn Coghlan, called Finn to all who knew him." He glanced at the index card, read from it: "We know him as the man who emigrated from Ireland in the summer of nineteen thirty-eight, made his way from New York to Atlanta in nineteen forty, met and married the lovely Dorothy Jean Cooper in nineteen forty-one, became the father of David Damian Coghlan in nineteen forty-two, and the grandfather of Cooper Finn Coghlan in nineteen seventy-three. He was a stone mason, a builder." He paused, looked over the gathering of mourners, then added, "And he was Irish to the core, a storyteller, a man of good nature, quick with a kind word for everyone he met.

"Finn Coghlan was the kind of man who could never disguise what abided in his soul," the Reverend Joyner continued. "He had what I like to call a billboard's face, and the message on Finn Coghlan's billboard was happiness. I'm sure he sometimes tested the patience of the Good Father by his teasing manner, but as far as I could tell it was never meant in a harmful way. I know this: he was proud of his heritage. He told me once that the first place God fashioned with his own personal touch after he had created the slosh and mud of the world—Finn's own colorful words, by the way—was Ireland, and what he had left from that work, he scattered about to make everything else look acceptable, and that was why the Irish had been persecuted by so many people. The rest of the world was jealous."

And then the Reverend Joyner veered off into a short, rote sermon about the sins of jealousy, and did not again mention Finn Coghlan's name until he said, "Since this is a memorial service, I want to invite anyone so inclined to say a few words about our brother in Christ, Finn Coghlan."

No one spoke. Only the damp breathing of sadness, and a single cough, invaded the strange, embarrassing silence of the sanctuary.

Cooper looked expectantly at his father, seated between his mother and his grandmother. His father stared numbly at the stained-glass window on the wall behind the Reverend Joyner. It was a rendering of Jesus, wearing an orange robe the color of autumn leaves. Jesus seemed to be in mid-step, seemed ready to slip off the glass that held him and to put his sandaled foot on the head of the Reverend Joyner.

"Anyone?" the Reverend Joyner asked.

Cooper heard another cough behind him.

"If not, then I'll ask us all to bow for—"

Cooper stood quickly. He said, "I've got something."

The Reverend Joyner frowned almost imperceptibly, then pushed a half-smile across his face and dipped a nod. He said, "Cooper."

Cooper could feel his heart racing. His face was flushed, his mouth dry. He licked his lips. He knew that everyone in the sanctuary was looking at him and in their thinking, they were seeing a younger model of his grandfather. And it was true. Everyone said so. Photographs proved it. Still, he was a pale model, a quieter model. Not so given to bluster, or the trigger-quick laugh, or the sweet sigh of melodrama. He did not have the poetry of his grandfather's Irish brogue—not until he began to tell his grandfather's stories, and then the mimicry was astonishing. Still, no one had ever affected him as his grandfather had.

"The Reverend is right," he said in a voice that trembled with a sudden, surprising energy. "My grandfather was a great storyteller, and I loved every word he ever said. I can't imagine being here and not having somebody say something about him." He paused and swallowed and heard the fading echo of his words. "He wouldn't have liked all this silence. He didn't believe in it. He believed that silence was like an empty room, just waiting to be filled with some good words." He paused again, looked at his father. His father had not taken his gaze from the stained-glass window of the orange-robed Jesus. "I didn't plan to do this," he added. "But that room—this room—needs some words about him, and I want to offer these, because I mean them, and because they're the kind of words my grandfather deserves: I loved him. I loved him for being who he was, and for the wonder of his dreams, and for his willingness to share those dreams with me." His voice became quieter. "My grandmother often tells me that I am like him. I hope so. I hope that, one day, I can pull my own grandson into my lap and tell him about Finn McCool and the Salmon of Knowledge, and about the Little People who dance on meadows of moonbeams, and about giants who make earthquakes when they walk.

"My grandfather never tried to buy my love by giving me material things. What he gave me was far better. He gave me dreams. And to me, that was magical. He was magical." Cooper's voice cracked. "I loved him so much. So very much."

He sat. Beside him, his grandmother brushed her eyes with a tissue. Her body convulsed once and she began to cry softly.

"Thank you, Cooper," the Reverend Joyner said. Then: "Would anyone else like to say anything?"

No one spoke.

3

In Dugan's Tavern, at a corner table in the deepest part of the room, Kevin Dugan raised his glass of imported Guinness over an empty chair—a leather-worn wingback that had been tilted forward against the table edge—and he said in a melancholy voice, "To Finn Coghlan. Him that's smiling down, wishing he was here."

A chorus of voices agreed: "To Finn."

Glasses clicked against glasses. Beer-mug glasses. Thick. A dull sound.

Cooper stood between Ealy Ackerman and Cary Wright, the two men who were his closest friends. Dugan's Tavern had been part of their lives since their freshmen year at Emory University, lured there both by the habits of classmates and by the presence of Finn Coghlan. Cooper had never been fooled by his grandfather's happy man-to-man treatment of him—and of Ealy and Cary—in Dugan's. In Dugan's, his grandfather could monitor their behavior, could keep watch on their moods, could control their drinking habits. In quiet times, the three had often confessed that Finn Coghlan had kept them from becoming professional idiots.

"The AA ought to hire him," Ealy once had observed. "I don't think it's possible for me to take more than one beer, not after being around Finn." He had paused, reflected, and then added, "Well, no more than two."

The tavern was off Ponce de Leon Avenue, leading into the Highland community. It was large and dark-paneled. A half-moon shaped bar curved from the longest wall in the main room, with a collection of wine glasses dangling upside down in the mockery of a chandelier over the center of the bar. On one side, raised above the entry floor, was a game room. Darts only. Kevin Dugan believed billiards attracted hustlers and went against the nature of a true Irish pub. Darts was a game of laughter, billiards a game of temper and quarreling. "This place is Irish," Kevin declared. "There'll only be the sound of somebody having a laugh here."

The tavern was not Irish, not true Irish. It was an American imitation, over-decorated with advertising premiums. A decent imitation, yet an imitation all the same. It had the look, and the happy aura, of the leavings of a St. Patrick's Day parade. Giant-sized cardboard shamrocks. Caricatures of leprechauns. Neon advertisements of Irish ales and whiskies.

Still, it had the sense of being Irish, primarily because it was loud, and because Kevin's voice—richly accented from his youth in Limerick—boomed happily from opening to closing.

Merriment. Dugan's Tavern was a place of merriment.

And it had been Finn Coghlan's place, where he took his afternoon glass of ale and told his mesmerizing stories, teased with humor and Irish legend. Stories told so often, they were like lyrics to a popular song. Could be quoted by any of the regulars, though no one could do them as well as Finn. No one except Cooper, and Cooper had an advantage. He had heard them from the crib, heard them before he knew that words were words.

The corner table in the deepest part of the room was Finn's table, the tilted-forward chair, Finn's chair. It was a house rule that only Finn could occupy the table or the chair when he was in Dugan's. Kevin called it the Emerald Rule, in honor of his fellow countryman.

"You can't thin the blood of an Irishman," was Kevin's philosophy. "And if you're born of the place, you're all of the same blood. Comes seeping up from the earth, it does. Them that's got it pure, there's always a seat in Dugan's."

Kevin placed his glass on the table, pulled the chair off its tilt, turned it toward Cooper.

"It's yours, young Finn," he said softly.

Cooper stared at the chair. "No," he whispered.

"You have to," Kevin insisted. "It's an Irish tradition. It's how we pass the torch. Irish to Irish, and though you've got the tainted blood in you, you're close enough."

"Listen to the man," Ealy said. He turned to Cary. "Tell him, Cary. You know all about that kind of stuff."

Cary smiled. He loved the smooth showmanship of Kevin Dugan. The only thing traditional about Kevin's tale was that it was from an Irishman, blithely invented.

"It's a touching ceremony," Cary said. "I've read about it. It's called the passing of the Chair of Honor."

A grin cracked on Kevin's face. "And what did I tell you? It's true, it is." He pushed the chair toward Cooper.

"All right," Cooper said, after a moment. He moved to the chair, sat cautiously in it, tested it with his body, then shook his head. "I'm not fit for it," he said. He tried to stand, was pushed back by Ealy.

"Finn," Kevin crowed. He lifted his glass again.

"Finn," the crowd echoed.

A mist coated Cooper's eyes. The mention of his grandfather was like hypnotic music to him. He raised his own glass. "Papa," he said quietly.

The men around him drained their glasses in unison and, in unison, put the empties on the table.

"A great man," Ealy bellowed, "and I don't care what the Presbyterians say about him." He motioned to a young waiter standing nearby and circled his hand over his head in a lariat of fingers, indicating another round of drinks. "When I die, boys," he added, "I want a sign put up at the wake: No Presbyterians Allowed."

"Best man ever to sit at one of my tables—present company included," Kevin said.

"Tell us one of his stories, Coop," Ealy urged.

Cooper shook his head. "I can't."

"One story," Ealy said. "For Finn, for your Papa."

Cooper slumped in his grandfather's chair. He touched at his eyes with his fingers.

"You know you can't leave without a story," Ealy pressed. "It would be—" He snapped his fingers as though beckoning for a word. He turned to Cary. "What, Cary?"

"A sacrilege," Cary said.

"That's it," Ealy bellowed. "A sacrilege. What would Finn think? His own grandson, carrying his own name, walking away from Dugan's without leaving a story behind? You can't do it, Coop. Not today. Not after the Presbyterians smoothed over him the way they did. We can't let you insult your grandfather that way. He was our friend. God, he was our family."

Ealy was a large man with a puffed face, giving him the appearance of always being short of breath. He was wealthy, the money inherited from his father, who, at the age of forty-three, had died from a fall on Mount Kilimanjaro. In dark moments, Ealy brooded that his father would have had a better life setting stone, as Finn Coghlan had done.

"Come on, Coop, don't make me beg," Ealy said. "I hate that."

Cooper smiled. He glanced across the room to the corner stage, and he saw Erin O'Connell taking her fiddle from its case as Davy Kildare unrolled a cord from the neck of a microphone and plugged it into a speaker. They had skipped their day jobs to play at his grandfather's memorial service, and when he had tried to pay them, they had refused, saying the offer was kind, but also an insult. "For Finn, you play out of the love of it," Davy had declared.

It was late afternoon. Outside, it was cloud-dark. Spear-drops of rain with ice-sharp tips beat against the windows of Dugan's. It would not be long until Erin and Davy began to play the music of Ireland. He knew he must be gone before then, or he would not leave. He knew the presence of his grandfather would appear with the first tender stroke of Erin's bow over the strings of her fiddle, or with the first bird-sweet cry from Davy's flute, and he knew he could not walk away with his grandfather's presence sitting in Dugan's, tapping time to the music.

"You tell him, Cary," Ealy said in mock exasperation. "He'll listen to you."

"One story," Cary said. "You know he won't let up on you. Just one."

Cooper inhaled slowly. His eyes blinked on the gentle-faced Cary. "All right," he said. "One story, but that's it."

"Our choice?" asked Ealy.

"Your choice."

A smile eased into Ealy's face. "Sally," he said.

"Yes, Sally," agreed Cary.

"Sally," other voices thundered.

"Ah, Sally," Kevin sighed. "I'll be crying in me beer."

"Dear God, don't do that," Ealy told him. "It's watered down enough as it is."

"Piss on you," Kevin said easily. He lifted a glass of maroon-dark ale from the tray the waiter held and handed it to Cooper. "Tell us, young Finn," he added.

Cooper held the glass with both hands, took one swallow, placed the glass on the table, then nestled back into the chair, his shoulders comfortable against the wings of the high back. He took a deep breath and exhaled slowly. His eyes became fixed on a large painting hanging on a wall near the table. The painting was of a shepherd and his dog crossing a rock-walled field, a desolate, yet peaceful scene. His grandfather had loved the painting, had sworn he knew the field and probably the fellow with the dog. A soft smile curled involuntarily across Cooper's mouth. He did not realize it, but the smile was the same as his grandfather's smile had always been when telling the story of Sally Cavanaugh.

The men gathered at the table quietly took seats, settled back, watched Cooper, waited.

How many times had his grandfather told him the story? Cooper wondered. Hundreds of times. Easily, hundreds of times. At first, it had been a bedtime tale and then it had become a game between them, like the game of the leprechauns. He would plea for the story and his grandfather would begin it, and he would interrupt with questions that led the story like words on a leash. And between the two of them, between the questions and the answers, Cooper had become part of the telling, and the telling had become a drama, a well-rehearsed play that was never tiresome.

He closed his eyes. He could sense his grandfather sitting beside him, his silk-white hair ruffled, his face red with gladness, his eyes as blue as morning sky.

And he could hear the exchange between himself and his grandfather.

14

Tell me about Sally Cavanaugh, Papa.

Who?

You know: Sally Cavanaugh.

Ah, Sally. The prettiest girl an Irishman ever looked upon.

How pretty?

Nut-red hair, light as air.

Her eyes?

Greenest green, like the heart of a leaf on a yew tree.

Fair?

Ivory, she was.

Who did she love?

Why, Finn McCool.

You were named for him?

And sure I was. Every Finn in Ireland is named for him. And you. You, too.

Who is Finn McCool?

The grandest man ever in Ireland—and that takes in the good St. Patrick, too. Thousands of years old, but never aging. Not a minute. The greatest warrior of them all—Finn of the Fianna. It was him that tasted the Salmon of Knowledge from out of the River Shannon, him that consorted with the enchanted ones.

And he still lives?

Sure he does. Making himself known when it pleases him.

Like a king?

King? Nay. It was in the bargain struck with the enchanted ones. When Finn returns, it's always as a common man, with not a penny to his name.

Why did he make himself known to Sally Cavanaugh?

Why, now, he couldn't help it, so lovely she was.

What happened?

Why do you want to hear it again?

Because I like hearing it.

Well, it was sad, it was. Finn wanted to marry the lovely Sally, and she wanted to be wife to him, but her family wouldn't hear of it. Not Finn

15

McCool. No. Not a man with a pocketful of holes. What could he give to Sally?

He was strong. He could give her that.

Strong? And where would they live? And what food on the table?

He had a job, didn't he?

Building fences of stone from a field? Is that a job, now?

Why didn't she just leave with him?

And bring shame down on her family? It's Ireland we're talking about, lad. Ireland.

Where did he last see Sally Cavanaugh?

On the cliffs of Moher.

Tell me.

She was standing there, in her white dress.

It was raining?

Yes, raining. One of them soft rains, like a good mist coming out of a low cloud. Off away, over the ocean, you could see the blue peeking through the rain-light.

But the rain was washing down over her, wasn't it?

Sure enough, it was, coating her white dress to her, white dress on white skin.

She was weeping?

True. Weeping.

And the sunset?

The only one of its kind ever.

Tell me.

It come falling out of the rain-light over the ocean—rich-red and marigold, like the bud of a morning rose that's right for cutting—and then it struck a cloud so thin that not an eye could see it, and it melted and spread itself out along that cloud, waving in a ship-pitched wind like a ribbon for a lady's hair. And then it seeped through the cloud and come back together in a sun ball that poured its light on Sally Cavanaugh.

What was it doing—the sun?

Bleeding. Its heart was broke open over the sight of Sally Cavanaugh's tears and over the sadness on Finn McCool's face.

And Finn McCool turned away and never looked back?

That he did. Never looked back.

And Sally Cavanaugh?

She is there still.

On the cliffs of Moher?

When it rains, misty-like, people have seen her.

In her white dress?

Sure, it is. Pasted to her by the rain.

And her hair?

Hanging down in ringlets, turned bronze by the rain.

And Finn McCool? What happened to Finn McCool?

Well, now, he went away, back to the other world—to a cave, some say—and there he stays, waiting.

Waiting for what?

The time to come back. And he will, my boy, he will.

When? When will he come back?

When Sally calls for him, there he'll be, with a pocketful of holes and little hope for riches.

Across the tavern, at the stage, Erin O'Connell pulled her bow over the strings of her fiddle in a single, sweet note.

Cooper heard his grandfather whispering.

He began to speak softly, his voice miraculously Irish, a voice pulled from his chest and from his throat like a Gaelic tide.

"Once there was a girl—lovely as any born of Ireland—whose name was Sally Cavanaugh, and she was in love with Finn McCool, she was…"

4

In his fitful sleep, Cooper dreamed a fitful dream crowded with faces floating against the black night-soot of space. Some of the faces he recognized—his father, his mother, Cary Wright, Jenny Gavin, Kevin Dugan, Ealy Ackerman, his grandmother, his grandfather. His grandfather seemed to be the only one with a look of happiness.

He awoke at 9:45, his head as dull and as sour as his stomach. He struggled to the window and looked out. The day was still wind-howling, still cloud-thick. He turned from the window and went to the bathroom and splashed water over his eyes, then dried his face and stood, leaning over the sink, gazing at himself in the mirror. He was thirty-two years old. Muscles ached that had never before ached. His eyes were red-streaked, as though damaged by a flash flood of blood. Thank God it was Saturday, he thought. Not a workday. Saturday.

Time to change my life, he reasoned. Too old for such nights. Too old.

And he thought of Jenny Gavin.

Jenny Gavin had ended her engagement to him because of such nights with Ealy and Cary.

Children, she had called them. Especially Ealy. Cary, alone—Cary, married—was one of the nicer men she knew, she had admitted, but not Ealy. To Jenny, Ealy was simply a fool.

"You don't get it, do you?" she had argued with Cooper on their last night together. "Ealy's buying you, and Cary. You're like toys to him. You've got his public relations account and Cary handles all of his insurance, and you think it's all out of friendship."

He had countered angrily, "It is friendship. Cary and I don't give a damn about the money. My God, what we make with Ealy is just a drop in the bucket compared to what we handle for other people. We like Ealy. We've been best friends since college. That's it. Nothing more."

Jenny had laughed cynically, had said to him, "All right, Cooper, name me one other account you handle."

He had sputtered the names of a few clients under contract to Boyles and Quigley, where he worked as a junior account executive.

"If I remember correctly, they're not your accounts," Jenny had said in a superior voice. "You simply work on them occasionally. Am I right, or not?"

She had been right, and he had gathered the embarrassment of the moment in a hand-rolling gesture of desperation. Had walked away from her. Had called Ealy. Had passed out on the sofa of Ealy's home from too much scotch. And he had remembered the night with sadness.

Cooper crossed to the shower, turned on the water, adjusted it, slipped out of his boxer shorts, and stepped under the steaming spray.

Maybe Jenny was right, he thought. Maybe he and Ealy and Cary— together—were no different than permanently disabled teenagers, three smart-ass, yuppie college students stuck in Fraternity 101, no better than young boys hiding in a closet with a flashlight to look at pirated copies of *Playboy* and *Penthouse*, whispering obscene jokes they had heard on the school ground. And, God knows, maybe it was a physical condition, as Jenny had bitterly suggested. Maybe it was nothing more than some clown-faced gene becoming drunk on the one hundred proof testosterone of puberty, never having another sober moment throughout the life of the man who carried it sloshing around in the scrotum sacks that dangled from him like ancient wine skins.

The water veined out of Cooper's hair and ran over his shoulders, tickled his lower back, curled at the ridge of his thighs, slipped off his calf muscles. He stood motionless, letting the water revive him, remembering the night in Dugan's.

His grandfather would have been ashamed of him, he believed. Drinking so much, even if the drinks had been hoisted in his grandfather's honor, compelling him to take another, and another, and another. Finn Coghlan never had more than one glass of ale, savoring it, then pushing the empty glass aside and waving off offers for refills. He had adopted his grandfather's ritual from his first high school beer. In college, he had been called the designated moralist.

Still, the night had been special. Finn Coghlan's night. He had been given his grandfather's chair, at his grandfather's table. It had been a ceremony, a rite of passage.

It had been the kind of night Jenny Gavin could never understand, and a night he could never give up. It was best that she had ended the engagement.

In the shower, he failed to hear the ringing of the telephone and there was a message from his grandmother on his answering machine. She wanted to see him. "Today, if possible." Her voice sounded tired, resigned.

Cooper returned her call, offered to take her to lunch.

"I've got more food here than I can eat in a month from what people have been bringing by," she told him. "Besides, it's too cold. I don't want to get out. I'll make you a sandwich."

"Good," Cooper said. "See you around twelve." He paused, asked, "Are you all right?"

"I'm fine, Cooper," his grandmother answered.

He made coffee and toast, ate the toast with blackberry jam, sipped the coffee, grateful for its heat and for the caffeine that jolted his body. He dressed casually in jeans and a white oxford shirt and a deep green cashmere pullover his grandmother had given him for Christmas. His grandfather had chosen the color, she had said. Had called it Irish green, which was not a surprise. Every shade of green on Earth had been Irish green to Finn Coghlan.

The thought of his grandfather caused a sadness to sweep over him, like the leaving of energy, and he went to the kitchen of his apartment and poured a second cup of coffee. He tried to read the morning edition of the *Atlanta Journal-Constitution*, a habit from seven years in public relations, but none of the stories went from his eyes to his brain, and he put the paper aside, leaving the business section on top as a reminder to read it again. He had not seen it on his glance-through, but there should have been a story about the Traber Trucking Company—a new account—and its state-of-technology tracking system. He had delivered the story on Monday, had begged for a Saturday release, and believed he had seen a nod of agreement from Francine Cofer, who was passionate about the integrity of her job. She did not publish releases from public relations firms to pad the scrapbooks of their clients; she published releases that had legitimate news value. Francine Cofer was not easily conned.

He did not know why, but he reached for his telephone and dialed the number for Jenny Gavin. There was no answer. Probably saw his name on her caller ID, Cooper thought. Saw his name and turned away from the ringing. He left a message: "Sorry I missed you, and I'm sorry I haven't called. It's been a busy week. Just wanted to say thanks for the note about Papa. He cared a lot about you." He paused, turned the phone in his hand, and added, "So do I. Talk to you soon."

He had thought that he would marry Jenny Gavin. If he had written a serious description of the perfect woman, it would have been Jenny. Bright-faced pretty. Sensible. Warm. A giving lover. In Jenny—deep inside—was a small girl with radiant goodness. There were times, quiet times, when he missed the small child more than he missed the lover.

~~~

Dottie Coghlan stood at the bay window which fronted her home and watched her grandson scramble from his car in the drizzling rain, pop open an umbrella, duck his head under it and begin his quick-step to the front door.

A single, sharp heartstroke pumped against her throat. There were times when Cooper so resembled his grandfather it frightened her. It was like a stagy illusion, something from a bizarre movie whose characters wandered about in a daze of flickering images and shrill music, bewildered by their surroundings, their minds so fragile they were doomed to madness.

Under his umbrella, taking his strong stride, Cooper was Finn Coghlan raised from the dead, full-bodied out of ash. Something—an invisible, cosmic hand—wiped away years in an eyeblink and Dottie Coghlan could see her new husband parading up the driveway, calling to her from a voice that had numbed and thrilled her the first day she heard him speak, a voice that turned meaningless words into sensuous poetry.

"Go away, Finn," she whispered.

She moved to the door and opened it and motioned Cooper inside the house.

"I think it's going to snow," Cooper said happily. He closed the umbrella, embraced his grandmother and kissed her on the forehead.

"You're wet," she said, pushing him away.

Cooper grinned. He shucked out of his overcoat.

"You must want something," his grandmother said.

"Why?" Cooper asked.

"The sweater."

A blush swept Cooper's face. He shrugged. "I like it. It's the only cashmere I've got."

"It looks good on you," his grandmother said honestly. "Come on, I've got your lunch."

The lunch was abundant, leftovers from platters of food delivered by neighbors and friends who had attended Finn Coghlan's memorial service. Sandwiches and salads, fruits and desserts. Tea made with cloves, the way Cooper liked it. Clove tea was his grandfather's recipe, a memory of holiday celebrations in Ireland.

"I can't for the life of me understand why people insist on bringing by enough food to feed Napoleon's army, when there's just me," Dottie Coghlan fussed. "You need to take most of this home with you."

Cooper knew it was useless to argue. "Sure," he said merrily. "It'll last about a day at my place." He winked at his grandmother. "I had a feeling this was why you wanted to see me. Worried that I'm starving, living on my own."

"Hush, Cooper."

"I do know how to order from a menu, Nana."

His grandmother's voice quivered. "That's got nothing to do with wanting to see you."

For a moment, Cooper did not speak. Then he said gently, "You miss Papa, don't you?"

His grandmother turned away, busied herself with covering a plastic container of egg salad.

"I do, too," Cooper said. "I miss him. I swear there are times I think I can hear him, like he's in the next room, telling one of his stories."

His grandmother stopped her work, looked Cooper. "The only time I hear him is when I'm listening to you," she said.

"I don't sound like him, Nana. Not at all."

"Yes, you do," Dottie Coghlan said irritably. "You don't have the brogue, thank God. Not until you start playing around, and then it's scary. I don't think I could bear it if it was natural for you. But you do have the same way of saying things." She waved her hand in the air, as if dismissing something that bothered her. "It's—like—like every word you speak is some kind of new thing that no one has ever heard, and you're the one who's been put on Earth to say it. That's from your grandfather. He was the same way."

Cooper did not reply. He sat, watching his grandmother. She pushed the container of egg salad aside and began to stack slices of ham on a plate. A frown of agitation was on her face.

"Don't hear me wrong, Cooper," she continued. "The reason I fell in love with your grandfather was because of his voice, and all those words that came tumbling out if it, non-stop. And I love that about you." She paused, touched the cheek of her face with the back of her hand. "Somebody told me one time that the first thing you forget about a person when they die is how they sound. It's the last thing I'll forget about your grandfather. I keep thinking how quiet this house is, now that he's gone. I don't hear him like you do, but I remember his voice, and when I hear you, I hear him all over again, like it's an echo."

"That's not bad, is it?" asked Cooper.

His grandmother shook her head slowly. "No, Cooper, it's not bad. Right now, it's a little sad, but it's not bad." She forced a smile. "You want another sandwich?"

Cooper shook his head. "I've had enough."

"Don't forget to take all this with you when you leave."

"I won't," Cooper said. He watched his grandmother move to the sink, rinse her hands, dry them on a towel. His grandmother was a remarkably majestic and healthy woman to be seventy-eight, lovely enough to pose as a magazine model for senior citizens who had defied age with whatever magic ebbed in their spirit. She would survive his grandfather's death with dignity, Cooper thought. Had she died first, his grandfather would have been lost without her. "Why did you want to see me?" he asked.

Dottie Coghlan turned to him, still holding the towel. "I've got something for you, something your grandfather wanted you to have."

"What?" Cooper said.

His grandmother folded the towel and placed it on the counter, then crossed the kitchen to a cabinet. She pulled open a drawer and withdrew two envelopes, one small, one large. She handed the small one to Cooper.

"Before you open it, you need to understand that I know what's in it," she said. "He had me write it for him the day before he died. I'm only sorry he was too weak to sign it for you."

Cooper turned the envelope in his hand, looked at it curiously, then frowned at his grandmother. "Why do I feel this is going to be something I'd rather not know about?"

His grandmother stood motionless, holding the larger envelope. She did not take her gaze from Cooper, did not speak. The expression on her face was regal.

Cooper fingered open the envelope and took out a sheet of paper. He read from his grandmother's familiar cursive handwriting.

My dear grandson,

I want you to take me back to Ireland. Let my ashes blow in the wind. You'll know the place when you come to it. I'll be there, telling you.

I beg you to do this for me.

I have dreamed about you many times lately. In every dream I have seen you where you were meant to be.

I love you to the very tender of my soul.

His grandmother had signed the letter, *Papa.*

Cooper folded the letter, put it on the table, reached for a napkin and touched it against the sudden bubbling of tears that coated his eyes. He could feel his body trembling, his mouth filling with sorrow. He swallowed hard.

"It's why he wanted to be cremated," Dottie Coghlan said softly. "He said he didn't want to be buried in the ground. He wanted to be turned loose in the wind in Ireland, and he wanted you to do it for him."

Cooper looked up at his grandmother. "I don't understand," he whispered.

"Neither do I," his grandmother said. "I thought it was the morphine, and maybe it was. But it was your grandfather talking, and I learned long ago that he believed what he said, even when it was nothing but one of his tales." She raised the larger envelope she was holding, seemed to weigh it with her hand, and then gave it to Cooper. "I don't know what's in this one. I've never opened it. Your grandfather had it when I met him, and he always kept it put away. He wanted you to have it. He told me about it the day before he died as though I'd never known it existed."

Cooper ran his fingers over the envelope and realized it contained more than paper. "You never asked him about it?" he said.

"No, Cooper," his grandmother said. "It was private." She paused. "Everyone deserves some privacy. Everyone. Never forget that. Whatever's in that envelope is now your property, but I don't want you to open it here. Wait until you get home."

Cooper nodded. He said, "I'm sorry Papa never had a chance to go back to Ireland while he was alive. I always thought he would."

"You're wrong about that," his grandmother said sternly.

"About what?"

"Your grandfather had a chance to go back—more than once."

"What do you mean?" Cooper said. "He always told me—"

"I know what he told you, Cooper, but you believed in your grandfather so much you never imagined he could—twist things. After the war, when your father was very young, I wanted to go there. I'd heard so much about it, I wanted to see it myself. I wanted our son to see it. And it wasn't money that kept us from going. I had an inheritance from my father. It was your Papa. Your Papa wouldn't hear of it. Then, on our fortieth wedding anniversary, your father gave us tickets to go. It was his anniversary present to us, but your Papa still wouldn't go. We cashed them in. We went to Boston instead—to Boston, Cooper, where the Irish nest like moles."

"Why?" Cooper asked in disbelief.

"Why?" his grandmother replied wearily. "Why ask me? I would be the last person on earth to know."

5

Cooper did not open the envelope until he returned to his apartment.

It contained five shards of rock, wrapped in strips of torn wool cloth, and two black-and-white photographs, faded to sepia with age. The first photograph was of four young men, dressed in rough clothing, standing outside a pub called Beckett's, smiling foolishly into the eye of the camera. Cooper looked closely. The second man from the left was unmistakably his grandfather. The second photograph, folded in a single sheet of paper containing the words *I want you to have this*, was of a woman sitting on a blanket in a meadow. A stone fence snaked up a hill in the distant background. The woman's face was turned profile. She seemed to be gazing at something far beyond the sharp border of the photograph, something as distant as a star, dot-marked against the sky. She was stunningly beautiful.

Cooper turned the photographs. No identifications had been written on the backs. He fanned them on the coffee table pulled close to his sofa and studied them, wondering who the people were. His grandfather's family, most likely. There had been a brother, Danny, and a sister, Joyce, both long dead from some forgotten fever that had swept the seacoast town of Dingle, where they had moved after his grandfather emigrated to America. It was the only real history Cooper knew of his grandfather's family.

He read again the line from the sheet of paper: *I want you to have this*. The handwriting, faded with age, was delicate, a woman's script.

He put the photographs aside and picked up one of the shards of rock and rolled it in his hand, touching his thumb over the chipped edge where it had been hammered away from a larger stone, and he remembered his grandfather's story of Fergus Sullivan, who could build a stone wall a mile a day, he was so powerful. "Toed the rock out of the ground as he walked, he did, flipping it up in his hands and breaking it to fit like it was dry-rot twigs. Sure, Fergus could wall in a herd of sheep whilst they was grazing and not so much as break a sweat, is how fast he was. There's some believe it was him that made the dirt of Ireland, grinding up so many rocks as he did."

Cooper slouched against the sofa, closed his eyes, and wormed his neck against the pillowed back. He thought of the rock shards and of the photographs and the sheet of paper with a message in a woman's thin handwriting. It was strange there were no letters tucked inside the envelope. Surely his grandfather had corresponded with his family, but there were no letters to prove it. Would he have destroyed them? If so, why?

And why did he not return to Ireland when there were opportunities to return? His grandfather had said it over and over, had whispered it so soulfully it had the sound of a moan: "Someday, I'll be standing again on that good island of rock, breathing in the air that freezes your lungs, it's so clear."

There was a reason. Cooper was sure of it. Uncertainty, perhaps. Afraid to be among his own people again, afraid that he had become a caricature of the real Irish, and if he escorted his Americanized family back to his home place, the real Irish would see through him.

There was another possibility, Cooper thought: The Troubles.

His grandfather had been a Protestant living in the Republic of Ireland, among strong-willed Catholics. There had been many conflicts. Torture. Killings. Cooper had thought of it as The Wars of God. From his childhood, reading of crusades against infidels, he had wondered about the brutality that had emerged from the gentle teaching of a gentle Jesus. The Troubles in Ireland were no different, and perhaps they were even more passionate than holy quarrels on the mainland of the European continent. No one, St. Patrick included, had been able to exorcise the pagan ancestry that rooted the Irish people to their land. It ran to the seabed of Ireland, was as stratified in the people as the epochs of time were stratified in soil and rock.

Still, he had never heard his grandfather speak harshly of the Catholics. To the contrary, he thought. His grandfather had often remembered his Catholic friends in a tender voice, saying there was great pity in the divide separating Christians.

Perhaps his grandfather's refusal to return to Ireland had to do with money, Cooper reasoned. Only that. Money. He had never been wealthy, had never held any position more important than foreman of construction sites. Perhaps he had mailed letters back to Ireland, boasting of his high place, or his abundant worth. Perhaps he had made himself a mayor, or other official. Nothing would be as damning as the truth, and there would be no reason for truth unless he, Finn Coghlan, returned to Ireland.

His grandmother had been bitter over the story of going to Boston instead of Ireland, and Cooper realized she had long been disenchanted with his grandfather. He had seen it in the impatient expression of her face, had heard it in the mildly quarrelsome complaints, but he had never considered the expressions and the complaints to be anything other than normal, the daily, irritating rub of marriage turned routine. What was abnormal, Cooper thought, was his own father's attitude toward his grandfather. His father, who had chosen the name David over Damian, had always behaved as though it was an embarrassment to be the child of Finn Coghlan. To David Coghlan, there was nothing special about a father who was a stonemason and a saloon storyteller. "After a while, you've heard all the stories," was how his father had dismissed the influence of his grandfather. Cooper had stopped himself before replying, "But have you ever listened to one?"

Cooper had not expected an inheritance from his grandfather. Not money. Not things. But he had received one. It was in an envelope. Photographs, rock shards, a sheet of paper with the line, *I want you to have this*. Vague history from a lifetime of experiences. Still, there were the stories, and Cooper knew the stories were in him, in his memory and in his soul. There was not an envelope in the world large enough to hold Finn Coghlan's stories.

And there was another thing.

Finn Coghlan's ashes.

Cremains, the funeral people called them.

Take them to Ireland, his grandfather had requested of Cooper. Shake them free to spin about in the Irish wind, in a place he would know only by intuition and by the imagined whisper of Finn Coghlan's ghost.

Cooper pulled up from his slouch, stood, braced his hands at the small of his back and arched, stretching the muscles. He wandered to the window of his apartment and gazed outside at the gray, wet landscape of a garden leading to the swimming pool and tennis courts. He saw a woman dressed for the weather in a thick red ski jacket with a pullover hood, tugging at a small, shaggy dog collared to a long leash. He had seen the woman and dog for months, knew their walking habits, yet he had no idea who she was, and it bothered him. She seemed nice enough. Middle age. A gentle face with webbed lines. A smile that nibbled at her mouth. Eyes that glanced greetings, then jerked away. Maybe he would stop her one day. Say to her, "My name's Cooper Coghlan. I'm your neighbor."

The woman opened the door to her apartment, and motioned for the dog to go inside. The dog backed against its leash, twisted to look toward the window where Cooper was standing, barked once, then gave way to the tug of the woman and disappeared into the apartment.

A thought struck unexpectedly at Cooper and he turned away from the window and looked across the room at a framed reproduction of an ancient map of the United Kingdom and Ireland that had been placed prominently above a mahogany secretary near the entrance door of his apartment.

Someone—Jenny, he believed—had once described the map as a bonnet-wearing woman pulling a dog on an invisible leash.

The bonnet-wearing woman was the United Kingdom. The dog was Ireland.

He thought of his neighbor and her dog. His grandfather had said there were signs and omens everywhere, if you gave your eyes permission to see them and your soul room enough to take them in.

"When you see three of them signs in a row—one after another, quick-like—you know it's for real, and only a man too dumb for his own good would deny what he's been told by them that know," his grandfather had said in a dramatic whisper.

And perhaps it was true.

The woman and her dog could be a sign, an omen, something done by those who knew, whoever they were and wherever they were.

The first sign.

Cooper smiled.

He enjoyed the thought of his grandfather's tale of the signs. As a child, he had believed the tale, had seen signs in everything. When he became older, he remembered the tale of the signs as playful, as sweet gullibility.

Still, he liked the idea of it.

Of signs.

Of omens.

An ancient map of the United Kingdom and Ireland.

The woman and her dog.

He would count the sightings as a sign and see if another followed.

Perhaps Ireland was calling to him, he thought.

Or perhaps it was his grandfather.

The thought was worth a second smile.

~~~

In the bookstore, at the travel section, he selected a half dozen books on Ireland and settled into a cushioned, beige-colored armchair provided for readers.

The books told him little he did not know, still he enjoyed the scan-and-pause reading and the gloriously vivid photography of castles and seascapes, cities and villages, bogs and rock-lined fields, the scrubbed-clean faces of children and the withered faces of the elderly. The faces were remarkable, Cooper thought. Grins, not smiles. Grins of erupting laughter. Tucked-away grins, still in the mouth. Eyes so bright they seemed to hold embers of sunlight. Cobwebbed lines at the lips and temples, made by wind and merriment and history.

He did not intend to buy the books. He wanted only to be with them for a time, to hold them, to hope there would be a line, a paragraph, an image—something—that would leap from the page and strike at him with a message telling him where to release the ashes of Finn Coghlan. His grandfather had promised, *You'll know the place when you come to it. I'll be there, telling you.* The only compass he had was a whim, and

Cooper believed the following of a whim in Ireland would be as useless as watering grass in a rainstorm. If what he had learned from his grandfather were true, Ireland was a land of whims, so many whims a man could become dizzy and easily lose his way by following his heart.

He would go to Ireland in May, he reasoned. His grandfather had emigrated to America in May, and returning his ashes in the same month would close the circle of time. Besides, his grandfather had often preached that Ireland in May was glorious, the time of year that God made a visit for a much-needed respite from watching over the rest of the world. "Before the tourists come calling," Finn Coghlan had said. "God's not much for all them tourists."

He randomly opened a pictorial book on Ireland, saw a valley field of rape, its brilliant yellow splashed against green hills. He glanced at the caption, saw the date: May.

He shivered.

A sign, he thought.

Another sign, quick-coming on the heels of his neighbor and her dog.

Two signs.

Two.

~~~

The day had tinted from gray to charcoal, still chilled by mist, when Cooper left the bookstore. He was hungry, but did not want to eat from the supply of leftovers his grandmother had forced on him. He went instead to a small Greek restaurant off Highland Avenue and ordered a salad and a glass of expensive Bordeaux. He left the restaurant at seven-thirty, checking his apartment for messages from his cell telephone. Jenny had called, apologizing for missing his earlier call, explaining that she had been shopping with her mother. She also issued an invitation: "A group of us are getting together at Café Intermezzo tonight, around seven. It's Hope's birthday. Why don't you join us?"

The sound of Jenny Gavin's voice saddened Cooper. There had been moments between them that still numbed him, still rushed into him unexpectedly, leaving him restless and regretful. His effort at maintaining a casual relationship was one of the unworkables in his life. Ealy had once observed that friends may become lovers, but lovers could never be friends. Cooper had laughed at Ealy's attempt to be profound. Now, he understood. Still, he wanted to be civil, wanted Jenny to think of him as a decent man.

He drove to Park Place, parked in the back lot and walked to the café. The café was crowded, noisy. A scent of coffee was suspended in the heated air—coffee and the faint presence of food and of perfume. In the rear of the café, at two tables pushed together, he recognized Jenny, though her back was turned to him. Knowing it was she, bothered him. Knowing her so well. Knowing her by the shape of her head, by the shimmer of her hair, by the way she moved. She was sitting across from Hope Marshall, her roommate from college and a friend who had lasted beyond college, as Ealy and Cary had lasted with him. A thin-faced man he did not know was seated beside her, leaning close. Not to hear, or to speak, but to be close. Another man was seated between Hope and a girl named Alysse. Cooper thought he had met the man at the advertising firm where Jenny worked, but could not remember his name. Gabriel, he believed. Yes, Gabriel. Jenny had called him a genius. Gabriel was telling an animated story. There was a spill of laughter from the table, a squeal. The thin-faced man sitting next to Jenny reached to touch her arm.

Cooper turned to leave.

A girl, Asian, model-slender, a flush of fatigue on her face, smiled at him. She was holding a tray with empty glasses on it. "Are you looking for someone?" she asked.

Cooper glanced toward the back tables where Jenny sat. The thin-faced man's hand was on her neck, massaging it.

"I think she's over there," the waitress said pleasantly.

"Excuse me?" Cooper said.

"Your date," the waitress said. "Over there." She motioned with a nod to the opposite side of the café.

Cooper saw a young woman sitting alone at one of the tables, scanning the room with the look of uncertainty. My God, he thought.

The girl was Irish. Cooper knew it. Deep auburn hair. Healthy, smiling face. Eyes the color of a delicate green stone having the rinse of joy. Radiantly pretty. She wore a green turtleneck sweater, the same color as the sweater that he wore.

"You are meeting someone, aren't you?" the waitress asked.

Cooper shook his head. "No."

"You look like you are. I thought—"

"No," Cooper said again. "I was just leaving."

"Too bad," the waitress said. "You look perfect for one another." She smiled, leaned close, whispered, "You could pull it off. She told me it was a blind date."

"I don't think so," Cooper said.

The waitress sighed. "She's so sweet. I just hate seeing her sitting there by herself, waiting for someone who probably got cold feet. She's been here an hour already."

"The traffic's pretty bad outside," Cooper said. "Maybe he got caught in it."

"Maybe," the waitress said. She flicked a smile at Cooper, walked away toward the table. Cooper hesitated a moment, watching. He saw the waitress pause at the girl's table, lean to whisper something. The girl blushed, looked up at Cooper, gazed at him for a moment, smiled sadly.

Cooper returned the smile, then turned and left the café.

Outside, the mist swirled, left a damp print of itself on the glass of the café's window. It was cold. The kind of cold that turned breathing into puffs of frost, like balloons in a comic strip. He paused at the window, looked back inside. The waiting girl at the table was still watching him, the sad smile still perched on her lips, and he thought suddenly of his grandfather and the asking-telling story of Sally Cavanaugh.

He heard himself ask: *And Sally Cavanaugh?*

He heard his grandfather answer: *She is there still.*

On the cliffs of Moher?

When it rains, misty-like, people have seen her.

The waiting girl could have been Sally Cavanaugh, Cooper thought. Signs and omens.

A woman and her dog.
A photograph in a book.
An Irish girl in a café.
Three signs.
Three signs.
Three signs.

~~~

On Monday, February 21, two days following the revelation of the three signs—as he accepted them to be—Cooper made application for a passport. That night, he returned to the bookstore and purchased eight books on Ireland. By May, he would have read all of them.

He said nothing of his trip to Ealy and Cary until mid-April, knowing that Ealy would insist on the three of them making the journey together.

A trip for the Boy Dogs, Ealy would call it. The Boy Dogs had always been Ealy's name for them. Moon-howlers. Bloodhounds after the scent of richly perfumed women. During their junior year at Emory University, there had been a ceremony to make the name official—a curiously Bacchanalian event in the small ballroom of an inexpensive motel, rented for a weekend by Ealy. He had hired strippers and a drummer who played bongos and an accordionist whose skin had been tinted orange by too much artificial tanning lotion. The strippers had presented each of them with a stuffed-animal basset hound while doing bump-and-grind to the best bump-and-grind music possible from bongo drums and an accordion. A sign hanging across the front of the ballroom read:

Boy Dogs
A Society of Gentlemen
Petitores Subuculas Puellarum

Loosely translated, *Petitores Subuculas Puellarum* meant Seekers of the Undertunics of Young Women, Ealy declared proudly.

The stuffed-animal basset hounds had long been discarded by the Boy Dogs, the night of ceremony and the bastardized Latin motto remembered only as absurdity, played to laughter. Still, the name had lasted: Boy Dogs.

And the discussion about Ireland had been as Cooper knew it would be: Ealy had wanted it to be a Boy Dogs adventure. He had argued vigorously that it would be something they would remember forever—the three of them together in Ireland, on a mission for Finn Coghlan that was close to being a holy command. He had even schemed to have the Ackerman Development Company investigate building shopping centers in Ireland. "That way I can pay for everything and write it off," he had explained. "I'm a CEO, for God's sake, and a CEO can pretty much order the peons on his payroll to do whatever the hell he wants, and unless I've missed something by never going to the office, the two of you are still on the payroll."

He had finally, reluctantly, agreed that Cooper should make the trip alone after Cooper had finally, reluctantly, lied, telling him, "It was something my grandfather wanted me to do by myself."

It had been an uncomfortable lie, yet he knew that having Ealy and Cary with him would be a distraction, a non-stop party dictated by Ealy. Ealy was a man who pushed, who bullied gently. Not from meanness, but from having a personality that seemed charged with high voltage current. It was a trait that could be as irritating as it could be charming. With Cary, it would have been different. Cary was calm to Ealy's storm. Still, he could not invite one without the other.

"I hope you guys understand," Cooper had said.

"Sure," Cary had answered.

"Yeah, I guess," Ealy had mumbled irritably. "But, damn it, Coop, I feel like I ought to be doing something. Finn was like a father to me, with my own father dying so young."

"Tell me where you think I should go when I get there," Cooper had suggested.

He had meant it as a causal remark.

Ealy had accepted it as a challenge.

And the Irish bible had been quickly compiled.

The bible was an eight-by-ten Corinthian leather datebook with a boarshide interior. It contained two weeks of intensive library-and-Internet research by Ealy and his personal secretary—a woman named Grace Ray—and included a neatly hand-written, day-by-day calendar of recommended events, beginning with touchdown in Dublin. The day-by-day calendar also had an hour-by-hour agenda, and the slip-jacket of the date book was crammed with maps and information on everything from lodging and train schedules to famous pubs.

According to Ealy's bible, Cooper would shake loose the ashes of Finn Coghlan on a cliff overlooking the Bay of Dingle on Friday, May 19, at 6:30 in the afternoon.

"I just wish I could be there with you," Ealy had said regretfully.

The Irish bible was one of two going-away gifts that Cooper had received.

The other was also leather-bound, a lined, blank-page book for journal entries, a beautiful book, soft to the touch. His father had given it to him at lunch on the day before he left for Ireland.

His father had said, "I don't know if you'll use this, or not, son, but I hope you do. You've always been a fine writer, if I remember your classroom days. It's a talent you get from your mother. Anyway, this will be a time to use it, even if you haven't planned on doing so. Years from now, it'll mean more than it does now."

Cooper had detected a longing in his father's voice. "Did you ever want to go to Ireland?" he had asked.

His father had smiled. Not his professional smile, but one that held warmth. "Once. When I was seventeen or eighteen. I had a friend who had ventured into genealogy for a class project. Her family was Irish, and she had talked them into letting her go there during the summer. She wanted two or three of us with Irish heritage to go along, but we really didn't have the money, so I stayed home."

Cooper had kidded, "Was she pretty?"

To his surprise, his father had answered, "Yes, she was. Very pretty. She's a doctor now, I believe." The hint of a blush, something from memory, tinted his face.

"Sounds like you've got a secret hidden away somewhere, Dad," Cooper had teased.

His father had shrugged slightly. "No secrets. Just privacy." He had touched the knot of his tie with his fingers. "It probably would have been a mistake. Besides, that was the summer I met your mother."

Cooper had watched his father closely, had seen the flicker of a remembered moment dim in his father's eyes. And he had imagined his father as a young man, aching for someone removed from him by an ocean. He had wanted to question his father, yet knew his father would dismiss the question. Instead, he had asked, "Why didn't Papa ever go back?"

His father had paused for a long moment, his gaze fixed away from the table and from Cooper, and then he had said in a soft voice, "I don't know, son. I don't know. Maybe he was waiting for you to take him."

"Maybe so," Cooper had replied. "Nana thinks there's not much difference between us, anyway."

His father had turned his look back to Cooper. "That's not true, Cooper," he had said. "You're not at all like your grandfather, not really. You look like him, and you can mimic the way he sounded, but you're not like him. He had hardships we never knew about, although I think he came close to telling you. You were the most special person in his life. I hope you find some answers on your trip, and if you do, I hope you share them with me."

6

The Delta fight from Atlanta to Dublin left at six twenty-five on Friday evening, May 12. In the west, a still-high yellow sun was jabbed like an open umbrella into a white beach of cloud dunes rising up from the blue water of sky. Cooper watched the umbrella sun from his window seat, then closed his eyes and leaned his head against the seat cushion. The slight force of the plane-lift pressed against his chest and throat. It was a sensation that always thrilled him. A tickle. A swoosh. A cold slap of air hissing from the vents above his face. The same sensation of rising up out of water after a deep dive.

He rooted his shoulders into the cushion and let a smile roost on his face. From the seats behind him, he heard a man say, "Can you believe it? We're going to Ireland." And a woman answered, "I'll believe it when we get there."

The tickle of the lift-off slid down Cooper's chest.

Ireland, he thought.

He could hear in memory his grandfather's voice: "It'll take your breath, it will. Leave you reeling like a drunk happy to be alive and loving the world and all them that's in it. Wait 'til you see it, Cooper. So many shades of green, you'd think a stripe of the rainbow had slid off and splashed plop down in the middle of it. Green on green, coming down them copper-brown hills. Like little grass ponds, they are. Why, you'd think there'd be little grass-green fish in them."

"You think the kids will be all right?" he heard the man ask the woman. There was fret in his voice. Worry.

"For God's sake, Harry, they're grown," the woman sighed.

"Joni was crying," the man said softly.

"Harry, there's more tears at an airport than at a funeral," the woman said.

"I guess you're right," Harry said.

"We'll only be gone for a week," his wife said.

"It's a long way away, that's all," Harry said.

"Yes, it is," the woman said. She sounded pleased.

Cooper thought of Ealy and Cary standing at the gate, waving their humorous waves of goodbye. He could hear Ealy's bellowing voice, "You need us, boy, just call. We'll be on the next plane out. And read the bible. Read the bible."

Now, in the air, the plane tilted in its angled climb, Cooper regretted his decision of going to Ireland alone.

Intuitively, he believed he would need the familiarity of his friends. He had never been to a foreign land, and though he had always thought of Ireland as a kind of spiritual home—knew it historically and geographically better than he knew his own home state of Georgia—he sensed it would still be a shock for him.

He thought of his first business trip to the city of New York. Remembered standing lost and bewildered on Avenue of the Americas. Remembered the street traffic and the rapidly moving crowds of pedestrians, the sharp sounds of shoe clicks and car horns and whistles, the snarls of passers-by elbowing their way into buildings. Remembered the rush of panic that crushed against his lungs, palpitating dangerously over the muscle of his heart. He had not thought of New York being different from Atlanta. Atlanta also had traffic and noise and elbowing people, yet Atlanta did not have the aura of threat that seemed to hang, suspended, over New York, a threat that, to Cooper, was as real as steel and concrete. He had admitted his panic to Jenny. She had found it amusing, had called it the Little Lost Boy Syndrome, saying it teasingly, saying it was an affliction that was incurable. "My God, I can't imagine what you'd be like in Hong Kong," she had added with a snicker.

Cooper shifted in his seat. His seatmate, an older woman with a kind face, smiled and said, "I'm glad we're flying at night." She had a faint Irish accent. "I have a terrible fear of water. Just the thought of looking out the window and seeing nothing but water is more than I can bear."

"I've never flown over water," Cooper told her.

The woman blinked in surprise. "This your first time to Ireland?"

"Yes," Cooper said.

The smile in the woman's face deepened. "Well, you're surely Irish. I can tell by the look of you," she said, the accent becoming stronger. "You're going to love it. It's beautiful this time of the year."

Behind him, the man named Harry said, "Did you call the paper to have them stop delivery?"

"Harry, the next sentence you say to me better have the word leprechaun in it," the woman answered wearily.

Cooper pinched his lips against a laugh.

Leprechauns, he thought.

He scrubbed his neck against the headrest of his seat, glanced at his seatmate. Her eyes were closed, her face lifted. She had the expression of someone remembering the sun on her face.

Leprechauns, he thought again.

He knew many leprechauns.

Or believed he did.

His grandfather had called them leprechauns. Had said leprechauns were as plentiful as birds and that a man who knew of such things could find them anywhere, yet a man not knowing—the average, walking-about man—could sit to tea with one and watch the leprechaun pay the bill out of his own gold-heavy, draw-string pouch, and still not have the slightest idea who he was. Yet, a man who knew of such things could see through the clever ruses leprechauns used in hiding themselves.

"You're a child who's been blessed, having somebody watching over you that's in the know," his grandfather had confided in a voice so low and tongue clucking and serious that Cooper could feel the words creeping across his skin like the footsteps of spiders.

His grandfather had had personal experience with leprechauns.

Or boasted that he had.

And it had seemed to Cooper that his grandfather was remarkably perceptive. He had marveled at the number of leprechauns his grandfather saw, pointing them out in an exaggerated act of secrecy and warning, saying to Cooper, "Watch yourself now. Keep close by me, and don't go gazing hard at him, or he'll put a spell on you, he will."

It had been a game from Cooper's childhood—grandfather and grandson with grand secrets between them, the grandfather giving story

41

to each sighting, the grandson listening in awe, holding tight to his grandfather's hand.

Cooper was certain that holding his grandfather's hand in the presence of a leprechaun was more important than breathing. Life-and-death import-ant, if the story was to be believed, and the story was too splendid not to believe.

As a young man in Ireland, Michael Finn Coghlan had come upon a leprechaun lazily napping under the cover of a hedgerow near Ross Castle in County Kerry. He had caught the leprechaun in a firm grip and the leprechaun, who gave his name as Bogmeadow, had struck a squealing bargain: To keep his freedom and his pouch of gold, Bogmeadow put a blessing on Finn Coghlan, protecting him and anyone touching him from the harm that could easily be done by other, more malicious leprechauns, particularly those pretending to be human.

"You can ask your grandmother if it's true," Cooper's grandfather had said seriously. "She'll tell you. With all of them that's about, there's never been one to give so much as a mean eye to either one of us."

Bogmeadow had further agreed to the granting of one wish, his grandfather had revealed.

Not three, which was customary.

One.

"And I've been saving it ever since," his grandfather had said. "Maybe I'll go using it on you one of these days, or pass it on for you to use on yourself. But it's a powerful thing, it is. Powerful. You'd have to be for certain that whatever it is you're wishing for is worth the wish. "

The memories of the game were warm for Cooper, and it did not matter that none of the leprechauns his grandfather spied in their walks together looked in the least like leprechauns were supposed to look. They all had resembled ordinary people. Cooper had known many of them by name. Neighbors, church people, shopkeepers. Even some of his teachers. Many were civil employees—postal workers, police, firemen. It was the nature of leprechauns to find such work and disguise themselves as real people wearing uniforms, Finn Coghlan had declared with authority. Yet, if you looked carefully, you could see them for who they were. At times it was in their gruff manner, but most often in their tricky charm. A certain give-away was the color of red. All of them would be wearing something shaded red, if not for the eye to see, then hidden. Red was their good-luck color. If you took the red away from them, they would vanish in a twinkle, like the last spew of a Fourth of July sparkle, leaving nothing to prove they had even existed except a little wisp of smoke that had a faint, gunpowder odor.

Still, it was best not to boast of knowing leprechauns, his grandfather had cautioned. If you made jest of them, you would never know of their magic, and their magic was more powerful than dreams.

"You won't go talking of them, now will you?" he had said to Cooper.

"No sir," Cooper had vowed. "Never."

"Not to a single person, ever. Is that a promise for certain?"

"Yes sir. I won't ever tell. Never."

"Good. And when I'm gone, you'll be the one having Bogmeadow's blessing, and if I find no reason to use it, you'll be having his wish, also," his grandfather had declared proudly. "There's only one wish, mind you, but the blessing goes on and on. It was part of the bargain that I could leave the blessing to another fellow, and I choose you, my own namesake, blood of my own blood. You're the only one I've ever told about it. Later on, you'll pass it on to some lucky fellow of your own choosing, and him to another, and on and on, and that's how it'll stay alive."

From his window, Cooper could see the sun spreading across the horizon—a red melon color. The airplane tilted into a turn, aimed its nose eastward, following the homing call of Ireland.

Beside him, Cooper's seatmate opened her eyes, made a small sound, a sound that carried a shimmer of joy.

~~~

It was eight o'clock in the evening—one o'clock in Dublin—when Kevin Dugan answered the telephone at his desk in Dugan's Tavern and accepted the international collect call. The caller was Sandy McAfee, an actor in his mid-fifties, a distant cousin to Kevin. "The man can talk

43

flowers off wallpaper," was how Kevin had described him to Ealy and Cary. "Had him a run at it for a time. Shakespeare, Ibsen, Shaw—did them all, he did. Good as they came, if you believed his tale of it. Even made a few movies, and there's always been some whispering in the family that Hitchcock tried to lure him to Hollywood, but he had too much principle to lower his standards. There was them that thought he'd be another Burton, but he made Burton look like a teetotaler, if you know what I mean. Now all he's got is his clippings and the memory of it. Does some street readings in Dublin, I hear. But he's the man we want, and he'll lap it up like a cat after cream."

For a week, Kevin and Ealy and Cary had negotiated with Sandy to perform a role that Ealy had created: to be Cooper's guide in Ireland.

"The boy's going to need help," Ealy had preached in enlisting Kevin and Cary in his conspiracy. "He won't let us go along, we damn well have to make sure he's got somebody looking after him."

Cary had argued against the plan, yet had finally surrendered. "If it fails, the blood's on your hands," he had said to Ealy.

"It won't fail," Ealy had crowed.

From Ireland, Sandy said over the speaker phone, "Kevin, me good man, and how are you?"

"Fit, Sandy, and you?" Kevin answered.

"Fine as a good-tuned fiddle," Sandy blared.

"You sound as though you might have drained a pint or two," Kevin said.

"A small ale, that's all. I'm reformed, or did I tell you?"

"You did, indeed," Kevin said. "Listen, Sandy, I've got my friends with me, the ones you've talked to before. Ealy and Cary. We're on the speaker phone, so mind your manners."

Sandy McAfee's voice purred: "Gentleman, and how are you this lovely evening?"

"We're fine," Ealy said anxiously. "We just got back from seeing our friend off at the airport. Sure appreciate you staying up so late to call us."

"For Sandy McAfee, it's the sweetest part of the day," Sandy crooned. "I've been at a reading most of the evening. King Lear, they're wanting me for."

"Oh?" said Ealy.

"But they'll not get me," Sandy said merrily. "A man can prance about in tights only so long, and, as the Devil himself knows, Lear's a bore. Give me Polonius any day."

"Then you're available?" Ealy asked.

"Well, now, I may be and I may not be."

"What's that supposed to mean, Sandy?" Kevin asked anxiously. "You gave your word—"

"Ah, you're sounding a bit put off, you are," Sandy said.

"Don't be an Irish shit," Kevin said firmly.

Ealy hushed Kevin with a wave of his hand, leaned close to the telephone and said, "Not at all, Mr. McAfee. We're not put off at all. We're simply looking for an answer here. Our friend's in the air, headed your way, and we still don't have this matter resolved." He paused, laughed easily, added, "You could say we're as much up the air as he is, and we thought we had a gentleman's agreement from our previous conversation."

Sandy sighed, said in a sorrowful voice, "Aye, I know, but the truth is—and God's truth it is, lads—I've had more of a time of it lately than I'd planned for, and with me agent on holiday, it's puzzling what to do."

"Why do you need your agent?" Kevin asked.

"Oh, dear boy," Sandy said proudly, "I'm an actor. You can't be an actor and not have an agent. There's percentages to account for, publicity to think about, preparation time, costuming, makeup. It's a demanding craft, it is."

Ealy smiled, nodded, winked at Cary. He said, "How much, Mr. McAfee?"

"Well, now, best I can figure it—without me agent, of course—is a thousand euro. You offered six hundred, if I recall."

"Jesus and Mary," Kevin cried. "You're my cousin, for God's sake. These are my friends. You can't go acting like a Brit to my friends.

You'd settled on six hundred, then, by God, it's six hundred, or I'll find me another."

"In such short time?" Sandy replied calmly. "Not so likely. Besides, I'd not thought of how long I'd be on the road."

"You've got it," Ealy said. "One thousand euro, three hundred up front, seven hundred at the end of the trip."

"Seven up front, three at the end," Sandy said.

Ealy laughed. He said, "You just crossed the line, Sandy. Now you can kiss my deep-South, redneck-Georgia ass." He added in a command, "Hang up on the son of a bitch, Kevin."

"Wait," Sandy said hurriedly. "All right, all right. Three up front, seven at the end."

"You're a fine man, Sandy McAfee," Ealy said triumphantly. "And I'm sure you'll keep in mind that there could be a sizable bonus at the end if you do your job."

"It'll be done, and that's a promise," Sandy said, suddenly eager. "You'll be talking about it when you're all old men, with drool dripping off your chins."

"I'm sure we will," Ealy said. "In fact, I look forward to it."

7

Ireland lifted out of the ocean in the early light of morning, a wiggle of land too far away and too dim to see clearly, and then the airplane tilted to lock on its path to Dublin and, suddenly, it was there, to the left, beneath the wings of the airplane, its shoreline gleaming in the yellow spray of the sun.

"There it is," Cooper's seatmate said softly, leaning near him, her elbow bridged on the armrest separating them. The look on her face was the look of awe. "Home," she added.

The airplane skimmed the coast line, past Arklow and Wicklow, weaving over stone-ridged fields of green and lush-yellow patching of rape and gorse, past Bray and Dalkey and Dun Laoghaire, tilted right again and dipped over the Irish Sea and slipped into Dublin Bay, where cargo ships crawled like toys on the heaving blue-green waters.

"Almost there," Cooper's seatmate said excitedly.

"Almost," Cooper said.

His seatmate was named Mavis Kolvoski. Kolvoski was from her marriage. Her maiden name was Mavis Gibbings, and she claimed distant kinship to the poet Robert Gibbings. She had married a Polish seaman at age seventeen, had moved to America at twenty-three. She had a kind face, gray hair, was plump from a lifetime of nibbling while cooking. For six years, as a widow, she had made an annual pilgrimage to Ireland in May, staying for a month with a younger sister who lived in Dublin. Only her children and her grandchildren compelled her to remain in America.

"I love America," Mavis Kolvoski said in a voice that was both melancholy and earnest, "but it's here that I'm at peace." A smile coated her face. "I've told my children that I want to be shipped here when I die, and be put to rest in Irish soil."

Cooper thought of the small, securely bound box in his briefcase— the ashes of his grandfather. He said, "Yes, I can understand that."

"Home," Mavis Kolvoski said again in a whisper.

Cooper leaned against the curved, soft cushion at his head and closed his eyes. He could hear the whistle of air spinning off the metal of the airplane, the groaning of the wheels untucking, the deep roaring of the jets. Home, he thought. Yes, he, too, was home. Not at the house of his parents, but home. The house of his parents was the place he had come from, but not a place to go to. There was no joy in the house of his parents. No laughter. No noise. No stories. The house of his parents was a house of order, of well-schemed routine that seemed always to conceal a terror as horrific as suffocation. When he returned for his occasional visits, he could see a cringe of fear in his mother's and father's face, as though his voice, his presence, somehow violated their order, their routine, and he had always imagined them collapsing in relief when he left. It was what had bothered him about Jenny. She, too, was orderly. She, too, lived by a routine as clean as a clock-tick.

"Look," Mavis Kolvoski said excitedly.

Cooper opened his eyes and turned to look out of the window. Below, Ireland rushed toward him. He heard his grandfather: "It'll take your breath away . . ." And he had a sudden sensation of his grandfather sitting beside him, where Mavis Kolvoski sat. Something visceral and primordial stirred in him, made him shift uncomfortably in his seat, and for a brittle moment, in the blink of a full and detailed dream, he could hear an ancient chant from a fierce and ancient people. He could see them below the roaring airplane, lining the runway, shaking their bony fists toward the sky. And his grandfather was standing among them, his glad face laughing a glad laugh.

The airplane skidded on the runway, bounced, touched again, and began its furious roll. The engines reversed to brake. The airplane shuddered.

"Ireland," Mavis Kolvoski said happily, said as exultation. "Can you feel it?"

"Yes," answered Cooper.

And he could. It was a chill, then an explosion of heat that trembled in his chest.

~~~

Cooper did not have to refer to Ealy's Irish bible to know his first duty in Ireland—a photograph to be taken at the arrival gate of the Dublin airport. Mavis Kolvoski's sister—Sarah Cockery—took the picture. Cooper and Mavis together, smiles peeling from their faces. He liked Sarah Cockery. She was spirited, loud, quick with a laugh. Favored her sister, but not so heavy. He took her telephone number, promised to call if time permitted, exchanged Atlanta addresses with Mavis, embraced her warmly, then excused himself to claim his rented car, a Nissan Vanette.

It was ten-thirty when he pulled to a stop in front of the Shelbourne Hotel on St. Stephens Green. The trip from the airport had taken longer than he had expected from studying the map. A strange drive for him, being on the opposite side of the road from the American system, and he was sure his slow speed had been an annoyance to other drivers. It did not matter. He was at his first destination—a hotel reserved and paid for by Ealy. Too expensive, yet he had not argued. "It's for Finn," Ealy had said. "Let him rest his first night back in Ireland in the lap of luxury." Standing in the lobby, he knew that Ealy had been right. The Shelbourne was magnificent.

Cooper did not see the small man sitting in an armchair, pretending to read a newspaper, a broad smile set in the frame of his flushed, pink face, his thick, silver hair combed in a lacquered wave over the peak of his ears.

It's him, thought Sandy McAfee, peering at Cooper. For certain, it's him.

He ducked his head behind the opened newspaper as Cooper passed, following a bellman to the staircase. And then he glanced at his watch. An hour before lunch, he reasoned. Time for a pint to quench the thirst. One only. He had a good-paying task to do and he would do it sober.

~~~

49

In his room Cooper unpacked, leaving the tape-wrapped metal box containing his grandfather's cremains and the envelope of rock shards and photographs locked in his briefcase. He had thought of asking for a security vault for the box but decided against it. He did not know how to explain its contents, was fearful of the reaction of the hotel staff. He imagined they would regard him as another odd American, afflicted with romantic madness about his Irish history, real or rumored. He imagined also there would be something offensive about carrying around the fine-ash leavings of a man who had been flesh and bone. In Ireland, religion was not a trifling matter; a lot of people had died committing transgressions against one belief or another.

He stood at the window and gazed outside. There was numbness in his body, a dull, tiring vibration that lingered in his muscles from the long hours in an airplane. In Atlanta, it was early morning, the stirring hour, the first slow-crawling of traffic into downtown parking lots. It would be a hot, muggy day in Atlanta, he thought. Cary would be in the traffic, probably beginning the day's business on his cell phone, leaving an instruction to himself on his office answering machine. Ealy would be at home, in bed still, blissfully recovering from his night at Dugan's, or possibly Joey D's near Perimeter Mall, which had become his second favorite gathering place. In Joey D's, he could mingle with people who amused him—lawyers and business executives and amateur politicians and sports figures. He could also watch the remarkably statuesque hostess named Lisa and make the soft, moaning sighs of fantasy that all men made in the presence of sensuality.

The thought of Ealy in Joey D's made Cooper smile. Ealy was a special man, a special friend.

Money had never impressed Ealy. It was there, like some monster amoeba dividing itself in the cold, locked chambers of bank vaults. There were those who believed Ealy had a Midas touch. He did not. He made money because he didn't touch it. He left it in the stocks and bonds his father had shrewdly—perhaps, illegally—selected. In fact, Ealy had no idea where most of it was. He knew only that he had more than he could reasonably spend and that his mother, Sarah, lived well and carefree on Hilton Head Island from its abundance. He knew that a pleasant, yet serious man named Asa Kimbrough ran the business from his president's office in downtown Atlanta, and that Hilda Kaufmann, a certifiably mad Certified Public Accountant, continued to fax to him summaries of the company's gain in monthly reports that not even the Internal Revenue Service could understand, which was the principal reason the Internal Revenue Service had never audited Ackerman Development Company.

Ealy's home was called Great Place, because, for Ealy, it was the simplest and most honest description he could think of. It was on twenty acres of prime real estate that overlooked the Chattahoochee River north of Atlanta. It was large and, when clean, spectacular. It was almost never clean. Ealy loved clutter. It had been Cary's belief that Ealy's divorce was because of the clutter. Jingle Ackerman had not sought the house in the divorce. "They can burn the damn thing for all I care," she reputedly had said. Instead, Ealy had built her a new home. "For the few good memories," was how he had described it. The home had cost two million dollars. Ealy had been surprised when Cooper and Cary questioned his judgment. "Well, good Lord, boys, she's got to have some place to live," he had argued incredulously.

In the years following college, and his divorce, nothing had pleased Ealy as much as the occasional visits and stay-overs by Cooper and Cary—before Cary's marriage. When the three were there, together, Ealy's home could be what he wanted it to be—the ultimate college fraternity house, where discarded clothing grew like giant African ant mounds in the corners of the rooms and dishware turned to mold on coffee tables and newspapers and books peppered the floor like confetti from a parade.

"Home, boys, is where the heart is," Ealy had crowed, "and, by God, there ain't no better heart beating on this green Earth than the three of us together. This ain't my place; it's our place."

And it was.

The best of the gatherings of the Boy Dogs had been at Great Place. Lazy, comfortable times. Never wild and absurd, as everyone had suspected. When the three were together at Ealy's home, it was for friendship, not to party with preening young women dressed for tease. Not even for Cary's bachelor party, a night when Cooper and Cary had feared the worse. Ealy had said, "Leave it to me, boys, leave it to me. Just don't think this is going to be one of those redneck occasions both of you like so much. Wear your tux." There had been merriment in his voice, and the merriment had terrified Cary. He had predicted a disaster: "You know him, Coop. Remember the Boy Dogs initiation. He'll have half the strippers in town there."

The party had been only for the three of them, a seven-course dinner catered by A Touch of Elegance. A quiet evening, gently nostalgic, in a spotlessly clean house, the three dressed in pressed tuxedos. Ealy's toast to Cary was still quoted among them: "To the best of moments for the best of men." Cooper would remember the ceremony of the toast—with the soft bell-clicking of crystal champagne glasses—as the warmest of their friendship, and as proof that men could love other men without fear of compromise.

Outside, the light that covered Dublin was spectacular. Seeing it, Cooper felt at peace. From his childhood, he had heard his grandfather's stories of the city, had read the history of its beginning by Norse Vikings settling along the bay under the shadow of the Wicklow Mountains, of the Norman invader Strongbow, of the rule of English law that ended in 1922, of the great writers—Ibsen and Joyce and Shaw and Yeats and Wilde and Synge and O'Casey and Swift and dozens of others. He was standing in the city that had hosted the first performance of Handel's *Messiah*, the city of Christ Church Cathedral, the city of men of passion, of warriors, the city of music, the city of happy liars and quick myth.

His grandfather had called Dublin blessed.

"It's the people," his grandfather had said longingly. "Ah, the people. Grand as you'll ever know, my boy. It's the people that's the make-up of Dublin. Without the people, it's nothing but a bunch of buildings that come out of the ground like them upside-down crystals I've seen in them caves in Virginia."

And seeing the people from his hotel window, seeing them exchange greetings, seeing their faces billowing in laughter, their gentle touching, Cooper knew his grandfather was right, and he was eager to be among them, to discover what his grandfather could never forget.

He took the journal his father had given him, opened it and wrote:

I am in Ireland. I know I should be tired from the trip, but I am not, only a little unsteady from being in the air so long. This is a spectacular place. The people are wonderful, like my Papa said they would be. I can't wait to get out among them, and I plan to do that immediately. I can always sleep when I am back in America.

~~~

Trailing Cooper was a pleasurable role for Sandy McAfee, and simple enough. He only had to imagine himself as being invisible, no more than a weak shadow under a filtered sun. Once he had played a private investigator in a low-budget movie about the infidelities of a politician's wife, and he had insisted on being photographed in shadows, giving him the appearance of an apparition. Surprisingly, he had received a few good notices about the role, though the movie, itself, was considered laughable.

Also, Sandy enjoyed watching the expression of awe that seemed to be glued to Cooper Coghlan's face. Cooper was like a child lost in a wonder-land. Face lifted. Wide-eyed. Lips slightly parted. To Sandy, what Cooper saw was as routine as breathing. Yet, he knew that to Cooper, the air was electric with magic.

It was a leisurely, predictable afternoon for Sandy. Cooper took lunch in a pub—Irish stew, from the look of the dish across the room—and then left, following the directions of a small map that he had taken from a leather notebook. Sandy knew the route. Tourists always took it. A stop for photographs at the statue of Molly Malone, with her low-cut dress and her bronze-hard breasts. A stroll across the grounds of Trinity College, pausing to watch a cricket match. A tour in the majestic Old Library and the sacred art of the Book of Kells. A meandering down Grafton Street, where street musicians—some of them children—rubbed spirited Irish music from fiddles, and punk street vendors, with orange and green and barn-red hairdos spiked like the dorsal fins of colorful aquarium fish, peddled their underground literature and juggled tennis balls for loose change. A sudden rain—suddenly there, suddenly gone—

drove Cooper inside a pub and Sandy inside a nearby clothing shop. Cooper would have hot tea and brown scones lathered with butter, Sandy guessed, and then he would return to the Shelbourne to sleep away the jet lag that confused his body.

Good enough, Sandy thought. He had overheard the waiter in the restaurant suggest to Cooper that he should visit Foley's, and Cooper had said, "Funny you would say that. It's on my agenda."

He would find Cooper at Foley's, Sandy decided. Make his move there. He was well known in Foley's, and being well known would help.

~~~

When he returned to the Shelbourne, Cooper set the alarm for seven o'clock on the small snap-open travel clock he had purchased in preparation for his trip. He undressed and slipped into his bed, turned to his side, closed his eyes and slept.

He dreamed of the Book of Kells and, in the way of dreams, he saw his grandfather sitting alone at a desk, patiently transcribing text in a large, ornate book, using a quill pen, dipping it in ink contained in a crystal bottle. He could not read the text, could only see it materializing. And there was an angel, tall, clothed in a brilliant white garment, with wings that bowed up over his shoulders. The angel stood at his grandfather's side, watched for a moment, then reached to touch his grandfather on the shoulder. His grandfather paused in his writing, inhaled suddenly. His body trembled. The angel turned, floated above the floor, faded away.

And then his grandfather was sitting on the trunk of a fallen tree in a grove of great trees with limbs that reached into clouds. He was holding a leprechaun in both hands, talking to him. The leprechaun was squirming against the grasp.

"Stay still now," his grandfather said with warning. "I've caught you fair, sleeping away like a man slosh-full of drink, not hearing thunder if it was over his head."

"A bargain, a bargain," the leprechaun squealed.

"And what would it be?" his grandfather asked.

"A blessing to keep you from harm, you and them after you," the leprechaun said, his voice turned to a begging whimper. He added, "And a wish to be used by you or by them that you grant it to."

"And how do I know I can trust you?" his grandfather asked. "You've got a lying look about you."

The leprechaun wagged his head sorrowfully. "My name is Bogmeadow. You have my word on it, the word of my people from time begun."

"Your word, you say?" his grandfather said.

"True," Bogmeadow answered. "My word for my freedom and my little pouch of gold. I'll shake your hand on it, and seal it. Put me down."

His grandfather laughed. "Well, now," he said good-naturedly, "it's a good enough bargain for me."

He set Bogmeadow on the ground and extended his hand.

Bogmeadow brushed the wrinkles of being held from his shirt. He stood erect, chest out, reached to touch the small pouch of gold tucked in his belt. A smirk began to grow in his face. He sang out, "Never give up what you've got in your hand, 'til the bargain's struck with another man." And then he leapt backward effortlessly, landed, cackled a shrill laugh, dove into the hedgerow and skittered away like a rabbit.

His grandfather smiled. He sat gazing at the hedgerow and he began to whistle softly. Then he reached into his shirt pocket and removed seven pieces of gold coin, fingered them gently. He stood, raised his arm, his fingers clutching the gold, and he shouted, "The bargain was struck while you slept, my friend. Look in your pouch. Stones for gold. Stones for gold. What you've said can't be untold."

From the hedgerow came a cry of great anguish.

And in his dream, Cooper heard his grandfather's voice, "Sleep light, sleep light, sleep light." He awoke, blinked, turned in the bed to look at the briefcase holding his grandfather's ashes. He whispered, "Papa?"

From outside, he heard the sound of moving traffic and muted voices.

~~~

Sandy McAfee stood before the cloudy mirror of the dresser in the small flat he occupied off O'Donovan Road and examined himself. He was still muscular for a man in his mid-50s, he concluded. One hundred and seventy-five pounds on a five-nine frame. On stage, he looked taller, or so he had been told by admirers. Sandy knew it was a deception of his shoulders. He had great shoulders, he believed—broad, strong—and he had learned at an early age to use them effectively when performing. Every stage movement was led by his shoulders, every counter turn, every open stance. He had learned to let his shoulders droop in sadness and rise up powerfully in triumphant moments. It was his shoulders that first moved toward the audience in a scene-stealing soliloquy, his shoulders coaxing him dramatically past the proscenium arch to the lip of the stage where the outer haze of spotlights bathed him eerily, leaving pockmarks of shadow on his face and body, causing viewers to gasp in awe. The viewers believed it was the language they heard, the melodies of Shakespeare and Shaw, but it was not; it was the appearance, the light-shrouded body of the actor conducting his audience with the hypnotic bobbing of his broad, strong shoulders.

Sandy wiggled his shoulders to the mirror. "But, soft, what light through yon window breaks? It is the east and Juliet is the sun," he whispered in a husky voice. He smiled, rotated his shoulders again, turned profile and cast a glance back to the mirror. He could see a wisp of his thick white hair waving free at his crown and he slicked it down quickly with his hand. Not bad, he thought. Not at all bad. "Aye, you've still got it," he said aloud. He added, "No matter what they say."

He turned again full to the mirror and tugged at the knot in his tie. It was his dandy suit, a double-breasted gray with broad, dark stripes, a suit that got attention. His tie was a green silk with the imprint of a winking, red-capped leprechaun in the middle of it. If it was Irish that would impress Cooper Coghlan of the southern state of Georgia in the United States of America, then, by the grace of the blessed Virgin, it would be Irish he would get. Sandy knew about Southerners, had observed Southern visitors in New York pulling the same trick, dressed in their white suits and string ties, deliberately exaggerating their Southern accents to charm gatherings of movers and shakers, and he would do the same. A little of Barry Fitzgerald at the right time would work wonders.

A car horn blared outside his window and Sandy moved to it to look out. He saw a group of young men dressed in rough clothing and leather jackets gathered around a car, circling it, pounding it with their fists, shouting curses. And then the car roared away, barely missing one of the men. An explosion of shouts spewed from the men as they chased after the car for a few steps, then bunched together to posture arrogantly and to brag among themselves of their bravery. Sandy stepped back quickly, instinctively, from the window and shook his head sadly. Dublin was becoming a mean, impersonal city, a dangerous city, he thought. It was time to get away, to find a smaller, less perilous place—Killarney, perhaps, or Limerick—and re-dedicate himself to his craft. His reputation outside Dublin was still intact as far as he knew, and theaters in places like Killarney and Limerick were hostile to the snobbery of Dublin directors. A good actor voluntarily leaving Dublin would be welcomed with open arms, especially if he brought with him gossip rich enough to enliven the monotony of green rooms during rehearsal periods.

He moved to his kitchen and poured a whiskey. Looked at his watch. It was ten minutes after eight. A few minutes of rest, of preparing himself mentally, and he would catch a shepherd's pie at one of the pubs on the way to Foley's. He swallowed the whiskey in a practiced gulp, then poured another and went into his living area and sat in the one comfortable chair he had. His eyes drifted over his apartment. Every piece of furniture in it had come from the set of some play he had performed. Every piece of art thumb-tacked to the walls was a poster advertising an opening night. He sighed. My life, he thought, is shit. He closed his eyes and wiggled his head into the chair's worn headrest. At least he could pay the last month's rent and have some spare jingling money after receiving the three hundred euro wired to him from Ealy Ackerman of the United States, and for nothing more than being who he was—an Irishman. The rest of the fee would give him some breathing room.

Such strange and gullible people, these Americans, he thought, and a smile crept across his mouth. He remembered his tour of the States, eight years earlier, giving readings from James Joyce's *Ulysses*. He'd been treated like a god—wined with the finest of wines, dined in the finest of diners, romanced by lovely, intense, thin-bodied women eager to celebrate the liberated Molly Bloom that each of them fancied themselves being. And not one of them had read the book, not cover to cover. But, God, who had? And who cared? A hot-tongued American woman, slippery with the heat of passion, believed any rambling that he whispered could have come from Joyce. And, of course, it could have.

He opened his eyes, stretched, and pulled himself from his chair. Ready, he thought. He presented himself a last time to the mirror on his dresser. Looked fine, dressed in his dandy. Fine. He felt a stirring in his abdomen, a singing. He lifted his shoulders proudly. "Go do it, Sandy McAfee," he cooed to the mirror. "Go break a leg, lad."

8

Finn Coghlan had been to Dublin in the year before immigrating to the United States. It was a week-long visit to seek construction work with the city's street-keepers, but the job had been more rumor than reality, the kind of teasing that often spread among Ireland's isolated field laborers who spent their time dreaming of merriment and riches, because dreams of merriment and riches were the only comforts for lives of hardship and poverty.

Finn had learned that glory jobs of the city, if they existed, went to Dubliners, not outsiders. Still, to Finn, the week in Dublin had been among the most memorable experiences of his life. He had talked of it with such energy and in such detail, it left the impression that he had been born there and knew its inhabitants intimately. His favorite story, told repeatedly in Dugan's, had been of Sean Malone, the incomparable bare-fisted fighter.

"Took on all comers, he did," had been Finn's way of describing Sean Malone to Cooper. "Throw your hat in the ring with Sean and you were a man looking for pain, and that's the truth. I saw him of a night when he took on five men, one after the other, and when he was finished there's not a mark on him and not a tooth left uncracked in the five who tried him. There were them that were saying he was a reincarnation of the great Dan Donnelly.

"But he was a sweet man, he was, and after the fights, when he went to a pub, they was always begging him to sing the songs of Ireland. He had an angel's voice, that Sean, and there was a saying about him: 'A man who can fight is a blessing to himself—being that living is mostly fight from cradle to grave—but a man who can sing is a blessing to the world.' And right it was. I spent some nights there in Dublin following him around, fight to fight, pub to pub. The fighting would make your blood run wild, it was so grand, and the singing—ah, the singing. When you listened to Sean Malone, you closed your eyes, so as to have nothing

59

but your ears working. It was that kind of voice he had, and since then I've never been in a pub that I couldn't hear him in the back of my memory, clear as a bird's song on the break of morning."

In Foley's, alone at a small corner table, sipping his second Irish coffee, Cooper remembered the story of Sean Malone and a warm shimmer swam through him. Two tables over, an older, white-haired man sat with his eyes closed and listened to a young tenor singing *The Mountains of Mourne.* For a moment, eerily real, Cooper believed the man was his grandfather. He put down his coffee and massaged his forehead with the tips of his fingers and the presence of his grandfather vanished.

Foley's was an upstairs pub. It was not large, yet it did not feel crowded, even when it was. A long bar ran along the west wall. A low railing split the room in the center, giving the illusion of separate seating areas. The stage was a wide, raised platform against the north wall. Tables, varying in size, dotted the floor space. It was a place that invited laughter and story, playfulness and intimacy, and when the flute and fiddle music began—the two instruments with a range of mourning and joy—Foley's became a cathedral of song, a celebration of the spirits that wandered into and out of its narrow downstairs door, leaving impressions as telling, yet as invisible, as fingerprints. It was music to be lived in, not listened to.

The music was a drug to Cooper. It seeped through the capillaries of his body and numbed him with pleasure. He was in Ireland. At last, he was in Ireland. Yet, somehow, he felt as though he had always been there. The only thing missing was being in the company of Ealy and Cary. If Ealy and Cary had been with him, he rightly could have called it the grandest evening of his life, and he imagined them there, seated at the table. Cary watching. Cary drifting like a buoy on the tide of all that was happening around him. Gentle Cary. And Ealy. At home in Foley's. But Ealy was always at home in a bar. In a bar, Ealy was a whale in a fishbowl. There was not a bar on earth where Ealy would have been a stranger. And, yet, it was deceiving. Ealy did not like bars because he liked to drink. Seldom had more than two. Ealy liked bars because he liked people. He liked their stories, their innocence, their dreams, their failures. He liked being the kind of person other people talked to freely. His father had wanted to conquer mountains; Ealy wanted to lift people up on his shoulders so they could see mountains.

He heard a man at the table next to him say, "Jesus, look at that character." The voice was from America. Northeast, Cooper believed. Boston, perhaps. The man pawed a motion toward the front of the room, near the door, and the woman sitting snug against him, turned her head to look. A knot of people was gathering around a man dressed in a double-breasted gray suit with dark, broad stripes, glad-handing him in the way that celebrities are greeted. The man's red face beamed in the frame of white hair that lapped in waves over his ears. He carried a silver-tipped walking cane. To Cooper, he seemed oddly familiar, like the face of someone he had seen in an advertisement.

"Must be somebody important," the man at the nearby table said.

"Looks like a leprechaun," the woman said, and she giggled.

"Maybe he owns the place," the man said.

Cooper watched as the man in the double-breasted suit drifted through the crowd, twirling his cane comically, accepting the tide of greetings that washed over him.

A voice flew up from a table near the bar: "Sandy McAfee, you weasely little bastard, I thought they'd run you out of town."

"Not a chance of it, Jerry," the man named Sandy roared. "The ladies would be rioting in the streets, now wouldn't they?"

"Indeed they would," the man named Jerry crowed. "Celebrating your leaving."

Sandy laughed heartily. He turned to a waitress. "Margaret, me love," he cooed. "Come give dear old Sandy a hug and a loving kiss, and then be off to finding me a pint."

The girl—tall, slender, pretty—embraced Sandy, leaned over to kiss him on the forehead, then turned away from a playful swipe at her ass. "You've not changed a bit, Sandy McAfee," she said over her shoulder. "Still fickle as the day is long."

"And faithful as the night is warm," Sandy called to her.

"Ho, Sandy," a woman from a table of women called, "will you be giving us a reading?"

"Not tonight, love," Sandy said gently. "I'm recovering from a small touch of the flu that's left me throat in a delicate way."

"Treating it with a pint, are you?" the woman said.

"Doctor's orders," Sandy answered, bowing dramatically. He looked around, as though searching for a table, saw the chair beside Cooper and moved toward it. "Say, friend, I'm wondering if you'd be holding that chair for someone?"

"No," Cooper said. "You may have it."

"You're sure now?" Sandy said, reaching the table. "There could be a lovely lady just turning the corner to make her way here, and fate could have her sitting snug up to you before you blinked."

Cooper heard the woman at the table near him giggle again. He glanced to the woman, saw her watching Sandy with amusement. It was the same look he had seen on many people in their first meeting of his grandfather. He looked back at Sandy. "I think I'm too late. It looks as though all the beautiful women are taken for the night."

Sandy nodded, slipped into the chair and leaned to Cooper. "You're talking to a man who understands such plights, indeed. The lovely ones are always arm in arm with some bloke what looks like a god out of your American movies."

Cooper smiled. "You've got me placed, sir."

"An Irishman can spot an American from a mile off," Sandy said. "It's how glad we are to see them, bringing in the money like they do." He extended his hand. "I'm Sandy McAfee."

"Cooper Coghlan," Cooper said. "I'm from Atlanta, Georgia." He added, "The South."

"Coghlan," Sandy said. "Well, there's Irish running in your veins, sure enough, and I might of guessed it, anyway. You've got the look of every Coghlan I've ever seen."

"My grandfather was from Ireland, near Killarney," Cooper told him.

"Lovely country," Sandy said. "Have you been there?"

"Not yet," Cooper answered. "I just arrived today."

"Well, I'm sure it's on your schedule."

"I don't really have any specific plans, but I hope to get there," Cooper said.

Margaret, the waitress, put the pint of Guinness in front of Sandy.

"Fetch another, love, for my new American friend here, Mr. Cooper Coghlan," Sandy said merrily. "Add it on my account."

"Now, Sandy, don't go making trouble for me," Margaret said. "You know you're on a pay-by-drink service."

"Ah, yes," Sandy sighed. "There's not an ounce of trust anywhere, it seems." He began to dig into his coat pocket.

"Put it on my tab," Cooper said quickly.

"Oh, lad—" Sandy said in an exaggerated objection.

"No, I'd like to do it," Cooper replied. He nodded to Margaret. "Bring us both another one on your next trip back this way."

"Sure, love," Margaret said. She winked at Cooper, dipped a nod of her head to Sandy and added, "Watch him. He'll talk you down to your last penny, if you let him." She pivoted away, deliberately rubbing her hip against Sandy's shoulder.

"Sweet girl, she is," Sandy said tenderly. "Flirts around in here shameless, but innocent as the Virgin Mother herself when she's off work."

Cooper watched Margaret glide through the crowd, dodging grabbing hands. She seemed as much a part of Foley's as the whiskies and ales that lined the bar, or the flute and fiddle that made the music.

"And what brings you to Ireland?" Sandy asked.

For a moment, Cooper hesitated. Then: "I guess you could say it's my grandfather."

"And how's that?"

"He died a few months ago," Cooper said. "I've brought his—" He paused again. "Well, his remains back."

"His ashes, I'm presuming," Sandy said. A look of kindness spread across his face.

"Yes."

"And where will you be leaving them?" Sandy asked.

"I'm not sure yet," Cooper told him. "He wanted me to find the spot."

"Ah, that's a lovely thing," Sandy said softly. He lifted his glass. "To your grandfather."

"Thank you," Cooper said. He clicked glasses with Sandy. They drank.

"And he was a Coghlan also, I'm guessing," Sandy said.

"Finn Coghlan," Cooper said.

"Finn," Sandy crooned. "A great name it is. After Finn McCool."

"That's right," Cooper said in surprise. "I used to think he was making that up, until I read about it."

"If we didn't have Finn McCool, we wouldn't have Ireland," Sandy said. "That's a truth, lad."

"And what do you do, Mr. McAfee?" asked Cooper.

"It's Sandy, me boy. Everybody calls me Sandy. I'm sure you wouldn't believe it, but I'm an actor."

"Really?"

"On my word," Sandy said lightly. "Theater mostly. A few movies, but I've always been partial to theater."

"Tell me about it," Cooper said.

"Are you sure, now?" Sandy asked.

"I am, yes," Cooper answered.

It was almost midnight when Cooper left Foley's, helping balance Sandy through the doorway. Margaret, the waitress, had been prophetic. Sandy's bar bill had reduced Cooper's budget considerably, yet he thought of it as money well-spent. Sandy had attracted a gathering at the corner table in Foley's, and what had been myth from his grandfather's telling had become real to Cooper. It had been an Irish night, the kind of night his grandfather had spent years celebrating in memory, a night filled with gaiety and with melancholy and with the sensation that it was eternal. Hypnotic, Cooper thought. Yes, hypnotic. He had watched the American couple being drawn into it, coaxed to slip their table nearer, eagerly telling of their lover's trip from Greenwich, Connecticut. He had listened in amazement as Sandy's voice flew over the crowd like a graceful cast from a fly rod, causing listeners to swim toward the bright, wiggling lure of his stories. He felt as though he had been caught inside the tender nucleus of music that was pure and haunting, coating him with a moist new skin.

On the sidewalk, Sandy pulled himself away from Cooper, raised his shoulders, and tried to stand steady with the aid of his walking cane. "Now, lad, off you go," he said to Cooper. "It's a fine hotel you're in. Go use it."

"I'll see you to your place," Cooper told him.

"I'll not hear of it," Sandy said firmly.

"Are you sure?" asked Cooper.

"It's Sandy McAfee you're talking to," Sandy crowed. "You could wrap a blindfold around me head and cover it with a sack and I'd find me way home without so much as a bobble." He waved his hand awkwardly. "Off you go, now."

"It was a pleasure meeting you," Cooper told him.

"The pleasure was mine, lad," Sandy said. "You're a Coghlan, all right. Good to the soul. And here's a toast for you: Know you're in the land of magic, sure as there's a heavenly father watching down on us with pity in his heart. And know it's him what puts the rainbow a-curling around our shoulders, and sets the pot of gold at our feet. May you find that place of magic, and may you stay still long enough to know you've been there." He bowed graciously, a wide, sweeping stage bow, and then he ambled off unsteadily, turned right down a side street, as though following the voice of someone calling his name. Around the corner, he paused, smiled, glanced at his watch. It was time enough to call his American cousin and report. He would say simply, "Landed him."

~~~

The Shelbourne was only a short distance from Foley's and Cooper walked it leisurely, letting the surprising chill of the May night brush away the voices and the music that seemed to cling to him like static electricity. The traffic that earlier had jammed St. Stephens Green, had thinned. A few people rushed along the sidewalk, their hands tucked inside coat pockets. Down the street, at a pub, he could hear a racing fiddle and laughter and song.

Approaching the Shelbourne, he saw a taxi veer from the street and stop at the sidewalk in front of the hotel. He watched as the driver jumped out and hurried to the trunk and opened it and pulled out a bulging hang-up bag, a small suitcase, and a large box wrapped in plastic. The passenger's door on the sidewalk side opened and a young woman, wearing a long dark skirt and a yellow pullover jacket with a hood covering her head, stepped out.

Cooper heard the woman say to the driver, "Thank you." She handed him some money. The driver looked at the bills, then reached into his pocket to make change. "No," the woman said. "Keep it."

"Well, now, that's kind of you," the driver said. "Give me a minute and I'll get the bellman."

"Don't bother," the woman said. "I can manage."

"Are you sure, now?" the driver asked.

"I'm sure," the woman said, moving toward her luggage.

The driver bobbed a nod, circled his car, got in and drove away.

Cooper watched as the woman draped the strap of her hang-up bag over her shoulder and then leaned to lift the box. The hang-up bag slipped comically from her shoulder and fell against the box, knocking it over.

"Why don't I give you a hand?" Cooper said, moving to her.

"I can handle it, thank you," the woman said without looking at him. There was a tone of threat in her voice.

"You don't have to worry," Cooper said pleasantly. "I'm a guest here. I was just going in myself."

The woman glanced at him and smiled weakly. "Thank you. It's a little heavier than I remember it being. It's a fault of mine. I've never learned when to quit packing."

Cooper laughed easily. "I'm guilty of the same thing."

"American?" the woman asked.

"Atlanta, Georgia," Cooper answered.

"It's in the South, isn't it?" the woman said.

"Yes," Cooper told her. He lifted the box and then reached for the hang-up bag.

"Oh, I'll take that," the woman said quickly.

"When you're from the South, and you're supposed to be a gentleman, you don't permit ladies to carry their own luggage," Cooper replied. He bowed slightly, felt foolish.

The woman did not reply. She smiled and reached for the small suitcase and then she turned and began striding toward the door of the hotel. Cooper followed. She opened the door and held it for Cooper, and then she moved toward the concierge desk.

"You'll need to check in around the corner," Cooper said. He motioned with his head. "That way."

"Oh?" the woman said, embarrassed. "Thank you. I've never stayed here before."

"You'll like it," Cooper said. "Very nice. Very old, of course."

"Of course," the woman said.

There was a pause, a cadence of awkwardness. The woman glanced toward the check-in desk, then back to Cooper. A smile flashed timidly. She pulled the hood of her jacket from her head and shook her hair free. Her hair was long and thick and wave-tumbled, copper and amber colored, glowing as though light had been trapped in it. She saw Cooper staring at her and the smile flicked again. She blinked and the rich, dark green of her eyes strobed over Cooper's face.

"Ah—" Cooper stammered. He paused, swallowed, tried to think of something to say, realized with embarrassment that his vocabulary had vanished, his entire storehouse of words deleted.

"Would you be checking in?" the bellman said from across the lobby.

The woman held her gaze on Cooper for a moment, then turned to the bellman. "Yes," she said. "This gentleman was kind enough to give a helping hand with my luggage."

"I'm sorry," the bellman said, rushing forward. "I was in the back."

"It's all right," Cooper told him. "I was just getting a breath of air."

"You have reservations?" the bellman asked.

"Yes," the woman said. "Kathleen O'Reilly."

"Very good," the bellman said, taking the luggage and the box from Cooper. "If you'll come with me, I'll show you to the desk."

"Right away," Kathleen O'Reilly said. She looked up at Cooper. "You've been most kind. Thank you."

"It was my pleasure," Cooper said. He could feel a blush covering his face.

"I hope you enjoy your stay in Dublin," Kathleen O'Reilly said softly.

"I'm here just for the night," Cooper replied. He paused, swallowed. "I'm off on a tour tomorrow."

"Really? Where to?"

"I'm not sure. Just driving, I think. Well, the southern part, really. My grandfather was born near Killarney. I want to see that. Down to Waterford first, though, and then I'll find my way from there."

The smile flowed back into Kathleen O'Reilly's face. "You'll like Waterford. It's very lovely."

"Oh? Do you live there?" Cooper asked politely.

"No. I do business there occasionally. Public relations."

"Do you really?" Cooper said with surprise. "That's what I do."

"Then you understand the running about," she said.

"I'm afraid so," Cooper said. "Do you specialize?"

A faint blush rose in her face. "At the moment, it's a project sponsored by a number of financial institutions. The planting of trees. That's what's in the box—seedlings. Giveaways, you know."

"Sounds interesting," Cooper said.

Another moment lingered. Kathleen glanced at the bellman, standing patiently, then turned her face back to Cooper. "Well, thank you again." There was kindness in her voice.

"You're very welcome," he said.

He watched Kathleen O'Reilly walk away, her wave-tumbled, copper-amber hair curling over her shoulders. He could feel a pulse-beat in his throat. "Jesus," he whispered. He thought of Ealy and Cary. They would not believe he had just met the most beautiful woman in Ireland.

9

Cooper had intended to have breakfast at seven, leave Dublin by eight or eight-thirty to avoid the Sunday church traffic. He overslept, deciding it did not matter. The schedule was from Ealy's Irish bible and it annoyed him that he felt somehow obligated to follow an agenda he had never thought about.

He had slept peacefully, expecting to dream again of his grandfather, but had not. Surprisingly, he had dreamed of Kathleen O'Reilly, a perfumed dream of her sitting beside him in Foley's, listening to Sandy McAfee's stories, the trapped light of her copper-amber hair shimmering in candlelight from the table. He tried to remember if there had been any candles on the tables, thought not, but the dream, even after showering and dressing, was still warm, still good. With luck, Cooper thought, she would be the only person in the dining room, there for an early breakfast before sprinting away to whatever business meeting had ordered her to Dublin.

In his journal, he wrote:

Sandy McAfee. Kathleen O'Reilly. Two people I met during my first night in Ireland. Sandy is a character straight out of Irish folklore, the kind of person who would drive my grandmother to madness. He's an actor, and pretty well known if the reaction to him in Foley's is any indication. I helped Kathleen O'Reilly carry her luggage into the hotel and talked to her a few minutes. She's in public relations, so we had some common ground. But that's about all we have in common. She has the beauty and spirit of someone who will have the wealthiest men in the country fighting over her. I don't fit in that company. Wish I'd had more time with her, though. It'd be something to brag about to Ealy and Cary. I'm ready to be on the road.

It was not Kathleen O'Reilly that Cooper saw as he pushed open the door to the restaurant; it was Sandy McAfee, dressed in tan cord pants, a red turtleneck sweater, a dark brown tweed jacket with leather elbow patches on the sleeves. A brown golf cap sat at a tilt on his head. His puffed face had the bleary look of a hangover.

"Cooper, my good man," Sandy said cheerfully. "I've been waiting for you."

"You have?" Cooper said, surprised. He sat opposite Sandy.

"I ordered a tea for you," Sandy said, pushing a cup toward him. "Still hot, I hope."

"Thank you," Cooper said.

"Maybe you're a coffee man, though, being from the States."

"Tea's fine," Cooper told him. "I like it." He added, "You're up early."

"It's the hand of fate," Sandy said.

"Fate?"

Sandy smiled broadly. "It's that for sure. Tugged me out of bed like a nagging wife, it did. I've a favor to ask of you."

"And what's that?" asked Cooper.

"You're headed for Waterford, I believe," Sandy said brightly.

"That's right."

"Would you mind if I tagged along with you?"

Cooper looked away from Sandy, dropped a cube of sugar into his tea. He felt suddenly uncomfortable, trapped. He said, "I—ah, I think that would be fine."

"You're a splendid man, Cooper Coghlan," Sandy said earnestly. "I've a chance to do some readings there, but I'm a bit short of traveling cash at the moment, and a lift would be a blessing."

Waterford was not far away, Cooper thought, and he did not want to appear inhospitable. "Happy to help out," he said.

"I'll be your guide," Sandy offered. "Believe me, as much as I've been on the road, I know half the folk of the country by name, and I know how baffling and confusing it can be, out on a road you've never traveled. Puts your wits on end, it does. When I was in your lovely country a few years back, doing readings from Joyce, it was the kindness of guides what kept me from falling off the edge of the world."

Cooper smiled. He was being conned and he knew it.

He remembered the woman in Foley's, saying to her husband about Sandy, "He looks like a leprechaun."

He thought of his grandfather and of Bogmeadow's charm and of the curious dream about his grandfather's trickery in taking Bogmeadow's gold.

"And so I'll be paying back that kindness a bit," Sandy added.

~~~

At nine-fifteen, the Nissan Vanette pulled away from the curb in front of the Shelbourne Hotel and bulled its way into Dublin traffic, with Sandy driving.

"Now, don't go to worrying about a thing," Sandy crowed in his best Barry Fitzgerald voice, swerving to miss two boys on bicycles. "I know these streets like the back of me own hand."

Cooper gazed out of the window of the Vanette and listened to the lyrical song-voice of Sandy McAfee as the city of Dublin thinned away in a blur of speed. Sandy seemed overjoyed at leaving Dublin. He drove like a madman being pursued by the law or by creditors or by attendants from a mental institution. Creditors, most likely, Cooper thought. Promises made, promises broken, and between the making and the breaking, enough of an Irish shenanigan to bring about the threat of bodily harm. The sprint away from Dublin on a bright Sunday morning was probably perfect timing. Sandy McAfee seemed to be a man who survived by perfect timing.

Cooper was not so blessed. Timing had never worked in his favor. He was an almost person. Almost at the right place in the right time. Almost first with an idea. Almost.

He had not said anything to Sandy about Kathleen O'Reilly, though Sandy might have suspected something. He had caught Cooper lingering in the lobby of the hotel, near the door leading into the dining room, as the bellman finished the loading of the Vanette, and he had said, "Looking for someone?"

"No, no, not at all," Cooper had answered too quickly. "It's colder than I thought. Just soaking up a little heat."

71

"It'll be warm enough driving," Sandy had said, letting his eyes scan the lobby.

Timing.

Almost.

He had not expected to see Kathleen O'Reilly, but he had. As the Vanette pulled away, he had glanced back at the Shelbourne and she had stepped out of the door, a flash of radiance.

Timing.

Almost.

Yet, perhaps the timing was as it should have been, he thought. He was in Ireland to deliver his grandfather's ashes to the wind. He did not need distractions.

He thought unexpectedly of Jenny Gavin and had an urge to call her. She would be surprised by the call, most likely irritated. It was only four-thirty in Atlanta. On Sunday mornings, she enjoyed sleeping until nine. It was part of her habit, her day-of-leisure routine. On some Sundays, she would go for a walk, or a workout, and on others, she would remember that she was Jennifer Suzanne Gavin and she would dress conservatively and go to the United Methodist Church near her apartment. On Sunday afternoons, she went to movies, or to art shows. Sundays, like every day, had patterns with Jenny. Once, he had been part of her pattern, and she of his, causing Cary to observe, "It seems to me, Coop, that the two of you are just together, but you don't necessarily belong together."

And what would he tell Jenny if he did call? Cooper wondered.

About Sandy McAfee, the free-loading actor? About the American couple in Foley's, the honeymooners from Greenwich, Connecticut? About Margaret, the teasing waitress? About the music of fiddle and flute, the music of tavern laughter? About watching college students gleefully rubbing their hands over the bronze breasts of Molly Malone, making lapping sounds as their fingers tipped the nipples? About Kathleen O'Reilly, the public relations specialist?

Jenny Gavin would not care about Sandy and the honeymooning couple and Margaret and music and Molly Malone and Kathleen O'Reilly. On Sunday, Jenny was refined. News to her would need to be of a refined nature.

He would tell her about the cricket match on the grounds of Trinity College, about the stunning display of the Book of Kells, about the slim, pale-faced young man standing on a chair on Grafton Street, making bubbles the size of a window by dipping a giant hoop into a flat of soap water and then lifting the hoop slowly, like a ballet dancer swimming in space with his arm-wings, letting the air fill the rainbow-streaked soap-film until it began to billow while the crowd oohed in wonder. He would tell her that he saw the young man pull the paisley-colored bubble over himself, bowing down gracefully as the bubble covered him like the thin, translucent skin of a caul, making him seem embryonic and mystical.

He would tell her Ireland was like that—bubble-covered and mystic.

~~~

Out of Dublin, Sandy steered the Vanette along N7, headed for Naas. At Naas, according to the map Ealy had provided, they would turn slightly southeast on N9, toward Kilcullen, then Castledermot and Carlow.

Sandy had no idea he was driving on N7 and he was amused by the map spread across Cooper's lap. "If it's Naas you're wanting to go to, then it's where I'll be taking you," he crooned. "You can fold that up. We'll not be needing it. The Irish know the places, not the names of the highways taking them there."

"So you know where it is?" Cooper said.

"Naas? I do, indeed. I've played it a number of times, it being so close to Dublin."

"What kind of roles?" asked Cooper.

Sandy laughed merrily. "Readings, mostly. For the horsey set, you know. They love the dirty parts of *Ulysses*."

Cooper wanted to know what Sandy meant by the horsey set.

"Why, lad, surely you know about the great race horses of Ireland?"

"I've read about them," Cooper said.

"Only the best of the world, if you'll forgive the bragging," Sandy said. "There's actions in Naas that'd make your head spin when the money starts piling in. I've been there, I have." He glanced at Cooper, felt the need to be more Irish. "Many of me dearest friends own racehorses," he added, rolling the words over his tongue. "There was one a few years back named for me. Footlight Sandy, it was called. Lovely beast. Lovely. Won a race or two, then broke its leg, dear thing. And wouldn't you know, it happened on the very same day I was there to watch the race. I'd stopped by the stable to have me photo taken with Footlight Sandy, and, naturally, me being an actor, when I was leaving I said, 'Now, go break a leg.' Well, who was to believe the blooming horse would take me serious?" He laughed.

"Is that true?" Cooper asked suspiciously.

"It's true, lad. It's true."

As he drove, Sandy rained stories about the McAfees and Ireland. He bounced excitedly on the seat, released his hands from the steering wheel to gesture dramatically at fields and small clusters of homes. Each off-road place had its own quaint and startling history and at least one McAfee of legendary status, and Cooper began to realize that being with Sandy could be a blessing. Sandy knew history, or he was the grandest liar in all of Ireland. Both, probably. Either way, it was better than riding alone, stopping on the roadside to read from the Irish bible. Also Sandy reminded Cooper of his grandfather, not in appearance, but in the lulling rhythm of speech, in the excess of expression, in the clean tenor of his voice when he broke into song, as he often did, and Cooper imagined that the spirit of his grandfather, still gathered in the ashes securely packed in his briefcase, was filled with gladness.

"There's not a spot of Ireland—not a rock, not a grain of sand, not a blade of grass, not a drop of water—that's not got a story fixed to it," Sandy said seriously, proudly. "Some of it as grand as anything the good Lord ever put voice to; some of it too sad to pass over lips. It's why our music stretches from jigs that'll put your feet to twitching to ballads that'll make your heart bleed with sorrow." He laughed quietly, a laugh of satisfaction. "Did your grandfather teach you the music?"

"Some," Cooper admitted. "The first words I remember hearing were from *Danny Boy*."

"I could have guessed," Sandy said. "It's what the Americans want to hear."

"He had a brother named Danny," Cooper explained. "I think they must have been close."

"Ah, I see," Sandy said. He drove for a moment, seemingly preoccupied, his head bobbing rhythmically. Then he asked gently, "And where would your grandfather's remains be?"

"They're in my briefcase, in a box," Cooper answered.

Sandy braked hard, pulled the Vanette to the side of the road, and stopped.

"What's wrong?" asked Cooper.

"Let's put him up front with us," Sandy said. He patted the space in the seat between them. "Here. It's a better view, and I'm sure he's wanting to take a look at all he's missed them many years."

It was a suggestion that pleased Cooper. He twisted his body and reached for the briefcase that he had placed on the seat behind him, pulled it to him, opened it and removed the box containing his grandfather's cremains. He placed the box on the seat beside him, closed the briefcase and put it again on the back seat.

"A small box for a man," Sandy observed with a hint of sadness. "Shows the great mind of the Almighty, starting us out as a little wiggle worm and ending us up as a cupful of dust." He pulled the Nissan back onto the road. "And what was your grandfather's name?" he asked. "You told me, but I've got a blank on it at the moment."

"Finn. Finn Coghlan," Cooper told him. "I was named for him. Finn's my middle name."

"It's as good a name as an Irishman ever carried," Sandy said. "And he told you about the great Finn McCool?"

"Many stories," Cooper said.

"And your favorite?"

Cooper remembered the night in Dugan's after the memorial service for his grandfather. Remembered the music of Erin O'Connell and Davy Kildare. Remembered the eerie sensation of his grandfather sitting beside him. Remembered Ealy's begging for the story of Finn McCool and Sally Cavanaugh. He said to Sandy, "For me, it was the one about Sally Cavanaugh."

"Sally Cavanaugh?" Sandy asked, letting a ripple of thought worm over his forehead.

"About Finn McCool being in love with her."

"I've not heard of it," Sandy said.

"My grandfather loved to tell it."

"Puzzling," Sandy muttered. "Didn't know there was a tale of Finn McCool that I've not heard." He repeated, "Puzzling." He glanced at Cooper. "But I do know some Cavanaughs. A crafty bunch, they are. I could tell you about a fellow named Patty Cavanaugh and how he broke the heart of a darling cousin of mine, name of Maggie McAfee . . . "

The story of Maggie McAfee flowed into the story of Frank McAfee and the story of Frank McAfee flowed into the story of another McAfee and another.

Cooper listened—half-listened—in amusement, knowing the stories were taken from imagination and bits and pieces of scenes that Sandy had played as an actor. He listened—half-listened—and gazed at the country-side of Ireland swimming past like a spectacular dream. Green-tinted valleys, pale to lush, laced in explosions of yellow from the gorse that grew at the skirt hems of pastures. Thin lines of bluebells hugging the ground like fine purple-blue stitching. Gray stonewalls meandering up and across distant hills, as though they were pebbles dropped by a child at play. Grazing sheep like dollops of white splatterings from the brush of celestial artists frenziedly working to obey the whispered command of God.

He wondered if Sandy was right. Wondered if his grandfather was also gazing at the countryside he had missed seeing for many years.

10

According to the commandments of Ealy's Irish bible, Cooper would make his first international telephone report on Sunday afternoon, one o'clock Ireland time. In Atlanta, it would be eight o'clock in the morning and Ealy would have gained sufficient consciousness from a Saturday night of celebration at Dugan's Tavern, or at Joey D's, to carry on a coherent conversation.

It was an instruction that had sounded ludicrous, yet Cooper knew Ealy was serious. He would, in fact, be awake in Atlanta, showered, alert, his mind alive with questions. It was one of Ealy's curious blessings that he had never had a hangover.

The telephone was outside a small restaurant called Marlowe's, south of Carlow. Sandy vowed he knew the proprietor, suggesting coyly that once he had enjoyed the company of the proprietor's wife in a younger, riskier period of his life. He called the wife ". . . a lovely memory." Sadly, no one knew what had become of her, he confided. One day, she had simply disappeared. "Most likely in the arms of a charmer," Sandy guessed. "She had a weakness for a soft word," he added, winking at Cooper before pushing open the door and striding inside.

The conversation that Cooper had with Ealy as Sandy took his place inside Marlow's, was long and rambling, a jabbering of questions that Cooper answered patiently.

Yes, the country was spectacular.

Yes, the people were the friendliest he had ever met.

Yes, he had been to Foley's, and Foley's had been everything Ealy had guessed it would be.

He told of meeting an Irish actor named Sandy McAfee, of Sandy weaseling a ride to Waterford. Was surprised that the information seemed to please Ealy.

"And the women?" Ealy asked.

Cooper smiled. It was the question he had been waiting to hear. He looked across the street and saw an elderly man and woman walking beside bicycles, carrying on an animated conversation about a row of flowers that were flashing colorful heads to the sun. The man held the woman's bicycle as she bent and touched one of the flowers, like someone touching the nose of a puppy.

"Coop?"

"Yeah," Cooper said.

"The women, boy, the women."

"They're very pretty," Cooper said.

"Beefy?" asked Ealy.

"Some, I guess. I haven't really noticed."

"Bullshit," Ealy said. "You meet one?"

Cooper thought of Kathleen O'Reilly, paused. He knew he would need to give Ealy a name, even if he invented one.

"Come on, Cooper, don't hold out on me."

"One. Briefly," Cooper said. "I helped her take her luggage into the hotel. Her name was Kathleen O'Reilly."

"Well, that ain't Italian," Ealy said. "How'd she look?"

"I think she was just elected Miss Ireland, or Miss Universe, or Miss International Playboy, or something like that," Cooper said. "I didn't pay much attention. We were discussing the aesthetics of public relations."

Ealy sighed heavily. "You know what, Coop, I think you're telling the truth. My God, you're a disgrace to every cod-carrying man over ten. Read the bible, boy. Call me at the next red-lettered hour."

"It's your dime," Cooper said.

"More than you know," Ealy replied. "More than you know."

An intense discussion was taking place around a large rectangular table when Cooper entered the restaurant. Sandy was seated at one end of the table, flanked by two older men. Pots of tea and small plates of scones covered the table.

The two men were introduced to Cooper as Timmy McFarland and George Molloy. They were not related, yet they looked like twins. Both had slender, long faces, red-lined by the abuses of age, or drink, or labor.

Both had clear blue eyes, large ears, white hair. Both were dressed conservatively, as businessmen might dress. Both, indeed, were businessmen, two life-long friends who had met for years on Sunday afternoons in Marlowe's. There they had tea and scones and discussed their respective businesses, and waited for strangers to wander inside. What Timmy McFarland and George Molloy enjoyed most in the world, was engaging strangers in the stories of Carlow.

"We're amateur historians, I suppose you could say," Timmy said.

"And good ones," Sandy offered with authority. "We were just discussing the bravery of the locals when Cromwell—the very devil, himself—come through slaughtering all that was in sight. That was back in the sixteen hundreds. The McAfees were in the thick of it."

"Well, now that's true about Cromwell," George admitted, "though I'm afraid Mr. McFarland and I are unfamiliar with the role of the McAfees."

"Why, of course you wouldn't know," Sandy exclaimed triumphantly. "And how could you? All but one of the McAfees was put to the sword, and the one that got away—badly wounded, he was—hid out in the Knockmealdown Mountains until he got his strength back, and from there he went on to Cork. It was in Cork that he married and saved the family name by the children born to him and his good wife."

Timmy McFarland looked at George Molloy. He blinked once. The blink said that a fool was talking.

"It was a bad time, for certain," George said. "There was a castle standing then, and Cromwell almost put it to ruin."

"True enough," Timmy said, taking up the story. "But the real ruin of it was in eighteen-fourteen."

"What happened?" asked Cooper.

George cleared his throat. "Well, now, there was a Dr. Middleton, who thought to turn it into a lunatic asylum, but was a bit of a lunatic himself."

"That he was," Timmy agreed with a bobbing of his head.

"He wanted to make the windows bigger," George continued, "so he got himself a sizeable amount of gunpowder, and when he set it off, he blew the whole thing apart."

"Boom!" Timmy boomed.

The two old men laughed heartily, slapping the table with the palms of their hands.

Sandy shrugged, arched an eyebrow toward Cooper. "Boom!" he said. He slapped the table and joined the laughter.

More tea was brought to the table by an older, arthritic woman—the second wife of poor Coleman Marlowe, who still yearned for the wife long gone, Sandy explained in a whisper—and the talk at the table turned to business.

Business was in a knotted-up fix, vowed Timmy and George, their twin-like heads bobbing in twin-like unison, and Ireland, always on the brink of sliding downhill from poor to out-and-out poverty, seemed hopelessly stuck in the bog of politics and stubbornness.

"Nobody wants to work," George complained. "Get on the dole, that's the thing."

"Too many old-fashioned ideas in a new-fashioned world," declared Timmy sadly.

"And what business would you be in, gentlemen?" asked Sandy.

"Banking's me business," Timmy answered, "but, at the present, me life is The Cause."

"Aye," said George in a heavy voice. "Me, I'm in farm implements, but like Mr. McFarland, The Cause is the thing that occupies me time."

Sandy blinked. The corrugated look of worry wrinkled across his forehead. The Cause had the sound of Irish terrorism. He said, "The Cause? Don't believe I know about it. Politics, is it?"

George chuckled. Timmy chuckled.

"Not at all," George answered, "though, like every blessed thing there is under the sun, there's some politics stinking things up now and again. No, no, The Cause is just that—a cause."

"A sort of project, you might say," Timmy added.

"And what would that be, if you wouldn't mind sharing with strangers?" Sandy said.

George and Timmy exchanged glances.

"Trees," Timmy said.

"Aye, that's it: trees," echoed George.

"Trees?" Sandy said.

"Making the whole of Ireland a forest, like it used to be when God put it down," Timmy said. "You look about. Not many trees left. The figures have it at eight percent on land mass in the Republic."

Cooper sat forward. He remembered the tree seedlings that Kathleen O'Reilly had in her plastic-covered box. "How does that work?" he asked.

As described by the ramblings of Timmy McFarland and George Molloy, the Cause—officially called NewTree—was a civic enterprise noble enough in its purpose to engage the energies of every true Irishman, politics and religion aside. They painted striking word pictures of desolate ground bolting to life with fuzzy stalks of yew and spruce and poplar and ash and birch and lodgepole pine worming their spindly roots into the earth, then muscling upward into the air, and, in time, providing an industry both beneficial and profitable.

"Goes hand-in-hand with the Irish Forestry Funds," said George.

"And what would that be?" asked Sandy.

"A group of companies with shareholders," George told him. "A fine undertaking. They find the proper land, buy it up, do the planting and care-taking and the harvesting, and the shareholders get their payoff."

"NewTree does the same, but it's for them people who want to keep their land and do their own planting," Timmy added.

"Like us," said George, "though we'll not see the harvesting, old as we are."

"It's for them that's not yet born," declared Timmy solemnly.

"Sounds good," Cooper said, "but I'm not sure I understand how it's to be done."

"Well, now, the sponsors provide the seedlings and the know-how of planting and things of that nature," explained George. "And there'll be contracts with the farmers on the harvesting, making a split with the farmers. They're working out the percentages now."

"Sharecropping," Cooper said.

"Aye, that's it," Timmy agreed. "A little like what used to be in your American South."

"It'll take time, it will," George added. "But time's the one thing we're rich in. Everything else crumbles and falls away; time just goes along being time, the same today as it was a million years ago, the same it'll be a million years from now."

Timmy leaned forward over the table. "We've got to watch the Brits, though," he whispered in a grave voice. "It's them that took the trees in the first place. Come over and cut us clean, they did. Why, there weren't enough timber to build a fishing boat, once they'd stripped us out."

The comment about the British stirred anger in George. "If the bones of every good and true Irishman who's lost his life in fighting the Brits could spring up as a tree, we'd be covered over, thick as wool on a sheep's back, like it was in the beginning." He cleared his throat and let his eyes drift over his listeners, pausing on Cooper. "Excusing me if any of you are from the British stock," he moderated. "I've some good friends who are Brits. Albert Daniels, down the street apiece. A fine man, he is, good as they come. What I'm talking about is history— bloody history."

"The lad understands," Sandy said sympathetically. "I'm sure he knows about the story from his grandfather."

Cooper did not know about the cutting of the trees, but he dipped his head in agreement. He thought again of Kathleen O'Reilly and her box of seedlings, remembered a logo circle with trees stamped into the box and the word NewTree printed beneath. He said, "You'd think there would be a big campaign going on for this."

"And there is, indeed," George declared. "There've been some news stories out, and meetings all over. I'll be going with Mr. McFarland to a gathering in Waterford tomorrow. Sure, now, there's lots of happenings. Lots. Big doings, indeed."

"In a year, we'll be planting, I'm sure of it," Timmy enthused. "I've got a few acres of land, myself, that I'm putting aside just for that purpose. It's the sheep we'll have to be watching. The sheep will graze them down."

Cooper drained the tea from his pot into his cup and half-listened to Timmy McFarland describe his land. It was coincidence—a quirk of timing—that he should meet Kathleen O'Reilly by accident and the next day have tea with Timmy McFarland and George Molloy in an off-road restaurant on the outskirts of Carlow. It wouldn't have happened if he had not called Ealy. He wagged his head in amazement and shifted in his chair. The drone of voices hummed over the table. What was it he had once read? Timing was the seesaw of coincidence. Off-timing, on-timing. Mere seconds of the clock had changed the course of history. If he put his own timing to a test, it would be more off than on. Almost-timing. Yet, he was in Ireland. In Ireland, his grandfather had preached, nothing happened because it happened. There were spirits about, all kinds of spirits—sky spirits, earth spirits, water spirits. Most of them playful busybodies who liked nothing more than meddling in the everyday affairs of mortals. "It's them that keep things hopping," Finn Coghlan had proclaimed. "Why, there's no way of fighting them, no way at all."

His grandfather would have loved the company of Timmy McFarland and George Molloy and Sandy McAfee, Cooper thought. His grandfather would have told them of trees that once grew as high as mountains in the Ireland of his youth, casting shades that cooled entire valleys, trees large enough to carve houses from their trunks.

Cooper stretched his shoulders. A light, gay laughter circled the table. He had not heard the words that invited the laughter, but still he laughed.

He was in Ireland. The spirits were playing.

11

It was a foolish thing she was doing, Kathleen O'Reilly thought. Still, she had made the agreement and she would honor it. And it wouldn't be as it might have been a few years earlier, when she was quick-tempered about such things. She was more mature now, a woman with a career, not a child with fantasies that changed on the tick of the clock. If she had learned nothing else at Raferty & Son, she had learned that patience was the art of survival, and survival was the art of picking and choosing. She had made her choice in the matter of Denis Colum: let him go.

A quick stab of anxiety struck Kathleen in the chest.

It was not letting Denis Colum go that had enraged her two years earlier. It was watching him leave in the company of Doris Hetherington.

I should not do this, Kathleen thought.

She stood in the insanity of movement that curled around her on Grafton Street, fought to compose herself. Why was she suddenly angry? They had talked it out in Cork only two weeks past, she and Doris. Had left one another with an embrace and with laughter and with the promise of the early lunch in Dublin—the three of them. It would be like old times, they had agreed. Three childhood friends together again. There would be no talk of betrayal.

"He'd really like seeing you," Doris had said urgently. "Talks about you all the time, he does. Feels badly about what happened."

"Nothing happened but the right thing," Kathleen had assured her. "It's plain as the sky you were meant to be together. Artist and writer. It's natural as breathing. Denis and I—we were a quick storm that flashed and ended."

And Doris had cried joyfully for the understanding. "I don't think I could live a minute longer if I lost either of you."

Kathleen glanced at her watch. It was twenty minutes after two. They were to meet at two-thirty in Colum's Pub. It would not last long, she reasoned. Thank God. An hour and twenty minutes at most. At four, she was scheduled to meet with a newspaper reporter from *The Dublin News*. If necessary, she could pry herself away early, citing a change in the reporter's schedule, saying the reporter had a Sunday dinner with family.

She crossed the street, side-stepping a juggler.

Of course, Denis Colum would want to meet in Colum's Pub, she thought. So like him. Any place to see his own name on the window and on the beer napkins. He'd most likely boast that the Colum of Colum's Pub was his own kin, and that he spent his days at a table in a dark corner, slouched over his notepad, writing the plays that would have the world forgetting George Bernard Shaw. But Denis Colum was not a writer; he was a pretender. Him with his brooding ways, with his dark, serious eyes, eyes so sensuous they could turn your mouth dry when he clicked them on you. Him with the body that was as lean and hard-muscled as a young lion, and how that body could move over you, like some warm, slow-falling water, trickling down your skin until your skin was oiled with the leavings of his touch.

Kathleen paused in front of a shop window and pretended to look at a display of wool dresses. She saw only her reflection. A new Kathleen, she thought. Dressed for business. Attractive, but not severe. Alluring, but with warning. The Kathleen O'Reilly of the shop window could preside over a director's meeting of a company and never give a glance to the likes of Denis Colum.

Denis was waiting for her at the bar in Colum's Pub. His long hair looked finger-combed, and its darkness matched the darkness of stubble that covered his face. He wore silver wire-rimmed glasses rounded over his dark, serious eyes. His gray-matched pants and jacket were loose-fitting and in need of pressing. His white, collarless shirt, buttoned to his throat, was dingy.

He said nothing to Kathleen when she stepped into the pub. He slipped from his chair and walked to her and folded his arms around her in a gesture of great sadness. His breath came in gulps against her shoulder.

"Will you forgive me?" he whispered.

"There's nothing to forgive," she told him.

He pulled his face back and looked at her. A smile of awe, of worship, seeped into his face. "You look lovely," he said softly. "Lovely." He brushed his fingers across her forehead.

"Thank you," Kathleen replied politely. "And you're looking fine yourself. Where's Doris?"

"I've got a table waiting for us in the back," Denis said.

"Anywhere's fine. And Doris? Is she not here?"

"I'll tell you about it," Denis promised. He took her arm and turned her toward the back of the pub.

"If she's not coming, I won't be staying," Kathleen said firmly.

"You'll understand it. On my oath," Denis said. He tugged at her arm and she followed him. "The day's crawled by, waiting for you," he added. "Like when we was little, waiting on Christmas. Remember them days, Kathleen?"

"We were children then," Kathleen said. "All children are like that."

They reached the table and Denis pulled out a chair for her. She sat properly, as she would sit in presiding over a business meeting. He sat across from her, slouched back in his chair—an artistic slouch—and gazed at her.

"Look at you now," he said gently. "The office lady, indeed. Ah, it goes well on you, Kathleen. It does. You're looking as successful as one of them lady television commentators."

The expression did not change on Kathleen's face. "You were going to tell me about Doris."

"Doris, yes," Denis said in a sigh. He pulled his body forward, propping his elbows on the table. "The fact is, she wanted us to have this time alone, the two of us. Talk things out, you know. She arranged an art class for this hour."

"Talk things out? What things?" Kathleen said.

"Why, us, for sure."

"What about us?"

A puzzled, hurt look clouded Denis's face. He fumbled for a package of cigarettes in his coat pocket, shook one free and held it between his fingers.

"We were—together, Kathleen," he said quietly, staring at the cigarette. "Surely, you've not forgotten that."

"No. I haven't. But that's over and done with. You chose someone else."

"Your best friend," Denis said painfully.

"It happens," Kathleen replied. Her voice surprised her. It was astonishingly calm. She added, "She and I have talked it over. It's best. You're more suited for one another."

"Have you no feelings for me?" Denis whined.

"None romantic," Kathleen answered. "How is your writing?"

Denis shrugged. He placed the cigarette between his lips.

"You can't smoke in here," she said.

He took the cigarette from his mouth. "I keep forgetting," he mumbled.

"The writing?" she said again.

"I put words on paper," he said pitifully. "Dip the tip of the pen into my soul and make scribblings of words. How can I know what it is? Some days it's like listening to music, it is, and other days, it's as drab as winter in Cork." He looked up, his eyes peering into her eyes. "I miss you."

"I'm sorry," Kathleen said quickly. "I don't miss you."

"You sound so cold when you say it like that," Denis protested. "Like you're talking to a stranger. We were children together."

"And now we're strangers together," Kathleen said. "What do you want of me, Denis Colum?"

His eyes did not move from her. He said quietly, "You. I want you, Kathleen O'Reilly."

Kathleen could feel his voice invade her, move inside her like some living thing made only of sound. She remembered nights when his voice covered her body with its warm blanket of air, purring on her skin.

"Could I get you something?" a waiter asked in a bright voice.

Kathleen turned to him. She had not seen him approach the table.

"Two pints of Guinness," Denis said. He reached across the table and took Kathleen's hand. "For the sake of good memories," he added.

Kathleen pulled her hand from his. "Nothing for me," she said. "I'll be leaving in a moment."

"I'll give you a little time," the waiter said, backing away.

"You can't be leaving now, Kathleen," Denis said desperately. "Not now."

"You want to take me to bed?" Kathleen said. "Is that it?"

"More than anything."

"And did you discuss this with Doris?"

"You know I didn't," Denis whimpered. "I'm being honest. You've been on my mind for days, since Doris came back from Cork and told me she'd seen you."

Kathleen laughed wearily. "I'm not believing you're saying such things to me."

Denis slumped in his seat. His expression was lined with pain. "We both know there's no one else for you," he said. "You don't have a man in your life. I'd know if you did. I could tell it on your face if there was."

"Well, look hard, Denis Colum," Kathleen snapped. "Because you're wrong. Wrong as you can be. I'm very much involved, I'll have you know. A fine man, he is."

There was a pause, as labored as the slow breathing from Denis. His eyes narrowed on her. "And who is this man?"

"He's with the firm," Kathleen said quickly.

"With the firm?"

"The company I work for. He's very high up. An officer."

"And would he have a name?"

"Peter," Kathleen answered defiantly. "He's as sweet and as gentle a man as you'd ever know and he treats me like a princess. I've dreamed of him since I was a child, and now I've found him."

Denis took his glasses from his face and looked away forlornly. He began to nod sadly.

"I'm sorry for my behavior," he said. "And I hope it's happiness you've got, because I love you. You know that. I always have. From when we was little."

Kathleen stood. "And I hope it's happiness you have. You and Doris."

Denis looked up. "What am I to tell her?" he asked in a begging voice.

"Tell her we had a wonderful time. Tell her we reminisced about when we were children, about the night we slipped the cat through old Mrs. Delanney's bedroom window and laughed over the fuss."

Denis smiled. "You're a beautiful person, Kathleen O'Reilly. The most beautiful person I think I'll ever know."

"Goodbye, Denis," Kathleen said. "Write well." She turned, walked through the pub and out onto the street, stopped, inhaled deeply, waited for the rush of anger and ache to spin through her. She turned to look at her reflection in the window of the pub. The ghostly, wavering image she saw was not Kathleen O'Reilly, object of pity. It was Kathleen O'Reilly, new person. Denis Colum was a thing of the past. Not a someone, but a thing, an incident. It would be easy to walk away from Denis Colum. She began to stride down the sidewalk, then she stopped abruptly. Why? she thought. Why in the name of God did I utter the name Peter? Of all the men I know, of all the names, why Peter?

12

The stories of Timmy McFarland and George Molloy had inspired Sandy, and before leaving Marlowe's he had launched into an elaborate history about the number of brave McAfees who lost their lives to Oliver Cromwell's forces in defense of the Castle of Carlow—an aggression Sandy compared to General Sherman's burning of the American South, only more horrible in its villainy. "The difference," Sandy had declared, "is that Sherman's work would seem like the warm comfort of a campfire on a chilly night to them that faced up to Cromwell. No doubt about it, Cromwell's fire was stoked in the furnace of hell, it was so hot. Melted rock, so I've heard."

Timmy and George had tilted their faces to Sandy during the telling, like flowers finding the sun. It was clear that neither of them had ever heard Sandy's version of the battle of Carlow, yet it was also clear that they were impressed by what they heard and would appropriate it—or the usable parts of it—for their own telling. To be kind, Timmy even admitted that he did have a vague recollection of the heroic character of the McAfees. Believed he knew of burial stones bearing the name.

"Time eats up some of the finest stories," Timmy had pronounced. "It's why you have to take all them facts you read about with a grain of salt. There's always more missing than's been found. It's why we keeping digging."

To Sandy, the battle of Carlow Castle was merely a warm-up. The stories were roiling in him, spilling like a waterfall from his imagination to his tongue, and Cooper sat relaxed against the passenger seat of the Vanette, listening. In Marlowe's, he had accepted that Sandy McAfee's plea for a ride from Dublin to Waterford was a con man's tale. Sandy McAfee was along for the free vacation the ride would provide, and he would find a way to stay with Cooper as long as possible. It made Cooper think of a Carl Sandburg poem called *To a Contemporary Bunkshooter*, a poem about a con-man evangelist, and how Sandburg thought it was all right to be conned if you knew it up front. Being conned by Sandy McAfee, the bunkshooter, was all right with Cooper. A little like having Ealy and Cary with him. Especially Ealy. Still, Sandy's game was different, his stories new and more outrageous than Ealy's stories would have been.

He touched the metal box containing his grandfather's ashes—still on the seat beside him—and he believed the spirit of his grandfather was in rapture over the stories of Sandy McAfee, believed his grandfather wanted to spin himself back into flesh and bone and blood and to join the merriment of the stories.

~~~

Cooper did not ask Sandy why he pulled the Vanette from the main road near Arthurstown, overlooking an inlet that ran into the Irish Sea. It would have been a foolish question. Cooper was now the passenger, the tag-along, and he knew it. He sat, waiting, watching the glow in Sandy's face.

"Lad, you're about to meet one of the world's grandest women," Sandy crooned, as he stopped the car on the gravel parking lot in front of the View of the Mist Inn. He quickly opened the door of the car and slipped out and stood, flashing a smile at a woman who watched from the porch.

And then a cry came from the woman: "Sandy!" She clasped her hands to her throat, like a girl giddy over a surprise, and then she ran-danced down the steps of the porch and embraced him joyfully.

She was stylish, appearing to Cooper to be in her late-forties to early-fifties. She had black hair, gray-streaked at the temples. Her slender face had the flushed look of health. Her dark eyes flashed. Cooper laughed softly. He had wondered why Sandy advised that they wait until Monday to drive into Waterford. Now he knew.

The woman's name was Lucy Lynch Butler Reid. She was the younger sister of Sandy's most cherished childhood friend, Colin Lynch, who had died four years earlier of tuberculosis. By her own admission—

proclaimed with the vigor of a town crier announcing good news—Lucy had been in love with Sandy since age thirteen.

"But he's a slippery one, he is," she said as she covered the table of her kitchen with slices of carrot cake and scones and serving pots of tea. "Oh, he's had his lady friends, and plenty of them. No doubting that, him being the celebrity he is, but none could hold a candle to his own true love—the blessed, blessed theater. Still in all, I've lived my life wishing for him."

Sandy loved the adoration. "Sure you have," he retorted. "And that's why there's two husbands you visit in the cemetery. Not one, but two." He looked at Cooper, mugged. "No, lad, this good woman was fighting off suitors before she was a teenager."

Lucy made an exaggerated motion of crossing herself. "Bless be the dead," she sighed. "Good men, both of them, and love them I did, but I never lied to either of them. I always told them that it was Sandy McAfee who'd be in my bed if he'd have me." She laughed merrily and sat beside Sandy and gently took his hand. Her gaze was soft. "We had such good times as children, didn't we?"

"That we did, Lucy," Sandy said quietly.

"Now, mind you," Lucy said to Cooper, "Sandy and my dear brother, Colin, was older than me by a few years, but they'd have me along with them, whatever they was doing."

Sandy nodded. "The Three Musketeers, we was."

There was a pause, a sweetly elegant moment, as Sandy leaned to kiss Lucy's hand. Lucy closed her eyes and smiled.

Cooper broke the silence. "You're sure you can accommodate us, Mrs. Reid? It's late in the day, and—"

"Hush," Lucy said gaily. "I've not another soul on the books, and if I did, I'd toss them out like yesterday's garbage." She released Sandy's hand and stood. "Now, find your rooms and take a little rest. I'll be about making the dinner."

"We wouldn't think of it," Sandy insisted. "You'll not be feeding us. We'll be taking you to dinner." He turned to Cooper. "Right, lad?"

"Of course," Cooper said.

"Oh, my," Lucy sighed. Her face beamed. "I've not been out since my last, late husband departed this earth. Two years ago, it was." She looked back at Sandy. "Sandy sent the loveliest flowers, a garden's worth."

"Well, put on your dancing shoes, love, for you've got two of us to share," Sandy chortled.

~~~

It was past ten when Cooper followed Sandy and Lucy out of a small pub not far from Lucy's View of the Mist bed and breakfast home. Outside, the air was clean and cool, holding a faint smell of the sea.

"I'm stuffed," Sandy said. "Best lamb chops I've ever had, I do believe."

"Wonderful," Lucy whispered.

They began to move in a languid pace down the sidewalk. A blade of moonlight, pale yellow, rippled across the waters of the inlet. Sandy and Lucy walked arm in arm, cuddled.

"Beautiful night," Cooper said.

"It is, yes," Lucy replied softly. She tugged at Sandy. "Would you like a walk along the pasture road?"

"You're up to it?" Sandy said.

Lucy laughed happily. "I'll be going alone, if you don't go with me. It's been so long since I've been out, I can't go in. Not now. Not with the moon hanging up there, cracking a smile." She looked at Cooper. "You've got your key?"

"Sure," Cooper told her. "I'm fine."

"Well, then, I suppose I'll be seeing you in the morning," Sandy said.

"Sure," Cooper said. "Early."

"Now, if you're feeling a bit lonely, you can find your way back to the pub," Sandy said. "I'd guess there's a lady or two who's looking for a warm companion on a cold night."

"Sandy," Lucy exclaimed. "Don't go corrupting the boy."

"You're right," Sandy said. "My own personal advice is to stay away from the ladies. They'll break your heart and never give you so much as a fare-thee-well."

"I think I'll leave you standing, after such remarks," Lucy said playfully.

"Now, love, you know I didn't mean you," Sandy whispered. He winked at Cooper.

"Behave yourself," Cooper said, grinning.

"If he does, I'll be locking him out," Lucy said. Her laugh flew into the air like a bird's song. She pulled Sandy away, guiding him down a pale gray road that followed the fence of a pasture.

~~~

In his room, Cooper again wrote in the journal his father had given him. Wrote of the wildness of Sandy McAfee, of the meeting of Timmy McFarland and George Molloy, of Lucy Lynch Butler Reid, of their dinner and how Sandy had cleverly avoided the check, of the night and of Sandy and Lucy disappearing on a path that followed a fence line. He concluded:

Papa would have loved this day.

As he slept, Cooper dreamed of Timmy McFarland and George Molloy. Dreamed that he was standing with Ealy and Cary on the same road he had walked with Sandy and Lucy, watching Timmy and George as they hobbled across a barren field leading to the Irish sea, dropping green seedlings of spruce. The seedlings sprang to life as they touched the ground, grew immediately into trees the size of sequoias, their low-swaying limbs sweeping Timmy and George into the darkness of their shade. And then he saw Kathleen O'Reilly emerging from the trees, holding an empty box. A light, like a halo, closed over her hair. Her eyes held the flame of small, burning candles—warm, soft. She paused, looked back at the trees, dropped the box, then turned and began to walk toward him. As she neared him, Ealy and Cary stepped away. She smiled. Her lips moved, but he did not hear her speak. A scent of vanilla swam around her face.

Cooper awoke suddenly. His heart was racing. A film of perspiration was caked to his forehead.

He rolled from his bed and glanced at his watch. It was two o'clock. He went to the window and looked outside. Below him, from the first floor window of Lucy Lynch Butler Reid's bedroom, he saw a yellow splotch of light puddled on the grass of the lawn. The faint fragrance of vanilla from his dream seemed to seep through the house. Candles, he thought. The light in Lucy Lynch Butler Reid's room was from vanilla-scented candles.

He went into the bathroom and bathed his eyes with cold water, dried his face and hands and went back into the bedroom. Without reason, he picked up his wallet and opened it, fanned open the plastic accordion picture-holder. He still had a photograph of Jenny Gavin, one taken on a New Year's holiday trip to Steamboat Springs, Colorado. She had just ended a run on a beginner's ski slope. A glad laugh was leaping from her face, the cold bite of winter was bright in her eyes.

Cooper remembered the night of lovemaking in their rented condominium. A night that both had called fantasy. Fire oozing up in yellow-orange flames from aged wood. Soft music, barely heard. Warm brandy. Candles. Dozens of candles. Jenny had insisted on them. Scented candles. A room dimly shadowed by fire and candlelight. The lovemaking had been both powerful and fragile—muscled, tender-touched, moist, warm as the light of the room—and when it was over, ebbed into exhaustion, they had curled together and slept.

He pulled the photograph of Jenny Gavin from its plastic holder, gazed at it. For months after their break-up, she had haunted him. Now, she was simply a memory.

He folded the photograph once and then dropped it into the waste can.

He wondered what Kathleen O'Reilly was saying to him in his dream.

13

Kathleen O'Reilly sat stiffly in the passenger seat of the Toyota, holding her briefcase in her lap, its handle uncomfortably buried beneath the seat-buckle strap crossing her hips. She tugged the strap loose, then pulled the hem of her short gray skirt down to mid-thigh.

Beside her, Peter Raferty smiled at the quick motion. His dark eyes moved back to the road, then again to Kathleen's thighs. The smile became a look of pleasure.

"Good trip, was it?" he said.

"You've asked about it once," Kathleen told him.

"I did, didn't I?"

"Yes, you did."

He laughed. "I must be brain dead. The traffic out of Cork this morning was enough to bring on madness." He turned to look at her and as he did, he could feel blood pumping hard in his body, gathering in his loins. The grass green, cable-knit turtleneck that she wore stretched across her breasts in perfectly pointed mounds. Her face was angelic. Her hair changed colors with the blips of sunstrokes that flashed into the car as it moved. Gold. Copper. Chestnut. Gold again. Her eyes were from crystals of a kaleidoscope. Green. Yellow. Yellow-green. Green-yellow. He had never seen a woman as sensuous.

"Peter, I'd be grateful if you didn't stare at me," she said without moving her eyes from the road.

He laughed again and drummed his fingers over the steering wheel. "Don't be pretending with me," he said in a teasing way. "You like being noticed. I know you do."

"You're wrong," she replied angrily. "It's an insult, the way you do it."

He mugged an expression of shock. "And would you be reporting me?"

"If you push me to it, I will," she told him.

"Well, now, you're giving me the shakes, for certain," he said playfully.

She turned in her seat to face him. He was not a tall man, yet his appearance was deceiving—stout in his arms and shoulders, his thick, dark hair oiled back and tied in a short ponytail at the nape of his neck. His face was the face of a man born to a rugged and daring life, having a long scar running off the corner of his left eye. There was rumor he had killed a man in a barroom brawl in Dublin, with the scar left on him as a Mark of Cain. When he smiled, his look was usually a sneer, a portrait of arrogance. From the first day of their meeting in Raferty & Son, she had been alert to his leering and, later, to the meanness that he wore like an aura. How could she have mentioned his name to Denis Colum? she wondered. Even being desperate for a name, how could she have done it?

"I have no fondness for you in the least, Peter," she said deliberately. "Truth be known, if your father didn't own the firm, and if I didn't need the job so badly, I would go directly to your wife and tell her about that little incident of exposing yourself in my office."

A crimson flush of anger flooded his face. "I was drunk, as you well know," he snapped.

"Of course you were," Kathleen said. "But there's nothing new about that, now is there? Not from the stories I hear."

"Stories, what stories?"

"Just—stories," she said, looking away.

"Who's saying such things?" he asked angrily.

"Everyone, Peter. Everyone," she replied.

"Not to my face, they're not," he growled.

"Of course not," she said patiently. "They live in fear of you." She paused, then added, "Why, in the name of all that's holy, do you do this to yourself? You could have asked anyone to meet me. Ian. Alfred. Maureen. All of them know this project a thousand times better than you do, and they all know how to find the rail station."

"I'm the vice president of the firm," he argued. "We needed someone here in a position of authority."

"Nonsense," she muttered.

"I don't like that kind of talk," he warned.

"Then take the job and give it to someone else, Peter," she said evenly. "Nothing's worth this."

"Is that a threat?" he asked.

For a moment she did not answer, and then she said in a quiet voice, "No, Peter, it's more begging than anything else. I'm asking you to stop harassing me. If you want to talk business, fine, but if it's going to be the other, then you'll force me to take measures neither one of us will like."

His smile returned to his face, and the sneer with it. He nodded, glanced at her and took a deep breath, inhaling the perfume she had dabbed on her neck. Its fragrance ran like an electric shock through his body.

"We do have some business to discuss," he said.

"Fine," she replied.

"My father wants you to sing at the gathering in Cork."

"No."

"And why not, may I ask?"

"I was not hired as a show girl. I was hired as a professional, and that's what I am. This project was my idea, in case you've forgotten, and singing was never part of it," she said. "When I sing, it's for my own pleasure."

"Doesn't matter to me what you do," he said caustically. "I'm giving you the wishes of my father. I'll tell him that what he thinks doesn't matter to you."

"For the love of God," she cried. "Stop it."

"All right, you don't have to sing."

"I never intended to."

They traveled in silence, in the awkwardness of being trapped in a space that was almost unbearable for Kathleen. The city of Waterford rose up like a mirage in a desert. Cars swarmed around them, crowding the street. "Tell me about Dublin," Peter said at last. "Did you make all your appointments?"

"I did," she replied coolly. "We should see some stories in a few days."

"Who interviewed you for the newspaper?"

"A man named Sean Kennedy."

"Good-looking, was he?"

Kathleen laughed wearily. She leaned back against her seat. "He was lovely, Peter. A god, he was. Handsome as a model. No, a movie star. A body like a Greek statue. Wheat-red hair. Sea-blue eyes. And a smile so grand it'd make your heart leap up into your throat." She paused, remembered the words she had said to Denis Colum about the man in her life, a man named Peter. The words—or words nearly like them—fit again in her mouth: "And kind, as sweet and as gentle a man as you'd ever know. He treated me like a princess. We had the loveliest dinner, and then he walked me back to my hotel and we spent the rest of the evening just talking."

"And where did this talking take place?" Peter demanded.

"Why, in my room, of course," she answered. She leaned toward Peter. "It had rained a bit, and my clothes had got wet, and I had to change. He loved that silk gown you gave me for Christmas, the one that arrived at my apartment with no name in the box."

Peter slapped the steering wheel hard with the palm of his hand. "You can be a real bitch when you put your mind to it," he hissed.

"So I've been told," she said.

"What was his name, again?" he asked in a rough tone.

A chill struck Kathleen. The man who had interviewed her was sixty years old, bald, a body that wobbled with fat. The man she had described was the American who had helped her with her luggage at the Shelbourne.

"Well?" he said.

"What?"

"His name?"

"I don't remember," she said in a whimper of frustration. "I don't remember."

~~~

In Waterford, Sandy parked the Nissan, excused himself and ducked into a grocery to make the phone call he had fretted about since leaving Arthurstown. "I've got an uneasy feeling in me bones," he had lamented.

99

"I'm chasing a ghost, for sure. You can't trust a producer, lad, not for a minute. They'll promise you everything short of absolution and glory over the telephone, and then not know your name when you show up to call their hand. I've a bad feeling, a bad feeling."

Cooper sat in the car with Ealy's Irish bible open on his lap. Its complicated text cross-referenced place and time. According to Ealy, he should have been driving west, toward Killarney, yet Ealy had not accounted for Sandy McAfee.

Outside the car, two old women wrapped in heavy, cloud-gray clothing were pushing a wobbly cart down the street, each with one hand on the cart. They seemed to strain, as though the cart was filled with stones. It was not. It was empty. As they neared the Nissan, they stopped and stared, huddled close, then moved on in their dragging steps.

Ealy would have jumped from the car with his camera in hand and he would have paid the two women an extravagant sum to pose for pictures, Cooper thought.

He felt suddenly lonely and he wished Ealy and Cary were with him. He glanced at his watch. It was ten minutes after eleven. In Atlanta, ten minutes after six. Maybe he would call them later, tell them about Arthurstown and Lucy Lynch Butler Reid and his odd, ethereal dream of Kathleen O'Reilly appearing to him from a forest of trees.

And maybe he would beg them to buy tickets on the next flight to Ireland. Tell them to find their way to Waterford.

No, he thought. Not enough time. He had a task. The task mattered. There was a place, a wind, waiting for the ashes of Finn Coghlan.

He touched the metal box holding his grandfather's cremains and remembered a childhood game he had played with his grandfather. Hot and Cold, it was called. His grandfather would hide a coin—a dime, a quarter—and Cooper would be given ten minutes to find it. If his search led him close to the coin, his grandfather would yodel, "Hot!" If he wandered away from it, his grandfather would say in a whisper, "Cold."

He had never failed to find the coin.

He ran his fingers over the top of the metal box. "Where am I, Papa?" he said softly. "Am I close? Am I hot?"

~~~

It was a woeful tale that Sandy McAfee shared over tea in a small rest-aurant.

The producer who had wooed him with lavish promises of stardom in a new staging of readings from James Joyce, had been arrested and locked away after being caught in a tryst with a fragile young actor who had attempted suicide over his shameful actions. The producer had lost his contracts, his wife, his children and, most distressing, the power of his promises.

"It's a damnable business, it is," Sandy moaned.

Cooper knew the story was only beginning. To rush it along, he asked, "What are you going to do?"

Sandy wagged his head, sighed. He leaned back heavily in his chair. "To be truthful, lad, I don't know, not at the moment, not with all that's happened." He looked away. A dreamy, melancholy look.

"Any immediate plans?" Cooper said.

Sandy sighed again. "Not the first one."

"You've got some time on your hands, then?"

Sandy chuckled softly, wearily. "Time? It's about the only thing I've got plenty of."

"Why don't you go along with me?" Cooper suggested.

Sandy looked back at him. A startled expression clicked across his face. Too startled, Cooper reasoned. Overplaying.

"Well, now, that's a thought, it is," Sandy enthused. He began to nod vigorously. "Sure, I can, and why not? It'd be a great pleasure." He leaned toward Cooper. "To be honest, young Finn, it's been heavy on me mind all this time being with you—about your grandfather's remains. Sometimes when we're driving, I think I can feel him creeping up out of his box, wanting to take hold of the steering wheel and put us on one of them winding little off-roads. I'd say he's wanting to be turned loose, and I know when you do it, you'll be in need of some comforting, and I'd be honored to lend an ear for listening. I know how it is. Me own sweet father was lost at sea, and there was nothing to do but row out on the water and float a spray of flowers over where he'd gone down." He paused, touched his eyes with a finger. "Geraniums, they was," he added.

"Then, it's settled," Cooper said. "My friends in Atlanta thought I needed a guide, and now I've got one. I'm sure they'll be happy to know it."

"Why, for sure they will," Sandy said blithely. "For sure, they will."

~~~

It was a wind-warm day, bright, green-laced, flowered. The sounds were the sounds made on playgrounds by children playing toss with their own squeals. If anything plagued the world, it was not in Waterford.

"One of the loveliest places you'll see," was Sandy's assurance to Cooper. "In my youth, I spent a number of summers here, studying for my craft in a small theater that took its final bow when I was twenty-five or so. Not many even remember it, but it was grand in its time. And I got to know the city, and since it's a walking kind of day, let me show it to you."

"Sounds good," Cooper said.

"You'll see," Sandy said. "There's more to it than a glass factory."

Sandy was ebullient. He had the bounce-walk of a prancer in a parade, the excited voice of an auctioneer. Cooper was both amused and amazed by his energy. The night before, Sandy had loved Lucy Lynch Butler Reid on a four-poster bed under the cozy light of candles leaving a scent of vanilla. An hour past, he had pulled his con about a disgraced producer, and now he was flying the con like a kite. Words, to Sandy, were like nicotine. He was addicted to them like a chain smoker of syllables.

Still, there was something touching about Sandy's love of Waterford. The great cathedrals of St. Patrick's and Christ Church and Holy Trinity seemed to numb him and he talked of them in a quiet, reverent voice. In the south sanctuary of Christ Church, at the sarcophagus of James Rice, he paused, gazed with awe, whispered the tale to Cooper: James Rice, mayor of Waterford in the late fifteenth century—about the time Columbus discovered America—had died and the sarcophagus had been carved according to his instruction. It was a body in decay, with worms crawling from his ribs. "Had it done to remind the unfaithful about the temporary nature of living on earth," he said softly. "There's them that finds it offensive, but it fascinates me. As a boy, I used to come and gaze at it, trying to hear the story it was telling to me."

At a late lunch in a small café, he fell into a somber mood and knowing it was on him, apologized to Cooper. It was from being in the presence of the cathedrals, he believed. The cathedrals always left him feeling unworthy, a dust-speck of existence. An aching festered in his soul over the killings that had ravaged his country from days so ancient they were real only in imagination. Clan against clan, family against family, Protestant against Catholic. "It's a struggle that brings a mist to God's eyes, it is," he said. "All them stories, Cooper, all them stories. Like the stars, they are. So many they can't be counted, but God's in them. Everywhere you turn. If you let your heart feel what you see with your eyes, or hear with your ears, you'll know he's there. Got his hand in all of it. I wouldn't speak of it outside a few of me dearest friends—and you're one of them, for certain—but it's not the Jews that God's got a tender spot for; it's the Irish, them that keeps his home here on Earth."

Sandy took a second ale to ease the depression of being unworthy, let it medicate him until a smile bloomed again on his face and he said to Cooper, "Let's go find a shop where there's some of the Waterford glass still to be had. Did you know it's made of sunlight? It is. The whitest white of sunlight that's been caught up and cooled down just enough to handle, and then put to shape by angels."

~~~

Kathleen O'Reilly stood under a thin stream of water that sprayed from the shower in her quarters at the Green Hills Bed and Breakfast. Her face was lifted against the water, her eyes closed. She could feel the water spinning down her body, spilling into the drain, a slurping sound. The water was cool, as she wanted it to be. Cool enough to take the heat of anger from her, cool enough to cleanse away the grime that was Peter Raferty.

As she knew he would do, Peter had ordered whiskey with the lunch she had arranged for businessmen in the Waterford area. Three drinks and he had become bullying and obscene, enough so that she had ushered him from the dining room—giving excuses of reaction to medicine for a lingering cold—and she had forced him, under threat, to leave.

"Go back to Cork," she had ordered, "or I'll call your father personally, and then your wife. As God is my witness, I will."

Peter had left angrily, driving erratically.

She was exhausted. More exhausted than she had ever been. The lunch. The after-lunch session of questions and testimonials. The distribution of spruce seedlings she had hurriedly potted, handing one to each attendee as they left the room. And then the walk-around to businesses in Waterford, leaving a seedling in each establishment. On the walk-around, an earnest young woman named Susan Dunne, on her first assignment as a journalist, had followed her. Susan Dunne had treated her as a goddess, had called her a Joan of Arc, and had vowed to do everything possible to make the story of the reforesting of Ireland the most important event of the new millennium.

Susan Dunne was wrong, Kathleen thought wearily. The shower she was taking was the most important event of the new millennium.

She turned off the water, toweled her body and hair, slipped into bikini panties and pulled a tee shirt over her head. The shirt advertised a 1997 music festival in Donegal Town.

It was 5:25 by the clock on the nightstand. A short nap, she thought. A short nap. She collapsed on the bed, tugged the pillow under her head, closed her eyes, slept.

14

Priscilla's was a large, comfortable tavern, designed to have a primary dining room and show area, and several isolated corners with small, private tables. There were two stone fireplaces, faced with sofas and armchairs. A weak fire flickered in each. The bar was in the center of the room. Recessed lighting, with finger-spots pooling over paintings and flower arrangements, gave the room a sense of warmth. To Cooper, it was more of a quiet American bar than an Irish pub. Only a few people were sitting at the bar and around four of the tables. The only sound was the sound of their voices and of their laughter, a friendly, inviting sound.

"It's not Foley's, but it's a grand place. You'll see," Sandy said. He was wearing his dandy suit. Did his dandy look-about with his dandy shoulder-pointing trick. "I'd say a seat in front of the fire."

"Sounds good to me," Cooper told him.

"A little favor," Sandy said quietly.

"Sure. What?" Cooper asked.

"Let's not go into what I do." He shrugged, touched at the wings of his hair. "The acting," he added. "I'm a bit weary tonight."

"You've got it," Cooper said.

They sat before the fire, in armchairs. A waitress in her mid-forties, pretty, hair that had a tint of pale straw, a smile as warm as the room, approached and asked for their drink order.

"What do you suggest?" asked Cooper.

The waitress smiled at the sound of Cooper's voice. "Well, you're in Ireland now aren't you?" she said pleasantly. "I'd guess a stout. A Guinness."

"Sounds fine," Cooper said. He turned to Sandy. "The same?" he asked.

"The same it is," Sandy said. Then, to the waitress: "And how's the dinner?"

"The best you'll find in Waterford," the waitress answered. "Want me to hold a table for you?"

"Sure," Cooper said.

"And will there be some music?" asked Sandy.

"A bit later," the waitress said. "Some of the locals, you know, playing for the fun of it and for a pint or two, and sometimes them from the audience joins in."

Sandy leaned forward, blinked a wink at the waitress that Cooper did not see. He said, "My friend here, why he sings like Caruso. Maybe he'll do a number or two."

Cooper blushed, looked in disbelief at Sandy.

"Well, it'll be an improvement over the locals," the waitress said.

"Wait a minute," Cooper objected. "His friend does not sound like Caruso, and his friend is definitely not going to insult the good people of Ireland by making a fool of himself."

The waitress laughed. "After a few pints, everybody's Irish and nothing's insulting. Why, they'll be cheering the effort."

"Or throwing bottles at the man making it," Cooper said.

"If they did, I'd have them cuffed," the waitress said.

"Are you Priscilla?" Sandy asked smoothly.

The waitress laughed again. "Oh, no, my name's Lizzy."

Sandy fell back in his chair. A look of shock flew into his face. "I'm not believing it," he whispered.

"What?" Lizzy said.

"It's the name of me ex-wife," Sandy moaned. "Lizzy, after Elizabeth. And wouldn't you know, tonight's the anniversary of her taking leave of me. Twenty years, it's been."

"Am I hearing a little run of blarney?" Lizzy said in a teasing voice.

"It's true," Sandy vowed. "And it's the name. Lizzy. Every Lizzy I've ever known, they've all been out to bring me to ruin."

"And do they?" Lizzy asked.

"Not yet," Sandy said.

"Now, could it be they've not tried hard enough?" Lizzy cooed. She blew a kiss toward Sandy, then pivoted gracefully and walked away.

"Lovely," Sandy said cheerfully.

"That true, about your ex-wife?" asked Cooper.

"For the moment, it is," Sandy answered. He ran his fingers over the lapels of his dandy suit, mugged a confident grin.

Cooper laughed quietly. "In America, we'd call you a work of art," he said.

"In America, I was a work of art, young Finn," Sandy bragged. "If I weren't so modest, I'd show you the nail marks of a charming lady I met when I was playing in your own good city of Atlanta. She loved me voice. Tried to claw it out of me, she did."

"And I wonder what Lucy Reid's doing at this moment," Cooper said, teasing.

"Why, boy, she's smiling at a memory worth keeping," Sandy said.

By nine o'clock, Priscilla's had become the center of the Irish universe—at least for those who had wandered through its doors during the cool May night. It was a gathering of the young mostly, and they quickly became amused with the gabbing that circulated among the regulars about the playful bantering between Lizzy, the waitress, and the aging, fancy-dressed gentleman sitting with an American tourist. It was a contest of flirtation between them, of winks and whispers, of sighs and promises, of come-ons and put-downs. Both knew it was being played for the crowd and both enjoyed the cheers of points scored. Lizzy was expert, as Cooper had suspected, yet so was Sandy, as he had boasted.

At nine-thirty, the music began—fiddle, flute and guitar—and Cooper could feel a comfortable, pensive mood closing over him. He was in the land of his grandfather, the land of Finn Coghlan and Finn McCool and all the other Finns, and the slow-moving brook of his third stout began to ebb gently against the landscape of his soul. Sandy saw the look in his face, the misty, sad-glad look.

"Ah, you're in it," Sandy whispered.

"In what?" asked Cooper.

"The place of the voices," Sandy said gently.

The fiddler, a rosy-faced young woman, plump at the jowls, stroked her bow across the strings and a soft, plaintive ballad began.

Sandy stood, bowed to Lizzy. "Lizzy, me love," he crooned, "it's our tune, it is. The first time we made love, it was what was playing."

Lizzy laughed.

"Surely you remember," Sandy pleaded. "On a rainy summer evening, with the wind whistling about the shutters, and the limbs of the trees slapping at the roof, and the music coming from the radio on the bed stand. The vow we took. If ever we heard it again, we'd dance to it."

"And sure I do," Lizzy said. She put down her tray of drinks and moved seductively to Sandy, her face almost touching his, and dared him with her eyes.

"Now, would you?" Sandy asked in a voice that only Lizzy heard.

"Yes," she said in a voice meant only for Sandy.

They began to dance slowly, comfortably, their bodies fitting close.

"Well, by the glory," exclaimed the bartender. "She's dancing. She's never done that before."

"Must be a good tipper," said a regular.

"Aye, or hung like Malone's ghost," said another.

"And what's that?" asked the bartender.

"Why, you know it's there, for sure, but you can't see it, so it's as big as a man's lying tongue, or a woman's wishful thinking."

A line of laughter rolled the length of the bar.

As they danced, Sandy could feel the dampness of Lizzy's hand against his own, could feel her ease into him, the strong thigh muscle of her leg stroking him. He could feel himself swelling and as her leg touched the swelling, recognizing it, her back stiffened and she lifted her breasts to tip against his chest. She placed her head on his shoulder. Her breathing was moist on his neck.

A woman at a table next to Cooper oohed audibly.

When the music ended, the room erupted in whistles and applause. For a moment—quick, unguarded—Lizzy gazed into Sandy's face, and then she stepped back and curtsied. "For a man full of himself, you're light enough on your feet," she said.

"And for a lady with the unforgiving name of Lizzy, you're a joy to behold, you are," Sandy replied, returning the bow. He turned to the musicians. "Do you take requests?"

"Indeed, we do," the guitar player said.

"Then I've a favor to ask," Sandy told him. He turned to Cooper, gestured grandly. "This fine young man from America is named Cooper Finn Coghlan and it's his first time in Ireland, but he's Irish to his soul and you have my vow on it. He's here bringing the ashes of his dear, lately departed grandfather to let blow free in the wind of his homeland."

The room became quiet and Sandy knew he was in command. He took a step toward Cooper. "It's an Irish thing to love the dead, since we've so many dead to love," he said gently. "Come. Tell these good people about your grandfather. We'll raise a glass to him, celebrate him being home."

"Here, here," a man at the bar said. A chorus of other voices repeated, "Here, here."

Sandy reached for Cooper's hand, pulled him from his chair to polite applause, led him to the bandstand, and positioned him in front of a microphone.

"These are your friends, young Finn Coghlan," Sandy said in his deepest voice. "Tell them." He stepped back.

For a moment Cooper did not speak. His eyes scanned the room, the faces watching him. The faces had the look of waiting gladness.

"My name is Coghlan," he said quietly. "Cooper Finn Coghlan. My grandfather, Michael Finn Coghlan, came to America in nineteen thirty-eight. He was a stonemason and a storyteller, and the stories he told were the stories of Ireland. He died three months ago, without ever returning here. It was his last wish that I bring his remains back to his homeland." He paused and let his eyes scan the faces of the people watching him, and he knew they were listening attentively, "When I was very small," he continued, "the first sounds I heard—the first sounds I remember hearing—were of my grandfather singing *Danny Boy* to me. I would learn later that he sang it because he had a younger brother named Danny, a brother he never saw again after boarding the ship for America. And though I know the Irish must think it's the only song from Ireland that Americans have ever heard, to me it's the song of my grandfather, and that's why it's special. I wish I had his voice. I would sing it. I would sing it for Finn Coghlan."

He paused again, turned to Sandy. Sandy nodded approval. He raised the glass he was holding.

"To Finn Coghlan," Sandy called.

"Finn Coghlan," the crowd answered in unison, raised glasses glimmering in the muted light of the tavern.

The guitar player fingered a note. The fiddler lifted her bow. The flutist blew softly into his flute. And the crowd began to sing: "Oh, Danny Boy…"

At the bar, an older man began to weep.

And at the door, holding her coat over her arm, Kathleen O'Reilly stood, watching in disbelief.

15

When Cooper saw her, she was still standing near the door, still holding her coat, still watching him as he moved through the people who crowded around him. She seemed trapped, uncomfortable. He wondered if she had just arrived or if she had been there and was leaving.

Go easy, he thought. Go easy.

She stepped closer to the door and glanced across the room as though looking for someone as he approached her.

"Hello again," he said.

She smiled uneasily.

"We—met before," he said hesitantly. "In Dublin. At the hotel."

"Oh, yes," she replied. "We did, didn't we?"

"You're Kathleen O'Reilly, if I remember correctly."

She nodded.

"I'm—"

"Cooper Finn Coghlan," she said. "I heard. It was lovely, what you said about your grandfather."

"Believe it or not, it was true," Cooper told her. Then: "Are you just arriving?"

"Yes," Kathleen said. "At least, I was thinking about it. Just for a quick glass of wine, but it's late and—"

"Late?" Cooper said cheerfully. "What is it? Ten-thirty? Eleven? That's not late."

"It's been a long day," she said.

"Planting trees?"

"Something like that."

"I'm here with a friend," Cooper said. He glanced at Sandy, who had paused at a table of laughing women. "The older gentleman who was with me on stage." He smiled, nodded with his head toward Sandy. "Him. Would you join us?"

Kathleen glanced over the room again. A worried expression flicked in her eyes.

"I'm sorry, you must be meeting someone," Cooper said apologetically. "Believe it or not, I met some gentlemen yesterday who were singing praises about your program."

"Really?" Kathleen said. She smiled nervously. "No, I'm not—meeting anyone." The smile twitched again on her lips. "One glass, then. A quick one."

"Good," Cooper said. He directed her to the table they had taken for dinner and introduced her to Sandy, explaining about their meeting in Dublin. He reminded Sandy of the conversation about the tree-planting project with Timmy McFarland and George Molloy.

"Well, indeed," Sandy crooned. "And this fine lady's making it happen, then? And it will, for certain."

The music began again, a lively, spirited tune.

"It's a little noisy here," Cooper suggested. "Why don't we move back to the fireplace so we can talk."

"I'd like that," Kathleen said, and the way she said it, Cooper knew she was self-conscious.

At the fireplace, partially isolated from the barroom by a curved wall, Sandy directed the seating—Cooper and Kathleen close in armchairs, he on a sofa opposite them.

"Do you live here?" Sandy asked.

"No," Kathleen told him. "In Cork. I'm here on work."

"Ah, Cork," Sandy sighed. "A grand city."

Lizzy approached. "Turn my back and you're off with another lady," she said to Sandy in a teasing voice.

"I'd never do that, love," Sandy said. "This young lady is a new friend of Cooper's. Her name's Kathleen." Then, to Kathleen: "This, my dear, is the enchanting Lizzy, who's promised to marry me and support me in my advancing years."

Kathleen smiled.

"Be careful what you ask for, love. You may get it," Lizzy countered. She turned to Kathleen. "Watch out for this one. He's the Love-Talker," she said. "And if you know the poem of the Love-Talker, you know it's death he's whispering in your ear. He's a flirt and a no-good, like most men, God love them. Take my advice and stick with this nice young fellow you're sitting near. I'd pour him into a perfume bottle if I could, just to pry open the top now and again and dab a bit of him on my neck. What he said about his grandfather was grand, too grand for this place. I've been passing out tissues to all the old men wedged in at the bar, most of them believing they knew Finn Coghlan as a boy."

"Do you think any of them did?" Cooper asked eagerly.

Lizzy laughed. "Not a one. It's the whiskey talking." She turned to Kathleen. "And what'll you have, dear?"

"I was thinking wine," Kathleen said, "but maybe an ale would be better."

"It's nippy out," Sandy said. "What would you think of a brandy?"

Kathleen nodded. She had slept a deep sleep, had awakened with the drugged hangover of a long, tiring day, and had taken a sandwich in the dining room of the Green Hill before deciding to walk to Priscilla's. The walk, in a cooling breeze, had refreshed her, yet it had also left a chill on her. Brandy sounded better than wine or ale. "Yes," she said. "That would be good."

"Three brandies, love," Sandy said to Lizzy. "The best you've got."

"You're talking to the best we've got," Lizzy said. She puckered her lips seductively to Sandy and waltzed away.

"Ah, another time in another day and she'd have me on my knees begging," Sandy said. He winked at Kathleen. "So, Kathleen O'Reilly of Cork, tell us about yourself. The whole history, from the moment of birth until you walked into this fine establishment a few minutes ago. Don't leave out a single detail."

A smile eased into her face. She liked Sandy. "Not much to tell, I'm afraid," she said. "Born in Cork. School. Job. And that's about it."

"Incredible," Sandy said in fake astonishment. "What great cinema it'd make."

Kathleen blushed. "Not very exciting, is it?" She fingered her hair from habit, flicked an awkward smile to Cooper. "I'm an only child. My father's name is Connor, my mother's name is Christine."

"Christine?" Cooper said. "That's my mother's name, also."

"Ah, now we have it," Sandy cooed. "Now, we're learning of the things that matter. What else, dear?"

"There's not very much more," she answered hesitantly.

"Some people keep things simple," Cooper said. "I think that's commendable." He frowned at Sandy. "And some people can be a little nosy."

"Oh, no, it's fine," Kathleen insisted. "I think of my life as being boring."

"Boring?" Sandy said. "Boring? This is what I think your life has been, Kathleen O'Reilly of Cork, daughter of Connor and Christine O'Reilly." And he began to weave a humorous story of birthright from nobility, of wealthy suitors, of intrigue, of retreat to the world of business. Words rolled from him in a rumbling voice, a soliloquy of words, and, suddenly, miraculously, Kathleen O'Reilly became a child, wide-eyed, mesmerized, bright with laughter.

"Love-talking you, is he?" Lizzy said, putting the tray of drinks on the coffee table separating the sofa and the armchairs. "Don't say I didn't warn you." She reached into her pocket and pulled out a small piece of paper and handed it to Kathleen. "A gentleman sent this over."

Kathleen closed her eyes in dread, then opened them and read the message. A surge of anger flowed red in her face. She wadded the paper and shoved it into her purse.

"Anything wrong?" asked Cooper.

"No," Kathleen answered evenly. She glanced toward the bar.

"Want me to tell him to bug off, dear?" Lizzy said.

"Thank you, no," Kathleen replied.

"He's a nasty one," Lizzy offered in a whisper. "I see them all the time. Come out from under the rocks at night, they do, always looking for a fight."

"It's all right," Kathleen told her.

"We've got a bouncer," Lizzy said. "And as rough-looking as your friend is, our boy's a head taller and a yard wider. It'd be like picking up a rag for him."

Sandy sat forward, gazed tenderly at Kathleen. "She's got two bouncers sitting with her," he said. "White horses and all, and if it's a damsel in distress who needs a strong arm, why we'll be providing it."

Kathleen smiled.

"What a talker he is," Lizzy said. "A good boo and he'll be diving for cover."

"There's nothing to worry about," Kathleen said.

"I'll keep a watch anyway," Lizzy promised. She left the table.

"Are you sure everything's all right?" Cooper said.

Kathleen nodded, picked up her brandy.

"Not a jealous husband, is it?" Sandy asked lightly.

Kathleen smiled again, a smile holding laughter. "Oh, heavens, no," she said. A light blush covered her face.

"I don't think we need to meddle," Cooper said to Sandy.

"You're not," Kathleen insisted. "It's just a co-worker who's a bit infatuated, and drunk, I'm sure." She shrugged her shoulders as though shrugging off the experience, then lifted her glass to Cooper. "Welcome to Ireland," she said.

"Believe me, I'm glad I'm here," Cooper replied.

"What we need is a photo of the two of you," Sandy said. "Did you bring your—" He paused and looked up to see a man staggering toward them.

"So, here you are," Peter Raferty hissed. His eyes were red-streaked and glazed. He wobbled a step closer and sneered at Cooper. "It's him, is it? Him that's followed you here. You'd be spreading yourself for the likes of him?"

Cooper stood, stepped between Peter and Kathleen. "I think you should leave," he said quietly.

"You do, do you?" Peter growled. He leaned to Cooper, an inch from touching. "And would you be showing me the door?"

"Now, lad, that's enough," Sandy said in a warning voice. He stood, lifted his shoulders and struck a bold pose. "Don't go making a fool of yourself."

From across the room a young man wearing muscles like a uniform moved quickly toward them.

"I'm not the fool," Peter said. He jabbed a finger at Kathleen. "She's the fool."

"Peter, leave. Please," Kathleen begged.

The bouncer reached them. His hand flashed like the striking of a cobra and he caught the muscle leading from Peter's neck to his shoulder, pinching it viciously in the vise of his fingers. Peter's mouth flew open in shock and in pain and he began to sink to his knees. "Come on, friend," the bouncer said in a light, up-beat voice. "Leave the good people alone and I'll buy you a farewell drink." He twisted Peter to face him. "But if you don't, I'll be obliged to tear your face from your skull and hang it up behind the bar for a little show-and-tell souvenir."

Peter gasped for air. He tried to lift his hand, but could not.

"And what was that?" Sandy said. "Was he trying to apologize to the lady?"

The bouncer smiled. "I do believe he was." He turned Peter to Kathleen, holding him like the dummy of a ventriloquist. "Could you manage a simple 'I'm sorry' for the lady?"

Peter gurgled.

"I didn't hear 'I'm sorry,'" Sandy said. He looked at the bouncer. "Did you, friend?"

"Not a syllable of it," the bouncer said. He pulled Peter's head back by his ponytail and snarled, "Me friends call me The Cat, as in 'The cat's got your tongue.' I'll hear an apology, or I'll have your tongue for fish food." He tightened his vise-grip on the muscle.

A cry of anguish came from Peter. He closed his eyes against the pain. "I—I," he stammered.

"I? I, what?" The Cat demanded.

"I—I'm sorry," Peter whispered weakly.

The Cat released his grip and effortlessly lifted Peter to a standing position and began to brush off his suit. "Now, you see, that wasn't so bad, was it, friend? And I'm a man of my word. Let's me and you find a drink." He winked at Sandy. "I'd say he was a Bushmills man, wouldn't you?"

"Indeed," Sandy crowed. "He's got the cut of one. Fact is, I'll bring me brandy along and join you. Just to keep an eye on him."

"Please," Kathleen said, "you don't have to do this."

"White horses," Sandy said proudly.

Kathleen smiled.

"Cooper, my boy, can I trust you with her?"

"I think so," Cooper answered.

"Then the check's yours, and so's the night," Sandy said gaily. He bowed to Kathleen. "Meeting you has been the pleasure of me life, Kathleen O'Reilly of Cork."

"No," Kathleen said quietly, "the pleasure's mine. Thank you."

"Say goodnight, Peter," Sandy instructed.

Peter looked away.

"Close enough," The Cat said. He began to escort Peter across the room. Sandy followed in his prance-step, his voice booming: "Lizzy, love, a drink for me very close friend, Peter."

16

Outside, it had turned cold. The wind coming from the River Suir and the Waterford Harbour twirled on the street and Kathleen O'Reilly walked close to Cooper, her hands pushed into the deep pockets of her heavy coat, her neck and chin wrapped by a plaid wool scarf. Still, they walked slowly, a stroll's pace, and talked in low voices.

She believed in coincidence, she told him, but it was odd— humorous, even—that, in two days, their paths had seemed as parallel as railroad tracks: the same road traveled, Cooper's meeting of Timmy McFarland and George Molloy and their praise of NewTree, her arriving at Priscilla's just as he was telling of his grandfather. That they were both staying at the Green Hill Bed and Breakfast made coincidence seem like predestination.

"My grandfather always told me that Ireland was a land of magic," Cooper said. "Maybe it's just the Fates having a bit of fun. You do believe in the Fates, don't you?"

"I'm Irish," Kathleen answered. "I'm supposed to, but I don't. They're all fairy tales. We export them, like wool." She smiled. "But you won't go reporting me, will you?"

"Not at all," Cooper told her.

"Sometimes things fall to chance," she said. "Chance. Nothing more than that."

"I don't disagree," Cooper replied.

They crossed the street and walked along the side of a building that shielded them from the wind. Rap music played its driving beat from behind the upstairs window of a shop advertising watch repair. Kathleen looked up.

"We're becoming Americanized," she said.

"Going to ruin, you mean," Cooper replied.

She smiled thoughtfully. "I don't know. I've never been to America."

"Do you want to go?"

"To see it, yes, but I don't think I could live there. I don't know how your grandfather did it without once coming home."

A police car crawled past, the driver straining to stare at Kathleen.

"May I ask you something?" Cooper said.

"Of course."

"The thing with Peter: What did he mean about me following you here?"

She did not speak for a few steps. Then: "Would you like to walk down to Cathedral Square?"

"Sure," he said. He did not tell her he had been there earlier.

"Really, it was nothing with Peter," she said. "He was drinking, that's all. Had it all muddled about an interview I had in Dublin."

"Why do you put up with him?"

Kathleen smiled at the question. It was one she had been asked often. "His father owns the firm I work for. We all put up with him."

"He's got a dangerous look about him," Cooper said.

"And he can be that," she said. "His father's got him out of more than one scrape, if the stories are to be believed. Temper and whiskey are a bad mix for him."

Cooper stopped walking. He glanced back in the direction of Priscilla's. "I shouldn't have left Sandy with him," he said with concern.

"I'm sure he'll be fine," she said. "He reaches a point in his drinking where he gets over his temper and becomes melancholy, and I'd guess Sandy's been around such people a few times in his life."

"You're probably right," Cooper said. He chuckled. "If he gets started on one of his tales, he'll have your friend begging for mercy." He paused, added, "He's an actor, you know."

"Sandy?"

"Yes. Sandy McAfee."

Surprise blinked in her eyes. "I do know him. I thought he was familiar, but I didn't make the connection. Our company's thought of using him for some commercial projects."

"He is what he is," Cooper said. "I think he could sell ice to Eskimos. He's been working a little shell game on me since I met him, but he's certainly not dull."

They began walking again.

"I think he had a fancy for our waitress," Kathleen said.

"Fancy? That's a good word for it."

"Then I take it he's not married?"

"Not that I know of."

Again, Kathleen paused, turned to Cooper. "And you? You're not married, are you?"

"No," Cooper told her.

"Is there a special girl? There, in America?"

"No," answered Cooper. "Not at the moment. Once, yes, but not now."

A smile teased across Kathleen's face. "And what does that mean?"

Cooper shrugged. "We were engaged. She ended it. And you?"

"I was engaged once, also," she said. "Had my head in a spin, it did. All silver moonlight and streaking stars and music coming out of the sky." She looked away, up, let her eyes scan the night sky. "It can be a little silly, can't it?"

"I guess," Cooper said quietly. "What happened? If it's not too personal."

"Not at all. His parents happened. Upper crust, they were, and a girl from Cork, with an address on a narrow street, was not of their choosing."

"And he gave in?" Cooper said in disbelief.

Kathleen laughed easily. "Not him. I did. It'd been a plague in my own family, the same sort of doings, and I suppose I knew it well enough from all the stories. He was married a few months later."

"Someone with an address on a very wide street?"

"With gates," Kathleen added.

"Does it still hurt?"

"No, it doesn't," she said. "I know now that I would have been miserable."

"One question," Cooper said.

"Yes?"

"Do you miss the silver moonlight and streaking stars and music coming out of the sky?"

She looked at him. Her eyes carried sadness. "Yes," she answered.

~~~

Kathleen rolled to her left side in the bed, tilted the pillow at an angle, burrowed her face into it. Her legs were curled. In her mind, she inspected herself and the bed. Pillow the way she liked it. Cover draped warmly to her back. Arms comfortable. Legs comfortable. Eyes closed.

Still, something was not right.

The t-shirt she wore, she decided. The t-shirt with the NewTree logo, a dark-green forest of tall spruces in a pale-green circle. It was too small, or too large.

She pushed away the covers and slid from the bed and shucked the t-shirt over her head and stood nude in the antiseptic light of the room. The light was from the window, from the moon that had spun up from the Irish Sea, dripping with clouds. The way the clouds filtered it, the way the window reflected it, the light from the moon was the color of silver.

"Oh, my God," she whispered.

She tossed the t-shirt across a chair and returned to bed and pulled the covers over her.

From the room above her, she heard the creaking of the flooring. It was a pacing, like the crunch of footsteps on snow. She wondered if the footsteps belonged to Cooper Coghlan, and if that were true, why was he so walk-about restless? She shifted to her back and stared at the spackled ceiling, squinting her eyes. She imagined she could see through the ceiling and the flooring, and she saw Cooper. He was wearing forest-green briefs, rounded full in front. The muscles of his body were like hard marble, shadowed gracefully in the same light of the same silver moon that seeped through the window of her own room. He was walking in a circle. Now he stopped walking, ran his hands through his hair, shook his head, inhaled deeply, his chest rising up. He held the breath, released it slowly. She could hear a soft sigh, or believed she could. Now he moved to the nightstand, picked up a glass. The glass had only a swallow of whiskey in it and he tilted it to his mouth and drank. He held the glass up to the moonlight, turning it in his hand. Now, took the bottle from the nightstand and poured more whiskey into the glass, then sat wearily on the bed and began to massage the long thigh muscle of his right leg. Drank again from the glass. Shifted his body forward, his elbows resting on his knees, both hands holding the glass. Gazed at the floor. She could see his face clearly. A worried look. And then his eyes narrowed on the floor. A frown of curiosity wiggled across his forehead. My God, she thought, he's watching me. Through the flooring and the ceiling and the bedding that covered her, Cooper Coghlan was watching her as she watched him. A smile eased into his face. His look was mesmerizing. Her hands caught the covers and pulled them slowly away from her body, exposing herself to the imagined eyes of Cooper Coghlan.

She blinked and she could no longer see through the ceiling and the flooring of the room above her.

"Damn it," she mumbled angrily. She jerked the covers over her again, gathered them at her throat.

Why did I tell him those things? she wondered. Nonsense, it was. Engaged? A great joke. A laugh. And where did it come from, popping up like that? Done so easily. Plucking an apple from the low-hanging branch of an apple tree could not have been easier. The same as her story to Denis Colum and to Peter Raferty. A make-believe man.

Silver moonlight and streaking stars and music from the skies.

It was the musing of a schoolgirl.

Her own father, who had kissed the Blarney stone more than he had kissed his own wife, could not have done it so well.

She could have eaten the bloody Blarney stone and not have told it better.

And all of that about being shunned by a well-to-do man was more of the same. Nonsense. Or mostly nonsense. It was from her family; that much of it was true. A sort of ghost story, the sort of story told in whispers and in sorrow, and sometimes in the roaring of her father's drunken moods. Her own mother found not fit for Robert Leary, and Robert Leary gone on to high places and great wealth, living in a country mansion with racing horses and servants, married to a proper name with a sour, thin-lipped face.

Kathleen knew about it.

She knew also that the flowers which occasionally appeared on the dining room table of the cottage where her mother and father lived, were from Robert Leary, and not purchased, as her mother adamantly claimed, from the small savings that she kept hidden.

But it was all right. It was good.

Her mother deserved the flowers.

Kathleen glanced again at the ceiling, imagined Cooper, squirmed against her bed.

How could she have feelings for a man she had known for fewer than three hours?

She didn't, she reasoned. Cooper Finn Coghlan was merely a diversion, nothing more than compensation, her way of erasing the bitterness of Denis Colum from her life, or perhaps countering the threat and fear of Peter Raferty.

She remembered that she had never liked American men, had seen enough of them over the years to know them for who they were— arrogant braggarts, thinking themselves God's present to women, thinking they could buy their way with stuffed wallets, all of them crude, all of them making fun of the Irish way. She had walked away from many of them.

There was no reason to think Cooper Finn Coghlan was different.

Still, he had been brave in standing up to Peter, she thought, and the thought calmed her, warmed her.

A sweet walk it had been.

Him close, their arms touching in the arm swings of the walk.

Gentle, his voice.

At the goodnight, in front of her door, he had said, "I still think it's the Fates." Said it in a voice that seemed to fold around her face.

She pulled the covers over her head.

He was an American. Enough had been lost to America.

And then she remembered.

It was her mother who had spoken of silver moonlight and streaking stars and music from the skies.

"When you truly love," her mother had told her in a quiet moment, after she had passed through the turbulent years of childhood, "you'll fancy silver moonlight and streaking stars and music everywhere. From the skies, it'll come. Music to make you dance in your very soul."

Damn Cooper Finn Coghlan.

Damn Denis Colum.

Damn Peter Raferty.

Damn them all.

She caught the pillow from behind her head and hugged it fiercely, and then she eased it to her face.

She wanted to see her mother.

~~~

The telephone conversation with Ealy Ackerman had earned Sandy a two hundred euro bonus to be wired to a bank in Cork.

Ealy had said, "Whatever you're doing, keep doing it. I want that boy coming back home with a smile on his face."

The report to Ealy, made on a whim and on the guess that it would be rewarding, had not required hyperbole. The truth was colorful enough, particularly in Sandy's telling of it. Cooper had met a young woman by happenstance, by the serendipity of place and time, and a second meeting had followed that meeting, also by happenstance. Further, he had come to her defense in a barroom incident, and had escorted her on a late night walk of Waterford.

Ealy had asked excitedly, "Where is he now?"

"That I don't know," Sandy had replied secretively. "But would you believe it? She's staying in the same lodgings as we are."

"Too bad," Ealy had mumbled.

"And why's that?"

"Without me, he won't know what to do."

"From the looks of it, he seemed to be managing fine," Sandy had replied.

"What's her name?" Ealy had asked.

"Kathleen," Sandy had answered cheerfully. "A lovely child. Lovely as a summer flower."

"Well, damn," Ealy had mumbled, remembering the name Cooper had given him in their earlier conversation. Either Cooper had lied or something strange was going on in Ireland.

The talk had been brief. For the additional two hundred euro, Sandy was instructed to make certain the happenstances continued. "If you have to bribe anybody to find out where she's going, you've got my permission to do it—just as long as it's reasonable," Ealy had added.

"You've got my word on it, as an Irishman," Sandy had promised. "It's not the money with me, mind you. It's seeing the lad take on a happy look. It's heartbreaking, the way he goes about with his grandfather's ashes all shut tight in a little box. I can see him gazing at it, like he's waiting for the old gentleman to speak up."

Sandy believed he had heard Ealy swallow a sob.

In his room, lounging on his bed, wearing only boxer shorts, Sandy took a sip of the brandy he had spirited out of Priscilla's, charging the bottle to Peter's account. A little quid pro quo, he thought. He had spent an hour listening to Peter's pitiable stories about his agonizing love for Kathleen O'Reilly—his mood swinging dangerously from shame bathed in tears to a roar of temper needing the warning look of The Cat for control. He was possessed of her, he confessed to Sandy, a hold that was surely demonic. He had risked his family, his profession, his own personal dignity, yet he could think of nothing but the splendor of touching her body, of having her pour herself over him like water made of silk, perfumed with wind blown through gardens of flowers.

And in his painful lamentations, Peter Raferty had generously provided Sandy with the schedule of Kathleen's business agenda.

In Cork, at eight o'clock on the following evening, there would be a NewTree ceremony featuring the mayor planting a spruce in Fitzgerald Park.

Kathleen O'Reilly would be in charge of the festivities.

Sandy smiled a triumphant smile. Such information was invaluable. He would charge Ealy another one hundred euro in the name of bribe money.

One hundred euro for tolerating the company of a miserably lost soul was little enough.

He pulled himself from the bed and crossed to the full-length mirror on the back of the entry door. Stood studying himself. In truth, there was a touch of sag to the muscles, a bit of flab over the gut, a puffing under the eyes. He'd had a slight resemblance to the late Richard Harris in his younger years, he'd been told, but age and the severity of the wind-drying Irish weather had taken its toll, as surely as Richard Harris had also become marked by time and elements. He rubbed a finger under one eye, remembered the advice of a fellow actor about the curative benefits of vitamin E. He stepped back from the mirror, rotated his shoulders. Not the man he once was, for sure, he thought. Still, he had appeal. Lucy Reid was proof. And Lizzy. With a little urging, he could have coaxed Lizzy to his room for a nightcap and pleasure. Yet, there was work to be done and he had to be in shape for it. He flicked his fingers through the wings of gray hair that flew out from over his ears, raised his chin, patted at the fold of skin wrinkled at his throat, then extended one leg in front of him, squatted unsteadily. He could feel the muscles straining. Time to start exercising again, he decided. Some pushups. Maybe light weights. Walking. Cut back a tad on the drink.

He gazed again into the mirror. "Ah, Sandy McAfee," he sighed, "you're getting along. Best make it all count."

17

Kathleen O'Reilly had checked out before breakfast, Veronica Hart, the proprietress of Green Hill Bed and Breakfast, explained to Cooper and Sandy.

"Something about catching an early train. A family matter, I believe," Veronica said pleasantly. "She seemed a little upset over it. But if one of you gentlemen happen to be a Mr. Coghlan, she left a note."

"I'm Cooper Coghlan," Cooper said.

Veronica pulled an envelope from a pigeonhole in the rolltop desk she used for business and handed it to Cooper. She smiled a smile that asked questions, and answered them. She had delivered such envelopes before.

"Well, lad, let's see what she had to say," Sandy suggested as they moved toward the dining room.

"I'm sure it's nothing," Cooper said. "A polite farewell."

"You've a bit of the devil in you, Cooper Finn Coghlan," Sandy said. "You know I'm wondering about it all, since you've not said a word about the evening."

Cooper paused in the dining room, found a table to his liking and moved toward it. "A nice night," he said casually. "We took a walk, talked a bit, said goodnight." He sat at the table.

"And you're asking me to believe such a tale?" Sandy said. He took the napkin from the table and snapped it open with a dramatic flick of his wrists. He sat opposite Cooper and smoothed the napkin across his lap.

"That's the whole of it," Cooper told him.

"The envelope, young Finn, the envelope," Sandy said.

Cooper shrugged. "Fine." He opened the envelope at the fold, removed the single sheet of paper, and silently read:

Dear Cooper Coghlan,

Thank you for such a pleasant evening. It was a pleasure meeting you and the gallant Sandy McAfee. I hope your visit to our country is memorable. I know you said you were going to Killarney today, but if you find yourself in Cork during your stay in Ireland and you need advice on lodging or restaurants (and pubs), I should be happy to make recommendations for you. You may try reaching me at Raferty & Son (the son you know well enough). I should warn you, my schedule is uncertain, due to the campaign I'm handling, as well as other commitments. If I don't speak with you, thank you again.

Sincerely,

Kathleen O'Reilly

P.S.: The walk was lovely.

Cooper folded the note and slipped it back into its envelope.

"Well?" Sandy said eagerly.

"A very nice note," Cooper answered. "I'm hungry. What about you?"

"Very nice note. Lovely," Sandy said in mock sarcasm. "Now, do I have to wrestle you for it, or do you let me read it? And surely you should know enough about the McAfee blood by now to know we're warriors at heart."

Cooper handed the envelope to Sandy.

The note was read and reread by Sandy during breakfast. "It's plain as a road post," he declared. "She's wanting you to come to Cork."

"She left out a few details, if that's what she wants," Cooper countered.

"Such as?"

"Telephone numbers."

"She's Irish. Irish women don't tease as shameless as your American women."

Cooper nodded thoughtfully. "I saw that last night, from Lizzy."

"That? In a bar, that's the selling, lad. But to leaving out the numbers, what do you think a telephone directory is for? I'd say she wants to see if you've got the courage to follow up."

"Maybe."

"You're talking to an Irishman, young Finn," Sandy said firmly. "I know a maybe from a no. Believe me, I do. I've had a go with both meanings." He paused and glanced at an older couple silently eating breakfast two tables over, pretending not to listen to the conversation he was having with Cooper. He added, "You're in the company of a man who's had his share of letters saying no. I could publish an anthology of them that would make *War and Peace* look like a prologue."

"And that I don't doubt," Cooper said. "But she also said her schedule was uncertain. It tells me she's being polite. She's busy."

Sandy sighed in exasperation. "It's a clever twist, that's what it is. And what about the line that says she'd be happy to make recommendations. It's a big word, it is. Listen to me, young Finn. What she's really saying is this: 'I want to be with you, but I can't be forward about it.'"

Cooper smiled. He drank from his coffee, watched the play in Sandy's face. Sandy was holding the note, gazing at it. He had the look of a surgeon studying an X-ray, wondering if what he saw was a smug or a dark spot on a lung.

"Tell me now, what was this about the walk?" Sandy said. "There's a message in it, believe me."

"It was nothing," Cooper answered. "A walk. Very pleasant. She's bright, a good conversationalist."

Sandy shook his head, folded the note, opened it again, glanced at it, folded it. He said in a grave voice, "My boy, my boy, you're either blind or you've been dumb-struck, or a bit of both. Know what your dear grandfather would be saying? He'd be telling you straight away that something was at work here, something none of us are keen enough to understand."

Cooper did not reply. He thought of his grandfather, knew that Sandy was right. His grandfather would have found a miracle in the note from Kathleen O'Reilly, a miracle as grand as the bargain of Bogmeadow.

"What happens, happens," Cooper said quietly.

"What happens, happens?" Sandy said incredulously. "Now, that's a thoughtful statement." He pushed away his empty coffee cup. "I'm not talking about marriage, you understand."

"Marriage? Who said anything about marriage?"

"Not me," Sandy said. "I'm not a believer in it. Too many of me friends have taken that waltz, and I've learned a thing or two from watching the troubles."

"Such as?" Cooper asked. He pushed away from the table and stood.

"Surviving with what little sanity God tucked into their brains." He also stood and cast a glance to the older couple and smiled pleasantly.

"I'll remember that," Cooper said. He began to walk away. Sandy followed.

"Someday, they'll do a serious study of it," Sandy continued in a deliberately loud voice. "And they'll determine that the survival rate of paddling through the Bermuda Triangle on a rubber duck is greater than surviving marriage. That's me take on it."

The older couple glared at him in disdain.

~~~

Connor and Christine O'Reilly's home was a ten-minute walk from Connor's Barber Shop on the outskirts of Cork. There were five pubs between the home and the shop and Connor had made it a habit of ducking into one of the five each day after work, alternating his visits among them to assure than none of the owners or patrons would be offended by an appearance of favoritism. Connor's own clientele came chiefly from the pubs, and his daily stopover for a pint or two was, to him, a matter of business as well as pleasure. In his more exuberant moments—which corresponded always with the amount of drink consumed—Connor swore that not one of them had made a new euro or pound in twenty years. It was money passed from pub to shop, then back to pub.

"Sure, when one of us dies, the rest will be wealthy," claimed Connor.

In her childhood, her father's routine had been as natural as any habit of the day to Kathleen O'Reilly, for it had been the same routine followed by the fathers of her friends—the fathers of Doris Hetherington and Denis Colum, of the Cunningham twins, of Ellen Lynch, of Barry Walsh. Their fathers also had taken their leisure in finding their way home, and when finally there, they, too, had made their families cower with the quick-meanness of their quick-moods. It was the nature of the Irishman, Kathleen had believed. The boasting and quarreling. The need to prove they were men. And what better place than their own home to be the men they boasted of being? Over time, Connor O'Reilly and the other fathers had broken the spirit of their wives and of their children, bleached them colorless, like rags washed thin over scrubbing stones. For the children, it was an encouragement to leave home. For the wives, it was condemnation.

Kathleen had always marveled at her mother's serene nature, even under the oppressive force of the bullying. Her mother did not answer her father's tirades with temper, but with silence. She would simply walk away—into another room, or outside to her garden—and she would will herself not to listen to the storm of Connor O'Reilly. When the storm subsided, she would return to its center of destruction and quietly repair its damage.

It was not the same with Kathleen. She had never been as forgiving, or as seemingly calm. Her fights with her father had been fierce enough to become legend, and the last, in Dorrian's House of Spirits, was still talked about with as much awe as a great sporting event.

She was sixteen, and she had tried quietly to lead him home from the bar, but he refused to leave and had shoved her rudely into Sean Dorrian, knocking a tray of drinks from him. It was, Kathleen believed, the moment that changed her life. She remembered it as a great release, a volcano of strength and pride erupting from her in a scream that caused people to coming running from the street. She had jumped to her feet and rushed her father, catching him by his shirt at his throat, and then she had jerked him to her and pelted him with her fists and clawed at him with her hard-tipped fingernails. He had recovered enough to strike her violently across the face, causing blood to spurt from a gash along her eyebrow. Sean Dorrian and some of the other men had tried to subdue Connor, but they managed only to distract him long enough for Kathleen to grab a heavy glass and smash it against his head. The blow had knocked Connor unconscious and had left him deaf in his right ear. It was the ear he turned to Kathleen whenever he saw her.

Her visits to see her mother were always carefully timed. She would drive past her father's barbershop, slowing to look into the window. If she saw him, she would drive on to her mother's home. And her mother would say politely, "Now, dear, you've got to come round when your father's home. Let by-gones be by-gones."

But it was nothing more than an exchange of words, the right thing for an Irish mother, and also an Irish wife, to say to a child. Kathleen knew her mother secretly was relieved when only the two of them were together.

And there were times when she needed to see her mother, needed the lingering, happy embrace, needed to sip the nectar of serenity that resided in her mother.

After returning from Waterford in mid-morning was one of those times.

She took a taxi from the train station to her apartment and then got into her car and drove across Cork and past her father's barbershop. She saw him through the window of the shop, cutting the hair of a small boy. The boy's head was ducked down and a scowl masked his face. Two or three men waited in chairs. Good, she thought.

Her mother was in the backyard of her home, digging in the soil with a hoe.

"It must be spring," Kathleen called cheerfully from the fence gate leading into the yard.

Christine O'Reilly turned to the voice. A smile blew across her face. "You gave me a fright," she said. "I must have been day-dreaming." She moved toward her daughter. "Come, come, let's have a hug."

Kathleen opened the gate and walked through it. She was always amazed at her mother's beauty. Her mother was fifty-one, yet so eternally young she seemed child-like. There were no lines in her face, no stoop in her shoulders. The only thing that betrayed her was her eyes. Christine O'Reilly's eyes had the sadness of seeing too much, weeping too often.

"How are you, Mum?" Kathleen said, holding tight to her mother.

"How else could I be on such a day as this?" her mother replied gaily. "It's lovely out." She stepped away from her daughter, studied her with a look. "And what are you doing here? I thought you were coming in this afternoon."

"I left early," Kathleen said.

"Is there a problem?" her mother asked.

Kathleen pushed a smile into her face. It was weak, fleeting. "No. I couldn't sleep, so I got up and took the early train out." She embraced her mother again. "Are you planting?"

Christine laughed and looked back at the plot of the ground. "Turning up worms for the birds more than anything. They've been chattering at me the whole morning, like a cheering section at a cricket match. Come inside. I was about to break for a cup of tea."

"I don't want to stop your work," Kathleen told her.

"Well, now, the birds—and I—would be grateful if you did. I need my tea and they need their worms."

Kathleen sat at the kitchen table of her childhood home and watched her mother prepare the tea. "A strong new blend," her mother claimed. "Your father found it in the market. Comes from one of them countries I've never been able to pronounce."

"And how is he?" asked Kathleen.

Her mother looked at her, then turned to pour the water over the tea strainers. "You'd be proud of him, for sure," she said. "He's stopped the drinking."

"Stopped? My father?" Kathleen said in astonishment. "Connor O'Reilly? Mum, we're talking about the same man who used to live here, are we not?"

Christine pivoted from the counter to her daughter. The smile was gone from her face. "Now, Kathleen, I'll not have you talking about your father in such a way. He's come to the changing days in his life. The only time he steps foot into a pub is with me, and he has his tea, as I do. He's learned he can laugh as well with a pot of tea as with a pint of stout."

"I'm sorry, I—"

"It's all right," Christine said, placing the tea on the table and sitting. "He's not as well as he used to be, and he's come to know—things."

"What things?"

"That he's mortal," Christine answered. "Come, do your tea."

"Has he seen a doctor?" Kathleen asked, swirling the tea strainer in the pot.

"He has."

"And?"

"They're not sure. At best, it's the migraine headaches he's having; at worse, it could be the Alzheimer's disease."

"My God," Kathleen whispered. "Mum, why haven't you called me?"

Christine poured her tea. "He'd not hear of it. He still feels bad for all that's gone on between the two of you. He'd not have you worry. I'm telling you now because I think you need to know, but it's something to keep between us."

"Tell me about it. What's been going on?"

Christine shook her head slowly. She blinked away a film of tears. "Little things. Forgetting what day it is. Lost his way home once, he did. I thought he'd gone back to one of the pubs, but he hadn't. Mickey Carey found him wandering down by the river. Said he'd gone down to look at the ships, but it was his way of covering up."

"Oh, my God," Kathleen whispered in shock.

"You're not to be worrying," Christine insisted. "I'm keeping watch on him. I go down each day at closing now and walk him back. He seems to like that."

Kathleen watched her mother absently stirring milk in her tea, gazing at the swirl. She seemed at peace. "Promise you'll let me know how it goes. Call me about anything."

"I will," her mother said. "You have my word."

"Mum?"

"Yes."

"You love him, don't you?"

Christine looked up. "Yes, I do. Of course I do."

"I didn't think you did. I never thought that," Kathleen said honestly.

"Love's such a trying thing," her mother answered. "Sometimes it takes being needed to know you've got a little love to give, and then it sprouts up like the flowers that'll soon be growing in my garden. You have to wait on the growing before you can see the blooms."

"Flowers?" Kathleen said. "But what about the flowers, Mum? The ones that you put in your vase?"

Christine dipped her head. She had long suspected that her daughter knew about the flowers from Robert Leary. "All flowers are lovely, dear—the ones that grow in the soil and them that bloom in a vase," she said. "The ones from the soil, they last longer. Sometimes they're not so pretty as what you put in a vase, but they stay."

Kathleen looked away from her mother. On the counter, under a cupboard, she saw the cut-glass vase that was used to hold the flowers from Robert Leary. The vase was a Waterford, and it, also, had been a gift. Kathleen was sure of it. Her mother had cheerfully explained that she had found the vase in a home sale, and that the seller was unaware of what it was. Asked only a half-dozen euro for such a fine item.

"Try the tea," Christine said.

The tea was superb. Strong, rich. And Kathleen tried to imagine her father in a market, selecting it. He had never shopped for anything, had never made the tender gesture of surprise. And perhaps that was what her mother had found in him to love. Stopping at market to find a new tea, presenting it as a gift. If it had happened that way, Kathleen was sorry she had missed the moment.

"Mum?"

"Yes, love."

"Do you remember telling me that love was a silver moon and streaking stars and music coming out of the skies?"

Christine laughed softly. "I did. For sure, that's what I said." She clasped her hands together. "You've met a man, have you?"

Kathleen nodded.

"And the moon?" asked her mother.

Kathleen did not answer for a moment. She could feel a smile growing in her throat. Then: "It might have been a little silver. More like a frost, I think."

"And the stars?"

"Bright."

"And the music?"

Kathleen let the smile play across her face in answer.

"Tell me. Who is he, this man?" her mother asked gently.

Kathleen turned to look again at Robert Leary's Waterford vase. It seemed oddly out-of-place. She said, "He's an American."

Her mother sat back against her chair, touched her throat with her hand. "Kathleen," she whispered. "Don't say it."

"It's all right," Kathleen said quickly. "He's on his way to Killarney. I won't be seeing him again."

"Oh, yes, child. You will. You will."

"No, Mum. It was just a little piece of happy time, that's all. I'll not see him again."

"You will," her mother said again. "You'll see him in your mind, and in your soul, if not with your eyes. And nothing's clearer than that, child. Nothing."

18

Cooper had packed away Ealy's Irish bible, with its detailed suggestions of directions from Dublin to Dingle, each route highlighted by must-see sites. There was no reason to consult it. He was with Sandy McAfee and Sandy McAfee was a rogue spirit who traveled as haphazardly as a playful whirlwind. Cooper knew the destination, yet the destination was not as compelling as the adventures that would take them there.

He did not object. At least, they were traveling west, toward the Dingle coast. At the right time, he would insist on driving into Killarney, and from Killarney to Dingle. In Killarney, he believed his grandfather's ashes would stir with recognition and his ghost voice would begin to speak.

First, they were going to Cork, Sandy announced as they packed the Nissan. Not because it was the home city of Kathleen O'Reilly—as Cooper might suspect, or wish—but because Sandy had arranged to pick up some money at a bank, residual payments for a television commercial.

Cooper objected mildly. He had to. It was his role, his dramatis personae, in the drama—or comedy—that Sandy was improvising. He said, "Cork's fine, but you can take that twinkle out of your eye. I've seen the last of Kathleen O'Reilly."

It was not subterfuge at work, Sandy vowed earnestly. Not in the least. It was an act of dignity, one that was necessary to assuage the embarrass-ment of being a down-on-his-luck tag-along. Cooper had been kind, understanding, trusting to take the risk of having such a traveling companion. It was only right that he, Sandy McAfee, should provide a share of the expenses.

"I've got me pride," he said, his voice trembling. "I'll not stand accused of living off the generosity of others, not Sandy McAfee."

Cooper bit a smile.

"I'll only be a few minutes in getting it," Sandy vowed. "Then we can move on if you wish, leave Kathleen O'Reilly to her work, put her away as a sweet memory. We can go to Blarney and kiss the stone, or ride on down the coast to Kinsale or Oysterhaven or Garrettstown. It's a sight to behold, seeing them places, there on the Gaelic Sea. It's like watching the coming of glory when them waves come crashing in. Water and rock, and the water's spitting anger and the rock's standing mean. I'm certain your grandfather stood in awe of it many times, many times."

"We'll see," Cooper told him.

Still, Cooper knew that Sandy was calculating delay in their trip from Waterford to Cork. He insisted on finding a florist and ordering a dozen roses to be delivered to Lizzy at Priscilla's, including a card that read: *Thanks for the dance. I'll be seeing you in my dreams.* Leaving the florist, he led Cooper into a book store and advised him on selecting post cards, and then suggested tea and scones in a small restaurant.

In the restaurant, he purchased a morning newspaper and discovered, on the front page, a photograph of Kathleen presenting a potted spruce seedling to the mayor. The accompanying story, written by Susan Dunne, was worshipful, shameless in its editorial praise. Susan Dunne, in a thousand words, had placed a dazzling crown of celebrity on the golden-red head of Kathleen O'Reilly.

"Well, maybe you're right," Sandy sighed after reading the story aloud to Cooper. "Maybe, now, she'll be too busy for the likes of us."

Cooper took the paper from Sandy, studied the photograph of Kathleen. He knew from his experience in dozens of public relations events that it was a surprisingly perfect shot taken at random, the shutter clicking as steady as automatic gunfire muted by a silencer. The flashed light bathed her face, froze a smile that was as radiant as any he had ever seen.

"It's a lovely likeness," Sandy said. "I'll not be surprised to see it used on the television."

Yes, thought Cooper. It could be. And perhaps he could help it happen. In Atlanta, he had a friend, a college classmate—Sidney Springer—who worked for CNN and had a fondness for offbeat stories. The NewTree project of Ireland was exactly the kind of material that would appeal to Sidney, and Kathleen O'Reilly was exactly the kind of woman who would command his attention.

He folded the paper. In the short time he had been in her presence, Kathleen O'Reilly had burrowed pleasantly into his thinking, invaded his dreams. She was as much the splendor of Ireland as the stories of his grandfather. He owed her a gift.

"Mind if I keep this?" he asked Sandy.

"A little reminder of what might have been?" Sandy said in a teasing voice.

"Something like that," Cooper told him.

It was past eleven when Sandy guided the Nissan out of Waterford toward Dungarvan. "Relax, young Finn," he crowed. "And keep an eye out for all the wonders you'll be seeing. You're going to learn more than books can tell you."

He was not boasting. The stories were remarkable, so many stories they crowded in Sandy's mouth, poured out in a geyser of words, stories colored in myth, stories of people and places Cooper vaguely remembered from the tales of his grandfather.

Crotty's Rock, named for William Crotty, Ireland's Robin Hood, a cave dweller, betrayed by his friend, David Norris.

Melleray Grotto, where a statue of the Virgin Mary was seen moving in 1985.

Dungarvan, spared Cromwell's torch because a woman named Mrs. Nagel fed him whiskey and pleasure, or so legend had it.

Youghal, where the motion picture *Moby Dick* had been filmed, where Sir Walter Raleigh had resided and served as mayor, the same Sir Walter Raleigh who introduced the potato and tobacco to Ireland—once being doused with water by a maid who believed he was on fire.

"It's pronounced 'Yawl,'" Sandy jested. "Easy for you Southerners. I'm surprised they haven't put up a signpost saying, 'Youghal come, now.'" He cackled. Said "Yawl" again, stretching the word, as though the word was made of taffy.

In Youghal, they stopped for lunch at the Whale Spout's pub, sat at a table near a vacationing family with frisky, giggling children, and Sandy again became suddenly melancholy, confessing to Cooper that his life was turning as gray as his hair. His profession was to blame—that and his own addiction to restlessness. There were moments, he lamented, when he longed for a simple existence, a steady employment, a wife and children, a tidy home. The misunderstanding of his lifestyle as an actor had cost him dearly, particularly with decent ladies. He was certain there was a network of women who met regularly to denigrate him by comparing notes, and, even worse, their gossiping tongues had flicked out to other women, spreading venom.

"They say there's no snakes in Ireland," he declared bitterly. "Well, there's some I know, only they don't have the look of a snake. The bite they've got, to be sure. Not the look."

Cooper listened patiently, realizing that Sandy, the performer, was in need of attention. "Doesn't every artist give up something for his art?" he asked sympathetically.

Sandy arched an eyebrow, as though hearing a great revelation. He dipped his head, whispered, "True enough."

"All the great ones, at least," Cooper added.

Sandy looked up. His eyes were damp. "You're an understanding man, Cooper Finn Coghlan."

The decision was made by Cooper to stay in Cork, surrendering to Sandy's appeal for a place to take a late afternoon rest. "To recoup myself," Sandy told him in a begging voice. "Shake the demons, them that come on me out of nowhere. An hour or two and I'll be set straight again, ready for showing you the sights."

"Sure," Cooper said.

"If you're wanting to find your lady friend, you can give it a try," Sandy added slyly.

"That's all right," Cooper said. "I think I'll rest, too."

"It'll do you good," Sandy agreed.

~~~

The Quayside Inn overlooked the north channel of the River Lee. Its rooms provided a spectacular windowed view of the river and the distant spires of St. Finbarr's Cathedral. A small garden, as delicately designed as a painting, curled to the river. Cork, like Dublin, was a city that seemed to be *in* Ireland, but was not necessarily of Ireland. As with any large city, it had assumed its own presence, and that presence had obscured the personality of the flowered green hills of the country, where herds of sheep and cattle grazed languidly, and people lived in small, clean homes growing like pods of mushrooms under isolated clumps of trees.

Cooper slept for an hour, being surprisingly exhausted from Sandy's rambling stories and dark-clouded somberness. When he awoke he showered and dressed and then wrote postcards to his parents and his grandmother, also to Ealy and Cary and Kevin Dugan. He had one card left. It was of a young street boy playing the flute. The face of the boy was happy and angelic, as though the music he played was clinging to him. He turned it over, wrote in large, sweeping letters, *It's more than I thought it would be, being in Ireland. You would like it more than you think.* He signed it *Love, Coop* and addressed it to Jenny Gavin.

Odd, he thought. Once he had wanted to travel with Jenny to Ireland, had even talked about it as a honeymoon. She had been amused by the suggestion: "If we're even thinking of heading in that direction for a honeymoon, it's going to be Paris or Rome," she had said. "I'm not about to spend my time driving around on the wrong side of the road, looking at sheep and rock piles and listening to the local drunks carrying on about how miserable their life's been."

It had been Cooper's first doubt about committing his life to Jenny Gavin, and he had shared the doubt with Ealy and Cary, offering it as a ball-and-chain joke, saying, "Well, she put the first leg in the family pants." And he had told them of her put-down remarks about Ireland, expecting them to laugh it off and to offer advice on controlling a high-maintenance woman.

Instead, Ealy had turned serious.

"Coop, I'll be honest with you," he had said. "I don't like her, and I hope you forgive me for being blunt about it. I don't like her, but I'm glad you do. I hope it works out for you, if that's what you want. I hope you get married and have a half-dozen babies who call me Uncle Ealy, and I hope I'll have a chance to wipe their snotty little noses when they're little and listen to their silly, lovesick blithering when they

141

become teenagers. I hope you'll let me steal them away for ball games and the ballet, and let me rent them limousines for prom night. And I hope you and I—and Cary—will have enough sense to sneak away to Dugan's a couple of times a month, just to be ourselves, to howl at the moon and lie about our youth and kick ass at the dartboard. In short, old friend, I want you to be happy, and I want to be happy with you. If that means being with Jennifer Gavin, the Irish-hater, then, damn it, that's fine with me. And I promise you, I'll be as civil as a spit-and-polish knight having audience with the Queen, but in my heart of hearts, in my soul of souls, I know she's not the woman for you."

There was another comment from Jenny that Cooper remembered, a comment he had not shared with Ealy and Cary.

Jenny had said, "Here's what it would be like to be in Ireland with you, Cooper: 'Papa would love this.' You'd say it a million times. Everything you'd see, you'd say it. Your grandfather may be a great Irish character to you, but he's not going on our honeymoon with us."

He looked across the writing table to the briefcase containing the ashes of Finn Coghlan, and he thought of playful exchanges he'd had with his grandfather from childhood. His grandfather had called himself the Man of Steel and had called Cooper the Boy of Mush.

"The Boy of Mush needs you, Papa," he whispered. "It's me and you. Like you always said it'd be. I just wish you'd start talking to me."

He stacked the postcards neatly and placed them beside the opened Waterford newspaper carrying the photograph of Kathleen O'Reilly. He touched her newspaper face and shuddered involuntarily. He had never been around anyone as intriguing.

He opened the telephone directory and searched for her name. To his surprise, it was listed. He picked up his pen and opened his date book and wrote Kathleen on a blank note page. Paused. Rolled the pen in his fingers. Closed the date book and the directory.

He pulled himself from his chair and went to the door of his room and opened it and stood gazing out over the river and the city. Kathleen O'Reilly was there, somewhere, perhaps only blocks away.

An odd sensation struck him: his age. He was thirty-two years old. By the time his father was thirty-two, his father had been married for nine years and had already begun his serious, steady climb in the solemn world of banking. He had never seen his father around friends such as Ealy and Cary. It was impossible to believe his father told jokes, played pranks, or had fantasies of making love to beautiful women. Compared to his father, Cooper had always felt immature, flawed, slightly retarded. Yet, he also had felt great sorrow for his father. Only rarely had his father ever expressed unguarded tenderness to Cooper—the kind of tenderness offered in the gift of the leather-bound journal.

His father did not seem to have laughter, did not seem to believe in dreams, Cooper thought. It was as though such happy, free sensations had been surgically removed from his father, perhaps because he was the son of a man named Finn Coghlan, who overpowered the laughter and dreams of others. And, yes, his grandmother's mumbling complaint was correct: Finn Coghlan's spirit had been injected into him—into the grandson—like an anointing from the gods. Finn to Finn. As though the name, itself, contained a command.

At thirty-two, Cooper was still a child. Kathleen O'Reilly was proof of it. He was becoming as unexpectedly attracted to Kathleen O'Reilly, at the age of thirty-two, as he had been to Marcia Brook, at the age of thirteen. There was no difference. None. It was a collision of impatience and serenity, bravado and fear. In the drive from Waterford to Cork, with Sandy raging about a battle of legend fought by Norsemen or Frenchmen or someone, he had sensed her as forcefully as he had ever sensed anyone or anything. It was as though Kathleen O'Reilly was not real, but simply a beam of light, a strobe from some distant star arching across space in search of Earth.

The thought had reminded him of a note he had written to Marcia Brook, leaving it in one of her textbooks.

If I cannot see you,
I only want to breathe the air you breathe,
Because I will know you have been there.
Silly words.
Marcia Brooks had giggled at him.

Cooper smiled at the thought of the beam of light and the strobe of a star. Childish. As childish as breathing the air that Marcia Brooks had breathed. Yet, he had always been childish. It was in his blood.

Finn to Finn.

He closed the door.

In a week, he would be home again, an ocean away. In a few months, Kathleen O'Reilly would be a trick of memory, an illusion.

There was no reason to call her.

The only thing that linked them was coincidence, or chance, as she had called it.

She was right about the Fates.

The Fates lived in the fancy of imagination, not in telephone directories.

Still, he could do one thing.

He went to the telephone and punched the number for the front desk.

"Do you have a fax machine?" he asked.

"But, of course," the clerk answered.

19

If she had looked out of her second-story office window in the building that carried the name of Raferty & Son, Kathleen might have seen them passing on the sidewalk below—Sandy in his bounce-walk, Cooper beside him, his step long and measured.

She did not have time for gazing from her office window. A man named Sidney Springer had called from America's Cable News Network, telling Kathleen that CNN would be broadcasting news of the NewTree campaign as a segment of its international coverage. He asked for information to be faxed to him, and for a schedule of planned events.

"Maybe we could do a follow-up with some footage," Sidney said.

"We do have a ceremony planned for tonight," Kathleen told him in her most professional voice, edged in nervousness. "Here in Cork. The mayor will be planting a tree."

"What time, your time?" Sidney asked.

"Eight o'clock," Kathleen answered.

"We'll see what we can do," Sidney promised.

"You're kind to consider it," Kathleen said. "We'll be sending you everything we have within a half-hour. If there's anything else you need, please call us."

"Will do," Sidney said. "By the way, that was an impressive story in the Waterford newspaper."

"Oh," Kathleen said in a surprised voice. "I haven't seen it."

"You should check it out," warned Sidney. "It put you square in the middle of the spotlight, and I have to warn you, the spotlight gets hot."

"I'm curious," Kathleen said on impulse. "How did you get a copy of it so quickly?

"Through a friend," Sidney replied cheerfully. "He's visiting there now. Sent me a fax."

A chill swept across Kathleen's shoulders and neck. "Oh," she said softly. "How—nice."

"He's a great guy," Sidney said. "I hope you get a chance to meet him."

"And what's his name?" Kathleen asked tentatively.

"Cooper," Sidney said. "Cooper Coghlan."

~~~

Sandy McAfee was in high spirits, having received his money wired by Ealy. He had used a portion of it to purchase for himself a sweater the color of gold and for Cooper a crimson jockey cap. The cap looked foolish on Cooper's head; still he wore it. It was the first money that Sandy had spent since leaving Dublin and Cooper did not wish to offend him.

Their walking tour of Cork could have been a two-man parade for an arriving circus, with Sandy playing the roles of everything from elephant to clown. He had insisted on photographing Cooper at every stop—at the Butter Exchange, the Opera House, the Crawford Art Gallery, The Statue, the English Market, Elizabeth Fort. He purchased postcards from sidewalk racks, shamrocks encased in plastic key chains, giving them to Cooper as mementos to share among friends back in America. He alerted Cooper to every woman in Cork who vaguely resembled Kathleen O'Reilly.

It was seven-thirty when they left St. Finbarr's Cathedral, the only place on their tour that subdued Sandy. The cathedral was beautiful. The air inside had seemed inordinately cool and holy, and Sandy and Cooper had walked through it quietly, reverently, stopping to gaze in wonder at stained glass windows illustrating the life of Christ, at mosaics that had been created by artists gifted with something more remarkable than skill and training and instinct. In whisper-voice, Sandy read the plaque commemorating the story of Elizabeth Aldworth, the only female ever admitted to a Freemason Lodge. In 1712, Elizabeth, then a young girl, was discovered eavesdropping on a Freemason meeting in her father's home. Rather than risk her telling the secrets of the society, she was initiated as a member.

"It's like being bathed in the light of the Almighty himself," Sandy said softly as they stood outside St. Finbarr's. "I tell you, young Finn, it'd be a hard man who couldn't be humbled by spending a minute or two in such a place."

Cooper remembered his grandfather's gentle ridicule of the Glendale Presbyterian Church, calling it little more than a tent on God's battlefield for lost souls. To Finn Coghlan, the stained glass of the orange-robed Jesus delivering his Sermon of the Mount in Glendale Presbyterian was the work of a child with a box of crayons compared to the art of great cathedrals in Ireland. And he had been right. Surely, he must have seen St. Finbarr's in his youth, Cooper thought.

Sandy turned away from St. Finbarr's and in the turn, his mood changed. "Are you up for some nourishment?" he asked merrily.

"Not particularly," Cooper answered.

"Good enough," Sandy said. He glanced at his watch and let his mind calculate time and distance. In Priscilla's, the drunken Peter Raferty had said Kathleen O'Reilly would be stage managing a NewTree program at Fitzgerald Park at eight o'clock. It was time to pull the puppet's string.

"Let's take a stroll over to Fitzgerald Park," he said to Cooper. "It's one of my favorite places."

"Is it far?" asked Cooper.

"Not at all," promised Sandy.

By eight o'clock, the day, which had been sun-bright and crisp, was graying and Fitzgerald Park—like all city parks, an oasis valley of grass and trees and flowers in a mountain range of buildings—was covered in the eerie off-color of street lights and seeping darkness. A few walkers ambled passively, absorbed not by the place where they walked, but by the time of day. The walkers did not seem to care about a crowd gathering near a pavilion that had been decorated with green-and-white bunting and with banners that had the outline of spruce trees growing majestically in a pale-green circle. A lectern with a microphone stood on a raised platform in the middle of the pavilion. A half-dozen chairs were in a semi-circle behind the lectern. In a corner of the pavilion, three musicians played lively Irish music, and the crowd, heavily populated by businessmen in overcoats, listened politely and watched as two television crews jockeyed for favorable positions in front of the platform.

"Seems like a party's going on," Sandy said. "Most likely political. Want to listen for a few minutes?"

"Fine with me," Cooper replied.

They moved closer to the pavilion. If he had timed it right, Sandy guessed that Kathleen O'Reilly would already be there, doing her stage manager's work. He stopped walking, pushed himself up on his toes to look over a huddled group listening to the music. He saw a group of men standing in a circle around a woman. The woman was Kathleen. She was holding a clipboard, referring to it as she spoke. Near her, Peter Raferty stood like a statue, a scowl fixed in his face. Sandy looked at Cooper. Cooper was listening to the music.

"Tell you the truth, young Finn, I'm not of a mood to listen to a lot of political haggling," Sandy said. "Besides it's a bit chilly. Why don't we slip away before it all begins?"

"Lead the way," Cooper told him.

Sandy began skirting the crowd, walking in front of Cooper to block his view. He saw the men who had surrounded Kathleen break away, saw her move to a table that had been placed nearby. The table was stacked with boxes of potted seedlings.

"Let's cut through here," Sandy said. He wiggled past a gathering of young people, all holding placards with slogans promoting NewTree. All on the Raferty payroll, Sandy reasoned. A little laugh stayed in his mouth. The tricks of the theater were everywhere.

And then he stopped walking. "Well, can you believe it?" he said in amazement. "Look who's here."

Cooper looked over Sandy's shoulder into Kathleen O'Reilly's startled face.

"Oh," she said in astonishment.

Cooper smiled foolishly.

"Now, will miracles never cease?" Sandy crooned. "It's sweet Kathleen."

"What—are you doing here?" Kathleen asked.

"We were just walking, seeing the sights," Cooper said weakly. He glanced at Sandy.

"It's the truth," Sandy said. "Heard the music and it pulled us in. We were just leaving. And yourself? What are you doing here?"

"Working," Kathleen said. She tried a smile, felt it wiggle ludicrously over her face. "Or trying to," she added. She sounded frustrated.

"The trees?" asked Sandy.

"Yes," Kathleen sighed. She tried to look away from Cooper, but could not. "The mayor's supposed to speak, and then we'll be planting a seedling and passing out the rest."

"You're planting a tree at night?" Cooper asked.

"You get the mayor when you can," she said. "We're calling it an ancient practice—planting trees at night, when the moon's looking down." She glanced away, then back to Cooper. Again tried the smile, again felt it wiggle ludicrously.

"Must be an Irish tradition," Cooper said. "Don't think I've ever heard of that in the States."

"That's what's grand about the Irish, now isn't it?" Sandy said lightly. "We've a story for every occasion, and if there's not one handy, we might take some liberties here and there."

"I thought you were off to Killarney," Kathleen said.

"A little change of plans," Sandy said. "I had a bit of business here."

"Oh," Kathleen said.

"I got your note," Cooper told her. "It was very nice of you."

Kathleen smiled, blushed. "I decided to take an early train out."

"I don't blame you," Cooper said. "I like traveling early."

Kathleen began to play with the seedlings, needlessly separating the pots. She thought: I should say something about the fax to CNN. She looked up, started to speak. Cooper interpreted her.

"We're keeping you, and I'm sorry," he said. "I know you're busy."

"Oh, no, that's all right," she said nervously. She had never felt as awkward. Worse than a young girl in her pre-teens, having the look of a graceless stork wearing the painting of a woman. All bone and teeth and nose. As sexless as a stick. "It's nice to see you again," she added in a rush.

"It's a real surprise," Cooper said. "A little shocking, to be honest."

"Yes, it is, isn't it?" she said in a forced, bright voice.

From near the platform, he heard a call, "Miss O'Reilly," and he looked toward the voice. It was Peter Raferty, standing behind the platform, his arms crossed, a hard glare fixed on his face.

"I think we've upset your friend," Cooper remarked quietly.

"Don't be bothered by him," she said. Then: "Did you find a place to stay?"

"At the Quayside Inn," Cooper answered.

"It's very nice," she replied, nodding. She picked up a potted seedling, put it back on the table.

"Why don't you join us there for a drink later?" Sandy said.

Kathleen forced a flickering, polite smile. She glanced toward Peter. He had not moved, had not changed expressions, and then she turned back to Sandy. "I don't think so," she said. "It's sure to be a late night. All this to clean up. I'm sure I'll be busy enough."

"A pity," Sandy said. "Still, if you get a chance, you'll know where we are."

"Thank you," she replied. She looked at Cooper. "You're off tomorrow?"

"Sometime in the morning," Cooper answered.

"Have a good trip," she said. She dipped her head, turned and moved hurriedly toward the waiting group of men.

Cooper watched her walk away, watched her approach the men, watched Peter Raferty step close to her and bend to say something, watched her face flare in anger. "She's in trouble," he said softly.

Sandy bobbed his head. "She'll be fine, lad. Don't be worrying about her. She's got some spunk. She'll take care of herself."

"I hope you're right," Cooper muttered. "You know, all of this is a little spooky to me. If I didn't have such a high regard for you, I'd say you arranged the whole thing."

Sandy laughed. "You're not a true believer, are you, young Finn?"

"A believer in what?" Cooper asked.

"In God's doing, my boy. In God's doing."

20

To Kathleen, it was almost a blessing to have Peter Raferty hovering over her, complaining about her wasting time with an American tourist when her duty was to Raferty & Son. With Peter, she was at least distracted long enough to manage the mayor's planting of a spruce seedling and to subject herself to a short interview from the CNN stringer without Cooper Finn Coghlan seizing her mind and controlling her.

Cooper was not stalking her, as Peter had insisted in his bitter accusation. She was certain of it. Cooper knew she lived in Cork, yes, and he knew she worked for Raferty & Son. They had talked about it in Waterford and she had left him a note reminding him, but he had given no indication of changing his travel plans to see her and he had not tried to call. And she had said nothing of the ceremony in the park. Nothing. Cooper could not have known about it. It was only a coincidence that he and Sandy McAfee had wandered into the crowd. Quirky, yes. Ironic, yes. Still, a coincidence.

She wished it were something else, something grander. Kismet. But she did not believe in kismet. Kismet was nothing more than a romantic notion, as fanciful and as improbable as a leprechaun hoarding a crock of gold. Kismet was the sort of dreamy nonsense that Denis Colum wasted his life believing.

Yet, Cooper had been there in Fitzgerald Park, inexplicably, the same as in Dublin and in Waterford.

And he was there still, even after the gathered crowd had wandered off, leaving her with the clean-up. His presence was there. Somewhere in Fitzgerald Park, Cooper Finn Coghlan watched her. As surely as the wind whispering from the leaf-tongue of trees was there—unseen, but felt—so was Cooper Finn Coghlan.

She took the empty box that had held potted seedlings and walked across the grass of the park toward her car. The dimple of a shadow fell over the grass from behind a tree, then disappeared, and she stopped walking.

"Peter?" she said in a tired voice.

There was no response from the shadow.

"Peter, I mean it. I know you're there. I can feel you crawling over my skin, like a bug."

Peter Raferty stepped from behind the tree and walked toward her. "I'm not hiding," he said arrogantly. "What makes you think that?"

She turned away and began walking again to her car, and he did a quickstep to follow her.

"I asked a question," he said in a harsh manner.

She stopped and whirled back to him. "Don't you know you're making a spectacle of yourself?" she said in anger. "The mayor, himself, was complaining about it. Whispering around about how ill mannered you were. He gave orders to have you watched."

"What have I done?" he demanded. "Nothing. Nothing at all. It's you that's the spectacle."

"What does that mean?" she asked.

A sneer curled over his face. "The American. You've got him sniffing around you same as a dog in heat."

She stood glaring at him, and then turned to walk away. He reached, catching her by her arm, spinning her to face him, causing her to drop the box she was carrying.

"Don't walk away from me," he commanded.

"Let go of me, Peter," she said quietly.

He closed his fist on her arm, causing a jolt of pain. "Who do you think you are?" he snapped. "You're nothing but an employee. I'll not have you treating me with such disrespect."

"Disrespect?" she said wearily. She tugged her arm away from his grip. "And what are you going to do, Peter? Rape me? Here, in the middle of Fitzgerald Park? Now? Is that what you've got in mind? Are you drunk enough or mean enough for that?"

"What kind of man do you think I am?" he growled.

She reached to pick up the box. "You're a beast, Peter. You love putting people in fear of you, but I'm tired of the fear. It's done with, Peter. You'll never put your hand on me again. Do you understand me?"

He inhaled deeply, suddenly. She could see the coiling of his body. His head bobbed menacingly. "He'll not have you. I'll see to that," he whispered.

"And what does that mean?" she demanded.

A sneer curled over his face. "It means what it means," he said in a low, threatening voice. He whirled on his heel and stalked away. "It means what it means," he said again.

~~~

On nights when his mood was tender and his longing for Ireland great, Finn Coghlan would often share his melancholy by telling the story of Patrick the Believer. It was a story Cooper had always loved, first as a child and then as a man, and now, being in Ireland, in the land of stories, the wonder of Patrick the Believer seemed eerily possible to him.

Patrick was the youngest of four brothers. He was small and slow-witted and his brothers took pleasure in ridiculing him. They would give him sticks and tell him the sticks were swords, and they would leave him at the edge of the forest bordering their father's farm, instructing him to stand guard against the fierce tree dragons that came at night to devour their sheep. And Patrick would march back and forth in front of the forest, as his brothers had taught him, singing, "The steel of my sword is sharper than wind. It can cut through stone and a dragon's hard skin." All night he would march, and at daybreak, his brothers would bring old wool from their father's barn and show it to Patrick and swear to him the wool was all that was left of the dragon's feast.

It was only one of many mean tricks his brothers used in their torment of Patrick.

Still, Patrick loved his brothers, and he believed what they told him.

As the years passed, each of the brothers took wives, leaving Patrick as the only unmarried son of the family.

"How can I too find a wife?" he asked his brothers.

"Well, now," said one of the brothers, "it's the same as with all of us. There's a great tree on the far hill, where the sheep love to wander in search of the greenest grass there is in all of Ireland. Under the tree, there's a stone, small as your hand. Now, you take it up and rub it and while you're rubbing it, you say, Angel of light from the night I was born, bring me a wife on a unicorn. And if you believe, young Patrick, why she'll be there in a wink."

"Is this so?" Patrick asked his other brothers.

"Aye, it's so," his brothers said.

"Then I must go find this tree," Patrick said.

And off he went to the far hill, where the sheep grazed on the greenest grass in Ireland, and there he found a great tree. To his dismay, there were hundreds of stones as small as his hand. "And which is the right stone?" he said. He picked up one and rubbed it and he whispered, "Angel of light from the night I was born, bring me a wife on a unicorn." He looked and waited, but nothing happened. So he placed the stone on a smooth spot of ground near the tree and picked up another stone and rubbed it furiously, again saying, "Angel of light from the night I was born, bring me a wife on a unicorn." Still, nothing happened. And he placed that stone beside the first on the smooth spot of ground near the tree.

And so it went for days, until all the stones under the tree, save one, had been picked up and rubbed and placed in a huge pile. And hidden in the distance, his brothers watched and laughed merrily, saying, "Stupid boy. Let us put a hag on a goat and send it to him. He'll not know the difference."

With the last stone, Patrick stood straight and looked into the sky. His hands, which were raw from so much rubbing, gently touched the stone he held and he said in a whisper that only the birds watching from the great tree could hear, "Oh, Angel of light from the night I was born, please bring me a wife on a unicorn." And, suddenly, there was a great flash, brighter than the sun's fire, and there, before young Patrick, was a white unicorn, more powerful than any horse ever to walk the Earth, and on the unicorn was the most beautiful woman any man had ever seen, dressed in a cloud whiter than finely spun silk.

"Come," she said sweetly to Patrick. "I am your bride, and I have come to take you to the Land of the Ever Young, where the believers live."

As his brothers watched, dumbstruck as dogs, the unicorn flew off with Patrick holding close to the beautiful, cloud-dressed woman.

And, still, on a far hill in Ireland, near a great tree, there is a stone heap called Patrick's Castle, and under the tree, lies one stone.

Those who believe, look for it.

It was the story of Patrick the Believer that Cooper told to Sandy McAfee in a shadowed corner of the Quayside bar.

The two had been exchanging stories in mellow voices—those of Finn Coghlan and those of Sandy McAfee—the same give-and-take Cooper remembered from childhood evenings with his grandfather.

"Ah, it's a great story," Sandy said reverently of Patrick the Believer. "A great story. One I've not heard. Like the other one you was asking about. What was it?"

"Finn McCool and Sally Cavanaugh," Cooper said.

"That's the one. You'll have to tell it to me."

"Another time," Cooper said.

"I'll hold you to it," Sandy said. He leaned toward Cooper, smiled his smile of devilment. "Now, when the lovely Kathleen O'Reilly shows up tonight, if she's riding a unicorn, wearing a dress of white clouds, I'll be rubbing every blessed rock in Ireland."

"She won't show," Cooper countered.

"She'll be here," Sandy said confidently. "Sure as young Patrick lives in the Land of the Ever Young."

"Wrong," Cooper said.

"A little wager, maybe?"

"Name it."

Sandy looked at his watch. "It's eight minutes after ten. I say she shows before ten-thirty. Now, if she does, you pick up the check. If she doesn't, it'll fall to me."

"You're on," Cooper told him.

At twenty-seven minutes after ten, Cooper saw her standing at the door leading into the bar, peering into the shadows. "I'll be damned," he said softly.

"Blessed is what I'd say," Sandy offered. "The check's yours, my boy."

Cooper stood at the table and waved across the room. Kathleen saw him, waved back timidly and began moving toward him.

"I'm feeling a bit under the weather," Sandy whispered as he stood.

Cooper turned to him. "What do you mean?"

"It's getting on to me bedtime," Sandy said, smiling.

Kathleen approached the table.

"You made it," Cooper said.

"I was driving nearby and thought I'd drop in quickly," she replied uneasily. "But if you're about to leave—"

"Leave?" Sandy said. "It's the shank of the evening for the young of the world. Come, sit. You look like a lady who could use a glass of spirits."

Kathleen smiled and took the chair offered by Cooper.

"So, how did it go?" asked Cooper, sitting.

A puzzled look waved over Kathleen's face.

"The tree planting under the light of the moon," Cooper said.

"Fine. It went fine," Kathleen said. "The mayor was a bit long-winded, but he put a spark in the crowd, and we got the tree planted without killing it."

"I think it's a great program," Cooper told her. "You should get it in the school systems. Give the kids a seedling and have them plant it. We did something like that when I was in school. The tree I planted is still living, believe it or not."

She tilted her head in interest. "That's a wonderful idea."

"It's called American enterprise, dear," Sandy said softly. "Now, what'll you have?"

"A coffee would be nice," she answered.

"Irish?"

"Yes, that would be good."

Sandy waved for the waitress, gave the order: three Irish coffees.

"And how's our boy, Peter?" he asked.

Kathleen glanced instinctively toward the door of the bar. "That's really why I came by," she said.

"Trouble?" asked Cooper.

"No," she answered quickly. Then, after a pause: "Not exactly."

"Something happened?" Cooper said.

"He was upset about the two of you appearing at the park," she said. "He's got it in his thinking that you're following me."

"Sounds like jealousy," Sandy said.

"It is, I suppose," she replied.

"From my little chat with him in Waterford, I understood that he was married," Sandy offered.

"Oh, he is," she said. "But he has this—this infatuation for me. And I'm not the first, to be sure."

"Why don't you report him?" asked Cooper.

"As I said before, it's his father who owns the firm, and his father's sure to take his word."

"Why don't you leave?"

"It's not that easy to find good jobs," she told him. "Not in Ireland. Not for women."

"Tell us about tonight," Cooper urged gently. "We don't want to be the cause of trouble."

And Kathleen told them of Peter's threat, without the mention of his rough treatment.

"I'm sure it means nothing," she added, "but I thought you should know. The Irish can let their emotions get the best of them at times and do foolish things without a thought, and as you've seen, he has a temper and the size to go with it. He's also got a history of brawling."

"I'm not worried," Cooper said. "I'm sure he was just letting off steam."

"Well, now, if he shows up again, we'll have to be a bit more forceful in our objections," Sandy said. "Have another little chat with him, remind him of Waterford."

They talked for an hour, nursing the sweet, strong Irish coffee, before Sandy stood, stretched and faked a yawn.

"Well, good people, the old need their rest, so I'll be bidding you a quiet adieu," he said.

Kathleen looked at her watch. "Oh, it is late. I should be going, too."

Sandy leaned to her, took her face in his hands, kissed her tenderly on the forehead. "No," he whispered. "It's not late for you, sweet lady. It's exactly the right time."

Kathleen blushed. She did not reply.

Sandy did his stage pivot to face Cooper. "As for you, young Finn, I'd say we have a leisurely rest in the morning. This is Ireland, not the blasted United States of America. You can get from here to there without spending a week on the road, and we're close enough to wherever we go next not to rush it."

"You're the guide," Cooper said.

"Indeed," Sandy replied, bowing. He said, to Kathleen, "I'm sure to see you again." Then he turned and left the room in an exit learned from the stage.

"He was in rare form tonight," Cooper said quietly.

"I do like him," she said.

"You know it's a plot, don't you? Him pretending to be sleepy. I hope it didn't embarrass you."

Kathleen shook her head.

"Would you like another coffee, or something else?"

"No, thank you. I really should be going. It's been a long day, for sure, and tomorrow's more of the same, thanks in great part to you."

"Me?" he said.

"It was you who put us in touch with your CNN friend."

"He called you?" Cooper said, surprised.

"He did. There was a crew tonight, taping for him."

Cooper laughed quietly. "I don't believe it. The story about you was so glowing, I thought he might have an interest, but you know that's a long shot, always."

"It worked. Thank you."

"You're welcome," he said. "So, what's next?"

For a moment—a long, deliberate pause—she did not answer. Then she said, "On the road again."

"Really? Where?" he asked.

"Killarney. They've put together a quick script and they want to do a taping in front of the great yew trees in the park."

Cooper grinned.

"What?" she said.

"I was thinking about you being in Killarney."

"You're going there, too?" she asked.

"Unless Sandy changes his mind," he told her. "It's my trip, but I'm at his mercy."

She gazed thoughtfully at the coffee cup. Then she said, "Do you get the feeling, Cooper Finn Coghlan, that we're in the middle of some grand prank?"

"It does have a strange sense about it," he admitted.

"Tell me true: is it your doing?"

"Not at all," he said. "Believe me."

"Amazing," she said softly. "It's that: amazing. I was shocked when I saw you tonight at the park. Shocked."

"Not as much as I was," he replied. "We were leaving, and that's the truth."

She moved in her chair. "And that's what I have to be doing," she said. "Or I'll find myself sitting and talking until the sunrise."

"I'd like that," he told her, "but I know you have to work, and I can sleep in, and that would be unfair." He stood. "I'll walk you to your car."

The night air was cool, the sky clear. The lights of Cork curved in an ethereal halo over the city, like the dull beginning of a sunrise. They walked slowly through the garden below the Quayside Inn to Kathleen's car, parked on a side street. Cooper joked about Peter hiding in the shadows with an Uzi.

"That's a scary thought," Kathleen said.

"Do you think he followed you?"

She shook her head. "He couldn't have. He was still marching across the park when I left."

"Does he know where you live?"

"Unfortunately, yes."

"Will he be waiting for you?"

"He could be, yes. He's done it before, slipping around believing I don't know he's there. James Bond, he's not."

"Would you like for me to follow you home?" Cooper asked.

She stopped at her car and turned to him. "That's sweet, but, no. There'll be no reason for it. He'll not harm me, if he's there."

"Will you call me if he bothers you?" he asked.

"Would you want me to do that?"

"Yes, I would."

"And, why?"

Cooper grinned, shrugged. "I'd wake Sandy and send him over."

"You wouldn't come yourself?" she said.

"I would. Of course, I would," he answered after a moment. "You'd think John Wayne was alive and well."

She stood gazing at him. She wanted to say many things to him, wanted to tell him about her visit with her mother and her mother's long, patient life settled between her love for two men. She said in a whisper, "I'm glad I saw you."

"I know I'm not Sandy, but do I get a goodnight hug?" he asked.

She stepped to him. He folded his arms around her and pulled her close.

"My mother used to tell me that a hug was the grandest thing on Earth," she said. "Sometimes when you're hugged, you can feel the other person pouring into you."

Cooper pulled back his face and looked at her. Light skated across her eyes, swirling, leaping. He leaned to her and kissed her softly. Could feel her lips quiver, then open as she took the kiss, tasted it, drew it carefully, slowly into her mouth, held it, fed from it. And then she turned her face and rested it on his shoulder. Her body trembled.

"Thank you," he said gently.

She did not answer. Her arms tightened around him.

"Where will you be in Killarney?" he asked.

She was quiet for a moment, and then she answered, "The Lake Hotel."

"Do you work the whole day?"

"It'll probably be over by four, maybe earlier."

"Now there's another coincidence for you," Cooper said. "I've always been a four o'clock man, especially for taking a walk around a new place. Do you have plans?"

She shook her head against his chest.

He nodded. "The Lake Hotel. I may see you there, in the lobby around four. Accidentally, of course."

"That would be nice," she whispered.

21

It was in Ealy's Irish bible that Cooper would place his second call to America on Tuesday evening, May 16, eight o'clock Daylight Saving Time, one o'clock in Ireland. The call would go to Dugan's Tavern, to Kevin Dugan's speaker telephone. Ealy would be there, and Cary and Kevin.

Cooper did not know that thirty minutes before he made the call, Ealy and Cary and Kevin had spoken to Sandy McAfee.

It had been difficult, and a bit costly, Sandy had reported with pride, yet he had managed to arrange a third serendipitous meeting between Cooper and the young woman named Kathleen O'Reilly, adding that he had left them huddled close in a pub, casting sweet glances at one another, fidgeting like school children caught up in their first giggly romance.

"Good man," Ealy had exclaimed with vigor.

"I'm afraid I'll be needing another hundred to keep it going, though," Sandy had suggested meekly. "I've a fellow inside her company who's supplying me with her whereabouts, but he's got a terrible thirst and a greedy soul."

"Fine, fine," Ealy had said. "I'll have it sent out in the morning. Where to?"

"The same place, here in Cork," Sandy had replied. "We won't be leaving too early."

Cooper's call was taken in the tavern, punched into Kevin's office, where Ealy and Cary and Kevin waited, celebrating the news from Sandy McAfee. Their greeting to Cooper was loud, the greeting of men for men, an exchange of one-upmanship—how the merriment of Dugan's Tavern had greatly improved with Cooper's absence, how serene Ireland was without the uncivilized behavior of such men as Ealy—and then

Kevin asked, "So, my boy, have you conquered the heart of one of the fine ladies of my country?"

"Several," Cooper answered. He thought of Kathleen, added, "They all seem to be love-starved since you moved to Atlanta."

Kevin laughed heartily. "And why do you think I had to move?" he roared.

"Wait a minute," Ealy said. Cooper knew he had moved close to the speaker on the telephone. "Didn't you tell me about some woman named Kathleen?"

"Kathleen?" Cooper asked.

"Yeah, cockroach: Kathleen."

"Oh," Cooper replied. "Yes, I did meet someone named Kathleen. She's in public relations. She's nice."

"Nice?"

"Very nice," Cooper said.

"Have you seen her again?"

"In fact, I have. Tonight. We were wandering through a park and she was there, promoting a project she's working on. I told you about it, didn't I? It's a tree-planting campaign." He paused. "We had coffee later."

"Let me speak to her," Ealy commanded.

"She's not here," Cooper said.

"What's wrong with you?" Ealy asked. "You're in the land of magic, boy. You better take advantage of it."

"That's not the reason I'm here," Cooper said. "Remember my grandfather?"

"Well, Coop, I know that," Ealy muttered. "Don't make me feel like an ass."

Cooper heard soft laughter in the background. Awkward laughter.

"You doing okay with that?" Ealy asked. "You know, having his ashes around."

"Fine," Cooper said. "Sometimes I think he's watching me from that box, and he's enjoying it."

"You're taking some pictures, I hope," Cary said. His voice sounded distant.

"When I remember the camera," Cooper said. "I've bought a lot of postcards. They're better than anything I can take. Put some in the mail to you guys today."

"We miss you, brother," Cary said gently.

"Yeah, we do," Ealy added.

"I'm keeping your chair turned up," Kevin said.

"Read the bible, boy," Ealy ordered. "We'll be waiting for the next call. And don't forget the name."

"What name?" asked Cooper.

"Kathleen. Sweet Kathleen."

After the call, Cooper opened the briefcase containing his grand-father's ashes. He took the box from the briefcase and placed it on the writing table in the room, and then he removed the envelope of rock shards and photographs his grandmother had given him, and he opened it and slipped the photographs out and spread them across the table.

"Am I getting hot, Papa?" he said quietly. "Are we close?"

He picked up the photograph of the young woman sitting in profile on a blanket in a meadow. She had a gentle face, the kind of face that portraitists would find irresistible in their paintings of pastoral scenes, and he remembered the reproduction of a painting he had seen in one of the guidebooks to Ireland. The artist was Gustave Courbet and the painting was called La Belle Irlandaise. A three-quarter profile of a woman whose expression was that of both child and seductress. It was the same with the photograph his grandfather had owned. Child and seductress. A gaze that was mesmerizing. Longing was in the gaze. And sadness. It was as though she was watching something magnificent disappear into the distance. Oddly, it was the same look he had seen earlier in Kathleen O'Reilly.

He slipped the rock shards and the photographs back into the envelope, closed it, put it again into the briefcase.

Ealy had said, "Don't forget the name."

Knowing, he had foolishly asked, "What name?"

"Kathleen. Sweet Kathleen," Ealy had said.

In Killarney, he would take his camera and photograph Kathleen O'Reilly, he thought.

On a blanket, in a meadow, perhaps.

In profile.

Or three-quarter profile.

La Belle Irlandaise.

For Ealy and Cary and Kevin, it would be proof of her.

For Cooper, it would be proof of the mystery of Ireland.

In his journal, he wrote:

When my father gave me this journal, he told me I was a good writer, and he urged me to do a daily accounting of my experiences in Ireland. I've had good intentions to do that, but those intentions have had competition. I think it's best to make notes now, with a promise to myself that I will write more in detail later.

Waterford: A beautiful city with beautiful churches. Glassworks are unbelievable. Agreed with Sandy McAfee for him to accompany me on rest of trip. Ran into Kathleen O'Reilly at a pub. We took a walk. She left me a kind note, saying she had to leave early for Cork. Found out from Sandy that he needed to go to Cork also, to get some money.

Cork: More sightseeing with Sandy. (If I didn't know better, I would think that Ireland was settled by McAfees and would have vanished into the sea long ago without the brave McAfees keeping it afloat.) One nice surprise: we again ran into Kathleen O'Reilly in a place called Fitzgerald Park. She was working on her tree-planting campaign. Later, she joined us for coffee. A nice evening.

Next: Killarney. Kathleen O'Reilly will also be there.

~~~

Kathleen saw the digital clock beside her bed wink 1:08. She had closed her eyes only in pretense, or from habit, or from hope that sleep would come automatically, that the act of closing her eyes would be like the off-switch of an electric light, breaking the current that flowed to it from some mysterious, humming generator. The off-switch of her eyes had failed and the current that flowed from Cooper Finn Coghlan did not stop.

She sensed him, sensed his touch. The current sizzled in her.

She turned in her bed, moved the pillow to fit over the cradle of her arm, pushed her face into the pillow and pulled her other arm over her face to sandwich it against the pillow. Closed her eyes again. Listened. She could hear nothing but the whirring of the refrigerator, and then the telephone rang again.

Damn Peter Raferty, she thought. She rolled onto her back and counted the rings. Two. Three. Four. Five. And then she reached for the telephone, lifted it, held it, dropped it. The ringing stopped.

The ringing had been constant since arriving at her apartment. She had answered the first two calls, believing they may be from Cooper, though she had not given him her number. Still, it was in the directory. No one had responded to her repeated hellos, and she knew it was Peter, wandering the streets of Cork City, pub to pub, making calls from his cell telephone. The calls were unspoken messages of warning.

She wondered if Peter would try to harm Cooper.

Not likely, she thought.

Yet, it was possible, having his reputation for brutality.

And it was ironic. Four days earlier, she had been consumed by her work, with no other interest on Earth, and no other distraction other than the overbearing, irritating presence of Peter Raferty. Now, she was inexplicably close to being consumed by a man she had seen exactly four times. It was as though she had made a wish at a wishing well—a tourist trap selling dreams for a lucky Irish penny—and the wish had materialized in a puff of smoke. If magic were more than illusion, then she had experienced magic. But it was not magic. It was chance, all chance. Stepping out of a taxi in Dublin and him being there. Walking into a pub in Waterford and him being there. Looking up in a park in Cork and him being there.

Chance. Only chance.

If she believed in the Fates, she would vow the Fates were toying with her.

Still, there was the kiss. Sweet. Warm as summer.

The bruise of the kiss was still on her lips, resting there like the sleep that would not come to her.

The telephone rang again. She picked it up.

"Peter, please," she whispered seductively, "you're interrupting the most glorious sex I've had since Dublin and Waterford." She held the telephone away from her and said in a moan, "No, no, not again. Please. I can't…" Then she slipped the telephone back onto its cradle. She rolled her legs over the side of the bed, sat, waited. She believed she could hear echoes of the telephone's ringing still in her bedroom.

She pushed from the bed, crossed the room, went into the kitchen, opened the refrigerator and took out a carton of orange juice. She found a glass on the drain board, poured juice into it, drank.

With luck, he would not call again, she thought. With luck, he would wander home, fall down before his disgusted wife like a sinner before God, and then beg her to punish him. It was office gossip that his wife had often assaulted Peter at his urging. A masochistic cleansing by a happily sadistic woman, the gossips said in giggly voices. You could tell it by the whelps on his face and the scrubbed look of redemption in his eyes. Always, after a cleansing, Peter Raferty was temporarily a changed man, promoting sobriety and family and all things beautiful and tender, candidly confessing that ruination for him would be in the first swallow of anything alcoholic. Always he took the swallow.

The telephone rang again.

God, she thought wearily.

She reached for the extension on the kitchen counter.

"Peter," she said evenly, "Tomorrow, I go to your wife. Do you hear me?"

Her mother answered: "It's me, dear."

"Mum?" She could feel her heart racing wildly.

"Are you having more trouble with Peter Raferty?" her mother said.

"The same, Mum. What's wrong?"

"It's your father."

"What?" Kathleen asked in an urgent voice.

"He's out on the porch, in the cold, just sitting there, looking at the night."

167

"Drinking, is he?"

"Not at all. I told you he'd stopped."

"Then, why?"

"He won't say. He won't say anything."

"What happened?"

"I don't know," her mother said. "I told him you'd come by, told him you'd sent your love. It seemed to please him, and then I found him outside, there in the cold."

Kathleen could hear her mother's voice break. Her mother added, "It's too cold to be outside, just sitting."

"I'll be over in a few minutes, Mum," Kathleen said. "Have you a blanket on him?"

"Yes," her mother said softly.

"He'll be fine. Put on some of that good strong tea. We'll get him in."

Connor O'Reilly was sitting leaned back in a porch chair, his face up-tilted, his eyes peering in wonder at the sky. The blanket wrapped over his shoulders, and the light of the stars covering him, made him appear strangely like a leper in a photograph Kathleen had seen. Sitting so, with the blanket on him, the light of the stars caught in his eyes, her father seemed frail, not the robust quarreler she had known. A suddenly old man. Lost in thoughts that swirled somewhere in cosmic dust, too far away to comprehend.

"Leave me with him," she said to her mother. Her mother dipped her head in a nod, turned and moved silently back into the house.

Kathleen knelt before her father, took his hands, said in a gentle voice, "It's late now, and cold. Let's go in."

Connor O'Reilly's eyes wandered to her.

"I'd like some of that good tea you bought," Kathleen whispered. "Would you have a cup with me?"

Her father blinked, but did not move from the chair. He turned his eyes back to the sky.

"What do you see up there?" she asked.

A damp film coated her father's eyes. "Lost nights," he mumbled.

"What lost nights?"

"All them years."

"They're done with," Kathleen said.

"I shamed you," her father whispered. "Shamed your mother."

"Don't talk about it."

"She had another life waiting. Better than she got from me."

"She's had the life she wanted," Kathleen said.

Her father shook his head slowly. "All them years, having a prize I didn't win, not knowing the luck of having it." He inhaled suddenly, as though swallowing a sob. A tremor shot through his body. "Nothing's worse than knowing you're not good enough, seeing them little gifts that come from elsewhere."

He knew, Kathleen thought. He had always known, and knowing had caused a great aching in his pride.

"Let's not have that kind of talk," she said in a soothing voice. She reached to stroke her father's face, to touch the ear gone deaf from the glass she had smashed against it. "Come. Let's go in, now. There's a lady inside who's worried enough, don't you think?"

Her father turned to look at her. A tear-string wiggled over one cheek.

"Do better than your mother," he said. "Stay with your heart and don't go giving in."

For a moment, Kathleen did not speak. Then she said, "Well, now, for the time being, you're my heart."

Her father took her hand, pulled it to his face. "I love you," he whispered. "You're my gift. Mine."

She leaned forward, rested her head in her father's lap. "I love you, too," she said softly.

22

Once, as a boy, Cooper had accompanied his grandparents on a vacation trip to the city of Savannah on the Georgia coast, and there, in a gift shop on East Bay Street, his grandfather had met an Irishman named Sean O'Keefe.

Cooper remembered the expression on his grandfather's face when he heard Sean O'Keefe speaking to a sales clerk, inquiring about an antique inkwell. The expression was a flash of delight, like the knowing of an animal for its master. His grandfather had broken away from his grandmother in a strong stride toward Sean O'Keefe, his voice unfurling like a sail. "Now, there's a sound from heaven," he had thundered.

And Sean O'Keefe had turned from the sales clerk, a startled look on his face.

"A true Irishman," his grandfather had said, extending his hand.

"True enough," Sean O'Keefe had replied, a weathered grin crossing his face. He had taken Finn Coghlan's hand in a crushing grip.

For a reason he had never understood, Cooper had turned to look at his grandmother and had seen a surge of anger in her eyes. She had taken a half-step forward, had lifted a hand in a gesture that seemed as though she wanted to swat away the words between the two men. Then she had paused. Her shoulders had seemed to sag in resignation, and she had walked away, motioning for Cooper to follow.

Deep in the store, while pretending to examine the delicate hand stitching on white table napkins, she had whispered, "The day's a waste now. He's found himself."

She had been right. The rest of the afternoon, Finn Coghlan and Sean O'Keefe had stayed together, with Cooper trailing after them. They had walked aimlessly along the squares of Savannah, stopping occasionally to sit on one of the benches, and their talking had been non-stop. Even as a small boy, Cooper had been enchanted by them, by their stories and by their laughter and by their tongue-clucking sorrow over the cloud of despair that stayed like sea mist over Ireland.

Sean O'Keefe had been a sheep farmer all his life, was in America for the wedding of a granddaughter to a Savannah businessman. "Jewish fellow," he had said in a voice used for secrets, adding, "A good enough man; well-off, for sure." And being well-off had seemed to cancel any objections to the thinning of the Irish blood, even among those whose beliefs regarded Judaism as heresy when put against the magnificence of the Virgin Mother and her blessed son, Jesus.

Cooper's grandfather had merely nodded in understanding and sympathy, and had observed, "It's the thing about the country that'll keep an Irishman reeling like a drunk, even when he's not had a drop. So much blood-mixing, there's not a history for anybody. Couldn't put a good sheep dog on the scent of it and raise a bark out of him. It's a hard thing to get used to, I tell you. Here they talk about what's on the television, not who they are or where they come from."

And so it had gone through the afternoon, until promises set by clocks forced the two men to part. A touching parting, Cooper remembered. Moist-eyed. Powerful handclasps, released reluctantly. Cheerful voices, too loud, a tremble in them. A scene that had caused passers-by to cast glances of puzzlement and humor.

Cooper had believed his grandmother was jealous of the time she knew she would lose to Sean O'Keefe, but it had been more than jealousy. It had been the irritation of hearing another voice from Ireland—"the Irish-speak," as she had once called it. And it was only after the death of his grandfather that Cooper had finally realized the great contradiction in his grand-mother's regard for his grandfather: the voice that once had mesmerized her with its wondrous flight of words, fluttering around her like colorful butterflies, was the same voice that had held so many empty promises.

Cooper loved his grandmother, in many ways felt closer to her than to his own parents. Still, he was bothered by the bitterness she seemed to harbor for his grandfather. She seldom spoke of him, and when she did it seemed always about a vow he had made and not kept.

"You'd be better off, Cooper, if you took after your father. His word's his bond," she had advised with great pride. "With your grandfather, words were just words, and if a promise got caught up in them, it was because the promise sounded good at the time. If you tried to hold him to it, he'd just make another and go about his way like he'd made a judgment that would've shamed Solomon."

Not returning to Ireland when the tickets had been purchased for him had been one of vows not kept, which was the reason Cooper had remembered Sean O'Keefe on the walk back to his room in the Quayside Inn, after watching Kathleen O'Reilly drive away.

His grandfather had said to Sean O'Keefe, "From the day I set foot in America, I've been looking to go back home, back to where people have some history to brag about. I'll tell you honest, Sean O'Keefe, nobody listens in this country. They don't want to hear you because they have no good stories to tell of their own place and their own people. It pains me to say it, but my own son—and I love the boy—can't give me the names of all his neighbors, living a stone's throw from him. And, bless him, he's not alone. Nobody can. It makes me long for Ireland."

Still, he had never returned. Not in flesh.

In a double-handful of ashes, but not in flesh.

~~~

Cooper awoke early on Wednesday, May 17, still with the memory of his grandfather and Sean O'Keefe. He showered, dressed, slipped into the dining room of the Quayside Inn before Sandy would appear, and ordered a take-out tray of tea and scones. Back in his room, he opened his journal and read from the notes he had made the night before, did not like what he had written, but did not want to cross through the words. He read them a second time. It's all right, he thought. It's a journal. Personal. Something only he would read, and only he would understand.

It was early. There was time to add a new entry. He picked up his pen and wrote:

Today, we go to Killarney, which is the home region of my grandfather. I hope I find the right place to scatter his ashes to the wind. Having been in Ireland now for a few days, I think that one place would be as good as another, because it seems the very soil is made of the ashes of the dead, and their spirits fly about everywhere—some happy and free, some bitter and tortured. I am beginning to believe that is what the Irish are always talking about in their stories. But I do not want to be hasty. My grandfather said I would know the place for his ashes and I have not yet had such a feeling.

It may be that I am too distracted. Sandy McAfee, the man who has worked his way into being my guide, is hard to keep up with and although I like his stories, he's more of a marathon talker than anyone I've ever known. If my grandfather's spirit is trying to communicate with me, it's having trouble getting a word in edgewise.

And there's the other distraction, a far more pleasant one than Sandy McAfee—Kathleen O'Reilly. As I have recorded earlier, I met her first by accident in Dublin, then again, also by accident, in Waterford, and a third time, again by accident, in Cork. I want to think it has to do with being in Ireland, with all the mystique of the land, but I'm guessing it's more coincidence than anything (although it sometimes seems like a set-up by Sandy, and I wouldn't be too surprised to find out she's an actress, hired by him to perform some kind of new style of theater). Frankly, I don't care. I keep bumping into her in my mind, even when she's not there. I like it. It's a good feeling. Today, I'm going to see her again, and it won't be by accident.

He checked his watch. It was seven-forty. He could be packed and ready to leave by eight, yet he knew that Sandy would find a reason to linger. For Sandy, the day began closer to noon than sunrise, even if he had been awake for hours. Cooper thought of it as a build-up period to replace the words he had used the day before, knowing the new supply would be needed on the drive from Cork to Killarney.

~~~

173

Cooper was half-right. Sandy did linger, making a second stop at the bank, citing an error in his earlier transaction. He emerged with a solemn look, one that Cooper had observed as noble fretting, almost comic in its seriousness. On the drive from Cork to Killarney, however, he was oddly restrained. Not completely silent. Restrained. There were no stories of McAfee bravery, no exaggerated tales of battle and conquest in the villages that dotted N22 along the route—Crookstown, Macroom, Ballymakeery, Poulgrom Bridge. He drove at a steady pace, his free hand often resting on the metal box containing the ashes of Finn Coghlan placed between them—a gesture from theater, Cooper thought. When he did speak, it was in a subdued tone, with more sigh than bluster. Casual comments. Questions about the American south. Chat-talk. Occasionally, his hand would sweep toward a passing scene and he would nod with pleasure, letting the scene speak for itself. Compared to their earlier travels, with Sandy blathering as non-stop as a hyperactive radio talk-show host, he was as low-key as a funeral attendant, and Cooper wondered if he had decided to become a mime and was rehearsing for the profession.

When Killarney appeared in the distance—to Cooper, an abrupt green feathering against a backdrop of cerulean-blue sky—Sandy glided to a stop on the roadside. "Where's your map?" he asked, his voice suddenly lively.

Cooper pulled a map from Ealy's Irish bible and handed it to him.

"Let's a have a look," Sandy said. He opened the map, held it up, read it in a glance. Then he folded it to a manageable size and leaned toward Cooper.

"Here we are," he said, pointing to the Killarney designation. He circled his finger to a jutting of land west of the city. "That's the Ring of Kerry and MacGillycuddy's Reeks. Put it in your mind."

"I know about it," Cooper said. "My grandfather talked about it a lot."

"Indeed," Sandy replied happily. "You can't come all the way from America and be this close and not see it. We'll do the circle, or the half-circle, then make it over to Dingle." He folded the map, handed it back to Cooper. "There's a reason for you to know where it is on the map."

"What's that?" Cooper said.

Sandy grinned. "Killarney's straight ahead, one of the loveliest places on God's Earth. So green, you'll think you're standing in the spot where Adam and Eve did their mating. But when you get to places in MacGillycuddy's Reeks—especially in the bleakness of winter—you'll think you're standing on the most desolate part of the moon. It's got the look of land that's been sewn together by stone, but it'll never leave your memory. And what's remarkable about it, young Finn, is how close the two are. It'll make your mind play tricks with your senses."

Cooper remembered that his grandfather had also described the region of Killarney, and the Ring of Kerry, very much the same. "They'll both humble you," his grandfather had said. "It's like the Almighty was saying, 'Here's what I can do with nothing more than a blink of an eye.'"

"It's got all you could want to see," Sandy added. "Hills and valleys and lakes and woods and the ocean pounding away like a sledge hammer. Trees standing like the ones from a thousand years ago, before the British come in, cutting them down. Everything from rivers to bog meadows."

Cooper looked with surprise. "Bog meadows?"

"Where they take the peat from, using it for fuel," Sandy said. He saw the smile on Cooper's face. "Have you not heard of bog meadows?"

"I have," Cooper told him. "Bogmeadow." He wiped his fingers over the smile perched on his face. "I've heard of Bogmeadow, not bog meadows."

"And how's that?" asked Sandy.

"He was a leprechaun," Cooper said casually. "My grandfather claimed to have captured him. He made a bargain with my grandfather to gain his freedom."

Sandy nodded. A fake-serious nod, a hint of humor in it. "And what was the bargain?"

"He would put a charm on my grandfather and all those around him, if my grandfather turned him loose."

"No wishes?" said Sandy.

"One."

"Only one?"

"My grandfather thought the charm was enough. He passed it on to me."

"So he used up the wish?"

"No," Cooper said, enjoying the exchange. "That's mine, too. I've still got it."

"Lovely," Sandy said.

"It was a story from my childhood," Cooper added. "I've never told anyone about it."

"And good that you haven't," Sandy said. "You'd be judged a loony. The only true leprechauns you're likely to find in Ireland are in the bottom of a pint of stout."

"I don't know," Cooper said, musing. "I think Bogmeadow was real."

Sandy laughed. "If he was, he carried a fighting name. A bog meadow can be a hard place." He ran his hands over the steering wheel of the Nissan, shook his head. "When I was a lad, living with my family up in Cornamona in County Galway, there was them who called me Bog Boy, said I had the stench of a bog," he added, his voice oddly flat, a voice Cooper had not heard from him. "Had me fighting all the time, which was part-why we moved away. It was my mother who brought me to the theater when we settled in at Limerick. One play was all it took." He paused. Cooper realized he was breathing heavily. "Nothing's been better in my life than going back to Galway City to do *Hamlet*."

Cooper did not speak. He watched Sandy's hands kneading the steering wheel. The only sound in the car was the purr of the motor and Sandy's breathing.

And then Sandy released the steering wheel and popped a smile. "And I've never told anybody I was once called Bog Boy," he said.

"Good that you haven't," Cooper mocked gently. "You'd be judged a loony."

"Given the two names, I'd take Bogmeadow," Sandy said. He arched his eyebrows comically. "It's got a ring to it. Bogmeadow. Like Puck. Always been one of my favorite characters—Puck. Bogmeadow's like that." He nodded with satisfaction. "Bogmeadow, the leprechaun. I'm sure I've looked him eye-to-eye in some empty glass on some empty night, just like Finn Coghlan." He pulled the car into gear, shot back onto the road without looking for oncoming traffic. "Bogmeadow and young Finn," he bellowed. His laugh was lost in the squeal of tires.

23

Kathleen had never been a guest in the Lake Hotel, though she had once attended a luncheon in its dining room for a client specializing in imports, and her memory of it had always been pleasing. It was a large and elegant facility, gracefully aged. From its windows, there was a spectacular view of Lough Leane, called the Lower Lake, and the ruins of the McCarthy Mor Castle. The National Park was near-by. It served as the perfect drive-away to the Ring of Kerry. Kathleen's married friends who had chosen it as a honeymoon spot, had called it romantic, the idyllic beginning for a new life. Kathleen had interpreted their descriptions as a blending of sophistication and sensuality—a proper afternoon tea in the Castlelough restaurant, uninhibited lovemaking on a four-poster bed in a luxury suite.

She wondered if she would see honeymooners, or lovers, at the Lake Hotel, wondered if, someday, she would choose it as the place to begin her life as a wife.

Tea and passion.

It was a dreamy thought, one that struck as she stood at the registration desk and she shook her head to clear it. She was not there for romance, or for dreaming. She was there for work. Important work. Not just for the NewTree campaign, but for her.

A video director named Ailish Fitzpatrick, hired as a free-lancer by CNN, had mapped out the segment. She would have Kathleen standing among the yew trees—a spot with a lush background—and Kathleen would say into the flat glass eye of he camera, "This is what Ireland once was." She would pause dramatically, then add, "And it is what Ireland will be again."

There would be a fade-cut, bridged by soft Irish music, and a voice-over announcer would tell the story of NewTree as a montage of shots played in the background—Kathleen gazing at the trees, dissolving to the bleakness of MacGillycuddy's Reeks, then to the shimmering waters of

Lough Leane, then to close-ups of fresh-planted seedlings, their spindly tips whipped by the wind. The announcer would talk about the history of ruin of Ireland's forests, and about the crusade—a word he would use often—to right the wrongs. He would tell of the Irish Forestry Funding and its civil, though unofficial, partnership with NewTree.

And it would end with Kathleen gazing into the camera from a different location. She would repeat, "What it will be again."

The script that Ailish Fitzpatrick had prepared directed Kathleen to pull her jacket together with her hands, turn and walk slowly into the woods until she disappeared.

It was, thought Kathleen, excessively melodramatic, an abuse of the seriousness of the campaign she had designed. Still, she knew it would work. It would be a story appealing to patriotism, and not just for Ireland, but as a metaphor for the rest of the world. Nothing stirred the blood of people as passionately as patriotism.

She did not want to think it, but she did: the spot, lasting for no longer than two minutes, would also elevate her position with Raferty & Son. Ailish Fitzpatrick had been blunt about it: "You're going to be a celebrity, want it or not." She had added in a close-face whisper, "And you'd be a fool not to use it to the fullest. You'll be striking a blow for the women of Ireland. Remember that."

She glanced into the restaurant and saw that it was crowded with people playing bridge, among them a number of priests.

An older couple standing near-by—Americans by their accent, their accent being much like Cooper Coghlan's—was taking photographs, their camera passed between them as they took turns posing. Kathleen heard the woman say in a voice of awe, "Queen Victoria stayed here."

And then she heard her own name: "Miss O'Reilly."

It was Peter Raferty. He was dressed in a black double-breasted wool suit, newly pressed. He held a raincoat across his arm, an umbrella in his hand. There was a dark look to his face.

"What are you doing here?" she asked.

"Supervising the account," he answered in a formal voice.

"I don't need you," Kathleen said.

A twitch rippled across Peter's lips. "My father thinks differently. So do I."

"Why?"

"We have the integrity of the firm to think about."

She wanted to laugh, to cry out, "What integrity?" She did not.

"And are you saying that I'm a danger to it?" she asked bluntly.

Peter licked his lips, composed the anger that blazed in his eyes. "No one's suggesting that."

"Really?" Kathleen said. "Then why does it sound that way to me?"

"Draw your own conclusions," Peter replied coolly. "I'm here as an officer of the firm, and seeing as how this is the most important exposure we've ever had, it only seems sensible that an officer of the firm be available." He added, smirking, "My father's in agreement."

"Then I should return to Cork," she said. "Let you take it over."

A blush of irritation rose in Peter's face. "You'll do your job." He shifted his umbrella to his other hand. "I simply wanted to inform you that I was in attendance." His head dipped in a bow. "I'm sure I'll see you later, Miss O'Reilly." He turned and strolled away, holding his shoulders erect, his head high.

~~~

The bed-and-breakfast inn, bearing the name Donoghue's, was on Muckross Road, not far from the Lake Hotel. A woman who introduced herself as Sarah Donoghue said that rooms were, indeed, available. She appeared to be in her late forties, had a thin, merry face, a cheerful voice, a playful look in her eyes. Her body seemed younger than her face, a body for dancing.

"You'll not find better accommodations in the region," she added. "And you'll be having a breakfast that'll bring you back just from the memory of it."

"Hearing you tell of it makes me want to move in permanent," Sandy said smoothly.

"You'd think it was a king's house, if you did," Sarah replied. She smiled at Sandy. "You look familiar," she added. "Have you stayed here before?"

"It's not been my privilege," Sandy said.

An expression of confusion blinked in Sarah's eyes. She tried to turn away from Sandy's deep gaze but could not. She blinked again. A girlish blink with a sigh in it.

Cooper saw the look, knew what it meant. He thought of Lucy Lynch Butler Reid.

"Well, then, I'd say you've got a couple of weary travelers looking for beds," Sandy said. "It's been a long drive from Dublin, leaving as early as we did."

Cooper turned away, knowing the smile would betray him.

"Dublin, you say?" Sarah asked.

"Dublin," Sandy answered. He gestured with his head toward Cooper. "My young cousin's in for a visit from the States, over to take a look at the trees of Killarney for a subject he teaches in university, and to see the place where his own grandfather lived as a boy."

"Indeed," Sarah crooned. "Then I'll put him up in the finest room we've got."

"You're a kind lady," Sandy said. "Maybe your good husband could give us some pointers on where to go for the trees."

Sarah blinked again, held her smile. "I've not had the joy of being married. There's just me and my mother, and she's room-bound."

"Ah," said Sandy. "You have my sympathy." He looked at Cooper. "We'll be whisper-quiet, not to disturb the dear lady."

"Oh, but she's deaf," said Sarah. There was a sound of delight in her voice.

"Sad," Sandy said in his saddest voice.

"You're kind," Sarah sighed warmly.

"My own dear mother was room-bound before she passed," Sandy added. "Broke my heart to see her in such a way. She loved sweets, and I used to sit beside her bed and feed her candies just to watch the smile warm up on her face."

Sarah Donoghue whimpered softly. "Such a lovely thing to do," she said. "My mother would be in heaven if I'd do the same, but I can't. She's got the diabetes."

"Sad," Sandy said again. He added, "But I know the risk of it. I've got the same disease myself."

Sarah oohed. She placed her hand on her throat as though holding back a flood of pity. "I'll get your keys and show you to your rooms," she whispered.

"We'll find them," Sandy told her. "Why don't you see to your dear mother?"

Incredible, Cooper thought. Incredible.

~~~

The rooms of Donoghue's were plain, yet comfortable, the kind of rooms Cooper remembered from small hotels on the perimeter of small Georgia towns during the two years he played baseball for a traveling youth league. To Cooper, a lived-in aura invisibly occupied such rooms, ghosts of other travelers, weary, glad for rest.

Still, he did not want to spend the afternoon in his room. He wanted to be outside, to get his bearings. He wanted to walk the same ground his grandfather had walked. He wanted to ask shopkeepers about the name Coghlan, and in the asking perhaps to discover distant relatives. He wanted also to listen for the whisper of his grandfather saying, *"Here, Cooper. This is the place. Here . . ."*

Patience. He needed patience.

He smiled at the thought, and then, oddly, unexpectedly, he remembered a prank he and Cary had pulled on Ealy during their junior year at Emory University. An unplanned prank.

They had persuaded Ealy that Katrina Wilson, the most beautiful woman on campus, was secretly in love with him.

"You're kidding," Ealy had said in disbelief. "She won't even speak to me."

"It's because of your money," Cary had told him. "Word is, she's afraid of people thinking her only interest in you is your money."

182

"How do you know that?" Ealy had asked suspiciously.

"She told Jodie Merrill, and Jodie Merrill told me," Cary had explained. "Jodie and I take an economics class together."

Cooper had added, "I've heard the same thing. I think Jodie talked to Sylvia Keefer. You know Sylvia, don't you?"

"Who?"

"Sylvia Keefer. She's a day student from Conyers."

"Good looking?"

"She's all right. Real smart."

"Naw, I don't know her," Ealy had admitted in his easy manner, leaning back against the booth in the pizza parlor where they had stopped for a late-night pizza. "The only women I know are night students." He had arched his eyebrows and grinned. "Funny how that works, but they're all good looking. They all grew up in Tit City, all graduated from Tit City High, or maybe it was High Tit City."

"Any as beautiful as Katrina?" Cary had asked.

"Not even close," Ealy had admitted. Then: "You really think she's got the hots for me?" It was a sincere question.

"That's the word," Cary had said. "Maybe it's just gossip."

"Well, Boy Dogs, I need some help here," Ealy had admitted. "What do I do?"

Cooper remembered the look he had exchanged with Cary. Laughing eyes, clamped smiles.

"P and D," Cary had replied after a moment.

"Yeah," Cooper had said, having no idea what Cary meant. "P and D."

"What the hell's that?"

"You don't know?"

"I wouldn't be asking if I knew, cockroach," Ealy had said irritably.

"Tell him, Cary," Cooper had urged.

And Cary had leaned forward at the table and had said in an earnest voice, "P and D stand for Patience and Delay."

Ealy's eyes had narrowed in thought, in the wonder of a revelation. "Patience and delay," he had repeated quietly. "P and D. Damn, that makes sense. Sometimes, I don't have a lot of either one." He had picked up another slice of the pizza advertised as The Kitchen Sink and nibbled from the crust, chewing slowly. "Where'd you guys learn about this?"

Cooper remembered Cary's under-the-table kick. The kick had been a signal, a message: *We've got him.*

"I've always known about it," Cary had said innocently. "I thought everybody did. Men, I mean."

"Me, too," Cooper had added.

"Not me," Ealy had sighed, dropping the pizza. "Every time I get around you guys, it makes me wish I'd grown up in the same shitty, low-rent neighborhoods you did. I missed out on a lot, being rich, Boy Dogs. So help me out with all that gutter knowledge you've got. What do I do about Katrina?"

And Cooper and Cary had improvised a scheme: send Katrina a single, long-stemmed red rose in a cut-glass vase with a note reading, *Beauty for Beauty.* Leave it unsigned to build suspense. Send her one a day for a week, same message, no signature. After a week, wait for her outside her dormitory with a single rose. When she appeared, hand it to her.

"She'll melt on the spot," Cary had said.

"A Katrina puddle," Cooper had added.

Eight days later, Ealy had been issued a warning by campus police for harassing Katrina Wilson. His only response to Cooper and Cary had been a question: "Boy Dogs, it was a great plan. Why didn't it work?"

"You got me," Cooper had answered. "Never worked for me, either."

"Same here," Cary had said sorrowfully.

Cooper smiled at the memory. He missed Ealy. Ealy had always had good-soul innocence. Life for Ealy had nothing to do with a straight-line, goal-inspired career path, posted with such directional signs as Paradigm, Policy, Procedure. Ealy would have laughed—sincerely believing it to be the punch line of some poorly told joke—if someone had suggested to him that he should embark on a pursuit of excellence. Ealy's philosophy was simple: Don't miss anything. It was why he had become obsessive about preparing the Irish bible for Cooper, never understanding that Cooper would miss everything by trying to see everything.

Still, the Irish bible was a generous gift. It was filled with information and good wishes and, Cooper believed, a little envy. It simply did not contain the things that commanded Cooper's attention.

Sandy McAfee.

Kathleen O'Reilly.

Especially Kathleen O'Reilly.

IIe needed to be patient, yes, but there was no time for delay.

And then a thought clicked, causing him to smile.

A single red rose in a cut-glass vase—maybe the Waterford he had purchased for his mother.

A note reading, *Beauty for Beauty.*

Unsigned.

He wondered if Sarah Donoghue knew of a florist.

~~~

It began to rain as Cooper and Sandy sat in Sarah Donoghue's dining room, eating a lunch of rich potato soup and shaved ham sandwiches made with fresh bread and a swipe of strong, brown mustard. It was not a regular-fare provision of Donoghue's, yet Sarah had insisted on serving lunch. A show of hospitality for the young American professor, she had declared. Cooper knew it had nothing to do with him. It had everything to do with Sandy.

Sandy did not need Patience and Delay.

Sandy only needed endurance.

Sarah Donoghue fluttered about them as they ate, replenishing their food, their tea. She had changed into a bright dress, had swept back her hair, and she wore a trace of perfume freshly applied. She had the manner and the appearance of a lady at a happy picnic, giddily flirting.

"Only a shower passing through," Sarah said of the rain. She darted to the window and looked out. "It's light off in the distance. It'll be gone soon." She returned to the table, took a chair near Cooper. "You teach about trees, do you?" she asked.

Cooper glanced at Sandy, saw a smirk of delight, thought of Ealy. The lie about his profession was a lie that Ealy would have told, and for the same reason. "Actually, my cousin is a little off about that," he said. "I'm doing an economic evaluation of the Irish forestry industry, and particularly the potential impact of the NewTree campaign that I'm sure you're familiar with."

Sarah smiled blankly. "I'm sorry, but I've not heard of it."

"It's quite an enterprise," Cooper said. "Getting some international attention now."

"Lovely," Sarah said. "And you teach at university?"

"University of Georgia," Cooper answered after a pause.

"Oooh," Sarah cooed. "University of Georgia. Last season we had some very nice people from there. Quite a lively group. I've a little bulldog and they loved him. Did a lot of barking with him. Confused the poor dear, hearing people bark as if they could talk dog-talk."

Cooper picked up his cup of tea and drank from it. Ealy would love this, he thought.

"It's sort of a password for a secret society," he said. "You hear it a lot at their football games."

"I see," Sarah said politely. She had no idea what Cooper was talking about.

"I wonder, Mrs. Donoghue—"

"Please call me Sarah," Sarah said.

"Thank you," Cooper replied. "I wonder if you know of any Coghlans in the area?"

Sarah's face brightened. "I do, indeed. Samuel Coghlan and his wife, Constance. They're good friends, a lovely couple. Protestants, but as kind as any Catholic I know. Now and again they come in to watch after my mother and give me a chance for a wee bit of free time."

"And what do you do with it?" Sandy asked in a teasing manner.

Sarah fanned away a blush with her hand. "Oh, I'm not talking of going off partying. I'm talking of shopping for necessities and the like."

"And your friends, the Coghlans, give you some time for doing it?" Cooper said to change the subject.

"Oh, yes. They're such caring folk. They operate a lovely little gift shop up near High Street. Would you like to meet them?'

"I would," Cooper said. "Maybe they can give me some information about my name."

"Then I'll give them a ring and tell them you'll be stopping in to see them."

"Thank you," Cooper said.

"You'll most likely find they're some distant relative," Sandy offered.

"I'm sure of it," Sarah said, studying Cooper closely. "He's got the Coghlan look about him."

They sat, talking, drinking tea, until the rain stopped and the clouds slipped away, leaving a startlingly bright sun. Sarah Donoghue spoke tenderly of her mother's suffering from what doctors had determined was Alzheimer's disease. It was something that had begun after the death of her father, ten years earlier.

"He'd had a hard life," Sarah said sorrowfully. "And it made him a hard man. He'd just found the holy church again after shunning it all them years. Died of a heart seizure while taking communion. Had the wafer still on his tongue. Having him die bowing before the altar makes it easier for me."

Sandy reached across the table and patted her hand, let his hand stay. He said, "You're a good lady, Sarah Donoghue. The world needs more people cut from your cloth. But you can't go around living in grief. It's easy to see you've got spirit, and you need to be sharing it."

A barely heard sound—the sound of a soft moan—escaped from Sarah Donoghue. Cooper saw Sandy gently squeeze her hand, saw her tilt her face to him, saw a rinse of gladness wash over her eyes. It was the same look that Cooper had seen from Lucy Lynch Butler Reid.

He's shameless, thought Cooper.

Shameless.

Or maybe not. Maybe Sandy had something—some hypnotic, curative power—that the women trapped in running the business of bed-and-breakfast inns found life-giving, and like the promises of a traveling medicine man, the elixir of his presence was enough to ease their drudgery.

Maybe it was his gift, his magic, his exchange for being who he was.

A little like Bogmeadow.

24

Peter Raferty stood away from the activity that swarmed around Kathleen O'Reilly, stood at a distance that he judged appropriate, a protected zone. He did not want to appear to be one of the gawkers who watched in awe as the scene was being arranged, yet, neither did he want to be mistaken for one of the workers who cowered under the lashing voice of Ailish Fitzpatrick. He wanted to be seen as the man he imagined himself to be—a responsible professional. If the scene to be videotaped had been a motion picture, he would be the producer.

He tugged at his tie, testing the perfection of the knot with his fingertip. His fingertip approved. He watched as Kathleen huddled with Ailish Fitzpatrick. A bitchy woman, he thought, holding his gaze on Ailish. Tall, stout, a menacing look. Lesbian, no doubt. From the way she constantly touched Kathleen, it was more likely than not. He sniffed, took a neat handkerchief from his pocket and dabbed at his nose. He was not accustomed to standing idly around in chilled, damp weather, watching such irritating people as Ailish Fitzpatrick pretend to be a genius. She was almost comic, standing there, giving instructions, her hands flashing in the air like semaphore flags. And Kathleen O'Reilly was into the act as well, her face furrowed in thought as a makeup artist—an anemic young woman—flipped at her forehead with something that resembled a miniature duster. Three young men, shabbily dressed, glittering in body piercings, fretted over lights and camera and sound equipment. They seemed anxious and irritated, their voices loud, their language foul. Peter could hear giggles and oohs from on-lookers, a number of impressionable young girls among them. He thought about stepping forward, confronting the foul-mouthed, shabbily dressed young men, admonishing them to behave. He did not. He had seen such boys in Cork and Dublin. He knew they would explode in anger if challenged, would shout threats at him, and that would cause more giggles, more oohing. Also, he did not want to let his temper get away from him. His temper was on probation from his father. He could not afford another accusation, not after the report of his behavior at the luncheon in Waterford or of the gossip floating around Cork about his interfering presence at the tree-planting ceremony in Fitzgerald Park. His father had threatened to relieve him of his position in the firm if he did not change his ways.

He reached into his pocket and removed a package of cigarettes, tapped one out, lit it, sucked the smoke into his lungs and let the smoke stream from his nose and mouth, and, for no reason, he remembered that, once, as a teenager, he had thought of becoming an actor. Had even auditioned for a role in a school play. The role had gone to Lewis Walshe, who had not auditioned at all. Lewis Walshe, soccer star, sex object for girls who glued themselves to him like bitch dogs in heat. A short life in the spotlight for Lewis Walshe, though, Peter remembered with pleasure. He drew again from his cigarette, felt the satisfaction of a smile building on his lips. Through an arrangement with two of his classmates, Peter had had the finger of accusation pointed at Lewis Walshe over a shoplifting charge two days after the play had closed, and in his fall from grace, Lewis had become a drug-dealer and, finally, a knife-carved corpse before the age of twenty-three.

The mighty fall mightily, Peter thought.

And, sometimes, deservedly.

He was under the shade of a tree, out of the after-rain brilliance of the sun. A drop of water slipped from a leaf and struck him on top of his head. He raised his hand and swiped the raindrop away with his palm, then moved from the spot, re-set himself, assumed his posture of authority.

Ailish Fitzpatrick bellowed: "All right, let's have a run-through."

Her crew dove to their positions.

"Nice and easy," Ailish said to Kathleen. "Don't pay attention to anything but the camera."

"We're rolling," the cameraman said.

Kathleen stared into the camera lenses, licked her lips. She seemed terrified.

"Anytime, now," said Ailish.

"This is what Ireland once was," Kathleen said weakly.

"No, love, that's not it," Ailish said in a kind voice. She glanced at the cameraman. "Keep rolling." She took two steps toward Kathleen. "Say it like you believe it, like it's the most important thing that's ever been uttered."

Kathleen repeated the line. The terror remained.

"Again," said Ailish.

The line was repeated a dozen times. A dozen failures.

"Keep rolling," Ailish ordered. She crossed to Kathleen, put her hands on Kathleen's shoulders, leaned close, and whispered something to her. A faint smile flashed in Kathleen's face. She nodded and Ailish walked away. "All right, this will be it," she announced to the crew, loud enough to silence the muttering of the on-lookers.

Kathleen lifted her face to the camera. The smile faded. She held her gaze, paused, and then said in a voice that was both honest and sensuous, "This is what Ireland once was." She turned her head slightly to gaze at the trees around her, then turned back to the camera. "And it is what Ireland will be again," she added. She blinked once, slowly. Her eyes held on the camera. Held as the cameraman triggered a slow zoom to a close-up. Held as her eyes invited the camera. Held. Held. And then she pulled her jacket to her chin, turned and walked toward the woods.

"Fock me," the cameraman muttered in astonishment.

"Cut," Ailish called.

Applause broke from the on-lookers. Ailish rushed to Kathleen, embraced her. No one heard her whisper, "You're going to have men all over the world playing with themselves."

It was a scene of jubilation, of high-fives and yelping, of hands reaching to touch Kathleen as though touching a celebrity.

Peter watched it with a sneer resting on his face. He thought: Whore.

He waiting until everyone had moved away, and then he approached her.

"I thought you'd never get it right," he said. "What'd she say to you?"

"I think you should be asking her," Kathleen replied coolly.

"You're my employee. I'm asking you," Peter said. "It's a civil enough question."

Kathleen stepped close to him. "She told me to think of being with someone who loved me so much, it'd make his heart weak just hearing my voice."

The blood-coloring of rage filled Peter's face. He said in a low, threatening voice, "You love the tease, don't you, Miss O'Reilly? You love it. But, mind you, this time, you've pushed me too far." He whirled and walked away quickly.

"What was that about?" Ailish asked.

Kathleen did not answer. She watched Peter shove his way through the crowd of the on-lookers. She had never seen him as angry.

"Are you all right?" Ailish said with concern.

"Yes," Kathleen answered. She turned to Ailish. "I'm fine."

"You don't look it."

"Oh, it's nothing."

A frown creased on Ailish's face. "Want my boys to have a little chat with him?" she asked. "If you haven't been able to tell from the looks of them, and by their ill-mannered behavior, I scraped them up off the streets in Dublin and taught them what they know, but they've not forgot the streets."

Kathleen laughed. "It's a thought, but no. He's just got his feelings a little bruised. Besides, he's got a temper. Best not to bother him."

"He does have that look about him," Ailish said. "Men like that, you have to watch."

"You do," Kathleen said. "Yes, you do."

~~~

In the side pocket of Ealy's Irish Bible was a map of Killarney printed from the Internet. It was a simple rendering, an overhead view of street lines and color-shaded landmarks with designations of public places by key symbols published in the top right corner.

From the rendering, Cooper realized Killarney had the map-look of hundreds of small towns in America, especially those in the South and in

New England—a clump of scattered buildings, arteries of roads, artistic puffs of trees, green swatches of parks, cut-and-paste church steeples and government buildings.

Killarney was not heavily populated—fewer than 10,000 by Sarah Donoghue's estimate—yet it was considered significant among the cities and towns of Ireland. Part of it was location, the Camelot setting of mountain ranges and lakes and preserved forests, and part of it—a great part of it—was the shrewdness of the citizenry in knowing that tourists arrived in the area with money-lined pockets. Location and money: a fail-safe formula, and it did not matter if the location and money applied to Killarney Town in County Kerry of the Irish Republic, or to a hotdog vendor in front of Yankee Stadium in New York City during an interleague baseball game between the Yankees and the Mets.

The place blessed with location and money was a place blessed with relative prosperity.

Coghlan's was in Killarney Town.

Location and money.

Coghlan's was a small shop, with narrow aisles and little walk-about room. It had the smell of new-leather belts and shoes and purses, and of the wool of shawls and suits and hats. The collection of small souvenir items seemed to hang heavily around the shop, like a Christmas tree drooping from decorations.

Still, the shop was cheerful, and the shop owners, Samuel and Constance Coghlan, had been eagerly awaiting the visit from Cooper. They were in their late fifties, or early sixties, and if Cooper had seen them on the street and had been asked to describe them, he would have said they were shopkeepers. It was in their look, in the mannequin smiles they had adopted from many years of being pleasant.

In the back of the shop, in a small office, Constance had opened a tin of sugar cookies and made tea. There was barely enough room for Cooper and Sandy and Samuel and Constance to sit.

No doubt that Cooper was related, Samuel declared with delight. Cooper had the fairness of the Coghlans and the strong jaw and clear eyes. "Why, you could've been born here in this very place," Samuel said.

"He has the look of your father," Constance said to her husband. "Taller, but the look's the same, don't you think?"

"Very close, yes. Very close," Samuel agreed.

"His grandfather was called Finn Coghlan," Sandy said.

"Finn?" Samuel said. "Seems I've heard the name."

"He left for America in thirty-eight," Cooper added.

"And he lived here?" asked Samuel.

"He did, yes. I understand his immediate family—his siblings—moved to Dingle soon after he left," Cooper told him.

Samuel stroked his chin thoughtfully. "Could be," he said. "It was a bit before my time. But you know how it is, even with family. Them that move away seem to disappear after a while." He laughed heartily. "It's the way of the Irish. They spend so much time talking to everybody else, they forget to talk to one another."

"Would you have any idea where my grandfather and his family might have lived?" asked Cooper.

Samuel and Constance exchanged looks. "Can't say that I do," Samuel said after a moment. "My own father owned this place before us, and he brought it late in life after he put in long years working here. His folk were farmers, and I've been led to believe that was the trade of most Coghlans. I do know this: being Protestant was hard on the Coghlans of them days, the family being excommunicated from the Catholics as it was."

"And why was that?" asked Cooper.

Samuel shook his head wearily. "Love," he said.

"Yes," whispered Constance.

"Goes back to our history," explained Samuel. "A great-great-grandmother, I believe it was. Out of Scotland. She was Presbyterian and she took a Coghlan in marriage. Him being Catholic meant being expelled by the Catholic church for marrying outside the faith, and that's been the way of it ever since. We're Presbyterian, sure enough, but there's the history of the Catholics still following us around."

"My grandfather was a Presbyterian," Cooper said.

"That he would have been, if he was from our line," Samuel suggested.

"I have a picture of him from when he lived here," Cooper said, reaching into the inside pocket of his jacket and taking out the photograph of the four men standing before the pub called Beckett's. "The second from the left, that's my grandfather," he added. "I don't know the other men."

Samuel gazed intently at the photograph, shook his head. "Wouldn't know them, either. But Beckett's I know, sure enough."

"Beckett's?" asked Constance.

Samuel touched the photograph with his finger. "The pub where they're standing." He held up the picture for Constance to see.

"Oh, yes," Constance agreed. "It's the same Beckett's all right. Hasn't changed much, has it?"

"And where would we find this Beckett's?" Sandy asked. "Maybe there's someone there who'd know one of them."

"It's down near Muckross House," Samuel answered. "Popular with the locals, but not much for visitors. If you go there, you'd best be careful."

For a half-hour, Cooper listened as Samuel and Constance talked in spillover sentences about the missing and dead of Killarney during their lifetime, about how Killarney had changed, how tourism had become the town's one great industry. It was easy enough to see during the season, Samuel offered. People crowding the streets, eager to find a bargain. "At night, the pubs are full-up, and there's plenty of pubs."

"My grandfather used to tell me there were two great institutions in Ireland," Cooper said. "Churches and pubs—both of them keeping the devil busy."

Samuel and Constance smiled politely. A bothered smile. Cooper knew he had offended them. He added, "I'm sorry. I didn't mean to make them sound equal, and I don't think my grandfather did, either."

"Don't be worrying about it," Sandy said easily. "Good Christian folk have no quarrel with pubs, as long as the pub's not the ruin of the man." He bobbed his head, sighed a heavy sigh. "The only hope is that the man who looks for himself in drink, finds himself at the altar."

"Yes," Constance said. "Like poor Davy Donoghue. His was a lost soul until he turned back to the church."

"Died the best a man could die," Samuel added seriously. "The wafer still on his tongue."

"Sarah's a saint, she is," Constance said. "Looking after old Mrs. Donoghue the way she does, and not complaining about a minute of it, and she'd plenty to complain about, I tell you."

"Now, love, don't go getting into all of that," warned Samuel.

"Well, it's true," Constance said stubbornly. She turned to Sandy. "Poor Sarah was engaged once to be married to a fine man, a dry goods salesman who used to call on us. Went to Davy Donoghue to ask for Sarah's hand, and Davy run him off with a gun, he did. So Sarah did the only thing she could. She took off with the man she loved. Did no good at all. Davy caught up with them down in Cork and beat the poor lad to a pulp. Drug Sarah back with him, and there she's been ever since, running that place, doing the work of a dozen. And now with her mother in such a fix, her hope's about run out."

"It's a painful story," Sandy said gently. "I was thinking of purchasing the dear lady a shawl."

"Sarah?" asked Constance.

"No," Sandy answered. "Her mother. What I'd like to do for Sarah is escort her to a dinner, if it fit in with your plans to watch over Mrs. Donoghue for a short time. Sarah's been so kind to me and my young cousin, I feel the need to return the goodness."

Constance's face brightened. "Why, that'd be lovely. Of course, we can." She looked at Samuel. He smiled his mannequin smile.

Sandy stood. "Show me the finest shawls you've got, then," he said brightly. "Irish linen. Lacy, I think, the kind that makes you wonder if it's been done by spider angels." He turned to Cooper. "And maybe you'd want to be finding some of the same for your new friend."

Cooper could feel the heat of a blush on his face. "I was thinking I should start with some flowers, if I can find a florist," he said.

"Oh, I know just the place," Constance said. "There's not a shop in Killarney Town that's even close to being as grand."

~~~

The single red rose in the cut-glass Waterford vase had been placed in Kathleen O'Reilly's room. The rose was enormous, its color deep and vibrant, dark as the petals of a ruby, against its green foliage.

Kathleen opened the note resting against the vase hesitantly

The note read, *Beauty for Beauty.*

It did not contain a signature.

Peter, she thought.

She dropped the card, turned away from the rose and crossed the room to the bed. Her clothes were still damp from the mist that had followed the rain, and she began to remove them angrily. Tomorrow, she would complain directly to Peter's father, she thought. She would threaten to resign unless Peter was permanently restricted from being in her presence, and if his father defended him again, she would file an official complaint of sexual harassment.

She stepped from her skirt and dropped it on the bed, then she looked back at the rose.

No, she thought: the rose was not from Peter. Peter had left the taping session annoyed, not full of himself. The full-of-himself Peter would have sent the rose—no, roses; a dozen of them at least. The annoyed Peter would send nothing but evil wishes.

She moved back to the rose, picked up the note, read it again.

Beauty for Beauty.

Ailish, she reasoned. Ailish had been extravagant in her praise of the shoot. Had oohed softly over the replay of the close-ups. She was lesbian, of course. Easy enough to know that. She had said it in every expression except words. Looks. Touches. Hovering. Little hints of meeting for drinks or for dinner. Maybe time together in the hot tub. The single rose would be something Ailish would do. *Beauty for Beauty* was something she would write.

She lifted the telephone from its cradle and dialed the front desk and asked if anyone had been present when the flower was delivered. The clerk said, "Oh, yes, I was here. It arrived about an hour ago."

"Do you know who delivered it?"

"Two gentlemen. One older, one younger. The older one was Irish, the other American. I had the impression it was from the younger man."

Kathleen smiled. "Thank you," she said.

"Is everything all right?" asked the clerk.

"Yes," Kathleen told her. "Fine. Everything's fine." She glanced at her watch. It was twenty minutes until four. "You don't happen to see either one of the gentlemen nearby, do you?"

There was a pause. Then: "I'm sorry, I don't. Should I watch for them?"

"No, thank you," Kathleen told her. She replaced the telephone on its cradle, reached to touch the delicate ridges in the Waterford vase. She thought of her mother and of her mother's Waterford and of the flowers of Robert Leary. A shiver struck her arms and shoulders.

Coincidence, she thought.

Many men gave flowers in Waterford vases.

25

Peter Raferty sat erect, his back hard against the chair. His hands were on the table before him, enclosed around a cup of tea. There was no discernible expression in his face, only a detached gaze.

A man sat across the table from him. He was in his mid-thirties, dark-hair, dark eyes, a bloodline from dark histories. He had given a name, but Peter had purposely put it out of his mind. To Peter, the name of the man did not matter—was better for him not to know. He only wanted loyalty, and was willing to pay for it.

"Do you understand what's expected of you?" Peter asked evenly.

The man nodded. He toyed with the small photograph of Kathleen O'Reilly that Peter had given him, then pushed it back across the table.

"Good," Peter said. He reached into the inside pocket of his suit coat and removed his wallet and counted out one hundred euro, then slipped the money across the table. "There's half of it now, the rest coming when you finish your duty."

"And what if things get a bit nasty?" the man asked.

The hint of a smile paused on Peter's lips. He said in a quiet voice, "You can kill him for all I care. He's an American. I don't have a great love for any of them."

"We're cut from the same bolt, then," the man offered.

For a moment, Peter did not respond, and then he said in a cold, even voice, "I doubt it."

The man shrugged. He took the money from the table without counting it, grinned an uneven grin revealing an uneven row of stained teeth, then he pushed up from his chair. "I'll see you back here around ten in the morning," he said. He paused, glanced around the pub, then leaned across the table and whispered to Peter, "And it's my advice that you don't go wandering off and start forgetting our bargain. I'm not always a gentleman."

Peter glared up at him. He touched the scar on his face with a finger. "Do you see this, friend?" he said in a low growl. "The man who put it there lies rotted in the ground, if you know my meaning of it. So it's my advice that you don't put a threat on the table that you can't take up and handle." The man blinked in surprise, then let a smirk crawl across his face. He turned and walked away, out of the pub. Peter picked up the photograph of Kathleen O'Reilly and slipped it back into his wallet.

It was her doing, he reasoned. Having the American following after her was all her doing. Had it plotted from Dublin, he guessed. Dublin to Waterford to Cork, and now Killarney. Leaving a trail for him with her whispering ways. She could lie if she wished, but he knew the American was there. Had seen him departing from the lobby of the Lake Hotel. The old Irishman had been with him. The old Irishman had made a fool of him in Waterford. He should have added the old Irishman to his deal. It would have been worth another hundred euro.

He was remarkably calm. The tea was warm, the taste of it rich in his mouth. He had never felt completely in control of his regard for Kathleen O'Reilly; now he did. A satisfying feeling. Powerful.

It was over, his obsession with her, he thought. Vanished as quickly as it had appeared in their first meeting. He always knew it would end in such a way. In anger. What surprised him was how unruffled he was, how composed. Anger had always turned to rage in him, making him a spectacle, a laughed-at punch line of a human joke.

At least, it had been that way in the past, he thought. His short-fuse temper, causing explosions loud enough to raise—or to bury—the dead, all of it brutal and blood-colored.

It had been that way, that shallow.

Had been.

Now the anger was deep enough to be deliberate, unseen, quiet, lethal.

Now he had enough control to hire the needed damage, and in a curious way, he believed the hiring would be more satisfying than his own joy of personal vengeance. It would leave him free of the despicable looks of disgust he got from women like Kathleen O'Reilly.

A slender waitress having a purple tint to her short-cropped hair and a silver ring attached to her left eyebrow, approached his table and asked if he wanted another tea or other drink.

"No," he said in a blunt manner.

"It's bad company you've been keeping," the waitress said lightly. "I know the gentleman. Watch him."

Peter shrugged. "He was recommended," he said.

"For something no-good, no doubt," the girl replied. "But it's of no interest to me. Live and let live is my way, and if you get lucky now and again, you're living in luxury." She smiled and winked. "If you need anything," she added, putting emphasis on anything, "give me a wave. You might get lucky." She did a little wiggle with her hips and walked away.

The signal was clear enough, he thought. He'd seen it since he was a teenager—part-time whores doing part-time duty by spotting and tagging a loner for a late-night date, finding a reason to call it celebration.

And perhaps that was how the night would go.

Perhaps celebration was in order—or would be.

He was handsome enough to catch a wandering eye and he knew it. He was also a man who would inherit position and power and money, and there were plenty of women who would leap at a chance for his company, even if it did not mean marriage. Not whores, either. Whores were plentiful, and if they were not eager, they were willing. He drank again from his tea. Nothing wrong with whores, though, he thought. They were always being hissed at by people who made a habit of hissing their objections to anyone, or anything, that offended them. Whores at least had some integrity, dealing as they did in an honest exchange. Supply and demand. Money paid for a task performed, all fair enough. He would never again fall to the spell of women such as Kathleen O'Reilly, women who looked down on him, contempt clouding their eyes, telling him with their sneers that he did not deserve their company. The right price would buy him no-rules sex with women far more beautiful than Kathleen O'Reilly, and when it was over, they would gather their belongings, blow him a kiss, give him a wink, and then leave him. And none of them would threaten to call his father, or go tattling to his wife.

He thought of his wife, felt a shiver of revulsion ice across his neck. A lumpy woman she had become, a face as stern as the face of a Priest in judgment. Sour as bitter fruit. In their dating years, she had been pretty in a plain, strict-Catholic way, gauntly thin, a shy, downcast look from large doleful eyes. Still, she had forgiven his flyaway temper and had offered him attention while other girls looked upon him with loathing, and from the attention he had become certain she would be an eager and giving sex partner. He had been wrong. The only sex he'd ever had with her, he'd been drunk, and necessarily so. She detested sex, tolerated it only from duty, performed it coldly, never with passion.

Peter pushed the cup of tea away from him, picked up the sugar spoon and balanced it on the edge of the saucer.

If he had learned nothing else from his wife, he had learned the cruelty of tolerance.

He lifted his hand above his head and waved it in a circle. At the bar, the waitress with the purple-tinted hair, smiled. "Yes, love?" she said cheerfully.

~~~

It was not deliberate that Kathleen was late for her four o'clock meeting with Cooper in the lobby of the Lake Hotel. She had showered and dressed quickly in a walking outfit. The phone call from Ailish Fitzpatrick was the delay. It was a call of more praise for Kathleen's work, of asking again about a late dinner, or an after-dinner drink. Something about her voice made Kathleen pause. It was the same sound, the same hint of fear, she had heard so many times from Peter Raferty. She knew the fear: rejection.

She told Ailish of Cooper, of the coincidence of the three unexpected meetings in three days, or nearly three days. Laughed lightly about it, then remembered that it was Cooper who had sent the fax to Sidney Springer at CNN.

"If I hadn't promised him dinner as a sort of thank-you for what he's done, I'd put it off," she said to Ailish, hoping Ailish would believe her. "But, as it is, I'm afraid I'm trapped."

"No bother," Ailish said. "It was just a thought. I've got to do a quick edit and beam the piece out tonight anyway. And I'm sure I'll be busy enough trying to keep my boys out of trouble."

"If I don't see you tomorrow, I'll call when I get back to Cork," Kathleen said.

"Sure, love," Ailish replied in forced gaiety. "Have a good night, but watch him. He's a man, and, worse, he's an American."

She saw Cooper standing at the doorway leading into the restaurant, positioned to watch both restaurant and lobby. He wore jeans and a red turtleneck pullover under a black windbreaker. He had a patient, engaged expression on his face, as though amused by the gathering of bridge players still engrossed by their games. Again, the sensation of being tugged by his presence struck her and she stepped back. She knew there was nothing sensible about being with Cooper Finn Coghlan. He was pleasant and friendly, but being pleasant and friendly were not exceptional qualities among most of the men she knew. He had a nice face, but she had known men who were more handsome. She liked his smile, liked the way he looked at her when he spoke. His smile and the way his eyes stayed on her made her feel comfortable.

Still, whatever tugged at her had little to do with the face or smile or eyes of Cooper Finn Coghlan, she thought.

Whatever tugged at her seemed mystical—a wish and a command caught in the same moment.

She wondered how she should approach him. It would be awkward after the kiss, she thought, the same as the day following her first kiss with Denis Colum, when they were fourteen. She had never forgotten the power of that kiss—exhilarating and frightening, leaving her quivering for a full night. The next morning, at school, she had been certain the nuns knew. Could see it in their disapproving eyes. She had prayed for the agony to pass away, for the blood of Christ to wash away the stain of her transgression. Seeing Denis, late in the afternoon with a gathering of her friends, she had said nothing, had avoided looking at him, and he had laughed at her, saying in a whisper that only she could hear, "You're no longer a virgin, Kathleen O'Reilly. Not after what we done in my dreams." And deep in her soul, she had believed him.

But Cooper Finn Coghlan was a better man than Denis Colum. She was sure of it, even in the short time knowing him. Still, he was a man, with the heritage of a man's floundering ways. A tourist, also. In a few days, he would return to America, and all that had happened between them, or would happen between them, would be over and done with. It would be best to keep him at arm's length, to behave as though the kiss in Cork had never happened.

She pulled at the scarf draped around her neck and began walking toward Cooper. He turned as she approached.

"Well, hello," she said. Her voice was too light.

He smiled, bobbed his head slightly. "What a coincidence," he said. "Fancy meeting you again."

"I was thinking the same myself," she said. She paused, waited for him to reply.

He did not. He stood, gazing at her, the smile lodged on his face. He looked boyish.

"Thank you for the rose," she added. "It's lovely."

Cooper blinked. "What rose?"

"The one in the beautiful Waterford."

"Someone sent you a rose?"

"With a note. I think it must be a line from a poem."

Cooper faked a frown. "Sandy was saying something about going by a flower shop. Maybe he sent it."

"Then I'll have to thank him for such a kindness," Kathleen said. "Where is he?"

"He's taking the night off from his duty as a shepherd," Cooper told her. He glanced at his watch. "At the moment, I'm almost sure he's entertaining a lady named Sarah Donoghue with some romantic story of his past."

"And I would say she's being charmed to the very quick of her soul," Kathleen said. "He has the gift, that one does. I was thinking of inviting him to pay a visit to my Granddear, just to cheer her up."

"Granddear? Is that your grandmother?"

She smiled. "Yes. It's what I call her. Granddear. I started saying it when I was a baby, but it's a perfect fit for her. Granddear. Grandeur. She's that fine a lady."

"She lives here?"

"Not here. Near Dingle," Kathleen said. "I was wanting to drive over to see her, but I don't know if I'll have the chance. Are you ready for your sight-seeing?"

"Sure," Cooper said. "If you're willing to put your life in my hands. It's the first time I've driven the car since I picked it up at the airport in Dublin."

"Then I'd better do the driving," Kathleen said.

"Fine. Where are we going?"

"There's a place I want you to see before we lose the light," she said. "But we have to get a move on."

"Sure," Cooper said. "Then I'd like to find a pub called Beckett's."

"Beckett's?"

"I have a photograph of my grandfather and three other men standing in front of it," Cooper said. He took the photograph from his pocket. "That's him," he added, pointing.

"You look just like him," Kathleen said in amazement.

Cooper thought of his grandmother, could hear his grandmother sighing. "I've been told that a lot," he said.

~~~

The place that Kathleen wanted to show Cooper was in the Killarney National Park, off N71, where the three lakes of Killarney were located. There the Torc River spilled sixty feet over majestic rock outcroppings into Muckross Lake. Bushes and trees lined the waterfall. It was a famous landmark, considered by many the most beautiful in Ireland. Cooper's grandfather had claimed it was where God had taken his first bath after creating the world—"Mainly to get the grime of England off him."

At the base of the falls, Kathleen stood away from Cooper, watching him. A look of awe rested on his face. "I love it here," she said over the noise of the water. "It's beautiful."

"Yes," Cooper replied. "My grandfather told me about it. He came here often as a boy."

"Did he live nearby?" asked Kathleen.

"I don't know," Cooper told her. "He never talked about the home he lived in."

Kathleen moved closer to the water. "Every time I come here I listen to the water. It always sounds like it's singing." She looked back at Cooper. "Can you hear it?"

Cooper stepped beside her, closed his eyes, listened.

"Some days it sounds sad, some days it sounds like a choir full of birds, it's so happy," Kathleen added.

The water over the rocks sounded distant to Cooper. Not the sound of music, but the sound of low, rolling thunder.

And then he heard something that startled him.

Or thought he heard it.

He heard the voice of his grandfather.

"Fingal," his grandfather said.

Cooper's body jerked violently, causing Kathleen to grab for him.

"What's wrong?" she asked.

He shook his head.

"Are you in pain?"

"No," Cooper said. "I'm sorry. I just— I'm sorry."

"What, Cooper?" Her voice carried worry. "Something just happened. What was it?"

"A memory. Just a memory," he said.

For a moment, Kathleen did not speak, then she asked, "Your grandfather?"

"Yes," Cooper answered, too softly for the word to be heard against the rush of the water. Still, Kathleen knew his answer.

"Good," she said. She moved close to him, slipped her arm under his arm and turned to gaze up at the cascading waterfall. The trees were damp from the earlier rain and from the mist of the waterfall and the late afternoon sunlight seemed to cling to the leaves like a clear spray.

Cooper believed he could hear the echo of his grandfather's voice, telling him the story of Fingal and the Waters of Life—Fingal, small of stature with pinched-in shoulders and long, uncombed hair, a face eroded by age and leathered by elements, a cackling, demented voice, eyes the color of boat tar.

He had wandered into Killarney carrying the tools of a silversmith and had taken residence in an ancient stone hut that had been occupied centuries before by a monk, and then by shepherds. From his hut he had created many fine objects from silver, including crucifixes of such exquisite detail it was said they were surely fashioned at night by angels who worked under the guidance of the Holy Mother.

Yet, there was a rumor that Fingal was the son of the Witch of Dingle, whose sister was known as the Hag of Beare, and he possessed powers beyond the ken of mortal man.

As the rumor grew in its telling, swelling from the yeast of whispers, the stories of Fingal became stories of fear.

There were those who swore they had seen him move trees with nothing more than a sweep of his hands, for in his old age he did not like the brightness of the sun—more proof that he was the son of the Witch of Dingle, who was well-known for keeping her head covered.

Others vowed they had seen him turn stone into bread. Still others had heard him calling fish from Lough Leane, had seen with their own eyes how the fish sprang from the water and landed into his fish basket. And there were those who vouched that the silver Fingal used in his work was nothing more than the acorns of oak trees, turned to silver nuggets by an incantation he whispered over them.

Yet, none of the stories were as remarkable as the source of Fingal's age, for it was believed he had lived for more than two hundred years, never aging more than he was when he hobbled into Killarney from the northwest, from the road that led to Dingle.

Fingal did not grow older because he knew the location of the Waters of Life, the stories declared. A daily drink stopped the aging.

"There's them that spied on him for years," Cooper's grandfather had said. "Trying to find where he went with his little pail. But he moved the trees so much to keep the shade on him, he'd soon be lost from them that followed him. All they could do was hope a tree wouldn't slide over them, leaving them buried in a bog hole. And then they'd watch him come up out of the woods, his pail filled to spilling over."

Only one other man in all of Ireland—and the rest of the world as well—knew the secret place of the Waters of Life, his grandfather had vowed, and that man was none other than himself, Finn Coghlan.

All due to kindness, he had explained in hushed tones to Cooper.

As a young man living near Killarney, he had befriended Fingal. Had helped Fingal build a stone fence around a small garden, and in exchange he had been given a map, written in Gaelic, of the whereabouts of the Waters of Life. "It's a little trickle of water coming up out of the ground close to where there's a waterfall that'll make you stand in wonder."

Cooper remembered the power of the story, the chest-aching awe of magic waters in a magic place, drawn on a map. He remembered asking to see the map, remembered how his grandfather had clucked his tongue and admitted in a grieving voice that the map had been lost on his journey from Ireland to America, most likely stolen by one of the ship's officers.

"They was always searching our things, but it doesn't matter which of them took it," he had assured Cooper. "It's burned in my memory, like it was drawn there by Fingal himself. When we go there, we'll find it together."

Hearing his grandfather's voice from the waterfall—standing in wonder as his grandfather had predicted—pleased Cooper. He again closed his eyes and listened. The sound of the water, with its echoes of Finn Coghlan, was very much the same as the sound of the wind on a gusty day. A hum. Steady. Mesmerizing. He could feel Kathleen rub against him.

"You have the look of a person listening to something far away," Kathleen said.

Cooper did not answer. He tilted his head, shrugged slightly.

"Your grandfather," she said. "You're listening to your grandfather."

Cooper opened his eyes, looked again at the waterfall. "It's almost like I can," he said after a moment. "But it's just a story I remember, one he liked to tell about this place."

"And what was it?" asked Kathleen.

"About an old man who lived a long time," Cooper said.

"Will you tell me?"

"Yes."

"Not now," she said. "Later."

"Why later?" he asked.

"I want you to keep listening," she told him.

~~~

Samuel Coghlan's warning about Beckett's was not exaggerated. It was a small, dim pub crowded with men who wore the rough dress, and the look, of a long day's labor. It smelled of ale and tobacco illegally smoked and, from the back, of stew-meat and fish and baked bread. It was loud. A hint of threat seemed to lurk in the heavy air.

Cooper wanted to leave after stepping through the door. Kathleen insisted on staying.

"It's just a true Irish crowd," she said, remembering the pubs frequented by her father. "A lot of noise, but that's the spirit of it. Let's stay for a half-pint, at least. Show the picture of your grandfather to the owner. Maybe he'll know something."

They found two seats at the end of the bar, next to an old man who seemed to be slumbering. Cooper ordered stouts and asked to speak to the owner. In a few moments, Theo Beckett appeared. He was a heavy man with a hedgerow of dark eyebrows, a brooding face that drooped into a frown, eyes that seemed permanently suspicious. Cooper handed him the photograph of Finn Coghlan and his friends, taken in the late thirties. "It's long ago," he said, "but I wonder if you'd recognize any of these men."

Theo glanced at the photograph, shrugged. "I've not the slightest notion," he said. "Why are you asking?"

"One of the men is my grandfather," Cooper said. "He was from Killarney, and he must have known this place."

"A lot of people have," Theo said.

"It was a long-shot, I know," Cooper said.

Theo leaned forward, over the bar, thrusting his face toward Cooper. "You'd be sitting beside the only man in the place who'd know," he said. "Buy him a pint, and maybe he'll help you." He arched one eyebrow, added, "Or maybe he'll give you a great, lying story."

"What's his name?" asked Kathleen in whisper.

"Padraic MacLaverty," Theo answered, also in whisper. "Everybody calls him Old Mac." He reached for the slumbering man's arm, shook him awake. "Look alive, Old Mac, there's a nice young couple wanting to buy you a pint."

The old man's eyes blinked. He looked from Theo Beckett to Cooper and Kathleen.

"You mind your manners, now," Theo warned. "I can tell by the looks of her, she's a proper lady." He signaled to the bartender to pour a pint for Old Mac, rolled his shoulders in a shrug and walked away.

Cooper made introductions, explained that his grandfather had lived in Killarney and had had a photograph taken in front of Beckett's before immigrating to America. He was not sure Old Mac heard him at all. His eyes seemed to float. The expression on his face was that of a daze.

"Let me show you," Cooper said. He held the photograph up for Old Mac to see.

The old man squinted his eyes, eased his face closer to the photograph, stared for a long moment. Then: "Mother of God, that's me." He pointed to the figure standing beside Finn Coghlan, at the end of the line.

"Is it?" Cooper asked in surprise. "Are you sure?"

Old Mac pulled his face back, turned his gaze to Cooper. "Coghlan. Did you say your name was Coghlan?"

"Yes sir."

"From Finn Coghlan?"

"Yes sir."

The face of Old Mac turned pale. "I could have told it," he said hoarsely. "You're the ghost of him, you are." He looked again at the photograph, gently touched the image of himself as a young man. "I know the day this was took," he whispered.

"You're sure, sir?" asked Cooper. "This is you, and you knew these other men?"

"Knew them? Like brothers, they was," Old Mac said, his voice rising, causing people near-by to turn their attention to him. "There's me on the end, next to Finn, and beside him, there's Devin Garrity, and that one's Arnold Hogan on the other end. We was all workers together, cleaning out the fields over near Muckross House in them days." He paused, shook his head sadly, wiped at his eyes with the knuckles of his hand, then looked up to Cooper. "And where is Finn?"

"He died a few months ago," Cooper answered. "I've brought his ashes back."

Old Mac tucked his head and sighed. His eyes watered again. "I'm the last, then," he said softly. "Devin and Arnold's gone. Died in their prime, both of them." He pulled the photograph close and examined it. A tremor ran through his body. Then he held the photograph above his head, turned in his bar stool. "Here I am, lads," he crowed. "Back in the good days of hard times. Me and me friends."

The pub fell silent. Theo Beckett moved back to the bar. He said, "Let me have a look."

Old Mac handed him the photograph, pointed to the image of himself as a young man.

"Well, now, you was a handsome enough fellow," Theo said.

A chorus of soft laughter rippled through the bar.

"You must of caught the ugly fever somewhere along the way," someone called from across the pub.

The laughter grew.

At the bar, Old Mac turned away. He rubbed the back of his head with the palm of his hand, as though trying to wipe the sting of the laughter from his skin.

"What was that?" Theo thundered. He slapped the bar hard. "Damn all of you. Damn you to blazing hell for behaving in such a way. You'll be paying some respect to your elders, or I'll clear the lot of you out with me ash club."

The laughter stopped. For a moment, there was only silence and the labored sound of Theo's hard breathing. Every eye in the pub watched him. He reached under the bar, took out a bottle of whiskey, poured a long shot into a glass and slid the glass across the bar to Old Mac. Then he poured another shot for himself. He lifted his glass. "To Padraic MacLaverty," he said. "A handsome young man." He circled his arm in a wave across the room. "Him that don't drink will never set foot in this good place again," he boomed.

Everyone in Beckett's raised a glass.

"To Padraic MacLaverty," Theo bellowed.

"To Padraic MacLaverty," the crowd echoed.

26

Padraic MacLaverty—Old Mac, as he asked to be called, saying he was used to the sound of it—sat at the table, taking small spoonfuls of onion soup that Cooper and Kathleen had insisted on buying. He was uncomfortable with the sudden celebrity that Theo had thrust on him because of an ancient photograph taken in an ancient time. Seeing it had been a spark of joy, a heart-leap back to youth and friendships, but the spark had quickly sizzled and died. He was an old man and he knew it, a pub character earning drinks for playing the fool.

Still, he liked the young couple that sat with him. The boy looked as if he had pulled the skin of Finn Coghlan over his body, the resemblance was so true. The girl was lovely and gentle-natured, like his wife had been. And they were kind, both of them. Treated him with dignity and high regard. Ordered the best from Theo Beckett's kitchen, though the soup was plentiful.

Cooper asked about the photograph he carried, and Old Mac gave an honest answer. It was from the day of Finn Coghlan's American wake.

"I don't understand," Cooper said. "His American wake? What was that?"

A cracked smile of memory settled over Old Mac's face. "It was started long ago, when all the Irish was leaving in them coffin ships for America," he said.

"I remember my grandfather and grandmother talking of them," Kathleen added. "The same as a funeral wake. Music and dancing and feasting and drinking, but not like it was a festival bringing out crowds for a celebration."

Old Mac bobbed his head. "It was grieving, is what it was—grieving whitewashed with partying. And it was done knowing them that was leaving was not likely to be coming back, like what happens when a man dies and is put in the ground. Sure, now, there was laughing. But there was weeping, too. I can still hear the wailing at Finn's leaving."

"He never told anyone why he left," Cooper said. "Do you know?"

"I've forgot if I ever did," Old Mac said. "It was sudden-like. I remember that. He come up to work one day with a bothered look on his face, and he said he'd got a ticket for America, and he was leaving soon—a week, I think it was. There was barely enough time to put together his wake."

"And this is where the wake was held?" asked Kathleen.

"That it was," Old Mac replied softly. "It was Theo's father running the place then."

"Was any of his family here?" Cooper said.

Old Mac paused in thought, holding his soupspoon over his bowl. "There was a brother."

"Danny," Cooper said.

"Seems that was it," Old Mac agreed. "He was crying hard through it all, begging Finn not to leave him." He wiggled the soupspoon in the air. "And there was a sister, too."

"Joyce," Cooper said.

Old Mac nodded, accepting the name. "She was doing her best to offer some comfort, but it didn't change matters. Heartbreaking, it was, seeing the boy cry out his soul."

"What of his friends? Do you remember who else, other than you, that might have been there?" Cooper asked.

"Devin and Arnold—them that's in the picture with us. And there was old Frank, the shoe cobbler, and seems there was a fellow named Tom—Tom Brennan—who had a sheep farm. Sure, there'd be the regular boys from the pub, though I'm the last of them now."

"All men, except the sister?" Kathleen asked.

"Aye," Old Mac said. "Best I remember, just men." He paused, cocked his head, then added, "No, there was some ladies, too. Some of them weeping as hard as his brother. Finn was liked by the girls, all right. Had his way of making them feel special, with all his stories and the look he had in his eye."

Cooper could feel a faint blush on his face. He glanced at Kathleen, saw her lips move in a smile.

"Now that I think of it, though, Finn seemed to be looking for somebody that night," Old Mac added. "Kept going to the door, looking out, gazing off down the road like he was expecting somebody to come walking up. It was Devin who asked him about it. Asked if he was leaving a lady keening away for him." He paused, looked off, letting his memory focus. "There'd been some talk around, people saying Finn was taken by some girl from a fine family, but Finn wouldn't talk of it. The only thing he said to Devin was, 'The keening's in me own heart.'"

Old Mac placed the spoon beside his bowl. He took his napkin and rubbed at his eyes. "Queer, how it is, remembering them words now. Like having him sitting on the tip of my ear, whispering them all over again." He shook his head in wonder, then said, "We saw him off a day or so later. Took the train over to Dublin, he did, and shipped out from there. We was surprised by that, thinking he'd go from Cork, like most did in that time, but it was Dublin he chose. There was some talk he wanted to put some tracks behind him."

"Did you ever hear from him?" asked Cooper.

Old Mac nodded once. "A letter or two. Filled with all kinds of stories, as Finn could do, saying how grand everything was, but I could tell he was longing to be home in Ireland." He looked at Cooper. "Wish I'd kept them. I'd give them to you, but like every other good thing in me life, they've been long gone."

"You're wrong," Kathleen said gently. She reached to touch Old Mac's hand. "Your memory's still with you, still warm, and there's nothing better than a warm memory."

The old man blinked. His eyes coated with a film of moisture. "Aye," he whispered. "Aye."

~~~

It was easy-earned money for Michael Doyle. And it came with a bonus that Peter Raferty had not mentioned: the woman called Kathleen was a looker, far grander in person than in her photograph. Watching her was not work. It was pleasure.

He had stayed his distance at the park, mingling with a tour group of Asians chattering away in a language that sounded to him like the driving of nails. The clicking of their cameras made insect noises.

In the park, he had watched the American and the woman called Kathleen standing at the waterfall, their heads craned up to the cascade, and then they had settled on a rock, sitting close, talking. Before they left, they, too, had taken photographs—he of her, she of him.

He had followed them in his aging Opel to Beckett's. Inside, he had joined a table of men he knew from his part-time construction trade, and to make himself welcome, he had used part of Peter Raferty's one hundred euro to buy a round of drinks. Three tables away, he had watched Old Mac talking to the American, most likely trading lies for drinks.

He rolled his hands on the steering wheel of his Opel, turned his wrist to look at his watch. Seven-twenty. Almost six hours until one o'clock. Plenty of time, he thought. No need to rush. He'd had his pints with his friends, and his meal of Irish stew and soda bread. He was comfortable. He reached into his coat pocket and touched the folded sheet of paper Peter Raferty had given him. The name Kathleen O'Reilly was on it, and beside her name, her room number at the Lake Hotel. In front of him, he could see the taillights of the Nissan turn onto the driveway leading to the hotel.

He smiled. Soon they would be in her room, undressing.

He imagined her body. Cream-white. Firm-breasted. Nipples like the tips of small figs. Muscled in her legs. Copper hair.

A shiver of excitement struck his chest.

If it was the girl that Peter Raferty wanted to impress, then he would get his money's worth. He knew how to make the girl remember the night.

~~~

For Cooper, the night seemed to be drugged. He could not ward off the sense of his grandfather's spirit, or the hollow, distant sound of his grandfather's voice, yet the presence of Kathleen O'Reilly consumed him. It was also confusing. He had known her only a few days—a few hours to be truthful about it—yet he felt inextricably connected to her. With every relationship he had ever had, there had always been a period of adjustment, of moving cautiously from moment to moment, discovery to discovery.

With Kathleen, there was only the awkwardness of a familiarity he did not understand, the same off-balance sensation of experiencing a sudden and jarring moment of déjà vu. Ealy would have called it the meeting of old souls—not because he believed in such accomplishments, but because it sounded romantic and because it made him appear spiritual. Cooper had heard Ealy use the expression often, his mock seriousness almost comical in its sighing pitch. "Maybe we're old souls finding one another again," was the line. Strangely, it had worked with a few women who were lonely and vulnerable, women who desperately needed to cling to something that had the word soul in it.

Cooper had never believed in old souls finding one another. With Kathleen, it seemed plausible.

They had left Beckett's and Old Mac and had driven back to the Lake Hotel to meet Sandy and Sarah Donoghue. Cooper had explained Sandy's ruse of being his cousin, and of the playful tale about being a professor researching the NewTree campaign. Sandy's way of teasing, he had said. She had laughed gleefully, had promised to carry on the deception.

In the lounge, they had found Sandy and Sarah sitting at a table, Sandy in his dandy suit, Sarah in an outfit that was more costume than evening wear, an imitation of the flapper style from the Roaring Twenties of America. Heavy makeup. The look of someone who had been dressed and waiting almost a century for an evening out. The look had greatly affected Kathleen, and she had poured her attention onto Sarah, offering her warmth and laughter and giddiness.

They had sat for almost three hours in the swarming of words that flew from Sandy's stories, from Sarah's astonished questions, from Kathleen's merriment, and Cooper had watched and listened in awe. A week earlier, he had been in Atlanta, preparing to leave for Ireland. Now he was in a lounge in Killarney, sitting with people who were strangers, yet seemed to belong in his life as naturally as his own parents, or his friends. It was as though he had wandered into a place made of dreams, a place found only in the secrecy of sleep.

And in the ballooning of words at the table, Cooper had sensed his grandfather's voice, or the memory of it. His grandfather telling of Bogmeadow, of Sally Cavanaugh, of Fergus Sullivan, of Sean Malone, of Patrick the Believer, of Fingal, of Finn McCool. There was no sound to his grandfather's voice, only the awareness of it. Still, when the conversation lagged with a pause, Cooper had expected his grandfather to say aloud, "There's a story I know…"

At ten-thirty, Sandy and Sarah rushed away, Sarah fretting over the late hour and the imposition she had wrongly heaped on Samuel and Constance Coghlan in caring for her mother and in borrowing their car for the drive to the hotel. In the aftermath of their leaving, a silence fell clumsily over the table.

"It was a dear thing for Sandy to do," Kathleen said after a few moments. "Bless her soul, she's never had such a night."

"I think you're right," Cooper agreed. He wanted to add, "And I'm sure it's not over," but he did not.

She turned to look at him. "How are you?" she asked softly.

"Fine," Cooper told her. "It's been a great day."

"For me, too," Kathleen said.

"Do you want to go somewhere else?" he asked.

She shook her head.

"A walk along the lake, maybe?" he asked.

"I'd like that," she answered.

Outside, it was a clear night, cold near the waters of the lake. An older man stood with a young boy. The young boy had binoculars and was scanning the skies, talking excitely of stars. The man grunted responses that had the sound of pleasure, and Cooper wondered if the man were the boy's grandfather. Likely so, he thought. The man smoked a pipe and the aroma of the tobacco was sweet in the air.

"Is it too cold for you?" Kathleen asked.

"It's fine," Cooper said. "You?"

She slipped her arm through his arm. "It feels good," she said. "I like the way the chill tickles on my face."

They walked slowly, close, toward the ruins of the McCarthy Mor Castle, and did not speak for a long time. Light from the moon skittered across the lake like transparent water spiders.

"What do you do tomorrow?" Cooper asked at last.

"I should be going back to Cork," she said, "but I'm thinking of taking the day off." She pulled closer to him. "Drive to Dingle to see my grandmother, like I was saying."

"Tell me about her," Cooper said.

"She's my mother's mother. In her eighties now, as beautiful as anyone you'll ever see that age. Still strong and lively. She was a teacher and still tutors some of the slow learners. She's been widowed for about thirty years, so it gives her something to do."

"And she probably spoils her granddaughter," Cooper suggested.

"She does."

"Then you do need to see her."

"I think so," she said. "And you? What are your plans?"

"I don't know. Drive the Ring of Kerry, maybe."

"It's beautiful," she said.

They walked a few more steps, then stopped and stood gazing at the castle. The mountains of MacGillycuddy's Reeks rose against the ash gray backdrop of the night sky across the lake.

"When do you go home?" she asked quietly.

"On Sunday," Cooper said.

"You don't have much time left."

"I know."

"And your grandfather's ashes? What will you do with them?"

"I'm not sure," Cooper told her. "I had the feeling today that I should scatter them at the waterfall, but I don't think so. Not yet."

"Maybe you'll find the right place tomorrow," she said.

He nodded, turned to face her. "Look, I know you'd like to see your grandmother, but if you're taking the day off tomorrow, why don't you go with us? I'd like that. I really would."

219

She stood looking up at him, did not speak for a long moment. Then she leaned forward and kissed him gently on the corner of his mouth. "I would, too," she whispered.

~~~

From a safe, secluded distance, Michael Doyle saw the kiss and smiled. He dropped the cigarette he was smoking, crushed it with the tip of his shoe. Soon, he thought. Soon.

He turned and walked toward the hotel. Peter Raferty only wanted him to leave his mark on the American—and it would be easy enough to do, from the looks of him—but the woman named Kathleen was the greater prize, and if he played it right, she would not put up a fight.

He began to whistle softly.

27

Ealy would have called him a fool, Cooper thought. Would have threatened to revoke his Boy Dog membership. Would have delivered a filibuster about his failure to recognize a gift from the gods, when the gods were slapping him in the face with it. Would have advised that Cooper resign from the Presbyterian Church and become a monk.

And perhaps he would have had a good argument, Cooper reasoned. Leaving a beautiful woman at the door of her hotel room—after an invitation to enter it—had the qualities of regret.

Still, it had seemed right to Cooper. He did not want to play games with Kathleen O'Reilly, did not want to trade the comfort of being with her for the possible reward of sex turned to regret. He had settled, instead, for a long-holding embrace, a tender kiss, a whispered, "Good night."

He had never felt as ebullient.

Once Ealy had described the perfect moment with the perfect woman as cloud-walking.

And it was that, Cooper thought.

Cloud-walking.

Even the cold slap of air that struck Cooper as he stepped outside the hotel was invigorating. In Atlanta, the air would be heavy, stifling. He paused, inhaled deeply, felt the cold of the wind bite at his lungs. His grandfather had declared that the air of Ireland came up from the floor of the ocean, wet and chilled and fresh, and that anyone who breathed it would always have a part of the ocean in him.

The voice startled Cooper.

"Would you have a light, my friend?"

Cooper turned, peered down the row of parked cars. He saw a lanky man standing in the shadows.

"I'm sorry, I don't," Cooper said.

The man took a step toward Cooper. "You're sure, now?" he asked lightly. "I'd trade a smoke for a light and call it even."

"I'm not a smoker," Cooper told him.

A grin broke over the cloudy face of the man. He said, "Well, damn you, then. Damn a man who'd turn down a friendly smoke."

Cooper heard the click of a knife snapping open, saw a splinter of light on the blade. He turned for the door of the Nissan. The man reached him in three steps.

"Now, what's wrong, friend?" the man said in a teasing voice. "The Irish not good enough for you?" He held the knife up, turned it in his hand.

"If it's money you want, you can have it," Cooper said.

The man laughed quietly. "It's not money I'm after. It's having me pride restored." He tilted the tip of the blade toward Cooper's throat. "So, why don't we take a little walk and have a talk about it." He motioned with the knife for Cooper to move away from the car, pushed at him with his other hand. "Go easy, now, like the little stroll you took earlier."

Cooper thought of Kathleen, knew the man had seen them.

"And did you have a fine time with her?" the man asked casually. He clucked his tongue. "A woman like that—a good Irish woman—giving herself to the tourist trade. It's a shame, it is. All the fit men of Ireland, wanting and waiting, and she pays them no mind, no mind at all. Could be I'll have a little talk with her about it, show her the true ways of the Irish."

Cooper said nothing. He was being guided to a covering of trees near the tennis courts. He knew he could not run, not with the man holding one arm, the knife close to his chest. He could only wait until the man released him. He scanned the parking lot, the tennis courts. A man jogged in the distance, following the road leading to the highway.

"Now, don't go thinking you'll be joining him for a little run," the man whispered close to Cooper's face. "You don't want to take the chance."

"No," Cooper said. "I won't do that."

"Good," the man said cheerfully. "I don't fancy sticking a well-dressed man. It's a shameful waste."

"What do you want?" Cooper asked. He could hear the weakness of his voice.

The man walked for a few steps, then said, "Pleasure. Aye, that's the word. Pleasure. And I think I'll get a double-portion of it tonight."

They had moved from the cars, past the tennis courts, to the trees.

"Far enough," the man said. He turned Cooper to face him. A smile blossomed in his face. He closed the blade of his knife and slipped it into his pocket. "See. I told you I didn't want to stick you." The smile vanished suddenly, and the man dropped in a slight crouch.

Cooper saw a flashing movement and felt the man's fist bury into his chest. The air exploded from him. He stumbled back and fell to his knees, gasping for breath. The man moved over him like a dark cloud and slapped him across his face with a rough palm. He could taste blood.

And then he heard a familiar voice: "That's enough." He raised his head to see Sandy standing beside the man, holding the barrel of a revolver at the back of his head.

The man started to turn and Sandy fanned back the hammer. The click was sharp.

"And are you ready to meet your Lord and Savior?" Sandy said in a growl.

The man froze.

"Now, that's better," Sandy said. He glanced at Cooper. "Are you all right, lad?"

Cooper nodded. He struggled to stand.

"I'm a little late, as they say in your American films," Sandy said. "But I had to know he'd put the knife away." He moved cautiously from behind the man, keeping the revolver aimed at the man's face.

"How?" Cooper said faintly.

"You don't think Bogmeadow would leave you to the likes of this sorry excuse for a man, do you?" Sandy said merrily. He nudged the barrel of the revolver against the man's cheek. "You're an ugly one, my friend, but I think you'd look better if you'd lay flat of the ground and put your hands behind your head." He tapped the man hard with the barrel. The man closed his eyes, then nodded and dropped to the ground and laced his hands behind his neck.

"Now, young Finn, why don't you take an inventory of what our friend could be carrying?" Sandy said. "I'll just keep my aim on him, hoping I don't start to shake, but if I do I'll want to know who it was I shot."

Cooper knelt beside the man and searched his pockets. He took the knife and slipped it into his own pocket, then he unfolded the sheet of paper with Kathleen's name and room number on it. "My God," he whispered. "He's got her name and her room number."

"And I'm sure he's the best of friends with Peter Raferty," Sandy said. "Look in his wallet."

The wallet contained sixteen euro and identification.

"Michael Doyle, is it?" asked Sandy.

Cooper looked up in surprise. "How did you know?"

Sandy smiled broadly. "I'm a leprechaun, lad, don't you remember? Leprechauns have the gift of knowing." He nudged Michael Doyle with his foot. "Sit up," he commanded.

Michael Doyle rolled into a sitting position, keeping his hands locked behind his neck.

Sandy squatted to face him. "How'd you like to walk away from all this, free as the day you were born?" he asked.

Michael Doyle frowned.

"I'll hear two things out of you, and you're off," Sandy said.

"What things?" Michael Doyle asked in a faint voice.

"First, you'll tell me if this is the doing of Peter Raferty," Sandy replied. "Second, you'll give me your word as an Irishman that you'll not try any harm on this lad, or the lady." He leaned close, added, "Or me."

Michael Doyle nodded.

Sandy placed the barrel of the revolver against Michael Doyle's nose. "Put it in words, or the bargain's off," he snarled.

"It was who you said," Michael Doyle stammered. "He offered me two hundred euro to work over whatever man she was with. Half up front, half when it was done."

"You keep poor company," Sandy said. "Now, the other part."

"I won't be bothering them, or you," Michael Doyle said earnestly. "You got me word on it."

Sandy stood. "See how easy it is when gentlemen talk things out," he said. "Now, you need to know one thing." He brushed his hand over the front of his dandy suit. "You wouldn't know it by the look I have— that of an easy-going man—but I've a group of lads who answer to me. It's a bit like a special club, you could say." He bowed close to Michael Doyle. "The Bogmeadow Boys, they're called," he whispered. "Before the night's over, they'll all have your name and know your deed, and if you break your promise, they'll come calling, and you'll be famous overnight, one of them that's talked about in every pub in Ireland, how there was so many pieces of you they had to have a hundred funerals just to give you a decent send-off."

Michael Doyle's eyes widened in horror.

"Do you believe me, friend?" Sandy asked softly.

Michael Doyle nodded once.

"Good. Now, be off with you," Sandy told him. "Hand him back his wallet, young Finn."

Michael Doyle stood cautiously. He took the wallet from Cooper, then crept away. Near the tennis courts, he began to run.

Sandy sighed heavily. He lowered the revolver he held. "Holy mother of Jesus," he whispered. He leaned against a tree. "Holy mother of Jesus," he repeated. "I could use a drink, lad."

"I'll join you," Cooper said. "After you tell me what just happened."

It was a simple story, Sandy said. As he left the hotel with Sarah, he saw a man sitting in a car near the Nissan.

"He had a bad look about him, and I mentioned it to Sarah. She recognized him for who he was, knew him by name and reputation. When we got back to her place, I had Samuel and Constance drop me off back here. There was something telling me he was up to no good."

"The gun," Cooper said. "I didn't know you had a gun."

Sandy laughed weakly. He lifted the revolver. "It's a stage gun," he said. "A prop. I carry it with me out of habit. I couldn't kill a flea with it, unless I smashed him in the head with the butt."

"Jesus," Cooper whispered. "I can't believe what you just did."

Sandy bowed his stage bow. "I'm really a splendid actor," he said proudly. "You should see the clippings. Once, I played Don Quixote in *Man of La Mancha*, another fellow who put himself up against giants. Now, let's go gather up sweet Kathleen."

"Do you think she's in danger?"

"Somewhere Peter's waiting to find out how well his money's been spent," Sandy said. "When his man fails to show up, he may decide to make a personal visit. I'd say he's past reason now, doing what he's done."

"I think you're right," Cooper said.

~~~

Cooper had expected Kathleen to be frightened. She was not. She was angry. She would not let the threat of Peter Raferty drive her from her hotel, she insisted, and the pleadings offered by Cooper and Sandy were wasted. She would not leave her room. She would only accept the compromise of Cooper staying with her, keeping Sandy's prop revolver for protection.

"He won't show up," she said firmly. "I know him. He'll not put himself in position to be caught, not with his record. He'd hire it done, as he tried, but he'll not do it himself."

There was a gleam in Sandy's eye when he left the suite. He did not have to say anything for Cooper to know what he was thinking. He would have Sarah Donoghue to himself, with no worry from her deaf and addled mother, and Cooper would be with Kathleen. The pairing was right. The gleam was for both of them.

"Now let me have a look at you," Kathleen said after Sandy closed the door.

"I'm all right," Cooper told her.

"Maybe you are, Cooper Finn Coghlan, but I'll rest better if I see for myself," she said.

She found a small cut on the cheek inside his mouth and forced him to rinse it with an antiseptic mouthwash that she had, offering to get a whiskey from the lounge.

"It's not necessary," Cooper said. "It's no more than a nick."

"Take off your shirt," Kathleen instructed. "Let me have a look at your chest."

He knew it was useless to object and he slipped his shirt over his head. There was a small bruise on his breastplate.

"We need some ice," she said in a fretting voice.

"No, really, it's nothing," he countered.

She stepped away from him. A shimmer of frustration flew across her face. "Have you never learned anything about women?" she said forcefully. "We don't worry because it's the expected thing to do; we worry because it's in our blood, and sometimes the only thing that makes sense is to put ice or a heating pad on the place of the hurt." She paused, swallowed a tremor, reached to touch Cooper's chest with her fingers. "And if it's somebody we care about—even if we don't know why—we have to think we can do the healing," she added. She blinked at the bubble of tears in her eyes. "Damn it, Cooper Finn Coghlan, let me do my healing. You could have been killed, and I'd never have it leave my mind."

Cooper nodded obediently, numbly. Her fingers lingered on his chest.

"I wish I could make you leave now," she said suddenly. "I do. I want to be in my safe place, and it's not here, having you standing in front of me, and me touching you. I don't want to hurt when you go home. I don't want to be looking for you, wishing you'll be there when I go into a pub, or a shop, or when I take a walk in a park. When you go home, I know I won't see you again by accident, or whatever it was that caused us to meet, and I think I'll feel so lost without the chance of that, it'll drive me mad." She stepped to him, brushed her lips across the place of the bruise on his chest. "I wish I could make you leave now, before all the aching begins, because I know it won't stop," she whispered. "But I can't. I can't because I want you with me, even if it's for a few hours."

He leaned his face against her forehead. "And it's where I want to be," he said.

It was late when she fell asleep, her body tucked against him in a curl, her body warm, love-scented. He listened to her breathing—rhythmic, soft—and he believed he would never again know such a night. Nothing in his history had been as complete. Not the escapades of friendship with Ealy or Cary. Not the lovemaking of Jenny Gavin. Not even the golden flight of stories from his grandfather.

He thought of his grandfather, of the letter his grandfather had dictated on his deathbed. *I have dreamed about you many times lately. In every dream I have seen you where you were meant to be.*

He wondered if his grandfather had seen him holding Kathleen O'Reilly.

It was possible, he thought. It was possible.

He had never belonged to anything as much as he belonged to the quiet of Kathleen O'Reilly's sleeping.

28

The day, Sandy observed, had been blessed by the spirits of his ancestors. "A McAfee day," he called it. A McAfee day was sun-bright and glorious and always occurred following an event of McAfee triumph.

The conquering of Michael Doyle was a triumph, as spectacular as war.

"He'll still be in hiding," Sandy predicted, "keeping a watch for the fearsome Bogmeadow Boys, wondering when it'll be safe to show his face again."

It was midmorning as Sandy guided the Nissan southwest on N71, transporting Cooper and Kathleen along the tourist route of the Ring of Kerry—Killarney to Kenmare, then right on N70 and into Tralee.

To his right, Cooper would see the distant humps of MacGillycuddy's Reeks; to his left, the Atlantic Ocean slashing against shorelines of rock. Once, in a dreamy mood, his grandfather had proposed to Cooper that the two of them stow away on the next ship to Ireland and, upon arrival, they would walk the Ring of Kerry. "It's the right way to see it," his grandfather had boasted. "Did it as a boy, me and two of me friends, and I'll take you the way we went. You'll see, boy. Every person we meet will be telling you something that'll have your feet dancing on down the road, and there'll be that clean air of ocean and mountain all mixed together, burning your lungs with its sweetness."

Sandy's praise of the route was a near-echo: "There's not a finer drive in the whole of the world," he crowed. "It'll make you forget all that's bothering you, all that's been dragging you down."

The morning had been rushed.

For Kathleen, it had been an email message to Raferty & Son, informing Peter Raferty's father that she would not be returning to Cork until the following week, and when she did, she would be submitting her resignation due to the unbearable behavior of his son—behavior that had changed from annoying to dangerous.

She had also gone to Peter's room and pounded on the door until he appeared, groggy from a hangover, surprised and disheveled. "You wasted your money last night," she had said in an angry, even voice. "I've got the name of the man you hired, and if you ever so much as speak to me again, I'll be pressing charges that'll bring you to your knees." She had whirled and walked away before he could speak.

For Cooper, it had been a quick call to Cary's office at eight-thirty Irish time—three-thirty in the morning, Atlanta time. He had said into Cary's answering machine, "Didn't want to wake you at home, but when you get in and hear this, call Sid Springer over at CNN and ask him when they're going to run the piece on the NewTree campaign in Ireland, then give Ealy the time, and the two of you watch it. Won't tell you anything else about it. You'll understand. I'm about to strike out for the Ring of Kerry with a couple of friends." He had paused and quietly added, "You should see this place, Cary. It's magical. I'm telling you, Houdini would be considered an amateur over here."

They had taken their breakfast with Sarah Donoghue, who wore the blissful look of being dazed, whose chatter was that of a young girl. The evening in the Lake Hotel lounge had been the finest of her life, she had assured Kathleen in confidence as Sandy and Cooper prepared the Vanette. Sandy had treated her as royalty would be treated, she had gushed—tender and loving, a Queen's treatment. "I know he's only passing through, and I'm not likely to see him again," she had said gently, "but he's leaving me with the feeling of being a woman again, and I'd almost forgot that. But I'm not shamed by it. Maybe I should be crying over the sin of it—acting like a Protestant the way I did—but I don't. There's not a minute of regret."

The drive from Killarney to Kenmare was measured not in distance or time, but in the stories that flooded from Sandy's imagination, embroidered by memories that were no older than the moment of saying them. He did not speak words. He conducted them with the baton of his tongue, and the music of his telling ranged from pianissimo to fortissimo. Kathleen was beside him in the passenger seat, Cooper behind him in the back seat. His audience, and his energy, had doubled, and the remarkable history of the McAfees became a saga of heroic acts so dazzling in scope that Sandy himself admitted to some degree of skepticism. A warring McAfee made tender by the forgiveness of God had escorted St. Patrick on his famous fast at Croagh Patrick, keeping watch over the great man, standing with him as he banished the snakes from Ireland and defeated the mother of the Devil, the demon Corra. Lost to history was the bravery of Cormac McAfee, who had stood alone at Ross Castle against invading Cromwellian troops, dying with a curse of the British on his lips, his ghost still lingering over the grounds to be seen on stormy nights when thunder boomed like cannon shot.

McAfees, Sandy declared, had been great sailors, great statesmen, great scholars.

And, he added with dramatic humility, there was sufficient reason to believe that it was a McAfee who first performed the works of Shakespeare in Ireland, having met, and assisted, the great playwright while studying theater in London. Sandy was certain that he was a direct descendent.

Cooper watched Kathleen as she listened to the stories, delight dancing in her eyes, laughter dancing on her lips. And there was nothing in the Ring of Kerry that held such wonder for him.

~~~

At eight-thirty in the morning, Atlanta time, Cary called Ealy and told him of Cooper's answering machine message. It was a simple matter to Ealy: there was no reason to wait for a broadcast. If Sid Springer had the tape Cooper had called about, then Sid Springer could order it up for preview. "I'll take care of it," he promised Cary. "What time can you be down at Sid's office?"

"Around ten," Cary suggested.

"Good. Be there," Ealy said. "I'll call Sid and get a quick shower and get on the road. Let's see what the Boy Dog's talking about. Ten to one, it's a woman. Naked, I hope."

Ealy had not talked to Sid Springer in two years, perhaps longer, and he had a tickle of guilt over imposing on a friendship that had, at best, faded gracefully. He liked Sid. Always had. Sid had almost made it into the inner circle of the Boy Dogs. Would have if he had not been so damnably taken by politics. Democrat, if Ealy remembered correctly.

Once he had annoyed Sid by challenging the notion that the president of the United States actually possessed as much power as he boasted of having. It had been during an election year—Dole against Clinton, before Clinton got caught intern-diddling—and Sid had been working on Ealy for a campaign contribution. He had said to Sid, "Do you believe it when somebody running for the presidency tells you he's going to do everything from repealing taxes to legalizing prostitution?" And Sid had said in argument, "It's the platform. It's what we have to believe." Ealy remembered laughing at Sid, remembered Sid's red-coated face of irritation. He had said to Sid, "Then what we're really doing is voting for a dictator, because what they're talking about is executive power. Not just your man, Sid, but every damn one of them. And what's really crazy, we buy it. Nobody ever stops for a minute to consider that Congress can override whatever son of a bitch we put in there. Once, just once, Sid, I'd like to hear that. I'd like to hear one of them stand up before the television cameras of America and say, 'Look, folks, the truth is, I'm going to try to do some of this stuff I've been talking about, but that bunch in the Congress will have their say, also, and we all know damn well what a mess that can be.' I'd vote for that man, Sid. Or woman. I'd throw money at him, or her. I'd run along in front of him, or her, with a little whisk broom and sweep the dust from where they're walking. Hell, if it was a her, I'd volunteer to be a gigolo."

The argument had ended with Ealy writing a five thousand dollar check, for no other reason than caring for Sid.

He hoped Sid remembered.

And Sid did. "All right, be here at ten," he told Ealy. "You and Cary. Nobody else. I'm sure I'm not supposed to do this sort of thing."

"Have you seen it?" Ealy asked.

"Not yet. I saw on the log sheet that it was in, but I haven't seen it," Sid told him. "Tell you the truth, I'm sort of eager to get a look at it myself. From the news article that Cooper faxed to me, that's a choice woman."

"Woman?" Ealy said.

"Yeah, woman," Sid answered. "I believe her name's Kathleen."

"Damn," Ealy mumbled. "I knew it. That cockroach found a way to rub it in from Ireland."

"What are you talking about?" Sid asked suspiciously. "Am I being boon-doggled?"

"By Cooper?" Ealy said. "God almighty, Sid, the boy's in Ireland to scatter the ashes of his grandfather. You know him. Do you really think he's in the mood to play jokes?"

"What was that about rubbing it in?"

"It was nothing," Ealy answered irritably. "You know me, too. If there's a woman involved, I've got a twisted mind."

~~~

The tape of Kathleen O'Reilly and the NewTree campaign to encourage the reforesting of Ireland was only one minute and twenty seconds long, and, according to Sid, was not as newsworthy as he had hoped. Too much like an ad for a save-the-whales crusade. Ealy did not care. There, on screen, in Sidney Springer's office, was a woman who could have campaigned for the preservation of malaria-carrying mosquitoes and he would have gladly dedicated his life to the cause.

His expression was, "Damn."

It was joined by a soft whistle of admiration from Cary.

"Bless his soul," Sid said in awe. "If Cooper's found that kind of woman after five days of being in Ireland, I'm going to quit my job, divorce my wife, put my kids in a monastery, change my name to O'Springer and get my ass on the next plane out."

"And what are you going to do when you get there?" asked Ealy.

"Who cares? Open a deli. There have to be a few Jews around," Sid said.

"Well, I can tell you what I'm going to do if Cooper comes home with her on his arm," Ealy said. "I'm going to kiss the boy on the lips, just so I can brag about tonguing the woman by proxy."

"Poetic," Cary said.

"I thought so, too," Ealy said. Then: "Re-run it, Sid. Hit the pause button when it zeroes in on her face."

Sid tapped the re-run button, paused on the close-up of Kathleen O'Reilly. The image quivered in its freeze. Kathleen O'Reilly's eyes seemed to melt in the intensity of her gaze.

"Boys, we are looking at a miracle," Ealy whispered. "All that cockamamie Cooper gave us about some woman who did public relations left out a few details." He turned to Cary. "What did he say about driving the Ring of Kerry?"

"A couple of friends were going with him," Cary said.

Ealy frowned seriously. His forehead wrinkled in thought. "We know about Sandy, but who's the other one?"

"Who's Sandy?" asked Sid.

Ealy did not want to waste time describing Sandy. "Just a guy he hooked up with in Dublin," he said. He rubbed the back of his neck. "She's the other one," he added. "That's what he meant when he said we'd understand things after seeing the tape." He paused, sighed, leaned back in his chair. "The boy's never lived a day when he was around that much woman. He needs some guidance. I can feel it." He looked at Cary, saw the smirk on Cary's face. "Needs me," he amended. "The two of you are married and are therefore ignorant of such matters as romance. Any advice you could give him would be useless."

"He'll be leaving in four days," Cary said patiently. "I'm sure he can survive it."

Ealy stood. "That's the point. If we—if I—can't be there, then we—I—need to do something to make her grateful that he's around."

"Ealy, leave it alone," Cary said.

Ealy swiped a dismissive wave toward Cary. He began pacing. "What do you know about this woman?" he asked Sid.

Sid opened his file, glanced at it and offered the information in contained: account executive for Raferty & Son out of Cork. In charge of the NewTree campaign.

"Got a phone number for that place?" Ealy asked.

"Yeah," Sid answered. He thumbed through the sheets in his file, found the number, copied it on a pad, ripped the sheet of paper away, and handed it to Ealy.

Ealy folded the paper and slipped it into his pocket. "Are they raising money?"

"Of course they are. You know anybody who's not?'

"What do they need it for?"

"How the hell do I know, Ealy? Buying seedlings, I guess."

Ealy nodded thoughtfully, glanced at his watch. "What time is it in Ireland?" asked.

"Ten-thirty here, three-thirty there," Cary answered.

"All right," Ealy mumbled. "Let's go, Cary, we've got work to do."

"What work?" asked Sid.

"Give me until this afternoon," Ealy told him. "You're going to have a little tag to go on that story of yours."

"Tell me the truth, Ealy," Sid insisted. "What's this all about? Getting Cooper laid?"

Ealy glared at him. "You've got a dirty mind, Sid."

"So I've been told," Sid said. "If you need some help, let me know."

Away from Sid Springer's office, in the lobby of CNN Center, Ealy called his secretary, Grace Ray, from his cell phone. He said, "Grace, have you got one of those financial statements around somewhere?" He paused, listened. "Yeah. That's it. Always marked private, sealed with about a mile of tape. Tear the latest one open and take a look at it. Tell me what the bottom-line is." He paused again, waited, his head bobbing as though listening to background music. Then: "What?" He whistled softly. "That's a lot of money," he added in amazement. "Okay, here's what I want you to do. Call this number in Ireland –" He pulled the sheet of paper that Sid had given him from his pocket and read the number for Raferty & Son to Grace. "Tell them the Ackerman Development

Company wishes to make a fifty thousand dollar donation to the NewTree campaign in honor of the late Finn Coghlan." Again, he paused, listened. "Yeah, that's right. NewTree. It's one word with a big T for tree. Tell them you want to talk to—" He looked at Cary and rolled his hand for help. "What's her name?"

"Kathleen O'Reilly," Cary said.

"That's it," Ealy said into his phone. "Kathleen O'Reilly. If she's not around, tell them to make sure she gets the message as soon as possible."

Cary tapped Ealy on his arm, then pointed to his watch. Ealy mugged a question.

"Remember what time it is in Ireland," Cary said.

"Oh, yeah," Ealy said. "Listen, Grace, you're going to have to make this call at—" He looked at Cary, shrugged.

"In the next hour, if she reaches them today," Cary said.

"Now," Ealy said. "You've got to get on the horn in the next few minutes, but I guess you'd better call the lawyers first—assuming we've still got one or two on the payroll. Let them put together the details."

Cary watched Ealy pacing, listening, his body bobbing with his steps. He knew that Grace was repeating Ealy's instructions. Probably terrified, Cary thought. He wondered if Ealy had ever before made a business decision.

"One other thing," Ealy said. "When you get it worked out, call Sid Springer at CNN—his name's in my book—and tell him about the donation. Tell him it was because your environmentalist employer was so impressed with Kathleen O'Reilly's appeal, that he wanted to honor the memory of his friend, Finn Coghlan." He winked at Cary. "If you need me, call me on the cell, and I don't care what time it is. I'll be at Dugan's Tavern at lunchtime, though. Our actor friend's supposed to call."

Cary shook his head in resignation. He thought: God help you, Coop.

~~~

It had taken most of the day to drive the Ring of Kerry and the arrival in Tralee, late in the afternoon, had been almost regretful. To end such a day of mirth—of roadside stops for sight-seeing and the taking of photographs, for idle shopping and lunch and refreshments—was very much like ending a spontaneous celebration that had no purpose other than celebration.

Yet, for Cooper, there had been an awareness to the day that would not leave him, something that had the sensation of the homing instincts of birds. He was in the Ireland of his grandfather's youth, with his grandfather's cremains in a box beside him, and there were moments—always, it seemed, in the telling of a story by Sandy, his sing-song voice as intoxicating as a lullaby—when Cooper would become warmed by his grandfather's presence. He knew, without understanding why he knew, that the time for releasing his grandfather into the winds of Ireland was rapidly approaching.

In Tralee, Sandy made a bothering discovery.

Or so he said.

He had left his medication at Donoghue's in Killarney.

The medication, he sorrowfully admitted, was for high blood pressure—the stress of his chosen profession. Cooper had never heard him mention it. Diabetes, yes, but not high blood pressure.

"If you wouldn't mind, I'll drive back over to get it, stay the night there, and join you back here in the morning," he said to Cooper.

"Sure," Cooper told him. "Do you want us to go with you?"

"No, no, not at all," Sandy replied quickly. "The way I'll go, it's only a few miles. I won't have to drive the Ring again. Besides, it's been a long enough day for you. We'll find a place close in and you can walk to the town if you'd like."

Cooper saw Kathleen's mouth move, as though tasting a smile.

The hotel was called The Evening House, located only a short distance from the center of Tralee. It was old and stately, with an outside appearance of being cold and severe. Inside, it was surprisingly warm, offering an atmosphere of comfort. An older man who identified himself as Brandon Heaney, manager of the Evening House, said to Cooper, "Would you be wanting one room, or two?"

For a moment, Cooper did not respond. He glanced to Kathleen. Kathleen looked away.

"Two, " Cooper said in a faint voice.

Brandon Heaney nodded. "I've got just what you'll be needing," he said. "Two rooms, side by side. Lovely, both of them."

"Good," Cooper said. "Good." He could feel the heat of a blush on his face.

The rooms were as promised—side-by-side, at the end of a long upstairs corridor.

"Very nice," Kathleen said as a tease. "I'm glad you're close by. Makes me feel safe."

"I should have asked you about the rooms," Cooper said apologetically.

"I think it's wonderful, what you did," she replied. "You're a gentleman. I like that."

They stood in the doorway of Kathleen's room, in the awkward silence of an awkward moment.

"Do you want a little rest before dinner?" asked Cooper.

"Oh, no, I'm fine," she said quickly. She took his hand and pulled him into her room. "Let me call my office and then we'll go see Tralee."

The call to Raferty & Son was transferred to Maura Mannion, Kathleen's assistant.

"It's a good thing you're calling," Maura whispered into the phone. "All sorts of things are going on here, and you're in the center of all of it."

"What things?" asked Kathleen.

Maura told her about the telephone call from a Grace Ray in America, pledging a substantial amount of money for the NewTree campaign in the name of Ackerman Development Company.

"She asked to speak with you," Maura added. "I told her you were on holiday, but when you called in, I'd give you the message."

"Why would they do such a thing?" Kathleen said.

"Just a moment," Maura replied. "I wrote down a name—yes, here it is. It's a donation to honor the memory of a Finn Coghlan."

Kathleen blinked surprise. She looked at Cooper, who was sitting on the side of the bed, leafing through a brochure about Tralee. "Finn Coghlan?" she said.

Cooper looked up.

"And what's the name of the company giving the money?" she asked Maura. She paused, listened. "Ackerman Development?" she said.

"Jesus," Cooper sighed.

"Hold a moment, Maura," Kathleen said. She cupped her hand over the telephone and turned to Cooper. "Do you know anything about this?"

Cooper shook his head. "No, but I have a good idea."

"Is it for real?"

"I'm sure it is," Cooper told her. "I'll explain it when you finish talking."

Kathleen removed her hand from the phone. "Call her back in the morning. Tell her you've spoken to me and I'm delighted at the news. Send her all the information we've got. I'm sure they'll need it for their board. Is there anything else?"

"Peter came back from Killarney this morning," Maura said secretively.

"And?"

"His father's having a fit with him."

"Over what?"

"No one knows, but I heard your name in the shouting going on in his office," Maura said.

"Good," Kathleen replied forcefully.

"Old Mr. Raferty's been melancholy the whole day," Maura added. "Is there something going on that I don't know about?"

Kathleen thought of her email announcing her intention to resign from Raferty & Son. She glanced at Cooper. She had said nothing to him of her decision. There was no reason. He was not to blame, yet he would believe that he was—would believe that it was his presence that had caused Peter's madness in Killarney.

"Is there?" Maura asked again.

"Nothing I can think of," Kathleen answered.

"Oh, we saw the tape, too," Maura said. "It's incredible, Kathleen. You were wonderful."

The sound of awe in Maura's voice was touching. "Thank you," Kathleen said.

"Where are you?" asked Maura. "Or maybe you don't want to tell me."

"In Tralee, now," Kathleen replied. She looked at Cooper. "I think I'll be going to Dingle tomorrow to visit my grandmother."

"Are you alone?" Maura asked in a whisper.

"No," Kathleen told her after a moment.

"A man?"

Her answer was stiff, formal. "Yes."

"The American?"

"And where did you get such information?"

"Peter, of course," Maura replied. "It's all over the office."

Kathleen inhaled slowly, composed herself. "Good," she said.

Maura's voice was barely audible and Kathleen could imagine her leaning over at her desk, her long-nailed fingers cupped around the telephone: "I'm proud of you, so proud I'm bursting with envy. Don't go worrying about this place. It'll be here, such as it is, but the days you've got now won't be."

"I know," Kathleen said softly.

The story that Cooper told of Ealy—describing him, qualifying him—was rambling and apologetic, having the sound of a lame excuse given by a child to a parent. To Kathleen, it was also amusing. "He sounds a bit like Sandy," she said.

"He is, I guess," Cooper admitted reluctantly.

"I think I like this Ealy," she said. "And I certainly like his generosity."

"How much was it?" asked Cooper.

"Fifty thousand."

"Dollars?" Cooper said in shock.

"Dollars," she replied.

"You know why he's doing it, don't you?"

"To honor your grandfather. He must have thought highly of him."

"Oh, he did," Cooper said. "But that's only a small part of the reason. You're the rest."

"Me?" she asked with surprise. "What does he know about me?"

"Nothing. That's the problem," he replied. "I'm sure he saw the tape, and because I'd mentioned your name to him, he's let his imagination go wild. He thinks his gift—and he can afford it, so don't worry about it—will somehow put us together."

Kathleen smiled. "Are you fibbing?"

"No. He's a very strange man."

"Oh, yes, I do like him," she said.

"So do I," Cooper mumbled.

29

It was a good deed he had done, leaving Cooper and Kathleen to themselves, Sandy thought as he listened to the ringing of the telephone in
Dugan's Tavern. He had done his work with them for the day, had taxed
himself with being in the spotlight, telling his stories for the sake of
entertainment. Now they needed some quiet time. Alone time. Touching
time.

Odd how he had come to like the boy, Sandy realized. Meeting him
had been hire for a job that was more prank than anything, yet the boy
had the makings of a good man. None of the arrogance that most
Americans wore like party hats. It was deserving that he had found
himself with a remarkable Irish woman.

In Atlanta, an ocean away, Kevin Dugan answered the ringing and
punched up the speakerphone, saying to Ealy, "You've got him."

"Catch me up on the news," Ealy said jovially. "Where's Cooper?"

"In Tralee," Sandy told him.

"Alone?"

"Not when I left him," Sandy replied.

Ealy laughed gleefully. "With the lovely Kathleen, I presume?"

"Indeed, he is. And happy for it, if I'm a judge of the look on a
man's face, and I pride myself in that regard."

"That's great, great," Ealy enthused. "Do they know about the
contribution I made?"

"Contribution?"

"I guess they don't, if you don't."

"And what would it be for?" asked Sandy.

"The NewTree campaign," Ealy answered, "but that's neither here
nor there. How's it going between them?"

"Well enough, though I'm not spying on them. There was a bit of an
incident, however."

"What?" Ealy demanded.

Sandy told of Michael Doyle's attack on Cooper and of his fortunate intervention, saving Cooper from a certain beating, or perhaps death.

Ealy whispered in awe, "I'm glad you were there."

"So am I," Sandy said dramatically. "I've grown fond of the boy."

"And you think he's all right?"

"I do," Sandy said. "Though I think he may be running a bit short of funds, and it seems a strain. I was thinking I might assume some of the costs over the next few days."

"How much?" Ealy asked.

"Well, now, I haven't given it much thought," Sandy said.

"Five hundred," Ealy suggested lightly.

For a moment, Sandy did not speak, then he said, "Sounds reasonable."

"Good," Ealy said. "You're a great man, Sandy McAfee, a great man. When are you going to see him?"

Sandy glanced at his watch. "It's a little after five, our time, so it won't be until tomorrow. I wanted to give them some time to themselves."

"Good thinking," Ealy told him. "You probably need some rest yourself."

Sandy thought of Sarah Donoghue and the surprised look of joy that would fly into her face when he appeared in her doorway. "It's what's on my mind," he said in a voice of exaggerated exhaustion. "Bed." He let a smile touch his mouth.

~~~

The day, warm for the season, had cooled, and the walking tour of Tralee that Cooper and Kathleen had planned was, by agreement, canceled. There had been enough sightseeing for one day. Instead, they took an early dinner in the small dining room of The Evening House, promoted by Brandon Heaney as equal to any in Tralee, and after the dinner they retired to a lounge having a fireplace and a raised platform crowded against the corner of one wall. They sat together on a sofa facing the fireplace and ordered brandy as they had in Waterford. The fire was warm, the brandy strong and sweet, and they sat touching-close without talking, taking as much comfort from the fire as from their glasses.

An older man played a guitar from the platform. He had hunched-over shoulders, a pale face behind large glasses, cropped gray hair, and the way he sat on stage—on a stool, a pin spot of light on him, his arms cradling his guitar like an exhausted soldier cradling a weapon—he seemed welded to the music that came from the delicate dance of his fingers.

"I like this," Cooper said. "Cozy and quiet. It's my kind of place."

"It won't last," Kathleen told him. "It's early. You'll see. There'll be noise enough."

She was right. Within minutes, a wedding party came into the pub, taking a large table that had been reserved for them. At a break between numbers, one of the men in the party—middle-aged, red-faced, a cloud of white hair that had the appearance of being permanently wind-whipped—stood at his table and blared an announcement: "Ladies and gentlemen, I'm inviting you to share in the happiness of this table by having a round of what you're drinking put on my bill." He paused, turned to the young girl sitting near him. "Here's to my dear, darling daughter, Peggy, and to her fine man, Kelly Neal."

A hoot of pleasure erupted from the room. Calls of good fortune. Glasses clicked.

The man then turned to the stage. "I've come to hear it, Rooney," he said in a strong voice. "To bring the charm of good life for these children, and I'm begging you to tell it. The greatest love story of them all, Rooney. Tell it again." He sat and the room became silent. Cooper nudged Kathleen. She smiled, nestled closer to him, rested her face on his shoulder and her gaze on the singer named Rooney.

From the stage, Rooney leaned to the microphone in front of him and began to speak. It was a voice shockingly different from the tenor of his singing voice. A voice deep in his throat, a voice that vibrated, rumbled, yet had the sound of whisper.

"Once, there was a man named William Mulchinock," he said, beginning the story of the high-bred William Mulchinock's ill-fated love for the housemaid named Mary O'Connor, the Rose of Tralee. The story was Irish-tragic, tearful, chilling in its sadness, and when he had finished the telling of it, Rooney lowered his head and his fingers ran a chord from the steel strings of his guitar.

The pub was hushed, as though hypnotized. A chill flashed through Cooper. He could feel Kathleen move against him, turned to look at her. A string of tears, small pearls of tears, rolled over her cheeks.

Rooney touched the strings again. "Join with me," he said in a voice so gentle it could have been an echo. He began to sing, and across the room, voices grew around the song.

The pale moon was rising above the green mountains,
The sun was declining beneath the blue sea;

Kathleen moved from Cooper, as though beckoned by the music. She sat forward on the sofa and began to sing with Rooney, with the room. Her voice was bell-clear and commanding.

When I strayed with my love by the pure crystal fountain,
That stands in the beautiful vale of Tralee.

Cooper saw faces gazing at Kathleen, saw the shock of amazement that numbed them, leaving soundless words in opened mouths, and he turned back to her. The pearl-string of tears glistened on her face. Her eyes were closed. Her voice rose with Rooney's voice, tempered with Rooney's voice, blended, caressed, coupled, until only the two of them could be heard.

She was lovely and fair as the rose of the summer,
Yet 'twas not her beauty alone that won me;
Oh, no, 'twas the truth in her eyes ever dawning,
That made me love Mary, the Rose of Tralee.

The song ended and Rooney rested the palm of his hand against the strings of his guitar. He bowed his head, then he looked up at Kathleen. Silence—fragile, ghostly—filled the room. He began to applaud, a slow music beat, building in rhythm. Someone from one of the tables joined him. And another. And another. It had the sound of the first drops of heavy rain in a storm, rain splattering on the leaves of a tree. Suddenly, the applause flooded, fell in torrents around Kathleen.

Cooper sat stunned, staring at her. She lifted her face, letting the rain of cheer wash over her.

~~~

She took his hand and pulled it to her face, nuzzling her face against the palm.

His hands fascinated her. They were large and strong and warm, hands an artist would paint if the artist wanted to tell a tale of power with the words of a brush. In his hands, in the ridges and lines, there were stories as hallowed as time, inviolate as prophecies. A reader of palms would see them, would read the mystery of their language. She believed she was there, somewhere in the ridges and lines.

She could still feel the traces of his hands on her body—had clasped her own hands over his as he stroked her, wanting not to guide him, but to follow. His hands had made shivers pulse through her like electricity, and when he touched her, her body had arched high against his hand, taking the heat from it.

She kissed the palm, closed her eyes against it, and drew in a breath that had the scent of his skin in it.

It was, she thought, only the second time she had taken love from a man's body. Love. Not sex. She had had sex with Denis Colum, believing it was love. It was not. It was an illusion, a quick-burning flame made from the friction of rubbing bodies, and it did not matter how dazzling, how exhilarating it had been, it was only sex.

There was a difference.

Cooper Finn Coghlan of America had loved her—loved her with his body, yes, but also with an aura that had enclosed her in such blinding colors she had felt powerless against it, and the sensation rested still against her chest, filled her throat with quivering. It was impossible to believe she had known him less than a week.

She opened her eyes, saw him gazing at her.

"What are you thinking?" she asked.

"I'm thinking that we rented one room too many," he answered.

She smiled.

"No, that's not it," Cooper added. "I was thinking about William Mulchinock and Mary O'Connor," he said. "It's a sad story."

"It is, yes," she replied.

"But I love the song. I remember my grandfather singing it."

"Did he sing to you a lot?" she asked.

"All the time," Cooper told her. *"Toora Loora Looral.* He used to sing it to me when I was a baby."

"It's one of my favorites," she said.

A smile crooked over his face. "Why don't you sing it to me?"

"No," she said softly. "I've done enough singing for one night."

"I'm still in shock," he told her. "You've got a beautiful voice." He paused. "It matches the rest of you."

Kathleen kissed his palm again.

"I think I should become your agent," Cooper said. "I have a friend who owns an Irish pub in Atlanta. He'd hire you on the spot. Probably make you a partner."

"It's a long way to commute for my day job," she said teasingly.

"The money you'd make singing, you could quit the day job."

"I sing for the love of it, Cooper," she said. "Not for the money. You'd be surprised how many pubs in Ireland get free entertainment for that reason alone. It's the love of it that matters."

Cooper moved his arm to cradle her neck against his shoulder, then leaned his body over her and kissed her shoulder. He pulled back, looked at her again.

"Why don't you sing to me?" she whispered.

"Are you in need of a laugh?" he asked.

"You're Irish. You must sing," she said.

"That was the one drop of blood that got away from me," he sighed. "No. I don't sing."

"I'll teach you."

He laughed. "You'd regret it."

"No, I will. I will teach you," she insisted eagerly. "Tomorrow. We'll start tomorrow on our drive. Sandy and me, we'll teach you."

Cooper rolled on his pillow, lay looking at the strip of pewter light that filtered through the curtains of the window and streamed across the ceiling. "I don't think there's enough time," he said at last.

She reached to touch his arm, let her hand rest on him, but did not speak. In three days, he would be leaving Ireland, she thought. But the aura would stay. It would follow her in its ghost presence, in an invisible shadow. She would feel its changing colors brushing warm against her body.

"I wish I had a recording of your singing, though," he said. "I'd like to take it with me."

Still, she did not speak.

"Or maybe I'll just call you and let you sing to me over the telephone," he added.

"Don't, Cooper," she said quietly.

He turned to look at her. "I'm sorry. It's self-pity, that's all."

"I don't want you to talk about leaving," she said. "The time for leaving will be here soon enough."

He pulled the bed covering over them, making a tent of darkness. He could feel her wiggling close to fit against him. The heat of her skin was like a fever. He ran his hand over her body, letting his hand memorize it. Her body was magnificent, he thought. Beautiful. Beautiful.

She shuddered at the touch, put her hand over his hand.

Very softly, Cooper began to sing in an off-key voice:

"Toora, loora looral,

"Toora Loorali,

"Toora loora looral,

"It's an Irish lullaby…"

30

She was still asleep when Cooper eased himself from the bed, dressed quietly and slipped out of the room, taking his journal with him. It was pre-dawn—light of the sun before the sun bubbles on the horizon—and still night-cool, but windless. He found a bench in a small garden that dimpled close to the sidewalk, and he sat and watched the sun nudge up in the distance like the tip of a bright raspberry-painted fingernail.

He saw no one. The only sound was from a nearby bird, singing happily. He opened his journal and wrote:

Friday, May 19. A week ago when I left Atlanta for Ireland I had a strange feeling that my life would never again be the same. I did not think of it then as a premonition, though now I believe that is what it was. From the first day, I have been guided by something I cannot pretend to understand. I feel like a leaf swept by the wind into a river, helpless to do anything but ride the water. It is like being a walk-on actor in a play that I have never read, or seen. Everyone I have met has been a player. Sandy McAfee has been chief among them, and well suited for his role, given his profession in the theater. Yet, no one has affected me as powerfully as Kathleen O'Reilly. There are moments when I believe she and I have rehearsed for this meeting from our birth. It makes no sense to say I love her, knowing her such a short time. Still, I do. Or I believe that I do, and it worries me that what I feel is nothing more than the pressure of too little time together. In two and a half days, I will be leaving for America. I cannot imagine not being with her. I believe she feels the same.

Last night, I dreamed of my grandfather again. In the dream, he was standing with a leprechaun who looked like a leprechaun—short, elfish, wearing the kind of watercolor costume I have seen in books for children. Both of them were smiling the way happy people smile. The leprechaun—who must have been Bogmeadow—said to me, "Make your wish." And then both of them disappeared in a sparkle.

I wonder if some dreams go beyond dreaming.

Today, I think I will find the place to release my grandfather.

Another premonition.

I hear his voice everywhere.

He closed his journal and looked up. The sun pushed against the membrane of sky and the chill of the air felt good against his face. It was a morning of peace and awe, blending so perfectly it had the sensation of an epiphany.

He turned to a noise, a faint shuffling noise, thinking it was an animal in the bushes. It was not. It was an elderly woman, bundled against the weather, puffs of white hair sticking from the stocking cap she wore. She was on the sidewalk, moving steadily toward him, her gaze already on him. She carried a thin walking cane that touched the sidewalk gently with each step.

"Good morning," Cooper said to the woman.

She nodded. Her face grew a smile. "Lovely day," she said cheerfully.

"Yes, it is," Cooper replied.

"It's the best time of the day," she said. "You can still breathe a little bit of God into your soul when it's this peaceful." She paused in front of him.

"I think you're right," Cooper told her. "I've been sitting here thinking the same thing."

The woman bobbed her body in acknowledgement, then turned slowly to look at the sunrise.

"Would you like to sit for a moment?" asked Cooper.

The woman turned back to him. "Thank you. I will. For a moment. Just to give me cane a rest." She sat next to him. "A visitor, are you?" she asked.

"Yes ma'am. I'm from America."

"So far away," she said softly. "And do you like our little island?"

"It's beautiful," Cooper answered. "It's my first trip. My grandfather was born in Ireland."

"One of the got-aways, was he?" the woman said.

"Got-aways?" Cooper said.

The smile on the woman's face mellowed. "It's what I call them that left for other places. Got-aways."

"Makes sense," Cooper said.

"And you've come back to see where he lived?"

"Yes ma'am."

"And to find who he was?"

The question surprised Cooper. "I suppose so," he said. "That's a good way of putting it."

The woman leaned forward, holding her cane with both hands, balancing with it. "There's only one thing you'll find, when you get to the truth of it," she said easily. "He'd had his last turn here, and there was nothing to do but go off looking in another place." She paused, let her gaze hold on the sun. "But if he's like all them I knew, he took a bit of Ireland with him, and tucked it away like it was a keepsake. The happy Ireland, I'm speaking of. The other's what they was leaving behind."

Cooper thought of the rock shards and the photographs his grandfather had harbored.

"And did he ever come back?" the woman asked after a moment.

"No," Cooper said.

"So few did, being so far away, and knowing if they did, they'd see what it was that drove them off," the woman said.

"Did you ever leave?" asked Cooper.

"Oh, no," she answered brightly. "No. I found my peace with it when I was just a girl." She pushed up on her cane and stood for a moment, her eyes closed, a look of radiance in her face. Then she opened her eyes and looked down at Cooper. "It was a good rest. I've enjoyed it."

"Me, too," Cooper said.

"But he did come back, you know," she said. "Your grandfather. He came back in you. Them that leave, they always send somebody back in their place. It's the only thing that's really Irish. You can't let go if you've been born to it." She began to walk away.

"Have a nice day," Cooper said in a weak voice.

She did not stop walking. "That I've had," she said. "That I've had."

Back in his room, Cooper found Kathleen still asleep. Or pretending sleep. He knew she had been out of bed. Had probably watched him from the window. She had filled the Waterford vase he had given her with flowers from the hotel's own vase, and had placed it on a writing table. He sat on the bed beside her and stroked the side of her face. She blinked, faked a frown of annoyance, then reached for him and pulled him to her.

~~~

Sandy arrived at The Evening House at nine o'clock. He was invigorated, eager for the day. His medication, he asserted, had leveled his stress and perked his spirits, and Sarah Donoghue—the grand lady that she was—had prepared a picnic basket for the three of them.

"She sends her love," he said merrily.

"And her mother?" asked Kathleen in a teasing voice. "How is she?"

Sandy clucked his tongue in sadness. "Suffering, the poor dear. We spent the evening sitting with her." He offered a sigh from a forgotten scene of melancholy performed in a forgotten play from a forgotten time. "I read some from the Bible. Seemed to comfort her."

The drive from Tralee to Dingle was a backward tour, going the northern route, skirting Tralee Bay and Brandon Bay, following the base of Brandon Mountain.

"Misnamed, it is," Sandy complained. "Should be Brendan Mountain, but there's two schools of argument on it. Some say Brandon, some say Brendan, and I'm of the Brendan school. It was on the mountain that he had his vision of land off to the west, far over the waters. It was him who was first to find America, a thousand years before Columbus set sail, and Brendan did it in a currach, which was nothing more than a skin-covered boat."

By Sandy's account, a McAfee was rumored to have made the trip to America. The tales of St. Brendan returning to Ireland with natives, however, were slanderously false.

"You can't believe all you hear from the Irish," he said, and he winked at Kathleen.

It was Sandy's decision: they would not stop in Dingle, choosing to first tour the peninsula, skirting Ballyferriter Village and the near-by Field of the Cutting, where more than six hundred Spanish, Italian and Irish soldiers had once been decapitated, their heads buried in the turf of the field, their bodies flung into the sea. Alleged to be among the executioners were Sir Walter Raleigh and the poet Edmund Spenser, author of *The Faerie Queen*. A McAfee had escaped the slaughter. Reportedly. According to the legend of family tales, as repeated by Sandy McAfee.

They took their lunch of Sarah Donoghue's picnic on the roadside overlooking the Dingle peninsula near Slea Head. To Cooper, it was the most spectacular view he had ever seen. Ocean as blue as pale ink, lapping against narrow strips of yellow beach and rock, cutting into the shoreline like the sweep of a scythe. Meadows lush green, fading to gray on distant knolls. Wiggling walls of chest-high stone climbing the knolls, disappearing over them. A stone house, long abandoned, ribs showing through its roof. Sheep grazing lazily, fat with flesh and wool. A sky to match the ocean, puffed with clouds. In the distance, the Basket Islands seemed to be adrift on the fog of the Atlantic.

Kathleen watched him, knew the disbelief that had seized him. "It's beautiful, isn't it?" she said quietly.

Cooper did not speak. He blinked his answer: Yes.

"You'll see things you'd think they made up in one of them studios you have in Hollywood, California," Sandy said. "Beehive huts, where the monks lived, so small you'd have to crawl inside them. And there's the Gallarus Oratory, just up the road a piece. Older than a thousand years, it is. Put together by stones with no mortar, millions of rainstorms beating hard against it, but dry as a bone inside. Makes you wonder about them that were here long ago. And there's a pub up the way where we'll have a pint, and you'll hear the Gaelic talked."

"I'd like that," Cooper said. He glanced at his watch. "But I know Kathleen wants to see her grandmother."

"We have plenty of time," Kathleen told him. "It's only a few miles. We'll do the loop and be back in Dingle long before the day ends."

~~~

Oliver Raferty was seventy-two years old. Like his son, Peter, he was tall. Unlike his son, his still-handsome face carried the look of kindness and dignity. His eyes were blue, his neatly trimmed hair, white. A number of his friends often chortled in private—and out of his hearing—that Oliver Raferty looked more like a stuffy British statesman than an Irishman. It was a comment made about the way he presented himself—stiff-backed, chin up, solemn, a slightly superior expression—and about his dress. His suits were tailored, pressed after each wearing. His shirts were never wrinkled, his silk tie bridged perfectly over his chest, secured to his neck by a single Windsor knot. He did not go anywhere without an umbrella, used to protect his appearance against the unpredictable Irish weather and also as a walking cane, not for need, but for affectation.

Sitting in the dining table chair in Elizabeth Finnegan's modest, well-kept home, Oliver Raferty was an imposing figure.

Sitting opposite him, Elizabeth Finnegan was his match. Tall, the lines of a once-great beauty still distinctive in her face, her own blue eyes clear and lively, her own white hair gathered in a bun at her neck, she considered the man who had arrived unannounced at her home a rare visitor. He did not have to speak for her to know he was a man of quality; the quality was in his appearance, the grace of his carriage.

He had come to find Kathleen, her granddaughter, he had said, understanding from his office staff that Kathleen had planned a visit.

It was true, she had replied. Kathleen had called earlier in the day, explaining that she was with friends on a brief tour of the peninsula.

"I expect her at any moment," she had told him.

254

She had invited him inside to wait with her, and he had reluctantly accepted, promising that his conference with Kathleen would require only a few moments.

"Is there trouble?" Elizabeth Finnegan had asked calmly.

"Not at all," Oliver Raferty had answered. "Just the opposite. She's an extraordinarily gifted young lady, a valued employee. I merely want to congratulate her on her very great achievement with one of our accounts."

"How lovely," she had said, knowing his explanation was only part true, and there was much more to be said to Kathleen. A man with the standing of Oliver Raferty did not make a drive from Cork to Dingle to express the same gratitude he could easily express over a telephone.

She had made tea, offered carrot cake she had baked for Kathleen, knowing carrot cake was a favorite of her granddaughter. He had accepted the refreshments appreciatively, praising the cake.

Elizabeth Finnegan had busied herself from early morning, cleaning her home, then re-cleaning it. Three dustings. She had realized the foolishness of it, knowing it was an old woman's doing, the spending of an old woman's impatience. And now there was a visitor, a distinguished man, and she knew there was something else she should have done, yet her mind would not let her think of it. Her mind seemed as locked as a vault with no combination to open it. It would not be long, she thought, until her memory faded and vanished.

They had talked politely, avoiding subjects of politics and weather.

He had spoken of the brilliance of Kathleen's concept for NewTree.

She had remembered Kathleen's curiosity and independence as a child.

He had inquired about her experiences as a teacher.

She had answered—too enthusiastically, she thought—that teaching had been the light illuminating her life.

"It's a grand duty, the noblest of them all, I think," he had said.

"It's given me pleasure," she had replied. "But there's a drawback to it. I see all these young men and women who've taken over the running of the town, and only remember them as small-faced children, flooding

255

over with so much energy their little bodies were barely able to contain it."

He had nodded agreement.

It was four-thirty when Kathleen arrived, alone. She was startled to find Oliver Raferty waiting with her grandmother.

"I'll give you some visiting time," Elizabeth Finnegan told them. "I've wanted to cut some flowers for the table, and forgot it." It was the truth, the duty she had forgotten in the routine of her dusting.

"I'll only be a minute," Oliver Raferty said apologetically.

"Don't rush," Elizabeth Finnegan insisted. "It's a lovely day outside." She looked at Kathleen. "Have some cake and tea, love, and cut another slice for Mr. Raferty."

"Thank you, but I'm afraid I've had my sugar quota for the day," Oliver Raferty said. He nodded a bow to Elizabeth Finnegan. "It was a pleasure to make your acquaintance, Mrs. Finnegan," he added. "I now know the origins of your granddaughter's charming personality."

Elizabeth Finnegan blushed, smiled appreciation, then left the room.

Kathleen moved to the dining room table and sat opposite Oliver Raferty. "Is there a problem?" she asked anxiously.

"I've come to apologize to you in person," Oliver Raferty replied, "and to ask you to reconsider your resignation. You're the bright light in our little company, and we need you." He paused. "I need you. The way you've handled the NewTree account has been exceptional. We've seen the tape. You were grand, and as I think you know, it's had a great impact. There's been a sizeable contribution from an American company as a result of it, with others already following suit."

Kathleen thought of Cooper's explanation about Ealy Ackerman's contribution and resisted the smile that wanted to mark her face. "I'm glad," she said.

Oliver Raferty paused, cleared his throat, lifted his face. "And there's the matter of Peter." He paused again, cleared his throat again.

Kathleen did not speak.

"I'm well aware of his—well, preoccupation with you," Oliver Raferty continued, "and I want to offer my apologies."

"It's unnecessary," she said.

"You're kind to say so, but it is necessary," he replied. "I want you to know that I've taken steps to assure that you don't have to suffer from it again. I've repositioned Peter in the organization. He'll be going to Limerick to open a small office there. But, first, he'll be in a treatment center for a time."

"Treatment?" she said.

"For the drinking," Oliver Raferty answered in a hurting voice. "I should have done it long ago. It'll be the ruin of him if he can't control it." He stood. "I'll be going now. Enjoy your time. You've earned it. We'll talk about your future when you return."

Kathleen stood. "Thank you, sir."

"Give my farewell to your grandmother," he said.

"I will."

"She's a remarkable lady. Like you."

Kathleen smiled. A blush tinted her cheeks.

Oliver Raferty paused for a moment, composing himself. "I'm sorry about my son," he said heavily. "I'm hoping you'll forgive him."

"I do, sir. I do," she replied.

She found her grandmother in the garden, as she had found her mother three days earlier. Standing at the gate, she was suddenly aware of the resemblance between her grandmother and her mother. The same peaceful expression, the same graceful movement. She wondered if, in time, she, too, would retire to a garden to find contentment.

"It's a shame to cut them, they're so pretty," she said to her grandmother.

Her grandmother laughed easily. "I've always found it hard, knowing what to do," she replied. "I love they way they look in the garden, like little drops of color, but they make a room so fresh and full of life, it's a shame not to have them on every table." She looked up at Kathleen. "Did Mr. Raferty leave?"

"Yes. He asked me to tell you how much he enjoyed the visit."

"A nice man, he is."

"Very nice."

"Oh, he was making a pretty speech about how important you are to the firm and how you've done something grand for the telly."

"I'm sure he was just trying to impress you," Kathleen said.

"Now, don't go making light of it. He was sincere. I could tell," her grandmother asserted. She handed the flowers to Kathleen. "And what of your friends you spoke of? Where are they?"

"I left them at Kieffer's place," Kathleen explained. "They wanted to clean themselves up a bit before meeting you. They're insisting on taking us to dinner. I'll go back for them later, after we've spent some time together."

Her grandmother smiled. "I could do the cooking, you know."

"I know, but there's no reason for it. You deserve a night out. If they weren't with me, I would insist on it myself."

Her grandmother took her arm and they started back toward the house.

"So, dear, tell me about this young man," her grandmother said.

"How do you know about a young man?" Kathleen asked.

"I spoke with your mother."

"Did she tell you he was an American?"

Kathleen could feel her grandmother's grip tighten on her arm. "No," she said after a moment.

"He's just a friend," Kathleen said. "I think you'll like him."

"I'm sure I will," her grandmother said softly.

~~~

Cooper needed the shower at Kieffer's Bed and Breakfast to clear his head of the pint of Guinness he had taken in a pub called Paddy's, where, as Sandy had promised, much of the conversation among customers was in Gaelic. The language had been like a code to Cooper. He did not know the words, had never heard them, still he believed he knew what was being said. It was as though the language, mixed with the Guinness, had intoxicated him, and he had left the pub surprisingly light-headed.

The shower had refreshed him and he had dressed in his most presentable clothes—khaki pants, a white, button-down collar shirt, his green cashmere sweater—and had joined Sandy for tea and scones in the restaurant of the inn.

Sandy had talked of a project that intrigued him—a translation of *Hamlet* into Gaelic. Sadly, he had confessed, the only Gaelic he knew from *Hamlet* was the line, "To be or not to be. . ." His deliverance of it was brooding, deep, serious, a voice that needed a furrowed forehead. To Cooper, it had not sounded Gaelic. It had sounded German, or bastardized German.

At six o'clock, Kathleen arrived, wearing a beige ensemble with a long tan coat, colors giving luster to the nut-red of her hair and shine to the pale sage-green of her eyes. Her appearance caused Sandy to sigh and to say, "I'm not certain me old heart can take such beauty."

Kathleen kissed his cheek.

Elizabeth Finnegan was waiting under the arch of the doorway of her home, dressed for the evening out. She watched as the two men escorted Kathleen from the car. With her failing eyesight, she knew only that one was young, the other older. Kathleen had said little about them, telling her, "You're going to be charmed by both of them. I promise you will." She had added, "And you're going to be surprised by one of them."

The older man seemed familiar as they approached the house—the beaming expression of his face, the way he walked. And then she knew: Sandy McAfee, the actor. She had seen him in the cinema and, years earlier, on stage during holidays to Dublin. A smile of delight flew into her face. "Oh, my," she said in an excited voice.

"You do recognize him, then?" said Kathleen.

"Of course, I do," her grandmother replied. She stepped forward, extended her hand to Sandy. "Sandy McAfee. What an honor."

Sandy took her hand, leaned to kiss it. He said in his actor's voice, "The honor, dear lady, is mine, believe me."

"Granddear, there's someone else I want you to meet," Kathleen said.

Elizabeth Finnegan looked past Sandy, to Kathleen, then to Cooper. "This is—"

A look of shock jerked across Elizabeth Finnegan's face, causing Kathleen to pause.

"Granddear?" Kathleen said in a worried voice.

Elizabeth Finnegan raised her hands in front of her, palms out, as if warding off a blow. She could feel the color of her face turn to ash. Her eyes were locked on Cooper. A light—brilliantly white—sizzled in her mind, swirled around her, lifted her effortlessly, and hurled her into the dizzying heights of memory. Images, exploding like star blinks, blew past her. Voices tangled with voices. She inhaled suddenly, a gasp.

"Granddear, are you all right?" Kathleen asked, stepping to her, catching her arm.

Her grandmother whispered, "Finn."

31

In his journal, late at night, Cooper wrote:

I now know the story of my grandfather. I know why he left Ireland. I know why he did not return. Most important, I know what he left behind when he stepped on the ship bound for America. And I know why he told the story of Sally Cavanaugh.

Sally Cavanaugh was not a myth. She was real. Her name is Elizabeth Cavanaugh Finnegan, called Sally by her childhood friends and by my grandfather. When they were young, they were in love. She is very open about that. Because he was a laborer and Protestant and she was Catholic from a family of middle-class means, her parents objected to the relationship and forbade her to continue seeing him.

It was that simple. No different than what has happened to millions of other people all over the Earth. Class separation. But in Ireland, with its history of The Troubles, violence seems to be part of it all.

One day, in a field near Dingle, he saw her for the last time because he knew it was hopeless. Not long after, he left for America.

But he did not leave with just a broken heart. He left thinking a charge of murder had been lodged against him. At least, I believe he did.

From the story told to me by Kathleen's grandmother, a group of men confronted him on his last visit to see her. Her brother, Wallace, who harbored a hatred for Protestants, was among them. A fight occurred and Wallace was seriously injured before my grandfather could escape. I believe that in Killarney, he heard a rumor that Wallace Cavanaugh had died and the authorities were looking for the assassin. It would have been only a rumor. Wallace Cavanaugh survived, although permanently crippled. I do not think my grandfather ever knew the truth, even from the correspondence he had with his brother and sister (he most likely never told them about it), but the fear of it was why he would not return to Ireland. (All of it reminds me of the story of the Rose of Tralee.)

I am numbed by what I have learned. Not because my grandfather never shared it with anyone in his family, but because of the incredible odds against my discovering it. I have to believe there is something at play here more powerful than coincidence. How else can I accept it? I have met and fallen in love with the granddaughter of the woman my own grandfather loved. How did it happen? Was it willed by my grandfather's spirit? Did he put me on the sidewalk of a street in Dublin at the exact time that a taxi delivered Kathleen O'Reilly to her hotel? Did he guide her to a pub in Waterford, just as I was talking about him? Was he acting in Sandy McAfee's decision to stroll through a park in Cork?

It is late. We did not go to dinner as we had planned. Instead, Kathleen made a stew (with Sandy's help), while her grandmother and I talked. It was clear Kathleen had never heard any of it. The story touched her deeply in what appeared to be a troubling manner. She was very quiet and asked no questions, although I believe she is talking to her grandmother privately as I write this. She will stay the night there. When Sandy and I left, her grandmother hugged me warmly. She is a beautiful and gracious woman. Maybe she couldn't help talking to me. She was so startled at the similarity between my grandfather and me, she kept staring at me, as though seeing an apparition.

But it is Kathleen I am concerned about. I could see many questions in her eyes, and I would not blame her for distrusting me, perhaps even considering my presence a curse in her life. In a way, I feel like a carrier of some killing disease.

To complicate matters, on the drive back to the inn, Sandy told me the truth about being hired by Ealy to watch over me. He had not bargained for such a turn of events, he said, and he had a compulsion to be honest. I should be angry, I suppose, but I'm not. I know Ealy. He did what he did because he loved my grandfather and he thought I needed some guidance while here. It wasn't a prank. I should have invited him and Cary to come with me. I didn't, and I got Sandy as a substitute. But I like Sandy. He has been the spirit of my trip. He saved me from a beating and it's possible he even saved my life. I doubt if he's told me everything, especially about manipulating my time with Kathleen, but it doesn't matter. I asked him what he thought of the events of the night and he said it was a night of miracles. He is as emotional as any person I've ever known. Maybe he has to be, being in the theater.

I have also been thinking about the old woman I met this morning, while watching the sunrise. One of the things she said to me was, "Them that leave, they always send somebody back in their place. It's the only thing that's really Irish. You can't let go if you've been born to it."

Maybe that is why my grandfather sent me off on this adventure. Even in death, he couldn't let go of the thing he had been born to.

Now I have a decision to make.

He closed his journal and put on his windbreaker and went outside. A chilled night wind crawled the streets and he stood for a moment listening to the low moaning that it made. It had the sound of someone in pain. He began to walk against it.

He had not told Elizabeth Finnegan of the story of Finn McCool and Sally Cavanaugh, but he had asked enough questions to know the story was his grandfather's way of remembering her. His grandfather had simply changed locations, from a meadow near Dingle to the cliffs of Moher, and his own name, from Finn Coghlan to Finn McCool.

Elizabeth Finnegan had described the leaving of his grandfather as the most confusing days of her life. She had defied her family, had helped his grandfather hide in an abandoned stone hut while recovering from the trauma of his own beating.

"It was there that I last saw him," she had said. "There was such anger, with my brother lying near death. If they had found him, they would have killed him for certain, him being Protestant and the great divide existing with the Catholics. And I couldn't let that happen, no matter the threats against me. I was an outcast for years in my own family, and the name Finn Coghlan was forbidden to be uttered in the presence of any of them.."

Cooper had asked if Wallace Cavanaugh had ever forgiven his grandfather.

"Never," she had answered. "He went to his grave a bitter old man, with the curse still hard on his heart."

"Curse?" Cooper had asked.

"It was against Finn and all his family," Elizabeth Finnegan had explained quietly. "There are those who believed it was the cause of death for Finn's brother and sister."

The description of the curse—bellowed by Wallace Cavanaugh as he lay covered in blood, his left leg bent grotesquely beneath him—had chilled Cooper. It was impossible to imagine his grandfather in such a fight.

"It's when I did the one thing my brother could never forgive me for," Elizabeth Finnegan had said quietly. "I left him to his friends, suffering with his wounds, and went after Finn, thinking to go away with him." She had paused, letting her gaze float from Cooper's face to a window as though beckoned by a memory, and then she had added, "It was Finn who made me stay. I would have followed him, but he wouldn't hear of it."

"Why not?" Cooper had asked.

"The curse," she had answered simply. "It was the curse. Finn was a great teller of stories. He believed in all such things." She had smiled warmly, added, "It's as Irish as anything on Earth. Sometimes I think this place doesn't exist at all, that it's all made of stories so grand you can't stop yourself from believing in them."

Cooper had asked if she remembered the day that his grandfather left.

She did, she had told him. Remembered it clearly. Late in the day. Rain-misty with breaks of sun. And as he listened, Cooper had heard his grandfather's voice from the story of Sally Cavanaugh. *"One of them soft rains, like a good mist coming out of a low cloud. Off away, over the ocean, you could see the blue peeking through the rain-light."*

And more, about the sun: *"It come falling out of the rain-light over the ocean—rich-red and marigold, like the bud of a morning rose that's right for cutting—and then it struck a cloud so thin that not an eye could see it, and it melted and spread itself out along that cloud, waving in a ship-pitched wind, like a ribbon for a lady's hair. And then it seeped*

264

through the cloud and come back together in a sun ball that poured its
light on Sally Cavanaugh.”

He wondered if his grandfather had glanced back in his leaving, and
if his last view of Sally Cavanaugh had been of the sun striking her.

Yet nothing that Elizabeth Finnegan said had intrigued him as much
as the answer to the last question he had asked her: “When was the last
time you thought of my grandfather?”

Elizabeth Finnegan had flinched in surprise. “Why, now, that’s a
remarkable thing to ask. It was only a short time ago. A few months
back. All those years gone, and I’d put him out of my mind, as it had to
be, but then he came back. Like a storm, he came back. For no reason at
all, and he’s been lingering around all this time, and then you.”

Cooper remembered the childhood of huddling against his
grandfather and the asking-telling of the story of Finn McCool and Sally
Cavanaugh:

“And Finn McCool? What happened to Finn McCool?”
“Well, now, he went away, back to the other world—to a cave, some
say—and there he stays, waiting.”
“Waiting for what?”
“The time to come back. And he will, my boy, he will.”
“When? When will he come back?”
“When Sally calls for him, there he’ll be, with a pocketful of holes
and little hope for riches.”

Sally Cavanaugh had called for Finn Coghlan, Cooper thought. For
the Finn of her memory.

And Finn Coghlan had returned as the Finn of his grandson.

He stopped on the street, let the wind spin around his legs, sting his
face. From a near-by house, he heard the sharp voice of a man, the bark
of a dog. The sounds were quarrelsome.

“Papa,” he whispered. “Tell me what to do.”

~~~

Kathleen sat on the floor beside her grandmother's chair, permitting her grandmother to slowly brush her hair. A table lamp and two candles, casting a mellow glow, lighted the room.

Her grandmother asked softly, "Do you love him, dear?"

Kathleen nodded.

"Then you'll do all that's in your power to have him."

Kathleen tilted her face to look at her grandmother. "Wouldn't you feel strange about that?"

"And why should I?" her grandmother said.

"Because of his grandfather and you," Kathleen answered. "All that went on. Wouldn't that make you feel strange?"

"Strange? No, love, no." She stroked Kathleen's hair with her fingers. "Not now. Not at my age. We did nothing foolish, Finn and I. We were young and we were in love. It was against us, and there was nothing we could do about it. Times have changed, and for the better. But who knows what would have been? We might have spent our lives bickering to one another if we'd been together."

"Couldn't that happen to me too?" Kathleen said.

"Sure it could. It could happen to anyone," her grandmother answered. "Nothing's certain, but why spoil sweet memories thinking in such a way?"

"Do you believe in the curse?" Kathleen asked.

The question caused her grandmother to pause. After a moment, she said, "It's why Finn wanted his ashes to be turned loose in Ireland."

"What do you mean?" Kathleen said.

"To take it away."

"The curse? That would take away the curse?"

"It's the tale of them who believe in such things," her grandmother said. "You free the spirit and the spirit makes amends."

"And you believe that?"

Her grandmother smiled. "Believe it? Oh, I don't know. It's a good enough thought. No reason not to believe it. This world is filled with mysteries, child, things none of us are meant to know. If we did, we'd have no need for wondering, now would we?"

"You never heard from him after he left, did you?" Kathleen asked.

"No, I didn't. Not directly. I knew about him some, from his sister and brother. They moved here after he left and I would see them from time to time, in a casual way. We were never close friends, and they died so young, both of them. They never knew about Finn and me, though they might have suspected something, with me inquiring about their brother."

"What did they tell you?"

"About his work. About his marriage," her grandmother answered.

"Did it hurt you to hear that?"

"Yes, it did. But I was also married by then."

"Do you regret your marriage?"

"Regret it? Oh, no, love. Not a moment of it. You were so small when your grandfather passed on, you wouldn't have a memory of him, but he was a wonderful man, as gentle as anyone you could ever meet. I loved him dearly. Not the same as Finn. I couldn't. No one can do that. When you first lose your heart, you lose something that no one else can ever have. Your grandfather knew that."

"Did you ever tell him about Finn Coghlan?"

"There was no reason. He knew the story. He was one of the friends of my brother."

"And it didn't matter to him?" Kathleen asked.

"He loved me for who I was, not who I'd been," her grandmother said. "He had the patience of Job. Never asked a question about Finn. Not one. It was him who got me back with my family."

Kathleen did not speak for a long time. She rested her head against her grandmother's leg and let the brushing soothe her. And then she said, "Tell me about my mother."

"Your mother?"

"My mother had the same thing happen to her, didn't she?"

Her grandmother paused in the brushing. "Your mother needs to tell you her own story," she said after a moment.

"But it really wasn't the same, was it?" Kathleen said. "My mother was the one who wasn't good enough."

"Your mother was good enough for kings," her grandmother said gently.

"Not everyone thought so," Kathleen said.

"But your mother had the grandest thing happen to her, didn't she?"

Kathleen looked up, puzzled. "What was that?"

"You, child, you. And you're not to go thinking that what's happened to me, or to your mother, is meant for you. It's not. We were of our time, and that's the answer to it. Your time is now. It's not the same. Not at all."

~~~

Cooper awoke from a bothered sleep at five o'clock and lay for a moment peering into the shadows of the room. On the night table beside his bed, he saw the metal box containing the ashes of his grandfather.

He had dreamed a dream of floating, of being weightless, yet of having the sensation of great weight. In the floating, looking down, he had seen his grandfather walking in a meadow beside Elizabeth Cavanaugh Finnegan, wearing a broad, beaming smile. A look of peace had been in Elizabeth Cavanaugh Finnegan's face. And then she had stopped walking, had stood watching his grandfather continue in his long stride across the field, toward the ocean. He had heard Elizabeth Cavanaugh Finnegan calling, "Finn! Finn! Finn!" But his grandfather had not answered, and a rain had begun to fall over her, and as Cooper watched from the height of his floating, the face of Elizabeth Cavanaugh Finnegan had become the face of Kathleen.

He rolled to a sitting position on the side of the bed. The fan of a heating unit hummed monotonously in the room. The hum seemed to come from the metal box, the mantra of a restless voice.

"Why did you do this to me, Papa?" Cooper said in a whimper.

The fan clicked off. The hum sighed to silence.

He pushed from the bed, went into the bathroom, showered, shaved, dressed, and then began packing. At five-thirty, he was ready to leave.

He took a sheet of the stationery that Ealy had supplied in the Irish bible and wrote:

Dear Kathleen,

I pray you understand what I am about to do. I cannot explain it, other than to tell you that, for the first time in my life, I feel great shame over being who I am, and for the confusion and hurt I have brought to your family, and surely to you. I am stunned by what has happened between us. It doesn't seem real, yet it is. My feeling for you is more powerful than anything I've ever known, but I'm afraid of adding to the confusion and the hurt.

Forgive me. Please forgive me.

How can anything so beautiful be so painful?

He signed his name, folded the sheet, slipped it into the large envelope containing the rock shards and photographs his grandfather had kept, and then he took his luggage to the Vanette.

At five-fifty, with the envelope in his hand, he knocked lightly on the door to the room occupied by Sandy. After a few moments, he heard Sandy's hoarse voice from behind the door: "Who is it?"

"Cooper," Cooper said quietly.

The door cracked opened. Sandy gazed out through squinted eyes. He looked surprisingly old and disoriented. "What is it, lad?"

"I need to talk to you for a minute," Cooper told him.

Sandy opened the door and Cooper stepped inside. There was an odor of alcohol in the room. Sandy turned on a light and pulled on a red silk bathrobe. "Seeing you dressed for traveling, I'm not sure I want to hear what you've come to say," he said.

Cooper reached into his pocket and removed money he had counted out in his room. He handed it to Sandy. "There's two hundred euro. I want you to use it to rent a car to take you and Kathleen back to Killarney, and then use what's left for a train ticket back to Dublin."

Sandy wagged his head. He held the money, looked at it. "And why are you doing this, young Finn? It's the wrong thing."

"I don't know what else to do," Cooper said. "I think the ghost of Finn Coghlan has done enough haunting, and I think I'd always be that ghost. That's what the curse means."

"And do you think your leaving will put him away from her family?" asked Sandy. "You can't do that, lad. You never chase off a ghost. Never. You've got too much Irish in you not to know that. No, you don't chase him off. You live with him long enough to be on friendly terms, and if you're lucky, you'll find him to be a comfort to you when you're all alone. It's why the old see spirits. It's why Mrs. Finnegan sees your grandfather from them bygone days. There's nobody else to cast an eye on."

Cooper ran his fingers over the rock shards in the envelope. "I'm not leaving to have him put away from her family," he said after a moment. "The reason I'm leaving is because I have to put him away from me. If I stay, I think I'll always hear him and it'll become a mocking, and I don't want that. I loved my grandfather. I don't want to stop loving him."

"What will you do?" Sandy asked quietly.

"I want to scatter my grandfather's ashes this morning," Cooper answered.

"And do you know where?"

"If I can find it, the place where Kathleen's grandmother last saw my grandfather."

"The meadow she talked about?" Sandy asked.

"Yes."

"I could take you. I know the place," Sandy told him.

"No," Cooper said. "I'll find it." He handed the envelope to Sandy. "Will you give this to Kathleen's grandmother? She'll understand it. There's a note in it for Kathleen."

Sandy nodded. "And when will you be going home?"

"My flight leaves tomorrow afternoon," Cooper told him. "I'll drive back to Dublin today and stay at the Shelbourne tonight."

"Go have a pint at Foley's," Sandy said. "It's luck to leave off at the place where you got started."

"I'll do that," Cooper promised.

"You'll be careful on the way, remembering which side of the road to stay on," Sandy said.

"I will."

"You're a fine Irishman, young Finn," Sandy whispered. "You'll not be forgetting old Sandy, now will you?"

Cooper could feel a shudder. "No," he said. "I can promise you, I won't forget. You've been with me on the best days of my life."

Sandy folded his arms around Cooper in a strong embrace. "You've still got your wish," he said softly. "The one your grandfather earned from Bogmeadow. Make it."

"A wish?" Cooper said.

"Sure, a wish."

"I wish things were the way I want them to be," Cooper said.

Sandy patted Cooper on the back, then released the embrace. "There you have it," he said. "A good wish. Now watch for the sign of it. You'll see the sign of it, I promise you."

"I think I've seen enough signs for a lifetime," Cooper replied.

"There'll be another," Sandy said. "Take me word for it. And when you see it, you'll know the answer has been given to you." He pushed the money Cooper had given him back into Cooper's pocket.

"You'll need that," Cooper protested.

Sandy smiled. "I've got me own crock of gold," he said in his deliberate Irish brogue. "In case you've not taken notice, that's a rainbow that's wrapped around me shoulders."

~~~

The meadow was east of Dingle on the north side of a knoll, shielding it from the howl of wind that whipped off the Atlantic. A cluster of trees grew stubbornly near a narrow road. Almost hidden among the trees was a small stone hut that appeared to have been abandoned for years. In the field beyond, rows of stonewalls ran haphazardly, like aimless stitching across a vivid green garment.

Cooper was certain it was the same meadow Elizabeth Finnegan had described as the last place she had seen his grandfather—*"Him walking off down the road, never looking back."*

He took the protective tape from the metal box containing Finn Coghlan's cremains, then carefully opened the box and looked inside. The powdery body of his grandfather was surprisingly small. He closed the box and tucked it under his arm and began to walk across the meadow toward the crest of the knoll.

On the eastern horizon, the appearing morning sun was orange-gold, filtered by fog rising up to become clouds. The wind flew in from the ocean, cold, carrying the scent of wet feathers, Cooper thought. It bit at his face.

At the crest, he stopped walking, stood for a moment to let the wind and the mist beat against him. In the distance, he saw a herd of grazing sheep and a car moving slowly along the road. Above him, an unseen gull spoke from a wind-draft and the cry, to Cooper, was like a Gaelic greeting, a language of song.

And then he lifted the top of the metal box and turned it over in his hand. The ashes of Michael Finn Coghlan fell, spinning crazily in the wind, leaping joyfully, vanishing.

"I love you, Papa," Cooper called painfully. "I love you."

He thought he heard a cry of exuberance from the ashes.

~~~

From his room, Sandy made a telephone call to the residence of Elizabeth Finnegan. It was seven-thirty, the early morning bright with sun spears that impaled his room from the windows. The day, he judged, would be clear and comfortable. A good day for travel.

Kathleen answered the call on the second ring. She said, "Cooper?"

"Not Cooper, love, it's Sandy," Sandy said.

There was a pause. Then: "Is Cooper with you?"

"I'm afraid not," Sandy answered gently. "Is it too early to come by?"

"Where is he?" asked Kathleen.

"I'll tell you all about it when I see you," Sandy replied. He asked again, "Is it too early?"

"No, not at all," Kathleen said. There was a tremble in her voice.

"I've called a taxi," Sandy told her. "I'll be there soon."

He thumbed down the connection on the telephone, lifted his hand and listened for the hum of the dial tone. "Ah, Sandy McAfee, you've got the touch of a genius," he said softly, and then he placed his call, taking the number from memory. In Dublin, Cameron Dickey answered on the sixth ring. His voice was heavy with sleep.

"It's Sandy," Sandy said.

"Oh, holy Jesus," Cameron sighed. "You calling this early puts a fright in me, Sandy. Where are you? In a lock-up?"

"Don't you be worrying about me, Cameron Dickey," Sandy said merrily. "I'm fit as can be, and, would you believe it, I've even got the money to pay for the call."

"And enough left over to pay back what you're owing me?" Cameron asked.

"That and more," Sandy said.

"It's early to be in the drink, Sandy," Cameron mumbled. "Even for the likes of you."

"Never been more sober," Sandy said. "Now, are you ready to listen?"

There was a pause. Sandy could hear Cameron's heavy breathing, the click of a cigarette lighter, the raspy inhaling of smoke.

"Go on," Cameron said wearily.

"I need you for your specialty," Sandy said warmly.

"Oh, fock you, Sandy," Cameron snapped. "I'm through playing it. Enough's enough."

"Don't be so quick," Sandy said. "There's two hundred in it."

There was no reply from Cameron.

"Did you hear me, my little friend?" asked Sandy. He paused, waited. Then he added, "It'll be for hour or so. One time only."

"Two hundred?" Cameron said warily.

"Two hundred."

"And why should I go believing you, Sandy McAfee? You're a lying son of a bitch, you are, and the whole of Dublin knows it."

"You have my word on it," Sandy said.

Cameron laughed.

"And I'll wire you a hundred of it this morning," Sandy added.

"A hundred? Try the two hundred," Cameron said.

"A hundred," Sandy insisted. "Another hundred when it's done— and if you do it right, the way I tell you."

For a moment, Cameron did not speak. Sandy could hear him blowing smoke from his cigarette, knew he was taking the bait.

"And when's this little game to be played?" Cameron asked suspiciously.

"Tonight," Sandy told him.

"If I get the hundred in advance," Cameron countered. "But if you make a fool of me, Sandy McAfee, I'll hunt you down like a dog starving for a bone."

"You'll be buying a round for us both when it's over," Sandy promised. "Now, here's the particulars."

~~~

He was merely performing a role, he thought, like the set-up of a first act in a wrenching drama, the kind of moment that takes a choking hold on the throat and brings a tear to the eye. In the playbook, his character would be recorded as the Messenger of Sadness. It would be the proper title. There was sadness in it, and not the kind borne of staged fakery.

He expected tears.

He was wrong. There were no tears. Or none to be seen.

"The pieces of stone and the photographs are for Mrs. Finnegan," Sandy said in a pitiful manner, after surrendering the envelope Cooper had left with him. "And the message is for dear Kathleen." He paused. "I've not read it," he added. "You have my word on it."

Kathleen smiled weakly and then she opened the note Cooper had written. She read it quickly and folded it again. She looked at Sandy and then at her grandmother, but she did not speak. The smile lingered awkwardly on her face.

"Are you all right, dear?" her grandmother asked.

She nodded. "Yes," she said. Then: "Do you know about the photographs?"

"The one of me, yes," Elizabeth Finnegan said quietly. "I gave it to Finn on the last day I saw him. It was taken not long before he left for America. The other one, I don't know."

"I do," Kathleen said. "It was taken at his American wake. We met one of the men who was in the photograph."

"And the pieces of stone?" Sandy said.

"Just part of Ireland, I would think," her grandmother replied. "Some little keepsake."

"A little keepsake," Kathleen said. "Strange, isn't it?" She turned to Sandy. "Thank you, Sandy, for the kindness you've shown." She paused. Her fingers played with the note from Cooper. "Would you have some tea?" she added in a sudden, rushed voice. "Granddear has it made, and some wonderful scones. She makes the best you've ever tasted."

"I'd like that," Sandy said.

"Would you make a tray, dear?" Elizabeth Finnegan said to Kathleen.

"Of course," Kathleen replied in a light voice. She smiled again at Sandy and then she left the room.

"Give her a minute," Elizabeth Finnegan whispered to Sandy. "She needs some privacy to compose herself." She sat in a chair near him.

"I'm sorry to be the bearer of such news," Sandy said.

"You're a good man, Sandy McAfee," Elizabeth Finnegan replied. She looked again at the photographs. A smile eased into her face. "I hoped the one I gave him would bring him back, I suppose." She paused. Her gaze stayed on the photographs. "But nothing could do that, him being the kind of man he was."

"And what was that?" asked Sandy.

Elizabeth Finnegan turned her eyes to Sandy. "Prideful. Had it in his mind that he wasn't good enough for me."

"The church, was it?" Sandy said.

"Only part of it was that," Elizabeth Finnegan answered. "No, there was more to it. Finn had so little, and that was a hard thing to live with when we were younger." She paused again. "But you know that, don't you? You come from the same kind of days, I'd think."

"I do, indeed," Sandy told her.

"It's not the same now, is it?" Elizabeth Finnegan said. "Not like the old ways."

"No," Sandy replied. "Thank God."

Elizabeth Finnegan nodded. She placed the photographs on a table beside her chair. "You have a thought about my sweet one, haven't you?" she said.

"I do," Sandy answered.

"And what would it be?"

"She needs to make a fight of it."

"And would you be helping her?"

"With pleasure," Sandy said.

"Where did he go?"

"To Dublin," Sandy answered. "He's to leave tomorrow for America."

"Dublin?" Elizabeth Finnegan said. "That's where Finn departed from."

"Was it, now?" Sandy said.

"If he had left from Cork, I might have gone there," she said. "Dublin was so far away, things being as tense as they were."

"Not as far now as it used to be, even if the miles are the same," Sandy said.

"It's only a day until he leaves. Is there time to do anything?" she asked.

"There's time to change the world in a day," Sandy said gently. "Or to be changed by it. There's a day in everybody's life that brings the change they'll be carrying forever, don't you think?"

For a moment, Elizabeth Finnegan did not answer. She turned to gaze at the photographs on the table beside her. Her smile faded slightly. "Yes," she said quietly.

From the kitchen, Kathleen returned with a tray of tea and scones, placing it on a serving table. Her face was flush, her eyes shining. "It's a strong tea," she said to Sandy. "The way you like it."

"Kathleen, I want you to do something for me," her grandmother said.

"What would it be?" Kathleen asked.

"I want you to gather your things," Elizabeth Finnegan said. "You're going to Dublin."

"And why would I do that?" Kathleen asked.

"Because I didn't," Elizabeth Finnegan said.

32

Cooper made the drive from Dingle to Dublin, through Limerick and Portlaoise, at a steady pace. He did not stop along the way, as he had done with Sandy in the meandering of their tour. He did not have the mood for sight-seeing, yet he was aware of the countryside, of subtle changes of landscape, of hues of plant-life, of quaint-sounding names of towns and villages—Nenagh, Tommyvara, Moneygall, Roscrea—and of the faces of roadside people, their gazes much like the gazes of pastured animals. Curious looks, quickly dismissed.

His thought was of Kathleen, and the great aching of his decision. At lunch, in a pub on the Dublin side of Portlaoise, a talkative waitress dressed seductively had asked, "Are you feeling well, love? You've got the look of sadness. Has there been a dying?" And Cooper had replied, "Yes." The waitress had sighed in sympathy, had said, "Funerals make me cry me eyes out."

In Dublin, he again checked into the Shelbourne Hotel. The Shelbourne was familiar. It would not require the ritual of investigation that had always seemed necessary to Cooper, and it was close to Foley's. He had spent his first night in Ireland in Foley's; he would spend his last night there also, as Sandy McAfee had urged. Still, it would not be the same. Sandy would not be there, dressed in his dandy suit, charming the crowd with his sweet stories.

In the afternoon, he slept, or tried to sleep. His dreams streamed aimlessly in abstract vignettes. Faces he knew and faces he did not know flew past his sleep-seeing. Nothing was sensible. Sandy was there in the garb of a priest, presiding over a cloud of ashes that had been his grandfather, the ashes hovering full-body above the ground, the lunch waitress standing beside Sandy, dressed in a short black split skirt with a black blouse tight over her breasts, crying desperately. Nearby, under umbrellas, Kathleen and her grandmother, watching with solemn faces.

Standing behind them, his own grandmother, wearing a bitter look. The dreams were shrill-voiced, dark-coated.

He awoke bothered, rolled to check his watch. It was five-twenty. He had been asleep only forty minutes.

He went into the bathroom and washed his face with cold water. He was not hungry and it was too early to go to Foley's. At the small writing table near the window, he opened his journal, picked up his pen and held it in his hand. From across the room, he could see himself in the wall mirror. He had a foolish, pretentious expression—that of someone posing for a foolish, pretentious photograph. He rolled the pen in his fingers, placed it on the table.

A muffled laugh, a woman's laugh, came from the next-door room. He had seen a woman earlier in the corridor, dark-haired, ink-blue eyes, a dimpled smile, a look of radiance in the glance and the nod she had given him, and he wondered if she was the woman of the laugh. It was possible. There had been a look of joy in the woman in the corridor.

Once Ealy had said he wanted to be reincarnated as a portrait hanging on the bedroom wall in the luxury suite of a great hotel—preferably European, and more preferably French. He did not care who the painting represented, man or woman, though he was impressed with the Mona Lisa. "Great eyes," Ealy had said. "Great eyes. She's got the eyes of a woman who is secretly getting off on what she's seeing."

The muffled laugh beyond the wall rose again, turned to giggle, trailed off, and then was followed by a man's laugh. Cooper wondered if any portraits were watching the laughing couple, and if they were, what was the delight of their voyeurism? Lovers, of course. Uninhibited in a strange room, locked away from whatever and whoever monitored them with expectations.

It had been so with Kathleen. The locked door freeing them.

He thought of Ealy, made the calculation of time zones in his mind. Five-thirty Dublin time, twelve-thirty of the noon hour in Atlanta. He wondered if Ealy was at his home. It was possible. Home, resting for the night. He picked up the telephone and made the international connection. Ealy answered on the first ring.

"How's my godfather?" Cooper asked.

"Come on, Coop, don't get on my case," Ealy said sourly. "And don't beat around the bush. I got a call from Sandy this morning, and I know you know all about him."

"You did me a favor," Cooper told him. "Sandy was like a three-ring circus."

"Forget Sandy," Ealy said. "What the hell are you doing?"

"Right now, I'm at the Shelbourne in Dublin," Cooper answered.

"I'm not talking about that. Why did you leave that woman?"

Cooper paused, fought a surge of anger. "That's personal, Ealy."

"My ass, it is," Ealy snapped. "It's me you're talking to."

"Ealy, I don't want to get aggravated on my last day in Ireland," Cooper said wearily. "I really don't."

"Aggravated?" Ealy said. "It seems to me you're forgetting Boy Dog rule number one. One Boy Dog does not get aggravated at another Boy Dog if that Boy Dog is being sincere, and in case you can't hear it in the question, I'll make it clear: I'm being so sincere I wouldn't recognize myself in a mirror."

"Okay," Cooper sighed. He took the telephone away from his ear, held it for a moment, then put it back to his ear. "Look, it's complicated. We'll go over it when I get back."

"Coop, tell me one thing," Ealy said.

"What?" Cooper asked.

"Do you care anything about that woman? Just yes or no. I don't want to hear any sentimental blithering, any maybes, any waffling at all. It's a simple question. Yes or no."

"Yes," Cooper said after a moment.

"Well, boy, do something about it."

"I have."

"I guess that's true," Ealy grumbled. "You tucked your tail and ran."

"Don't go there, Ealy," Cooper warned. "Boy Dog or not, don't go there."

"Well, to be honest with you, Cooper, right now I don't much give a happy hoot in hell," Ealy said. "I love you like a brother, and you know that. And I know you well enough to know you think you've done something fine and noble—something that a sloppy-drunk, over-emotional Irishman would do—and that, Boy Dog, is just plain laughable. What you did was stupid."

Cooper held the phone, waited.

"Okay, okay," Ealy mumbled. "I've had my say. We'll talk more about it tomorrow night when I pick you up, and I promise I'll be calmed down. What are you doing tonight?"

"I thought I'd go back to Foley's," Cooper said.

"Have a pint for me," Ealy said.

"Sure."

"See you tomorrow night."

"Yeah," Cooper said. "Tell Cary I'll talk to him on Monday."

"Glad you mentioned him," Ealy said quickly. "Big news. Rachel's pregnant."

"She is?" Cooper said in surprise. "Good. I'm glad to hear it."

"We're about to be uncles, Boy Dog."

"That'll be a change," Cooper said.

"Just shows you what love can do, don't it?" Ealy said. He added, "With the right woman, that is."

~~~

Cooper chose a light dinner in the restaurant of the Shelbourne—broiled trout, carrots, spinach, a glass of Chardonnay, followed by coffee. Eating alone seemed eerily quiet without Sandy's remarkable stories. He was not hungry and he picked at the food, consuming only enough to express appreciation for the waiter's theatrics. Feeling guilty, he left a sizeable tip.

Outside, it was cool with a brisk wind and he hurried his walk to Foley's, worried that he had waited too late to find a seat. If so, maybe he would be invited to join a table with a spare chair, he thought, and he would find himself surrendering to the merriment of the table, giving himself over to the conversation, to the chortling, to the singing. It would be an enjoyable way to fill the hours before sleep, giving in to the sprint-energy of partying, pushing himself to exhaustion. Then maybe his sleep would be dreamless, a heavy, peaceful sleep, with the sorrow in his soul dulled by drink and by the ringing of voices and music. Tomorrow he would be gone from Ireland, back to the routine of work and after-work, back to the companionship of Ealy and Cary and Dugan's Tavern, permitting Time, the omnipresent healer, to correct the off-balance of pain that lived in him like a sour fever. It would happen. Nothing was as curative as Time. He would only have to fear being alone.

The stairs leading from the street to the second floor were not as crowded as Cooper had expected. He could hear a racing Irish song spilling down the stairwell, the frenzied music of the fiddle pitched ceiling-high over the singing. He took the steps slowly, wading into the music. At the top step, he paused, scanned the room. The crowd, many of them in locked arms, swayed rhythmically to the beat of the music, singing lustily. In a far corner, he saw the table he had occupied a week earlier. It was empty and he began to weave his way toward it.

Near the bar he saw the waitress named Margaret and wondered if she would remember him. Not likely, he decided. He had been with Sandy McAfee and Sandy McAfee was the kind of man people remembered, not those around him.

He was wrong. Margaret waved to him, a glad smile blossoming in her face. He pointed to the table, mouthed, "A Guinness." She lifted a bottle of Guinness from the bar, held it up. He nodded yes, then angled to the table and sat.

Around him, the swaying, locked-arm crowd, caught the last note of the song, held it, yodeled it, then broke away from it like the jettisoning of a rocket into space. The crowd cheered its own release, settled again to their seats, to their drinking, to the loud, giddy conversations they had left waiting during the singing.

Cooper watched the musicians relax from their playing, watched them lean close to one another in a laughing exchange. The fiddler rolled his shoulders, took a sip from a glass of dark beer. He lifted his bow, examined it, put it aside, took another from a carrying case near his feet, and drew it once across the strings of his fiddle. The sound was like the squeal of an insect.

Margaret approached his table, carrying the glass of Guinness stout in one hand and a white gift bag in the other.

"I was getting worried about you," she said cheerfully.

"Worried?" Cooper asked.

"That you'd not show up," Margaret replied.

"Were you expecting me?" Cooper said.

Margaret smiled, put the stout on the table, then handed Cooper the bag.

"What's this?" Cooper asked.

Margaret leaned close. "I'm supposed to say it's from a Mr. Bogmeadow, but it's only Sandy calling himself that, playing the fool like he does. He said you'd know what it was all about."

Cooper opened the bag. Inside was a small, stuffed unicorn, white with a gold horn. He pulled it from the bag. He thought of the sign that Sandy said he would see, but it was not a sign. It was a teasing, gently meant.

"Is he here?" he asked.

"Sandy?" Margaret said. "He was by earlier."

"Is he coming back?"

"He didn't say, but I wouldn't think so," Margaret told him. "He looked a bit under the weather. Said he'd just come in on the train from Tralee."

"Do you know where he lives?"

"No, and I'm not wanting to know," Margaret said. "He moves about I'd guess."

Cooper sat, holding the unicorn. He thought: Patrick the Believer. He heard the incantation from his own telling of the story: *Angel of light, from the night I was born, bring me a wife on a unicorn.*

"What's it about?" Margaret asked playfully.

Cooper looked up, forced a feeble smile. "Just a story."

"I'm sure of it, coming from Sandy," Margaret said.

Cooper stood, reached into his pocket and took out some money. "How much for the stout?" he asked.

"Are you leaving?" Margaret said.

"Yes."

"You haven't touched it," Margaret said. "There's no charge. Believe me, it'll not make it back to the bar."

"Thank you," Cooper said. He put the unicorn back into the bag and tucked it into his coat pocket. "When you see Sandy again, tell him I'm grateful for the gift."

"I will, love," Margaret promised. "From his talking about it, the week he's been with you was special to him."

"It was for me," Cooper said.

"You'll visit us again someday, I hope," Margaret said.

"Someday," Cooper told her.

Margaret watched him leave, letting a smile grow across her face. She moved to a nearby table, placed the stout before a man sitting with three women. "Here's one on the house, Artie," she said merrily. "From all the women who love you so." The man named Artie brayed in delight.

She turned away, crossed quickly to a deep corner of the bar, to a heavy curtain that partitioned a storage room from the customers.

"He's gone," she whispered to the curtain.

Sandy stepped from behind it. He was again dressed in his dandy suit. A silk shamrock was pushed through the buttonhole of his lapel. "And what did he have to say?" he asked.

"To give you thanks for the gift," Margaret answered.

Sandy beamed.

"You're up to no good," Margaret said. "It's stamped on your face like a tattoo. You're a trouble-maker, Sandy McAfee. A trouble-maker."

Sandy squared his shoulders proudly, touched the shamrock. "No, me love," he said. "You're looking at a wish-maker."

~~~

Cooper walked for an hour, aimlessly, without realization of where he was, knowing only that other walkers were on the street, rushing along in the cool air, ducking into pubs and restaurants and still-open shops. The cool air made his eyes water. He thought of his night walks with Kathleen. Cathedral Square in Waterford. Along the banks of Lough Leane in Killarney. Kathleen, close to him, touching, the chilled night air of Ireland curled around them. His chest ached, causing his breathing to be shallow and hard. It was like a drowning, the way his chest begged for air.

He did not know he had made a circle—had not sensed he was walking in such a pattern—yet he found himself again in front of Foley's. He paused for a moment, considered going back into the company of revelers, then shook off the thought and began his walk to the Shelbourne.

Two blocks from the hotel, he came upon a crowd gathered around a small man—a dwarf, he believed—who was dressed as a leprechaun. The man was performing magic tricks in a high-pitched voice that had the sound of off-key singing. The voice reminded Cooper of the Munchkins in *The Wizard of Oz*. Cameras flashed from tourists who were watching.

The man was amazing, Cooper thought. The costume made him appear eerily unreal, a drawing that had leaped from the pages of an illustrated book. Yet, he labored. His breathing was hard. A film of perspiration seemed lacquered to his forehead.

The man did a wobbling skip-dance to a young girl standing near the front of the watchers. The girl was the man's height. The expression of her face balanced delicately between horror and fascination, smile and scream. The man waved his hand over the girl's head, reciting, "Gold of air is everywhere, everywhere, everywhere." He reached to the girl's ear to pluck an imitation gold coin. Dropped it ceremoniously into his pouch. Whirled on his heel and glided away while pulling a brilliant red scarf from his small, closed fist and waving it over his head like a banner in a parade.

The crowd applauded. The man turned, wrapped the scarf around his neck and tied it. He bowed a stage bow, low and graceful, then he stood erect and let his eyes scan the crowd. His gaze paused on Cooper. A smile exploded on his face. He lifted the leather coin pouch hanging from his neck and shook it. A dull sound of metal against metal rose from the pouch. He began a strange, exaggerated movement toward Cooper, a waddle. The crowd of on-lookers became silent and stepped away from the little man's path. When he reached Cooper, he bowed again, his hands disappearing behind his back under the coat flap of his costume. His body swept up out of the bow and he opened his right hand in front of his mouth and blew across his palm. A puff of white glitter dust swirled in the air, catching the light of street lamps, billowed on an air current and waved its way toward Cooper, falling around his face and shoulders. The man tilted his head, winked.

"The wish," he whispered. "The wish."

He turned and sprinted away, his laugh curling in the air.

Cooper could not move. He could feel the bloodrush of his heart, could hear its thunder.

Bogmeadow, he thought.

Bogmeadow.

Around him, he could hear the delight of on-lookers, could sense them wading into the small glitter cloud that drifted slowly to the sidewalk. A woman said, "Janie, don't get that in your hair."

The laughter of the man who could have been Bogmeadow echoed, faded.

Cooper blinked. An image of his grandfather flashed hot, then disappeared. "My God," he whispered. "My God."

A block away, in the shadow of a building, Cameron Dickey stood panting beside Sandy McAfee.

"That's it," Cameron said bitterly. "Never again, Sandy, so don't go asking me. Not even for a crock of gold."

"You're a beautiful man, Cameron Dickey," Sandy said. "An artist." He handed Cameron an envelope. "It's all there, as promised. What I've owed you and the other hundred."

Cameron took the envelope, opened it, counted the money, looked up at Sandy, snarled, then turned and wobbled off.

"And goodnight to you, too, my little friend," Sandy called. He reached into his pocket and withdrew a roll of bills. A good profit, he thought. Ealy Ackerman was a generous man. Five hundred euro for emergency needs. Two for Cameron, three for himself. It was fair. Without him, Cameron would have nothing, and Cooper Finn Coghlan would be returning to America with only his memories. "Ah, Sandy McAfee, you're a fine man," he whispered. "A saint, you are." He did a pivot turn and began striding away, toward Foley's, whistling a tune.

33

Near the Shelbourne, Cooper saw a taxi brake to a stop. He paused and watched a woman slip out of the back seat. From the distance, the woman could have been Kathleen. And then the woman leaned back into the car and helped a young boy struggle to the street. He stood, waiting until the woman and the boy had entered the hotel. He glanced at his watch. It was twenty minutes after ten. In Atlanta, it would be twenty minutes after five. Ealy would be dressing for his night out at Dugan's or Joey D's. There would still be time to call him before he left. Maybe if he talked to Ealy again, he would shake the unsettling sense of things being off-balance.

And it was that—being off-balance, he thought. Foolishness. A street actor dressed as a leprechaun, blowing glitter dust on him, leaving him dizzy. Sandy would call it a sign, but the talk of signs and omens was only the fancy of imagination. His grandfather had said to watch for three signs in a row. Sandy had promised one, had tried childishly to deliver it in the gift of a stuffed unicorn. He could not fault Sandy for the effort, yet it was nothing more than the way of an Irishman, as his grandmother had lamented. In Ireland, magic—or the promise of magic—was a commodity as saleable as wool or ale, and there were so many buyers it was surprising there were no McMagic shops with drive-through windows. If magic existed, it was in the gullibility of the mind, in the dreamy blur of hope.

The street-actor leprechaun with his whispered line about wishes was not Bogmeadow.

Bogmeadow was a tale invented to charm a child.

The street actor was only that—an actor—saying a line for the effect of it.

And there was something sad about all of it, he realized.

He had wanted the leprechaun to be Bogmeadow.

He had wanted magic.

In the hotel lobby, he saw the woman and the boy. They were with an older man, but not too old to be the boy's father. He was holding the boy on his left hip, slightly tilted to his right to balance for the weight. The woman was fingering the boy's hair in darting fingertip strikes, fluffing it. The boy was pulling back from the strikes, his head leaned against the man's shoulder. A family gathering, Cooper thought. The husband at a conference in Dublin, his wife and son joining him for a Sunday of leisure, of sightseeing. For the woman and man, an hour of locked-door love, perhaps. Quiet with their passion, while their son slept. No one watching except the unblinking people of the portraits.

He took the stairs to his floor, meeting a waiter carrying an empty food tray. The waiter dipped his head in greeting and Cooper returned the gesture. He paused at the door to his room, slipped the key into its lock, turned it, opened the door, stepped inside, closed the door and reached for the light switch.

"Don't turn it on, Cooper."

Cooper jerked his hand away from the switch, stumbled back against the door, the jolt of surprise striking him like a gunshot.

"Kathleen?" he said in shock.

"Stay there," she answered. Her voice trembled. "I don't want you to see me now, not until I say the things I have to say."

"All right," he said weakly. He looked in the direction of her voice, saw only the hazy outline of her body against the curtain that had been drawn over the window. "How did you get in here?"

"You'll have to ask Sandy that," she replied in a terse voice. "I don't know. I didn't ask him."

"It's all right," he said. "I'm glad you're here."

"You may be, but I don't know that I am," she said. "I thought I would be, but now I feel like a silly schoolgirl slipping around to see some boy who's turned her head for no reason at all."

"You don't have to feel that way," he told her gently.

"You're not letting me say what I came to say," she protested.

"I'm sorry."

She moved against the curtain, positioned herself to stand erect, facing Cooper. "I am not my grandmother," she said, her voice stronger than she intended. "And you are not your grandfather, even if you are acting like him." She paused, thought desperately to remember the speech she had prepared on the train from Tralee, a speech fashioned and coached by Sandy. She had spent the day vacillating between tears and anger, and Sandy had warned her against such uncertainty. Sandy had cautioned her to be firm, to stand her ground, and now Sandy was nowhere around, having left her to blunder her way in the dark. She felt a sudden pulse of fury for Sandy. Being there in a dark room was his idea, the persuasion of his soft-talking pleas. And now that she was there, she knew it had as much to do with Sandy's sense of drama as her own needs.

"If you leave me," she added, "it will be for a better reason than something that happened sixty years ago. I'll not live my life like my grandmother, wondering what might have been. Do you understand me, Cooper Finn Coghlan?"

"Yes," Cooper said. He thought he saw her move toward him.

"I have no hold on you, and I know it," she continued. "And if you ask me to walk away, I'll do it, but I'll know I've had my say." She paused again, drew in a breath to calm the tremors. Don't rush, Sandy had advised. Don't rush. Make him want to listen. "I love you. I don't know how it could have happened, not in such a short time. Do you know I met you almost exactly—to the hour—one week ago? One week, Cooper. It's not enough time to be on good speaking terms, but it's far beyond that for me."

"For me, too," Cooper whispered.

"Do you know what you've had me thinking, Cooper? Do you know what little girl fantasies have been flitting about in my head, like I was playing with paper dolls, making up happy-ever-after lives for them before putting them back in their box? Have you any idea, Cooper?"

"No," he said.

A surge of energy shot through her. "That we'd have two children, a girl and then a boy. We'd name the girl Christine, after my mother and your mother, and we'd name the boy anything on God's Earth other than

289

Finn. I'll not have a son of mine cursed with some lame excuse to run away from his true feelings."

Cooper did not reply. Did not want to speak. The distant between them was too brittle for words. In his mind, he could hear the fading laugh of the street-actor leprechaun. Bogmeadow, he thought.

"That's the kind of nonsense you've put in my mind," she added. "And I feel like a fool for saying such things out loud, even worse for having them lodged in my head. Talk about curses. It's a curse that I'm feeling, letting Sandy McAfee talk me into this."

"Where is he?" asked Cooper.

"How should I know?" she answered irritably. "He said he had some things to take care of, but he could be standing outside the door, for all I know, listening to every word, having a grand time of it." She raised her voice, directed it toward the door. "Him and his sweet-talking about wishes coming true."

Bogmeadow's wish, Cooper thought. The actor in Sandy had taken on the role of Bogmeadow, and he was improvising a script that would play for the run of his life in the pubs of Ireland. In Sandy's telling of it, it would be a love story as tender as *Romeo and Juliet*, but without tragedy. And the hero would be a leprechaun in the disguise of a man, playing his tricks with glitter dust.

"I have two questions," Kathleen said after a moment.

"Yes," Cooper said.

"The first is this: Do you love me?"

"Yes." The answer was given quietly. "I do."

"The second is this: Who is Patrick?"

Cooper thought of the unicorn in his pocket. "Why did you ask me that?" he asked.

"Sandy said I should."

Cooper reached to the light switch and turned it on. He stood looking at Kathleen. She was dressed in forest green slacks, a white blouse with a vest sweater that matched her slacks. Her face was flushed, her eyes moist.

"Patrick was a man who believed in magic," he said.

"And do you, Cooper Finn Coghlan?" she asked.

"I have to," he said.

"Why?" Her voice was a whisper.

He crossed the room to her, touched her face, kissed her gently.

"Why?" she asked again, again in whisper.

"Because you're here," he answered.